# SKANDAR
## AND THE
## SKELETON CURSE

BOOKS BY A.F. STEADMAN
*Skandar and the Unicorn Thief*
*Skandar and the Phantom Rider*
*Skandar and the Chaos Trials*
*Skandar and the Skeleton Curse*

# SKANDAR
## AND THE SKELETON CURSE

# A.F. STEADMAN

SIMON & SCHUSTER

First published in Great Britain in 2024 by Simon & Schuster UK Ltd

Text copyright © De Ore Leonis 2024
Illustrations copyright © Two Dots 2024

This book is copyright under the Berne Convention.
No reproduction without permission.
All rights reserved.

The right of A.F. Steadman and Two Dots to be identified as the author and illustrator of this work respectively has been asserted by them in accordance with sections 77 and 78 of the Copyright, Designs and Patents Act, 1988.

1 3 5 7 9 10 8 6 4 2

Simon & Schuster UK Ltd
1st Floor, 222 Gray's Inn Road
London
WC1X 8HB

Simon & Schuster: celebrating 100 years of Publishing in 2024

www.simonandschuster.co.uk
www.simonandschuster.com.au
www.simonandschuster.co.in

Simon & Schuster Australia, Sydney
Simon & Schuster India, New Delhi

A CIP catalogue record for this book is available from the British Library.

HB ISBN: 978-1-3985-2471-2
eBook ISBN: 978-1-3985-2473-6
eAudio ISBN: 978-1-3985-2472-9
ANZ PB: 978-1-3985-3611-1

This book is a work of fiction. Names, characters, places and incidents are either the product of the author's imagination or are used fictitiously. Any resemblance to actual people living or dead, events or locales is entirely coincidental.

Typeset in the UK by Sorrel Packham

Printed and Bound in the UK using 100% Renewable Electricity at CPI Group (UK) Ltd

*For my brothers, Alex and Hugo*
*– who showed me that love soars through our*
*skies, just as easily as it crosses our oceans*

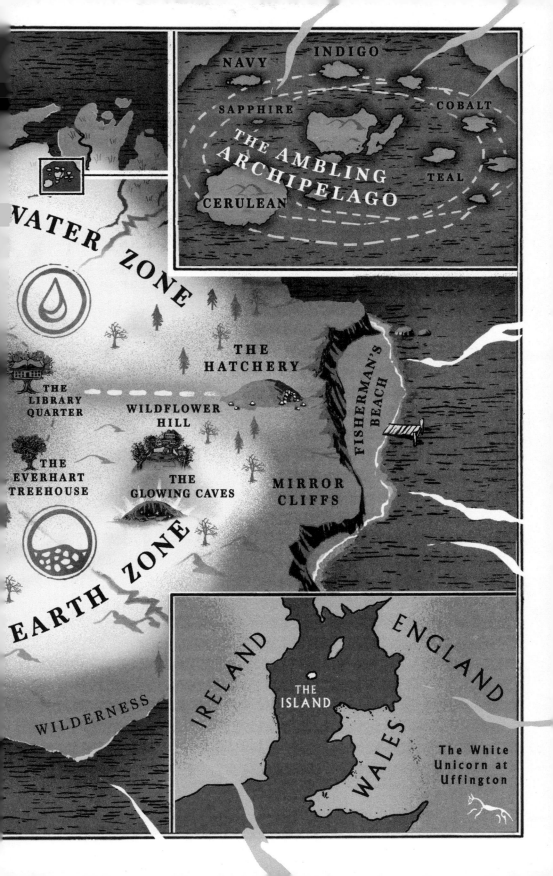

# CONTENTS

| | |
|---|---|
| Prologue | xi |
| *Chapter One:* **The Earth Festival** | 1 |
| *Chapter Two:* **New Rules** | 15 |
| *Chapter Three:* **Acting Skills** | 29 |
| *Chapter Four:* **Poisoned** | 41 |
| **Kenna – Haunted House** | 56 |
| *Chapter Five:* **Rider Revolt** | 62 |
| *Chapter Six:* **A Commodore's Revenge** | 76 |
| *Chapter Seven:* **Sacrifice** | 93 |
| **Kenna – Old Friends, New Tricks** | 113 |
| *Chapter Eight:* **The Skeleton Curse** | 119 |
| *Chapter Nine:* **Sapphire** | 139 |
| *Chapter Ten:* **The Water Keeper** | 153 |
| *Chapter Eleven:* **The Vaults** | 167 |
| **Kenna – Originals** | 180 |
| *Chapter Twelve:* **The Lioness and the Puppy** | 187 |
| *Chapter Thirteen:* **Registration** | 197 |
| *Chapter Fourteen:* **Battle Lines** | 212 |
| **Kenna – Born to Lead** | 229 |
| *Chapter Fifteen:* **The Qualifiers** | 238 |
| *Chapter Sixteen:* **Vanishing Act** | 258 |
| **Kenna – No Place Like Home** | 273 |
| *Chapter Seventeen:* **Resistance** | 282 |
| *Chapter Eighteen:* **Children's Warning** | 298 |
| *Chapter Nineteen:* **The Spirit Yard** | 309 |
| **Kenna – In Too Deep** | 322 |
| *Chapter Twenty:* **Parley** | 328 |
| *Chapter Twenty-One:* **Blackout** | 345 |
| *Chapter Twenty-Two:* **Lucky Thirteen** | 359 |
| *Chapter Twenty-Three:* **The Chaos Cup** | 371 |
| *Chapter Twenty-Four:* **Immortal Secrets** | 381 |
| **Kenna – Brother** | 391 |
| *Chapter Twenty-Five:* **The Silver and the Spirit Wielder** | 394 |
| Epilogue | 400 |

# PROLOGUE

*A* rider galloped her wild unicorn through a deserted graveyard. The girl was more skull than skin, the unicorn more skeleton than flesh.

They passed unseen like the tormented ghosts of those buried beneath the trees, unmoved by the crackle of an air-allied leaf or the whisper of a seaweed-strewn trunk.

Woodland creatures sheltered from their anger under earth-allied roots. Each blaze of blood-red leaves dulled at the depths of their bitterness.

They reached a tree, as white and smooth as their own bones.
Goshawk's Fury rested her nose against the carved bark that read:

## BLOOD-MOON'S EQUINOX – DIED IN BATTLE – CHAOS CUP

*Kenna Everhart ran her fingers over the letters of her mother's name.*

# ERIKA EVERHART – DIED – MIRROR CLIFFS

*Kenna pulled a knife from her belt and attacked the spirit tree with a feral cry.*

*White whittled bark fell like summer snow until* Mirror Cliffs *had been obliterated and* Died *had been overlaid with . . .*

# MURDERED.

*She allowed herself one more howl of grief before mounting her wild unicorn.*

*It was enough now. Erika's body was not here. Had never been here.*

*And Kenna had work to do.*

*As Goshawk carried her under the colourful trees, Kenna rode on faster.*

*This place was an elemental memorial to a bond she did not have.*

*Kenna was allied to all five elements.*

*And Goshawk would live for ever.*

*No.*

*They must both live for ever.*

*Only two things interested the Weaver's successor now.*

*Revenge. And immortality.*

*For Kenna Everhart would never feel powerless again.*

CHAPTER ONE

# THE EARTH FESTIVAL

Skandar Smith watched the rays of the setting sun dance through the Eyrie's armoured trees. From the doorway of the treehouse he shared with his three best friends, he could hear the familiar chaos of them attempting to leave for the Earth Festival on time.

'Bobby! You haven't even got your jacket on yet!' Flo Shekoni cried in despair.

A thump as Bobby Bruna's boots landed on the metal floor. 'I refuse to change until the very last second – green just isn't my colour.'

'Yes, and yellow matches your sunny personality so perfectly,' Mitchell Henderson said sarcastically.

'There's no need for that,' Flo scolded, and Skandar suspected Bobby had made a rude gesture at Mitchell. 'I know you prefer the air season, Bobby, but we do need to leave now, or we'll miss the festival altogether.'

'Why do you care so much?' Bobby grumbled. 'You hate crowds.'

'Flaming fireballs,' Mitchell cursed. 'I'd forgotten about the rip in this jacket. You can practically see my whole shoulder!'

'You can wear my jacket,' Bobby said innocently. 'I'll keep my yellow one on—'

'Mitchell Henderson, if you let her give you that green jacket, I will—'

'Ooh, go on, Flo!' Bobby whooped, and then there was laughter and running footsteps.

Smiling to himself, Skandar finally turned round in the doorway. 'Oi! We're Rookies now – practically fully-trained, fully-grown unicorn riders.' He stepped inside the treehouse, narrowly dodging Flo, who was chasing after Bobby, who was hurtling after Mitchell. 'If you carry on like this, I might find myself some more mature friends. *Branch out* a bit.'

Flo, Bobby and Mitchell stopped dead, looked at each other and then . . . ran at Skandar and tackled him on to the pile of beanbags, hooting with laugher.

'I hate to break it to you, spirit boy,' Bobby cackled. 'But nobody else would have you.'

Skandar sighed dramatically. 'I suppose I'll have to put up with you three then.' And for one blissful moment, lying on the colourful beanbags surrounded by his friends, Skandar could almost pretend that he was fine.

Eventually – after much swapping and repairing of jackets – the quartet were riding through the crowded streets of Fourpoint. Skandar and Scoundrel's Luck had Bobby and Falcon's Wrath on their left, Mitchell and Red Night's Delight on their right, and Flo and Silver Blade shining ahead of them, among the sea of green-clad Islanders making their way towards Element Square.

'Is this festival actually going to be any fun?' Bobby said.

'What do you mean?' Flo spoke over her shoulder as Blade

# THE EARTH FESTIVAL

stormed ahead. The silver unicorn seemed to be as worried as his rider that they might be late.

'Well . . . earth wielders aren't exactly known for being party people. If it was the *air* festival—'

'Bobby, will you please stop complaining about the season changing?' Mitchell said, Red's wings colliding with Scoundrel's as they squeezed through the narrow street.

Flo looked a bit offended. 'It's not that we don't *like* parties – it's just more effort for us than for air wielders. *You* could turn any situation into a party.'

'Aww, thanks Flo!' Bobby said, genuinely touched.

Mitchell chuckled. 'Yes, I bet Bobby could even turn a *burial* into a party—'

Flo shook her head at Mitchell, as Bobby raised an eyebrow.

'Sorry, Skandar.' Mitchell sounded horrified. 'I didn't think. I didn't mean . . .'

'It's fine,' Skandar said. 'Really, I'm all right.' He'd been saying this since June, and he knew nobody believed him, but sometimes he wished his quartet could treat him less like his mum had died, his sister had betrayed him, and his aunt was on the run. It was why he longed for moments when they were all just silly together, and also why Skandar looked forward to letters from Dad.

Robert Smith was still writing to his son about how proud he'd been watching the Air Trial at the end of Fledgling year. He knew nothing about the terrible events that had followed it. So when Skandar wrote back, he could pretend he was living an ordinary life at the Eyrie with his sister. He could imagine that the story he was making up for Dad was true.

'I mean, this looks like rather a good party to me,' Mitchell said, attempting a return to normal conversation as they arrived at Element Square.

– 3 –

# SKANDAR AND THE SKELETON CURSE

It was the first Earth Festival Skandar had managed to attend, and he'd never seen the square quite so beautiful. The earth wielders had grown a knee-high wildflower meadow across it, with colourful blooms bursting through the long grass, which seemed somehow resistant to the trampling of hundreds of unicorn hooves. The whole place smelled fragrant and fresh, and the stalls dotted around were just as strikingly earth-allied: some were cave-like, filled with gems where customers could choose precious stones and have them made into jewellery, while others boasted soil-filled beds, with flowers or vegetables ready to be picked right from the soil and roasted. And there were, as usual, activities to keep restless riders and unicorns amused – a tug of war with flowering vines, an obstacle course involving giant magnets, and a sand-modelling competition boasting ambitious creations. Skandar could already see a replica Hatchery, complete with perfectly round door.

Listening to the cheerful chatter of the festivalgoers, Skandar felt a twinge of jealousy. How could nothing have changed for them, when only a few weeks ago his whole world had been irreversibly altered? Erika Everhart – spirit's dark friend, the Island's greatest enemy, the Weaver – was dead. But no matter how many names she'd been given, she'd been Skandar's mum too, and losing her hurt more than he'd thought it would. Even after everything she'd done to the Island. To his sister. *With* his sister.

The quartet dismounted – even Bobby looked awed – and they looked around. Skandar pushed away his dark thoughts. He was just about to ask whether anyone wanted to share a sizzling tub of roast potatoes, when three Eyrie riders approached.

Skandar recognised them all. Marcus, with his unicorn Sandstorm's Orbit, had been chosen as the new squadron leader of the Peregrine Society – the Eyrie's elite flying squad. Marcus

– 4 –

## THE EARTH FESTIVAL

was flanked by Patrick, a fellow Grin, on Hurricane Hoax, and – bizarrely – Bobby's younger sister, Isabel Bruna, riding her brand-new unicorn, Tsunami's Herald.

It was easy to tell that Bobby and Isa were related – they had the same severe brown fringe, the same olive skin. But Isa wore her hair long, trapped neatly in two braids, and her eyes were bigger and brighter – as though constantly surprised by whatever trouble she'd started. And where Falcon was slate grey, Herald was as white as snow.

'Isa!' Bobby hissed. 'What are *you* doing at the Earth Festival? Hatchlings aren't allowed!' Skandar had never heard Bobby sound so like Flo in his life.

Isa tutted. 'Wrong as usual, hermana. The Commodore changed the rules.'

'Oh.' Bobby looked taken aback, but turned her attention to Marcus and Patrick instead. 'Okay, new question. Why are two Preds hanging around with a Hatchling?'

'We're not *hanging around* with her,' Patrick protested, his mutated hair sticking up as though freshly electrocuted. 'She won't stop *following* us.'

'Harsh but accurate,' Isa said, patting Herald's neck.

'Isa—' Bobby started, but then breathed in deeply as though trying to calm herself. Flo looked on approvingly; she'd been encouraging Bobby to turn over a new leaf with her sister now she was on the Island. The trouble was – as Skandar had realised the moment Isa arrived – Bobby's sister was really, really annoying.

'I'm looking for a Rookie,' Squadron Leader Marcus said, ignoring the sisters. 'An earth wielder called Elias – rides Marauding Magnet. Have you seen him?'

Nobody had.

'Is everything all right?' Flo asked.

'I'm not sure,' Marcus said, his face creased with concern.

– 5 –

# SKANDAR AND THE SKELETON CURSE

'Elias had a lot of friends declared nomads after their Chaos Trials. Instructor Webb hasn't seen him for days – he's worried.'

'He'll turn up, mate,' Patrick said reassuringly. 'Then we can go back to discussing how you *betrayed* me and chose Fen as your flight lieutenant.'

Marcus groaned good-naturedly as they said goodbye and moved to the next group of Eyrie riders. Bobby managed to grab Herald's reins before Isa could follow them.

'How about some sister bonding time?' she asked in an enormous effort to be nice. 'We could visit one of the gemstone caves? How about something blue for your element?'

Isa rolled her eyes. Skandar wondered which sister had started the habit.

Stomach rumbling, Skandar turned to Flo and Mitchell, but Mitchell was already riding Red towards a group of blacksmiths listening to a bard singing about the coming harvest. 'I said I'd meet . . . I'm just going to see if Jamie . . .' Mitchell's voice was swallowed up by the festival crowd as he went in search of his boyfriend.

'Potatoes?' Skandar asked Flo, and she nodded enthusiastically, the silver in her Afro flashing.

As they started to queue, Skandar saw Rex Manning nearby, surrounded by members of the Silver Circle. A shiver went down Skandar's spine when he spotted Nina Kazama's mood ring on the Commodore's pale white finger. Rex had shown his true colours back on the summer solstice when he imprisoned any spirit wielder he could lay his hands on. The other Eyrie instructors had protected Skandar, but he worried about how long Rex would allow that to last.

He turned to Flo. 'Why isn't anyone investigating Nina's death? I'm *sure* Rex killed her. How can they let a murderer be Commodore? Has Rex said anything to you? About Nina? About

– 6 –

me? About Agatha? About what his plans are for the spirit element once—'

Quick as a lightning attack, Flo placed her fingers to his lips and Scoundrel growled. 'Skar, you have to stop this,' she said, ignoring the black unicorn. 'There's no evidence that Rex killed Nina.'

'Apart from the fact he's *wearing her ring*?'

Flo shook her head. 'There could be so many reasons for that. Maybe it's out of respect – weren't they in the Peregrine Society together?'

'Yes, but—'

'I don't trust Rex either, okay? Not after he tried to arrest you and Agatha. But I really don't think he's a murderer. And he's no more prejudiced against the spirit element than most people on this Island. Remember how he saved us from his father at the end of Nestling year? And he still has Dorian locked in the prison, apparently.' She swallowed. 'Rex is a complicated person, I think. I've heard rumours within the Silver Circle that he didn't have an easy time of it growing up.'

Skandar grunted in disbelief. 'Well, I'm not exactly having an easy time growing up either. And *I* haven't killed anyone!'

Flo sighed. 'I don't believe he's as bad as all that. I think he'll keep Aspen's word and bring spirit wielders back if you make it to the end of your training. He keeps promises, Skar. I think he just wants the Island to be safe, that's all.'

Skandar didn't want to keep arguing. Flo always believed the best in everyone – he loved that about her – but he was convinced Rex Manning was one of the most dangerous people he'd ever met.

'We're starting Rookie training in a few weeks,' Flo said, smiling at Skandar in that way that made him forget where he was. 'Enjoy what's happening now, rather than worrying.'

– 7 –

# SKANDAR AND THE SKELETON CURSE

Skandar shrugged, knowing she was also talking about Kenna. He'd noticed Flo paying close attention to him over the last month. Perhaps she'd guessed how he kept going over and over the events from June: Kenna's betrayal, her attempt to forge a new generation of riders, and – worst of all – the moment she'd killed Agatha's unicorn, Arctic Swansong.

'Take it from someone who knows,' Flo continued. 'Worrying doesn't help. What flavour do you want?' She pointed to the sign above the kiosk.

Underneath the words RITA'S ROLLICKING ROASTIES, were various decisions that customers had to make before ordering their potatoes: crispiness – from doughy to jaw-crunching, saltiness – from sprinkle to seawater, and finally flavour, of which there were at least twenty – everything from rosemary to lemon to beef to chocolate.

'Do you think chocolate and roast potatoes taste good together?' Skandar wondered.

'Only one way to find out.' Flo winked at him and kneeled down by the wooden planter, searching for a potato hidden within its soil.

Skandar was about to join her when he noticed something odd about the statues at the centre of Element Square. The lightning bolt, waves, and flames were all their usual concrete grey, but the jagged rock for earth was painted with a long white stripe down its centre.

Skandar's heart beat wildly, his quickening breaths loud in his ears. As panic flooded his senses, the happy chatter of the emerald crowd faded to a low hum. Was painting the statue part of the festival? Surely not. Surely the organisers would have realised the panic it would cause. It looked exactly like that mark. *Her* mark.

'Flo?' Skandar said, his voice shaking.

– 8 –

# THE EARTH FESTIVAL

She looked up at him, alert. They'd been through so much together – she knew fear when she heard it in his voice.

'Please tell me the earth statue's been like that the whole time.' Skandar pointed at the rock. 'Tell me it's someone's idea of a really bad joke.'

Flo stood to look. 'It wasn't like that a few minutes ago, Skar.'

Without another word, she scrambled up on to Blade's back. Skandar mounted Scoundrel, who sent a pulse of calm through the bond, sensing his rider's unease.

Others were starting to notice the statue now – some pointing, others staring in disbelief, as worry rippled across Element Square.

Within seconds, Falcon and Herald emerged from the sea of festivalgoers, and stopped by Blade and Scoundrel. Skandar was relieved to see Mitchell approaching too, with Jamie sprinting alongside Red through the wildflower meadow. Scoundrel shrieked, as though urging his fiery best friend to hurry up.

'I don't understand,' Isa said, as the quartet moved their unicorns into a defensive circle, shielding Tsunami's Herald behind them. 'It's just paint on a statue, why is everyone—'

'It's the Weaver's sign.' Bobby's voice was tense. 'Like the stripe she had down her face. Like a spirit unicorn's blaze.'

'But isn't the Weaver dead? The Islanders in my quartet told me Commodore Manning killed her!' Isa insisted.

'*He* didn't kill her,' Skandar growled. 'But yes, she's dead. I saw her die.'

Isa stayed silent.

'Who would do this?' Jamie sounded angry.

'I can think of someone,' Mitchell said, glancing in Skandar's direction.

'But she wouldn't try anything, would she?' Flo said softly. 'It's too risky. Too many sentinels, silvers everywhere. The entire

– 9 –

# SKANDAR AND THE SKELETON CURSE

Council of Seven is here. And the Commodore.'

Then, all across Element Square, unicorns began to collapse.

Riders yelled in shock as they were thrown from their unicorns' backs. Distress flares exploded from the saddles of earth-allied sentinels as they were unseated, filling the square with green smoke. Islanders screamed as unicorns that had been flying over the festival plummeted to the ground, ploughing through stalls and sand sculptures. Sandstorm's Orbit fell on top of a gem cave and it collapsed, spewing colourful jewels as Squadron Leader Marcus pulled himself from the wreckage.

Scoundrel bellowed in confusion, as he and Skandar watched stone-haired Gabriel leaning over the light grey body of Queen's Price, pleading with her to wake up. Aisha was calling to Dagger's Emerald over and over, the flowers in her hair wilting with anguish. Freya was pulling at Earth-Bound Raptor's mane in floods of tears. Panicking, Skandar jerked his gaze back towards Marcus, where Orbit was lying on a sea of gemstones.

'It's the earth wielders,' Mitchell cried. 'It's only affecting earth unicorns!'

'Apart from Blade,' Flo breathed, winding her hands into his silver mane as though trying to keep him upright.

Time in the square seemed to slow. Skandar scanned the motionless bodies, wings spread across the ground at odd angles like fallen angels.

'They'll be okay, right?' Isa asked, her face stricken, arms round the white neck of Tsunami's Herald, as though worrying her water unicorn would collapse too. 'They're not dead, are they?'

Skandar opened his mouth to reply but the fallen unicorns answered for him. As one, the earth unicorns rose like ghosts from shallow graves. But they weren't dead. As their transparent horns glowed eerily in the torchlit square, Skandar realised it was far more terrifying than that.

– 10 –

# THE EARTH FESTIVAL

All the earth unicorns had turned wild.

Scoundrel bellowed, Falcon and Blade screeched, and Herald and Red reared up, as the putrid stench of wild unicorn blasts filled the air. Mitchell was pleading with Jamie to run, and he sprinted away, shouting to nearby blacksmiths that they should take cover in the forges.

Earth wielders across Element Square were all frozen in shock. The unicorns they had loved since they'd first locked eyes in the Hatchery had turned into the monsters the riders had been taught to fear. Coats that had glistened only moments before were now dull. Wing muscles that had taken years to build were wasting away, as well-fed bodies began to shrink and shrivel, the lines and bumps of their bones becoming visible in seconds.

Some riders fled from the square in panic. Others stayed – pleading, begging, sobbing – as their beloved unicorns blasted at anything in range and tore through the square causing chaos. Commodore Manning and his Council of Seven had organised themselves into a defensive line and were firing lightning bolts to try to move the wild unicorns out of the crowd.

'Stop! He's not himself! Don't hurt him!' Farooq was shouting at them, trying to protect Toxic Thyme from their air magic. But Thyme just snarled at him and barged right past, sending him flying into the tall grass of the meadow.

'This is horrible!' Flo cried, as she summoned a sand shield to defend against a wild unicorn's blast of stinking smog.

'But how?' Mitchell threw a fireball in the general direction of Dagger's Emerald, trying to head her off without injuring her. 'This is impossible. Bonded unicorns don't just turn wild for no reason . . .'

A wild unicorn swooped low over their heads.

A wild unicorn with a rider.

– 11 –

# SKANDAR AND THE SKELETON CURSE

There was a white stripe painted down the middle of the rider's face from the crown of the head to the tip of the chin. But that was where the similarities to the Weaver ended – for this rider had thorned vines curling up her arm, ice spikes at her throat, lava in her veins, feathers at her ears, a head that was half skull. And even if Skandar had seen none of those things, he would have recognised his sister anywhere.

Kenna Smith landed Goshawk's Fury amid the chaos of stampeding unicorns, begging riders and fleeing Islanders – and she laughed. And laughed.

Skandar was barely aware of riding Scoundrel through the crowd of screaming earth wielders. He was scarcely conscious of the elemental shields he was raising to deflect blasts from the newly wild unicorns. He hardly heard himself yelling his sister's name. 'KENNA!' A fierce desperation to reach her boiled in Skandar's veins, even though he had no idea what he was going to do when he got there. Attack her? Hug her?

'Stop her!' Rex Manning's authoritative bark rang out over the bellows of the wild unicorns. The Commodore and his entire air-allied Council of Seven galloped towards Goshawk from the opposite side of the square.

Kenna stopped laughing as she rode Goshawk's Fury forward – away from the Commodore but towards Scoundrel's Luck. Goshawk's rotting wings snapped out, the meadow wilting as her skeletal knees brushed its flowers. For a moment, Skandar thought she was going to collide with Scoundrel, but seconds before impact the wild unicorn took off and soared right over his head.

Skandar fought off tears. Not because Kenna had painted herself to look like the Weaver. Not because she was almost certainly responsible for the earth unicorns turning wild. But because his sister hadn't even looked at him. He missed her –

– 12 –

# THE EARTH FESTIVAL

that was the truth. Even though he knew he was supposed to think of her as the enemy, all he really wanted was to talk about what had happened in June. Was she hurting too? Was she angry – like he was – about Erika Everhart leaving them behind all over again?

Skandar was only vaguely aware of his quartet catching up with Scoundrel.

'We need to get out of here,' Bobby said through gritted teeth. She was having trouble protecting her sister from the swirling blasts of the earth unicorns. Isa had barely started Hatchling training and her attempts at magic were doing more harm than good. 'Herald can't fly yet; we'll have to ride for the Eyrie.'

Fourpoint was in complete chaos as the quartet fought their way through, young Tsunami's Herald sandwiched protectively between them. The earth unicorns didn't appear to be as wary of human settlements as normal wild unicorns, and Skandar saw at least a dozen tearing through the narrow streets. Others had already set fire to wooden treehouses, or smashed shop windows. Some of their riders were attempting to catch them; others were cowering in doorways or hiding in trees.

'From bonded to wild. It's impossible,' Mitchell said again, as they reached the base of the Eyrie's hill.

'Mitchell, it just happened,' Bobby snapped at him. 'Clearly, it *is* possible.'

'Why wasn't Blade affected?' Flo's voice was barely audible.

'It could have something to do with Blade being a silver,' Skandar guessed. 'Silver unicorns aren't as affected by spirit magic.'

'Blade's the only earth-allied silver, right?' Bobby checked.

'Apart from Elora and Silver Soldier,' Mitchell said, already planning. 'We should get a message to Agatha and see what the situation is with the Wanderers. Is it *all* the earth unicorns, or

– 13 –

only the ones who were in Element Square tonight?'

Flo was still worrying about Blade. 'So you're saying Kenna used the spirit element to do this? That because Blade is a silver he definitely won't be affected?'

'We'll know for sure once we talk to Elora,' Skandar said carefully, but he was already thinking about how wild unicorns had an affinity with the spirit element. How only spirit wielders could see and break bonds to kill unicorns. And how that *didn't* work against silvers.

'Why would your sister do this?' Isa asked Skandar accusingly.

He bristled. 'Kenna's been through . . . a lot. I'm not sure she knows *what* she's doing right now.'

'Are you really defending her?' Bobby asked, incredulous. 'After Arctic Swansong?'

'Leave it, Bobby. Okay?' Flo said more forcefully than usual.

Mitchell ploughed over the tension with practicality. 'Rather than *why* Kenna's done this, the scarier question is *how*. How has she been able to affect so many unicorns at the same time? That kind of magic, that kind of power, it means . . .'

'We're all in danger,' Skandar finished.

Because Kenna was more powerful than any rider Skandar had ever seen. And she was grieving – just like he was.

A combination both terrible and terrifying.

Chapter Two

# NEW RULES

Numb with shock after the Earth Festival, Skandar's brain kept short-circuiting and going back to his sister. Nobody outside of his trusted circle knew she was Erika Everhart's daughter, but – with that white stripe down her face – she had reminded him so much of the Weaver. Had she really turned the earth unicorns wild? Was it all of them? How had she done it? How long would it last? What was her next move?

And when Skandar's quartet tried to settle their unicorns in the stables – brushed them down, filled their water buckets, tossed them a couple of goat legs – the Eyrie was already full of fearful whispers.

'The Commodore is here,' Benji hissed from a couple of stables down. The air wielder was treating a wound on Cursed Whisper's neck – although if it was from wild magic, it would never heal.

Art shrugged. 'Rex is the air instructor – that's not exactly unusual.'

'Well, he's calling a meeting.' Benji raised a winged eyebrow.

# SKANDAR AND THE SKELETON CURSE

'I heard that too,' Mariam murmured, bolting Old Starlight's stable door.

'What? Now? It's almost ten,' Niamh said.

'Could *you* sleep after what happened tonight?' Benji capped his ointment bottle.

'How's Farooq?' Mariam asked gently.

Niamh, Benji and Art looked at each other. Farooq was the earth wielder in their quartet.

'Toxic Thyme bolted from Element Square. I told Farooq it was too dangerous to look for him, but –' Niamh glanced at Snow Swimmer – 'you couldn't stop me searching for my unicorn, no matter how wild she was. And Elias? You were added to his trio for the Chaos Trials, weren't you?'

Mariam adjusted her headscarf. 'I haven't seen him or Marauding Magnet for days. He took losing Walker *and* Romily pretty hard. I told him we could stick together – the two of us – even though the trials were over.' She shivered despite the warm summer evening. 'After what happened tonight, I'm obviously a *lot* more worried about him now.'

The four riders drifted out towards the Eyrie's forest, still talking in low voices.

'Did you hear that?' Skandar asked Mitchell.

Mitchell nodded, leaving Red's stable. 'Elias is still missing.'

'No, not that. Rex is holding a meeting by the Divide. Right now.'

'Let's see what Rowdy Melon has got to say,' Bobby said, smoothing the feathers along her arm.

'I wish you wouldn't call him silly names like that, Bobby,' Flo said uncomfortably. 'He *is* the Commodore.'

'He's also a murderer,' Bobby shot back, 'so I'll call him whatever I like.' Bobby was as convinced as Skandar that Rex had killed Nina Kazama. Especially after hearing the story

– 16 –

## NEW RULES

about how Rex left the Peregrine Society when Nina was chosen as squadron leader instead of him.

'I mean, even I was a bit dramatic when that stupid bird club chose Skandar over me,' she'd said.

'A bit dramatic?' Mitchell had scoffed. 'You practically left our quartet!'

'Didn't kill anyone, though, did I? There's jealousy, and then there's pure evil.'

The problem was, Skandar thought – as they were ushered towards the Eyrie's clearing by some officious Preds – that nobody else believed Rex Manning *was* evil. And now he was Commodore, head of the Silver Circle *and* the Eyrie's air instructor. The man was impossible to avoid.

The clearing was packed by the time the quartet arrived. Lanterns swung from the branches and bridges above, lighting up the riders on the moonless August night and illuminating the deep grooves of the fault lines. Skandar watched as a platform was raised on ropes. The same platform Aspen McGrath had used when she'd given her speech about rooting out the spirit element three years ago – the thought of it made Skandar feel very old and very tired.

Commodore Manning stepped off a swinging bridge and on to the suspended platform, closely followed by Instructors Anderson and O'Sullivan. Skandar noticed the glint of sentinel masks lurking like armoured ghosts between the leaves.

'Oh no, look at Instructor Webb,' Flo whispered, and there was deep sorrow in her voice. It took Skandar a second to spot the moss-haired instructor, his hunched form emerging from the shadowy trees behind Instructor O'Sullivan. His shoulders were shaking, his green cloak was askew, and tears were streaming down his lined face.

'Moonlight Dust must have turned . . .' Bobby tailed off at the

– 17 –

# SKANDAR AND THE SKELETON CURSE

awfulness of the whole Eyrie peering up at the earth instructor in his grief.

Then Rex Manning stepped in front of the other three Eyrie instructors and held up a hand for silence.

'Well, that's not on,' Mitchell said, pushing his glasses back up his nose crossly. 'Rex might be Commodore, but the four elemental instructors are supposed to be equal.'

'I don't think he cares,' Skandar murmured, as Commodore Manning began to speak.

'First, I wish to address all the earth wielders here and offer my sincerest apologies. My duty as Commodore is to keep *all* riders and unicorns safe. And I have failed you. Can you forgive me for allowing this terrible atrocity to happen? I am not sure I'll ever forgive myself.'

Bobby rolled her eyes. But most riders appeared to be hanging on Rex's every word, and many earth wielders were crying and nodding along.

'I promise you that my researchers will be working round the clock to reverse what has happened to your unicorns. We *will* find the answer. To the rest of you here, I say this—'

Rex paused, his cheeks sparking with threads of silver electricity. Somehow it felt like he was looking at every rider individually, and Skandar cringed away from the intensity in the Commodore's green eyes.

'The Eyrie is the future of the Island. *You* are our future, and out there tonight –' he pointed down towards Fourpoint – 'that was an act of war. The Weaver has a new name and that name is Kenna Smith.'

Riders near Skandar inched away from him; others turned to stare, whispering behind their hands. Mitchell put a protective arm round Skandar's shoulders.

Rex continued. 'Kenna Smith is far more dangerous than

– 18 –

## NEW RULES

Erika Everhart ever was. The dark power she used tonight has affected every single earth unicorn on the Island. Not just the ones at the festival this evening. Every. Single. One.'

'Except Blade,' Flo whispered.

More anxious murmurs spread across the crowd. Instructor Webb let out a haunting wail from behind the Commodore.

*Oh, Kenna. What have you done?* The words cycled around in Skandar's head.

A slight breeze ruffled the Commodore's wavy blond hair as he went on. 'I am not telling you this to scare you, but to prepare you. For we *must* be prepared. And therefore I –' he glanced behind him at the other instructors – '*we*, at the Eyrie, will be adapting to this new threat. Which means introducing some changes that will keep us united, strong and focused in the fight against our new enemy.'

Fear flooded Skandar's body. Change was dangerous. He was the brother of the new enemy, a spirit wielder. Change might mean getting rid of *him*. And he wasn't the only one thinking it. Mitchell's arm tightened round Skandar's shoulders, Bobby moved sideways to block him from view, and Flo gripped his arm tightly.

'Instructor Manning, we have not discussed *any* changes.' Instructor O'Sullivan's voice carried across the clearing. 'We are not your Council of Seven. At the Eyrie all four instructors must agree before new measures are implemented.' Skandar had the feeling the water instructor was talking deliberately loudly so that everyone clustered round the Divide would hear her.

'Naturally,' Rex said silkily. 'But – as I'm sure you understand, Instructor O'Sullivan – what happened tonight was highly unusual. The changes I am making will keep us all at our strongest, so we may best protect ourselves from future attacks.'

Most riders were too busy looking up at Rex's confident face

SKANDAR AND THE SKELETON CURSE

to notice his fingers gripping Instructor O'Sullivan's wrist, forcing her behind him. But Skandar noticed, and the water instructor's face was pale with shock as Rex began to speak again.

'Kenna Smith has access – through her theft of Goshawk's Fury – to five wild elements. In that lies her power. But also her weakness. A bonded unicorn's greatest strength is in its allied element – and that is something our new enemy cannot truly understand.'

'What is he on about?' Bobby hissed, at the exact same time that Mitchell said, 'I do *not* like where this is going.'

It felt like the whole crowd was holding its breath. Skandar's heart hammered impossibly fast.

'Until this new threat has passed, Eyrie riders will train *only* in their allied element,' Rex announced.

Whispering erupted across the clearing. Skandar looked for the other instructors but they were no longer on the platform. Had they left in protest? Or had they been removed by the sentinels before they could object?

'There will now be two Eyrie instructors for each element. All water wielders will be trained by Instructor O'Sullivan and a water-allied member of the Silver Circle. All fire wielders will be trained by Instructor Anderson and a fire-allied member of the Silver Circle. All air wielders will be taught by me and another air-allied member of the Silver Circle. All earth wielders –' there was a horrible pause – 'will resume training with Instructor Webb and an earth-allied member of the Silver Circle as soon as their unicorns return to normal.'

'But – but *I'm* the only earth-allied member of the Silver Circle,' Flo whispered in shock. 'He can't be expecting me to—'

'What are earth wielders supposed to do until then?' Gabriel yelled across the clearing, and other shouts echoed his anger.

'Florence Shekoni and Silver Blade will undertake training

– 20 –

# NEW RULES

sessions in the Silver Stronghold.' Rex nodded to Flo, who frowned deeply. 'All other earth wielders will attend theory classes at the Eyrie provided by Instructor Webb, and then—'

'What about our unicorns? We can't just leave them in the Wilderness with the other wild ones!' It was Marcus who called up to Rex this time. 'They're not the same!'

Commodore Manning held up a hand for quiet. 'For now, they *are* the same. And you must treat them as such. I do understand the horror of what has happened and some of my – our – changes will be unpopular at first. But we have to be united in the face of this new threat.'

'Chan*ges* plural?' Bobby glanced at Skandar.

'Therefore –' Rex raised his voice further – 'elemental separation will not be limited to training sessions. From tomorrow morning, all quartets will be disbanded. New quartets will be formed from wielders of the same element.'

There were cries of distress this time. Skandar, Bobby, Mitchell and Flo stared at each other in absolute disbelief.

'I AM AWARE,' Rex shouted, trying to regain control of the crowd, 'that this is very different from how we usually do things. But there is no better way to unify and strengthen our allied elements than by sharing every piece of knowledge we have. I believe that *allied* quartets are key to winning this war against the new Weaver. Therefore any rider found breaking these new rules will be treated as an enemy of the Island. Thank you in advance for your co-operation and understanding. Together we *will* prevail.'

And, with that, Commodore Manning disappeared across the bridge behind him, flanked by sentinels.

The clearing exploded with frantic conversation. Skandar was shocked to find that shouts supporting the Commodore outnumbered the outraged voices. Many believed the Commodore when he said this was the only way. They trusted

## SKANDAR AND THE SKELETON CURSE

Rex to protect them. Skandar, on the other hand, trusted him about as far as he could throw him – which was not very far given how many muscles the silver rider had.

'Let's get out of here,' Skandar murmured to his quartet. A few riders were pointing aggressively towards him – particularly those with earth mutations. Were they wondering if he knew what Kenna had planned for their unicorns? If he could reverse what she'd done?

As Skandar entered the quartet's treehouse, a lump rose in his throat. He took in the elemental paint they'd splashed on the trunk in Nestling year, Mitchell's blackboard tucked behind an overflowing bookshelf, the noticeboard filled with messages they'd left for each other over the years.

Gone to the Trough because STARVING – see you later. That was Skandar.

At water library for book on solstice stones. Mitchell from last year.

Flo, can you get more raspberry jam after your silver circle thing? Bobby, of course.

It will all be okay, I promise! I'm at the stables. Flo from Nestling year.

The quartet slumped on to their beanbags and simply stared at each other.

'Flaming fireballs!' Mitchell exclaimed eventually, sounding half furious, half terrified. 'What kind of sadist decides we should live with people wielding the *same* element? Oh yes, great idea, Rex. Let's put all the air wielders together – extroverts, thrill-seekers, rule-breakers – all in one treehouse, which they'll probably explode for fun within minutes.'

'You're right, Mitchell,' Flo said. 'We all need to be balanced out, learn from each other. You've all taught me so much – how to be more confident in myself, how to face my fears, how it's

– 22 –

# NEW RULES

okay to be rude sometimes.' Her voice sounded wobbly. 'I don't know what Rex thinks he's doing.' It was one of the only times Skandar had heard Flo criticise the head of the Silver Circle.

'What if we just refuse to join a new quartet?' Bobby said suddenly. She'd taken off her battered green jacket and all the grey feathers on her arms stood up on end, as though readying for a fight.

Mitchell's voice was quieter when he spoke again. 'You heard what Rex said. Anyone who breaks the new rules will be treated as an *enemy of the Island*. That might even mean prison. And we can't risk the Commodore having any excuse to arrest Skandar. I hate to say it, but we have to do what he wants.'

'But maybe not for ever.' Flo's eyes were alight with an idea. 'Skar, you could investigate the bonds between the earth unicorns and their riders – use the spirit element to see if they're still connected! If we reverse what Kenna has done, won't everything go back to normal?'

'An excellent plan,' Mitchell announced happily. 'We'll all be back together in no time.'

Skandar was desperate to believe this and copied Mitchell's upbeat tone. 'Let's visit Agatha before we start Rookie training. There might be earth-allied Wanderers whose unicorns are still with them – they've always been better at living alongside the wild ones. Like Flo said, I could take a look at their bonds up close.' Skandar was the only spirit wielder left with a unicorn, so he alone would be able to see if any trace of the earth bonds remained.

There was another stressed silence as they tried to process the shock of being separated.

'I wish we didn't have to leave here,' Flo said, looking around the treehouse.

Skandar felt his anger building now. 'Separating us doesn't

– 23 –

# SKANDAR AND THE SKELETON CURSE

even make sense! My sister is *allied* to all five elements. She's as strong in fire as she is in water. Why does Rex think restricting us to one element is going to help? Kenna will still win. And Rex must have had reports from his sentinels – he must know how powerful she is. The separation is pointless!'

Bobby blew her fringe out of her eyes. 'Exactly what I was thinking, spirit boy. I don't think these new rules have anything to do with uniting against Kenna's power or whatever rubbish he said down there. Don't you see? Only allowing us to train in our allied elements gives pure magical strength an advantage over skill. You've said it yourself, Flo. Switching between elements is one of the hardest things for silvers to do. But if everyone is forced to stick to their own element – their *allied* element – then a silver is unbeatable.'

Mitchell was nodding. 'Not many people on the Island have *seen* Kenna's power up close. I think Rex is taking advantage of that. With these new rules he can appear to be doing something against Kenna *and* establish silvers as top of the food chain.'

'But Rex is Commodore! He's already at the top!' Flo argued.

'Yes, and he wants to stay there,' Mitchell said ominously.

Skandar felt fear grip his heart. Bobby and Mitchell were right. There was no way Rex was ever going to allow training or quartets to go back to normal – even if Skandar and his friends reversed what his sister had done. Because Kenna's attack was an opportunity for more power – and the Commodore had seized it.

Rex Manning didn't waste any time. The following morning, Skandar and Mitchell were awoken by loud conversation coming from the next-door treehouse. They both swung quickly out of their hammocks and rushed to open the circular window halfway down the trunk.

'What's going on?' Flo's voice floated up from the living area –

– 24 –

## NEW RULES

Skandar could see her sitting cross-legged on the green beanbag below, leaning over a pile of something colourful.

'The instructors are next door,' Mitchell called down.

'Already?' Flo croaked.

Skandar looked out of the open window at Sarika, Gabriel, Zac and Mabel standing with the instructors on their treehouse platform. Aside from Skandar's and Niamh's, they were the only other full quartet left after the Chaos Trials.

Mabel was pleading with Instructor Webb, her frosted freckles sparkling in the morning sun. 'But Queen's Price only turned wild yesterday. *Please* can you just let us stay together a bit longer – for Gabriel?'

'I wish I could.' Instructor Webb's voice was very solemn, and it looked as though he wanted to say more. He glanced sideways at Rex. 'But it's for the good of the Island. Be ready to leave this treehouse in one hour.'

It took a surprisingly long time for the instructors to knock on the door of Skandar's treehouse. He and Mitchell had woken Bobby, got dressed and then they'd all had time to stare ominously at the door for a few minutes before the instructors arrived.

*Knock. Knock.*

'What if we refuse to open it?' Bobby said fiercely. 'What if I fight them? What if—'

Flo pulled the air wielder into a hug. 'It's all right, Bobby. It'll be all right.'

Mitchell turned to face them all. 'What we have to remember – no matter what they say or do – is that we'll always be a quartet. We chose each other. And we can keep choosing each other. They can't take that away from us.'

'Forking thunderstorms, Mitchell, open the door before you make me cry,' Bobby said. And when Skandar saw her stricken expression, he realised that – for once – she was serious.

– 25 –

# SKANDAR AND THE SKELETON CURSE

'Good morning!' Rex greeted them with a wide smile and a sparkle in his cheeks, as though he was about to deliver exceptionally good news. 'Wonderful to see you all awake already. Change is exciting, isn't it?'

The quartet glared back at him. Even Flo didn't return his smile.

Rex cleared his throat a little awkwardly. 'Right then. I'll go first – Roberta? Ready to hear who will be in your air-allied quartet?'

'My *name* is Bobby,' she said in a voice filled with venom.

Rex ignored this and peered down at his yellow clipboard. 'Your new quartet will be Anoushka and Sky Pirate, Zac and Yesterday's Ghost, and Ivan and Swift Sabotage.' Rex looked up at Bobby expectantly.

She put a hand on her hip. 'What do you want me to say? Thank you?'

Skandar saw again that dangerous flash in Rex's green eyes, but the Commodore simply moved out of the doorway for Instructor Anderson and his red clipboard. The fire instructor's usually merry expression was completely absent, the flames at his ears burning very low. When he spoke, his voice was gentle. 'Mitchell? Your new fire-allied quartet will be Art and Furious Inferno, Ajay and Smouldering Menace, and Meiyi and Rose-Briar's Darling.' Mitchell tried to stifle his choke – Meiyi had been a member of the original Threat Quartet.

'You okay?' Skandar checked, but Mitchell was looking down at his boots.

Then Instructor Webb listed the members of Flo's new earth-allied quartet, but the only pair Skandar recognised was Marcus and Sandstorm's Orbit. Flo looked bewildered and Instructor Manning stepped forward to explain. 'I thought it would be beneficial for you to live with Preds. You'll need to learn as much as you can from the older riders. As the only earth silver in the

– 26 –

# NEW RULES

Circle, you and Blade will be taking on teaching duties as soon as the other earth unicorns return to normal.'

Flo took two deep breaths, something she often did when gathering the courage to speak her mind. Then: 'This is madness, Rex. What are you doing?'

Skandar tensed. Mitchell's hair flared. Bobby clenched a fist in silent celebration.

Rex didn't respond but Flo wasn't finished. 'I'm a Rookie. You can't expect me to *teach* other riders. They'll never respect me, and why should they? I'm nowhere near the best in *my* year, let alone among the Predators.'

Rex frowned as though confused by Flo's reaction. 'Of course they'll respect you. You're a silver, Flo. Never forget that.'

'But I don't *want* to teach!'

'You will because I'm asking, Florence. And I am the Commodore, and you swore your loyalty to the Silver Circle. There is nothing further to discuss. Instructor O'Sullivan?'

Rex waved the water instructor forward as a way of ending the conversation. Flo was shaking from head to foot – though with fear or anger, Skandar didn't know. He put a gentle hand on her arm, and she shut her eyes for a moment, steadying herself.

Instructor O'Sullivan's cerulean cloak filled the doorway and her swirling blue eyes held Skandar's. There was some kind of battle raging across her face. Finally, instead of reading from the clipboard, she lowered it to her side.

'Skandar, I have always treated you as an honorary water wielder, so I will assign you to a water-allied treehouse should you wish it. But the truth, so far *unacknowledged* –' she glowered at Rex – 'is that you are a spirit wielder, and the Eyrie has permitted you to train as such for the last two years. The decision is yours.'

Everything had happened so quickly in the past twelve hours – Kenna, the earth unicorns, Rex's new rules – that

– 27 –

# SKANDAR AND THE SKELETON CURSE

Skandar hadn't even thought about which quartet he would be joining. Would he be alone if he chose spirit? Who would train him with Agatha gone? Where would he live?

'Skar?' Flo prompted, and he realised they were all waiting for him to choose.

He imagined the training sessions he and Scoundrel's Luck would have to endure. They'd only be allowed to train in the water element – Scoundrel would hate that. It would be like going back to Hatchling year, unable to be themselves.

'I won't hide who I am,' Skandar answered. 'I'm not a water wielder – I never have been and I never will be. It's kind of you to offer, Instructor,' he added. 'But Scoundrel's Luck and I are allied to the spirit element. So, well, that's . . . that.'

There was fierce pride in Instructor O'Sullivan's eyes. 'Very well. As the only spirit wielder, I think it's probably best that you move into Instructor Everhart's old treehouse.'

'Persephone, we have not previously discussed this—'

She rounded on Rex, her cloak swishing. 'Just as *you* failed to discuss any of *your* changes with us before introducing a completely new and, may I say, extremely damaging system to the Eyrie. Vexing, isn't it?'

'I *can* have you replaced, you know.' Rex was smiling – his voice was steady, polite even – but it sent a shiver down Skandar's spine.

'I dare you to try,' Instructor O'Sullivan growled, her words as spiked as her grey hair.

The air fizzed with tension, until Rex broke it by addressing the quartet as though nothing had happened. 'You have one hour to gather your belongings. We will be back to direct you to your new treehouses shortly.'

Bobby took the opportunity to kick the door shut so it slammed in Rex's face.

CHAPTER THREE

# ACTING SKILLS

Once the instructors had left with their clipboards, Skandar, Bobby, Mitchell and Flo had no choice but to prepare for their quartet's separation. Packing up took much longer than they'd expected. Skandar in particular had acquired so many more belongings than the few he'd brought in his black rucksack from the Mainland three years ago. He had to borrow two more bags from Mitchell.

Finally the quartet heaved their things down the treehouse trunk and gathered in the empty space. Everything was bare, and far too tidy.

'I've decided we're all being very overdramatic about this,' Bobby announced, as she crammed her last jar of Marmite into her rucksack. 'Let's meet at the stables in an hour. The treehouse is just where we sleep; it's really not that big a deal.'

'That's true!' Mitchell said, visibly cheering up. 'They can't stop us spending time together. It's only training and sleeping when we're required to be apart.'

'They didn't technically say that we can't *meet* in treehouses,'

# SKANDAR AND THE SKELETON CURSE

Flo said, looking excited. 'And Skandar's got one all to himself. We can all go to Agatha's later, can't we?'

The relief made Skandar laugh out loud. 'Flo! You rebel!'

She beamed at him, delighted.

Bobby bowed flamboyantly. 'She learned from the best.'

*Knock. Knock.*

'Florence?' It was Instructor Webb.

'No!' Flo cried, her smile vanishing. 'Not yet! Stall him, please!'

'Sorry, Instructor Webb. We're all naked right now!' Bobby yelled. 'Give Flo a minute to put her clothes on.'

Mitchell and Skandar muffled their laughter, while Flo pulled a fistful of something out of her green jacket pocket.

'Do you all have the bracelets I made you for your birthdays last year?' she asked.

Bobby, Skandar and Mitchell each held up a wrist. Not one of them had taken Flo's gift off.

'Okay, give them to me. Quickly!'

They slipped the circlets off their wrists, and Flo dropped to the floor and started laying out more bracelets. There were twelve in total, each made with all five elemental colours.

'Is this why you never came to bed last night?' Bobby asked, her eyes wide.

Flo nodded and began giving out the bracelets. She pressed three into Skandar's hand – one with the words *Bobby and Falcon* accented in yellow thread, one with *Mitchell and Red* in scarlet, and Flo's own, threaded green with Blade's name. Skandar saw that she slipped the white threaded bracelet he'd been wearing on to her own wrist, and gave Mitchell and Bobby two new *Skandar and Scoundrel* bracelets.

For a moment they fiddled silently with the saddler knots to secure the bracelets under their green jacket sleeves.

– 30 –

# ACTING SKILLS

'It's like Mitchell said.' Flo showed them the bracelets stacked on her arm. 'We'll always be a quartet, and I thought it would be nice if we had these to remind us of that. You know, when we're sleeping in different treehouses.'

'I love them,' Mitchell declared immediately.

Bobby looked down at her own bracelets in wonder. 'These are so deeply unfashionable, but somehow I never, ever want to take them off.'

'They're perfect,' Skandar said, and hugged Flo for so long that Instructor Webb cleared his throat from outside the door.

'It's time to go, Florence.'

Skandar felt stomach-churning panic as Flo moved out of his arms. There was so much he'd wanted to say to her since the end of the Chaos Trials, but he'd never quite managed to find the words.

'I'll see you all a bit later,' Flo said – though she was looking only at Skandar, and he thought perhaps there were lots of things she wanted to say to him too.

Mitchell was collected next, clutching the bracelets on his arm like a lifeline. And when Rex came for Bobby, she refused to say one word to him.

Skandar waited on the blue beanbag, staring at the seascape he'd painted two years before, and trying to fight off the waves of sadness that now hit him whenever he was alone. In recent weeks he'd found that he needed constant distraction – by his friends, by Scoundrel – just to keep his head above water. And now his quartet had been separated, he didn't know how he was going to deal with these times when there was nowhere to hide from his jumble of confused emotions. He should be happy that the Weaver was dead, but most of the time he swung between anger and sadness. He should hate Kenna for killing Arctic Swansong, for turning the earth unicorns wild, but all he could

– 31 –

# SKANDAR AND THE SKELETON CURSE

do was wonder whether she felt like she was drowning too.

In fact, he had done more than just wonder.

Not long after the Weaver's death, Skandar had snuck out from the treehouse and attempted a Mender dream with Scoundrel. It was the only way for him to check on his sister. But it hadn't gone well. When Skandar's dream presence had first collided with hers, Kenna's emotions had been in such furious turmoil that he'd thought he'd somehow ended up colliding with a wild unicorn instead.

When he'd eventually managed to separate himself, Skandar had sat next to Kenna on a strange treehouse platform made from different shades of metal. For a moment he'd forgotten that people couldn't have conversations in Mender dreams; that this wasn't really Kenna. He'd talked to her, his phantom words hanging in the air unanswered. And her silence had been overwhelmingly awful. He'd sobbed so loudly that he'd woken himself up and out of the dream altogether. He had not tried it again.

Now the bond with his unicorn filled with an emotion that wasn't his own – a pulse of playfulness, a dose of hope and boundless love. 'Thanks, Scoundrel,' Skandar murmured. Even though the unicorn was metres below, he could feel his rider's emotions spiralling and he was helping as best he could. For a few seconds, Skandar felt brighter, but then another wave of sadness arrived, and not even Scoundrel could keep it from crashing over him. As a result, when Instructor O'Sullivan came to collect him, Skandar practically ran out of the treehouse.

As they made their way to Agatha's old treehouse, the water instructor and spirit wielder edged past other riders clutching belongings. Thinking of his aunt made Skandar feel even sadder. He'd been out to see her with the Wanderers, but it wasn't the same as being able to pop over for a cup of fire zone tea anytime he liked – and Agatha was different too. The first time Skandar

– 32 –

## ACTING SKILLS

had visited her after Swan's death, she'd barely been able to speak for grief. It was no surprise. She'd lost her sister and her unicorn in one fell swoop.

Instructor O'Sullivan's face was as grim as Skandar's thoughts when they eventually reached the treehouse. But it didn't stop him asking a question he hadn't been able to in front of Rex.

'Instructor, you know how you called this whole new quartet thing "damaging" earlier?'

'I did say that, didn't I?' Her eyes were deep whirlpools.

'How come you – the Eyrie – are letting Rex get away with this? I thought the Commodore didn't have power here; I thought—'

'You thought you were safe,' Instructor O'Sullivan finished for him, and her voice was so desolate that it chilled Skandar to his bones.

'I just mean, I thought the instructors had the power to stop something like this.' Skandar was aware that he sounded like he was blaming her. Perhaps he was.

She sighed and faced him in the doorway. 'The problem is that Rex Manning *is* one of the instructors. He has power here, power as Commodore *and* power as head of the Silver Circle. I was worried about him the moment he searched your treehouse unsanctioned last year, but then when he announced his temporary leadership after Nina's death . . .' She grimaced. 'The Island never envisaged that one person would have all three roles.'

'So will he replace you? Like he threatened?'

'I don't think so, although I'm sure he'd like to. He wants to make everything look peaceful. He wants to appear like he has everything under control at the Eyrie, at the Stronghold, in Council Square. I considered resigning in protest, but . . .' She hesitated. 'As long as I'm here, I can at least try to protect all you riders, as best I can.'

– 33 –

# SKANDAR AND THE SKELETON CURSE

Skandar frowned. 'From Kenna, do you mean?'

Instructor O'Sullivan shook her head. 'No. From the Commodore. In my experience, sometimes the most dangerous men are the ones who style themselves as our saviours.'

Dread settled in Skandar's stomach. 'Will he even *try* to reverse what Kenna has done?'

'Oh, I'm sure he'll make some effort,' the water instructor said dismissively. 'But it won't be for the earth wielders – it'll be to make himself look good. Even better, I should say. He's very popular inside the Eyrie and outside it. That's part of the problem.'

'But doesn't he care about the unicorns going wild? About what their riders are going through?'

'No,' she said simply. 'Because it's not happening to him.' Instructor O'Sullivan pushed the door open for Skandar and placed one of his bags in the doorway.

'Well, he's never going to reverse what Kenna's done if he's got an attitude like that,' Skandar said angrily. 'Not if he doesn't even care about the earth wielders.'

'Correct,' Instructor O'Sullivan agreed. 'But then perhaps it falls – as always – to the kind of people who do care. The ones brave enough to bend bad rules. Those with courage and recklessness running through their veins?' She raised a sharp grey eyebrow and left Skandar standing on the treehouse doorstep.

Had Instructor O'Sullivan really just *encouraged* him to break the rules?

---

For the rest of August, the atmosphere at the Eyrie was the strangest Skandar had ever known. The Hatchlings restarted their training, separated by allied element and forbidden from summoning any other. This worked when the Instructors' domes

– 34 –

## ACTING SKILLS

were up, but at all other times the baby unicorns ignored this rule and blasted any of the four elements they fancied. Bobby's sister, Isa, found this very funny, and Skandar supposed she hadn't known anything different. Even the quartet separation wasn't such a big deal for the Hatchlings – they'd known each other less than two months.

Meanwhile nobody would have known that Skandar, Bobby, Flo and Mitchell were no longer an official quartet. Rookie training didn't start until September, so – much to Skandar's relief – they spent every possible moment together, carefully avoiding Rex. Agatha's treehouse became their regular meeting place, and on most balmy earth-season nights they slept in their unicorns' neighbouring stables, rather than in their new allied treehouses. This wasn't technically against the rules . . . yet. As Flo had said, it wasn't that the riders in her new quartet were horrible – they just weren't Skandar, Mitchell and Bobby. Mitchell, however, didn't share her opinion. He avoided his new treehouse at all costs, convinced that Meiyi would murder him in his sleep.

It was terrible to see earth wielders aimlessly wandering the Eyrie. Many had abandoned the training school altogether – like Gabriel, who'd gone off to search for Queen's Price despite the warnings in the *Hatchery Herald* about stampeding wild unicorns and the curfews in Fourpoint after dark. Interestingly the earth unicorns seemed to feel a pull towards places where humans gathered – unlike true wild unicorns who stuck largely to the Wilderness.

Skandar decided to take this behaviour as a good sign. Perhaps it showed their unicorn–rider bonds were not gone for ever? He was desperate to visit Agatha and talk to the Wanderers about using the spirit element to investigate. But the challenge was getting out of the Eyrie.

– 35 –

# SKANDAR AND THE SKELETON CURSE

After Gabriel and some of the other earth wielders had left to search for their unicorns, Rex had introduced a whole raft of new 'safety measures'. Preds had been put on rotas to patrol the Eyrie walls, riding after dark had been banned, and four silver-masked sentinels had been stationed at the Eyrie's entrance. The measures were supposedly for everyone's protection, but they also made it almost impossible to get beyond the elemental walls without a valid excuse.

Jamie had also struggled to get *in* to the Eyrie, since he visited much more often than other blacksmiths. Mitchell had spent hours inventing new excuses for him, but one evening Skandar found the fire wielder with his face buried in Red's mane, distraught because Jamie had been turned away.

'Everything is wrong,' Mitchell choked out, as Skandar guided him to sit down on the straw. Red blew a comforting warm breeze over the two of them. 'I don't . . . I don't like change. I hate not having a treehouse I can go back to. And I miss Jamie, and missing him feels like –' he paused, struggling to voice it – 'like someone is pressing on my chest and I can't take a deep enough breath.'

Since Mitchell and Jamie had got together, Skandar had listened very carefully when Mitchell spoke about the blacksmith. And he had found himself searching – in the way the two whispered to each other, or held hands so effortlessly – for how to solve the puzzle of his feelings about Flo. Something had shifted for Skandar at the end of the Air Trial. And he found himself thinking about her all the time, as well as choosing to sit next to her rather than anyone else when they were in Agatha's treehouse. Whenever she touched his arm now, it was as though her hand was fizzing with the air element. But he didn't know what he was supposed to *do* about any of that, and he felt too shy to ask anyone.

– 36 –

## ACTING SKILLS

Out loud Mitchell continued to worry. 'And how will we ever get out of the Eyrie unseen? The sentinels aren't exactly going to miss us, are they? We *need* to talk to Agatha and work out what Kenna has done so that everything can go back to normal. I miss normal! I took normal for granted. Erm, Skandar? Are you even listening to this rant? I need a response if it's going to be at all satisfying.'

'I'm sorry, but I've just had an idea about how we can get out of the Eyrie!' Skandar's mouth twitched into a smile. 'Among the riders we know, who would you say is most capable of causing a very loud and annoying distraction? Apart from Bobby,' he added.

'Isa, of course,' Mitchell answered immediately. 'Those sisters were raised on raw confidence with a side helping of sarcasm.'

'Exactly. If anyone can distract those sentinels, it's a Bruna.'

On the last day of August, Scoundrel, Falcon, Blade and Red waited near the Eyrie's entrance, hidden in the shadows of the armoured trees. The quartet had eventually managed to strike a bargain with Isa, who was a very tough negotiator. It turned out that what she wanted most of all was to be chosen for the Peregrine Society in her Nestling year – something her older sister had never achieved. Therefore, in return for distracting the sentinels, Skandar had agreed to give her tips about fast flying. She'd also demanded ten emergency sandwiches – not because she liked them, but because she wanted to irritate Bobby.

'Come on, Isa,' Bobby muttered, as they waited between the trunks. 'It would be just like her to go back on her word *after* she's eaten my sandwiches.'

'Try to trust her, Bobby. Remember?' Flo encouraged.

Mitchell snorted. 'I'm with Bobby on this one. Isa's attitude doesn't exactly shout reliable, does it?'

– 37 –

# SKANDAR AND THE SKELETON CURSE

'OH NO, MY UNICORN IS COMPLETELY OUT OF CONTROL!' Isa's voice was so loud that Flo winced, as Tsunami's Herald came careering out of the trees in a white blur.

'OH NO, PLEASE HELP, I'M GOING TO COLLIDE WITH THE ENTRANCE TREE. I'M NOT SUPPOSED TO LEAVE THE EYRIE, OH NOOOOO!'

'My sister has many talents, but acting is not one of them,' Bobby whispered, as Isa slowed Herald to a complete stop, leaned down to place her palm on the trunk, and opened it in a whirl of water. She glanced over her shoulder, nodded once towards them, and then galloped Herald through the gap.

'Stop her!' Skandar heard one of the sentinels yell from the outer wall.

'HELP ME, I'M A HELPLESS HATCHLING! I CAN'T STOP! I can't . . .' Isa's voice grew fainter as Herald carried her further away from the colourful entrance. And, as predicted, two sentinels chased after her. But the other two remained – just visible through the open entrance. That was where Skandar came in.

In a perfect imitation of Rex Manning's voice, Skandar's spirit speech sounded in their ears. *Report to the Silver Stronghold immediately.*

One of the sentinels looked over his shoulder, as though he thought Rex had perhaps called the instruction through the entrance.

'Better not argue with the boss,' the other sentinel said – and they too left their posts at the Eyrie's gate.

'Quick, before it closes!' Mitchell cried, and the four unicorns barrelled through the opening Isa had left in the trunk.

Even with the sentinels gone, it was still too risky to fly, so the quartet galloped down towards Fourpoint.

'Well, Isa definitely committed to her role. You can't argue

– 38 –

## ACTING SKILLS

with that,' Bobby said, once they were safely hidden within Fourpoint's narrow streets.

'My ears are still ringing.' Flo tipped her head from side to side.

Skandar chuckled. 'She must *really* want to be a Grin.'

As the quartet passed through the final fragrant rosemary field and on to the rougher moorland of the earth zone, Skandar blew the cuckoo whistle to alert the Wanderers. He was painfully aware of Kenna doing the same along the earth fault line the previous year, and for a moment he could hardly breathe thinking of how much had changed since then. *Kenna's betrayal. Swan's murder. His mum's death.*

'I've just had a terrible thought,' Bobby said, sounding appalled.

'What?' Mitchell asked, and Skandar was pulled from his own dark thoughts.

'If all the air wielders are training together, I might have to partner up with Amber *every single day.*'

'I thought you were going to say something dreadful,' Flo scolded over her shoulder.

Skandar laughed. 'She isn't that bad, Bobby. Give her a chance.'

'I *did* give her a chance – I saved her skin at the end of the Chaos Trials, but that doesn't mean I signed up for seeing her smug face all the time.'

'I still don't really understand why you— FLO! ' Mitchell interrupted himself. 'Watch out!'

At the front of the group, Silver Blade was rearing up, hooves flailing.

'What's he seen?' Skandar asked, confused.

'Back him up!' Bobby called.

– 39 –

# SKANDAR AND THE SKELETON CURSE

'I can't!' Flo cried.

And when Falcon skittered sideways, Skandar saw the problem.

Ahead, roots had risen through the crack of the fault line and wrapped themselves round Blade's legs like living chains. Green vines then burst from the roots themselves, flowering with black honeysuckle, and encircled the silver unicorn's stomach as though trying to pull him down on to the line.

Blade went berserk. He bellowed and blasted magic and attempted to buck. Flo was thrown over his silver head as he struggled to escape. She landed with a thud right on the fault line just in front of his great hooves.

Skandar, Bobby and Mitchell flung themselves from their unicorns and ran towards Flo; she was surrounded by an eerie green glow radiating from the fault line.

Bobby was the first to reach her, but she suddenly rubbed her hands over her eyes, as though trying to wipe something away. 'Arghhhh!' When she turned back round, her whole face was plastered with thick mud.

Mitchell had barely taken a step into the green glow when he was forced backwards – his body covered from head to toe in sand, like he'd walked through a desert storm.

'You won't get through!' Mitchell cried, as Skandar stepped towards the glow himself. 'We need a different plan.'

'I'm not leaving her!' Skandar called, before dropping to his knees and making his way along the deep groove of the fault line towards Flo's motionless form.

Chapter Four

# POISONED

Even though he was surrounded by the green glow, Skandar met no resistance as he made his way towards Flo. No mud. No sand. No vines. Just the overpowering smell of pure earth magic – for him it was newly dug soil, pine needles, and sun-baked rocks. His heart thundered as he got nearer. Black honeysuckle vines had grown over her body, as though she were a chrysalis not yet ready to become a butterfly. It was some of the most extraordinary earth magic Skandar had ever seen, but all he could think as he reached her was:

*Not Flo. I can't lose Flo.*

When she whimpered Skandar thought his chest might explode with relief. 'I'm here, Flo. I'll get you. I'll get you out.'

Skandar pulled frantically at the vines. His palms blistered, the thorns cut his fingers, but he didn't stop until he was able to hook his hands underneath Flo's arms and drag her out from the black-flowered cocoon. She slumped against his chest and Skandar had to half crawl, half stagger to get them safely beyond the green glow.

# SKANDAR AND THE SKELETON CURSE

Once free, they collapsed into a clump of purple heather to one side of the fault line. Bobby rushed to them, as Mitchell and Red reduced the very last root trapping Blade to cinders.

'How are you not covered in anything?' Bobby asked Skandar, as she dropped to her knees next to a barely conscious Flo. Both girls were absolutely caked in mud and sand – Flo looked almost mummified with it.

'Is she breathing? Is she okay? She made a sound before but I—'

Then Flo let out a hacking cough, followed by another whimper. Blade stormed over with Mitchell, and stood protectively by his rider.

Skandar put a hand to Flo's deep brown forehead. 'She's burning up. We're going to have to get her to a healer or—'

Unicorns were galloping across the moorland towards them.

'They're Wanderers,' Bobby breathed in relief. 'Thank all five elements for that.'

The Wanderers – none of whom Skandar recognised – constructed a stretcher to carry Flo back to their earth-season home. On the journey, Blade kept so close to her that his silver nose nudged against her cloud of hair.

When they finally entered the dark mouth of the Glowing Caves, Skandar was so panicked that he barely noticed the ethereal blue light from the glow-worms above his head, or how many more people were gathered inside the cave system than the last time he'd visited. Instead, his eyes were fixed on the campfire ahead and two figures rising behind its smoke. One was tall, with white hair cut into a sharp bob. The other was shorter, with grey-brown hair pulled into a tight bun.

'What's happened?' The first figure stepped in front of the fire and resolved into Elora Scott, the Pathfinder of the Wanderers. Her amethyst eyes darted behind Scoundrel and

# POISONED

fixed on Flo in the stretcher.

'Can you help her?' Skandar asked.

Mitchell explained quickly what had happened to Flo and Blade on the fault line.

Elora listened intently, her face turning an even paler shade of white than Skandar's, and then called for two Wanderers called Otto and Cat to assist her.

'We must not be disturbed,' she said, before heading towards a small cave separated from the main cavern by a string curtain of rose quartz. The gemstones clinked as all three Wanderers disappeared behind it, carrying Flo's stretcher between them.

'Skandar, what are you doing here?' The growl of a question came from Agatha Everhart – grief for her unicorn and her sister still etched across her features.

'Flo,' Skandar choked out, and somehow he found himself in his aunt's arms.

'She'll be all right, little spirit wielder. You'll see.' Agatha patted his head awkwardly – the pair were still getting used to the idea of hugs. 'Although you're not so little now. You're actually . . . crushing my ribs?'

Skandar let go, clearing his throat. 'Sorry, I—'

'Why don't we all sit down and have some fire zone tea while we wait?'

'You do realise that you almost always suggest having tea in life-or-death situations?' Mitchell said dryly, sitting down on one of the smooth flat rocks by the fire.

'I do.' Agatha shrugged. 'And have any of you ever come to serious harm?'

'Depends on what you mean by harm,' Bobby mumbled, glancing at Skandar, who had his head in his hands.

'Skandar, you haven't answered my question.' Agatha

– 43 –

nudged his wrist with a steaming mug so he had to look up and take it. 'Why were you summoning the Wanderers?'

Skandar's eyes kept flicking to the gemstone beads of the curtain. Blade was outside it, on guard. 'I wanted to talk to you about the earth unicorns going wild. I thought you might have an idea how Kenna –' Skandar hesitated as Agatha recoiled at the name of Swan's killer – 'how she did it, whether there might be a way to reverse it.'

'Without the spirit element, without Swan –' Agatha paused, as though willing herself to carry on – 'I haven't been much use on that front.'

'What about Elora?' Mitchell asked, between sips. 'Did Silver Soldier turn wild along with the other earth unicorns?

Agatha shook her head. 'No. All the other earth unicorns among the Wanderers did, but not Soldier. I'm guessing since Blade is still his shiny self, whatever Ken— whatever *she's* done, couldn't affect silvers.'

There was a long silence while Agatha stared into space – like the pain of losing her unicorn had hollowed her out. It reminded Skandar horribly of another spirit wielder whose unicorn had been killed – Joby Worsham, who'd taught him as a Hatchling and then joined the Weaver.

Bobby broke the spell. 'It smells proper fruity in this cave.' She wrinkled her nose and looked around at the rocks crowded with people. 'Did washing suddenly become too mainstream for this lot?'

'The Wanderers have taken in a great many of the earth wielders looking for their unicorns,' Agatha said softly. 'They use this as a base before searching the zones or the Wilderness.'

'Have any of them found their unicorns?' Mitchell asked hopefully.

'A few,' Agatha answered, then her focus snapped back

– 44 –

# POISONED

towards Skandar. 'In fact, since you've risked coming all the way out here, let's take a look at them. You can summon the spirit element, see if they're still connected.'

'What about Flo?'

'You sitting here fretting isn't helping anything. And frankly there are two outcomes that will emerge from behind that hideously garish curtain. One, Elora heals Flo and she needs rest. Two, Elora can't heal Flo and there is nothing you can do. Neither of those options requires your presence, does it?'

Even Bobby winced at Agatha's bluntness. 'Absolutely brutal.'

Skandar knew there was no arguing with his aunt when she was in this kind of mood. And he also felt relieved that the haunted look had momentarily disappeared from her face – even if she was ordering him around. So, with Bobby and Mitchell promising to fetch Skandar if anything changed with Flo, he led Scoundrel back through the cave and out into the late-August sunshine.

Skandar glanced sideways at his aunt in the bright light – and it was only now that he noticed her cheeks. The white mutation marks on her face that he'd once mistaken for scars were definitely a little . . . fainter. Another memory of Joby surfaced: of the spirit wielder pulling off a sock to reveal his own faded mutation. Skandar hadn't realised it would happen to Agatha so soon after Swan's death.

'What?' Agatha asked aggressively when she caught Skandar looking. Then she sighed. 'Sorry.'

'You never say "sorry"!'

'Well,' Agatha croaked, 'I'm being an old grump and you can't be having an easy time of it either. How are you holding up?'

Skandar knew she wasn't talking about Flo. He shrugged. 'Not great,' he said eventually, knowing Agatha would see right through a lie.

– 45 –

'You can talk to me,' she said uncharacteristically gently. 'I know you probably blame me for killing your mother, but—'

Skandar grabbed his aunt's hand. 'Don't say that. I don't blame you, okay? It wasn't your fault. You didn't know what was going to happen.'

Agatha squeezed his hand tighter. 'You're kind for saying that.'

'I'm saying it because it's true,' Skandar said stubbornly. 'How are *you* holding up?'

Agatha shrugged in a perfect imitation of her nephew. 'Not great.'

He waited.

'Sometimes I forget, Skandar,' she confessed in a rush. 'I was separated from Erika and Swan for so many years that sometimes I wake up and – for a single blissful moment – I forget that they're both gone for good.'

'I'm sorry.' Skandar blinked back tears.

Agatha chuckled, though the sound was sad. 'You *always* say sorry, little spirit wielder – even when none of this is your fault.'

Aunt and nephew continued in companionable silence until they emerged at the edge of a field filled with wild unicorns. But Skandar's eye was drawn to a high rocky shelf that jutted out from the neighbouring mountain's side, which was populated with half a dozen tattered-looking tents.

'Elora has had to keep the earth unicorns separated from the other wild foals the Wanderers take care of,' Agatha explained. 'The earth unicorns are very volatile and confused, and of course they have no prior relationship with the Wanderers. Once a rider finds their unicorn, Elora helps herd it to this area here. It's certainly brave of her.'

Skandar watched as a boy came out of a tent, attached himself to a rope and abseiled down the rock face to the pasture below. A boy with hair as still as stone.

– 46 –

# POISONED

'That's Gabriel!' Skandar exclaimed.

Agatha nodded. 'He was one of the first to find his unicorn. Try the spirit element now?' There was a hungry intensity to her voice. 'You're probably safest summoning it in the air. Once the wild unicorns spot the white glow, they'll be over here like a shot.'

Usually, when Skandar and Scoundrel flew together, the black unicorn was so full of joy that the bond vibrated with it. But today, as they took off, it was filled with Scoundrel's confusion instead, and he made short shrieking noises at the wild unicorns below. Skandar was sure he knew they weren't natural wild unicorns; perhaps he recognised some of his Eyrie stablemates?

Skandar summoned the spirit element into his palm and – as it glowed white – he focused on Gabriel standing at the base of the rocky overhang. The bond running from the earth wielder's heart burst into his vision, and Skandar tracked it to a light grey unicorn that was making its way towards the earth wielder. Queen's Price was barely recognisable. The bones of her skeleton flashed as she walked, wings hanging limply like a bird's rotting carcass. But it was Price, Skandar was sure, because the bond at Gabriel's heart led directly to her own.

For a split second Skandar felt a huge rush of joy and relief, but then his heart plummeted. There was something wrong. Gabriel and Queen's Price were earth-allied so the cord between their hearts should have been bright green, but it . . . wasn't. Instead, the bond that had formed the moment Price had hatched was ghostly and empty.

Scoundrel swooped round and Skandar widened his vision to the rest of the field. More empty bonds hovered in shadowy lines, leading from the hearts of the wild unicorns to the tents on the ridge. Looking at them more closely, Skandar thought that the transparent outlines reminded him a little of a spirit bond.

– 47 –

# SKANDAR AND THE SKELETON CURSE

Scoundrel landed and Queen's Price was now sniffing at Gabriel's hand, blood crusted round her nostrils.

'The bonds are still there,' Skandar told Agatha breathlessly as he dismounted.

'And the bad news?' she asked, seeing his distress.

'There's no colour in them,' Skandar said quietly. 'It's like they've been drained.'

'Drained? *How* has she done this?' Agatha sighed deeply. 'It is good news, though. Reversing it feels more possible if you can still see the link between their hearts. I suspected there was still a connection – the wild ones definitely recognise their riders and prefer to stay near them once they're reunited, though that doesn't stop them— GABRIEL!' Agatha yelled suddenly. 'Get out of there!'

The wild unicorn was hurtling towards the earth wielder. Price's eyes were now a deep, angry red, the bones in her legs visible as she moved. She reared up, ghostly horn striking the air and sent five elemental blasts from her mouth right towards Gabriel's head. As quick as a flash, he was climbing the rope to the relative safety of the ridge.

'The recognition doesn't stop them attacking, I was going to say,' Agatha grunted, as she scrambled up the side of the mountain to the tents, gesturing for Skandar to follow. Scoundrel stayed sheltered at the corner of the field below, wisely keeping out of the way.

'Still alive?' Agatha barked, though there was a note of worry in her voice as they reached Gabriel, who was breathing hard at the edge of the ridge. Below, Queen's Price stampeded around the field, hurling blasts in a confused rage.

Other earth wielders had emerged from their tents to check on Gabriel – but Skandar got the sense that they were getting used to near-death experiences with their wild unicorns.

– 48 –

## POISONED

'Skandar?' Gabriel stood up, dusting off bashed knees.

'Hi, Gabriel, are you all right?'

'Physically, yes – only a few grazes this time. But otherwise.' He gestured to Queen's Price down below. 'Otherwise I'm not fine at all.'

'Skandar Smith?' Another earth wielder approached. He had straight brown hair and a constellation of freckles across his nose and cheeks. Skandar recognised him as Charlie – whose unicorn was Hinterland Magma. Charlie had been declared a nomad back in Skandar's Nestling year.

'Why are you here?' Charlie asked suspiciously. 'Is it something to do with your sister?'

Skandar was careful as he answered, remembering that Charlie had been in the Glowing Caves last year when Kenna had sheltered with the Wanderers. And now it was her fault that Hinterland Magma was wild. 'I want to help you; I came to take a look at your bonds. I'm a spirit wielder, so I can see them.'

Charlie's face went from wary to excited. 'You mean we still have our bonds? You saw them?' He raised his voice. 'Everyone, get out here! There's good news!'

'I knew I could still feel something with Price!' Gabriel punched the air. 'I knew our bond wasn't gone for ever!'

Tents unzipped and a dozen more earth wielders emerged – some Eyrie age, others much older. Skandar recognised Aisha, a fellow Rookie, as well as Fatima, who'd been declared a nomad after the Chaos Trials – her unicorn, Moonstone's Venom, was down in the field. One of the last riders to appear was Peter Whitaker, who'd raced Hallowed Hussar in last year's Chaos Cup.

Skandar swallowed nervously, glancing at Agatha. She gave him an unhelpful shrug. 'Umm . . . hi. I'm Skandar.'

'You're the brother of the one who did this to our unicorns,' Peter said gruffly. 'We know who you are.'

– 49 –

# SKANDAR AND THE SKELETON CURSE

'Right, right,' Skandar said, flustered. 'Anyway, I came here to help. I checked your bonds using the spirit element, and they're not *gone*. They're just . . . empty. Empty of colour – of magic, I guess.'

'So there's still a connection?' Aisha asked hopefully, the flowers of her mutation rippling through her dark hair. Fatima nudged her friend, and Aisha signed the question she'd just asked.

'Yes,' Skandar said quickly, as Aisha translated for Fatima. 'But it looks different. They're usually bright green, but now they're transparent, sort of ghostly – like a wild unicorn's horn.'

Smiles broke over both of the girls' faces and they hugged each other, relieved their bonds still existed.

'Can you *fix* them?' an older earth wielder asked, his hair mutated to spikes of short green grass.

'I don't know yet,' Skandar admitted. 'But I'm going to try to find out.'

Peter Whitaker grunted. 'Well, that's better than what that preening Commodore's doing.' There were murmurs of agreement. 'He's more focused on the Eyrie than actually helping us earth wielders. But then it doesn't look like the wildness affects silvers.'

Agatha answered this time, her voice clipped and precise. 'Silver unicorns are the only kind that spirit wielders cannot kill – we have always found it impossible to break their bonds. Elora has a theory that the structure of silver bonds somehow makes them resistant to the spirit element, and this allowed both Silver Blade and Silver Soldier to escape the fate of the other earth unicorns.'

Fatima tapped Aisha on the arm, then faced Agatha to sign a question she wanted answered. 'So the spirit element's responsible for this happening to our unicorns?' Aisha voiced for Fatima.

– 50 –

## POISONED

'As it involves bonds, that's what we're assuming.' Fatima nodded solemnly, as Aisha translated Agatha's response.

Skandar suddenly heard Scoundrel make the joyful shriek he reserved for greeting his best friend. And, sure enough, Skandar spotted a scarlet flash as Mitchell rode Red Night's Delight through the gap between the two mountains.

He waved up at Skandar on the ridge, beaming. 'FLO'S GOING TO BE OKAY! SHE'S AWAKE!'

Relief flooded Skandar, and – promising the earth wielders he would find out what he could about their bonds – he and Agatha scrambled off the ridge and followed Mitchell back into the Glowing Caves.

A few hours later, Skandar sat by the Wanderers' fire. Flo leaned against his shoulder, snoozing. Many of the Wanderers had gone out searching for food but Elora, Agatha, Bobby and Mitchell had stayed, talking in low tones. Skandar had filled them in about the empty bonds he'd seen, and now they were puzzling over what had happened to Flo.

'I've never seen anything like it,' Elora was saying. 'It was as though Flo's body had overdosed on earth magic – been poisoned by it.'

'Perhaps that's why it didn't affect the rest of us so badly?' Mitchell guessed. 'Our bonds aren't already full of earth magic?'

'It didn't affect me at all,' Skandar said quietly, trying not to disturb Flo. 'But the whole place felt . . . off. Unnatural. And there was that green glow.'

'The fact she suffered these injuries in the earth zone cannot be a coincidence,' Elora mused. 'I'll ride there with a team tomorrow to check out the site.'

'I'll come with you,' Agatha said forcefully.

Skandar thought perhaps his aunt was determined to busy

– 51 –

# SKANDAR AND THE SKELETON CURSE

herself with the mystery of Kenna's attack.

'Will you keep allowing the earth wielders to use the Glowing Caves as a base while they look for their unicorns?' he asked Elora. 'We could tell other Eyrie riders about it – ones who want to go looking for their own wild unicorns.'

Elora nodded, her amethyst eyes serious. 'We welcome anyone who needs us. And the wild ones appear to want to stay near their riders once they find them – that's why we move the reunited pairs out to the ridge. But it is a dangerous thing to seek the unicorns while they're wild. Some have . . .' She hesitated. 'In truth, some riders have been killed searching the Wilderness.'

'Killed?' Mitchell's eyes went wide behind his brown glasses.

'That hasn't been in the *Hatchery Herald*!' Bobby protested.

Elora and Agatha gave each other a significant look. 'No,' Elora said finally. 'It hasn't.'

Flo stirred against Skandar's shoulder.

'How are you doing?' he asked gently.

'Better,' she whispered.

'Do you think you can ride?' Mitchell asked her. 'Ideally we'd get back tonight. That way we can at least *pretend* we were visiting the Fourpoint libraries until they closed.'

Flo nodded and was attempting to stand when a white unicorn thundered towards the fire. The rider flung himself to the ground and sprinted towards the group.

'Is she here? Is Kenna here?' It was Albert, his blond curls loose and unkempt, sweat glistening on his slightly pink forehead. 'I was out riding and I heard Skandar was here, and—' He stared round at them.

Elora's eyes were both kind and troubled. 'I'm sorry, Albert. Skandar and his friends came to see if they could help the earth wielders. And I'm not sure we would welcome Kenna even if—'

Albert looked thunderstruck. 'But you wouldn't turn Kenna

– 52 –

# POISONED

away? If she asked for our help; if she said she was sorry? Everyone makes mistakes, right?'

Elora appeared to consider this, glancing at Agatha. 'She has now made several very large mistakes.'

Skandar had forgotten how close Albert and Kenna had become last year, how much time they'd spent together. He swallowed. 'I saw her at the Earth Festival, Albert. She looked well; she looked healthy, sort of, but—'

'Then she did something unthinkable,' Agatha said fiercely.

'Maybe she didn't mean to! Maybe it was—' Albert's blue eyes were wild, frantic.

'She laughed, Albert,' Bobby said bluntly. 'She rode Goshawk into the middle of Element Square and she *laughed*.'

'Well, if that isn't a cry for help, I don't know what is!' Desperation laced Albert's voice. 'Have you got any idea what it was like for Kenna last year? To be so hated? To be hunted by Rex? And yet the Wanderers –' he glared at Elora – 'do not move against the silver Commodore. They just hide in the zones like cowards.'

Elora attempted to interrupt him, but Albert was ranting now.

'And what about the riders with wild unicorns? You say they can stay, but you don't invite them to join us as Wanderers. Oh no. You keep them at arm's length – out on that ridge – just like you did with Kenna last year. You're a coward, Pathfinder!' He spat the title and stalked off with Eagle's Dawn into one of the cave's darker corners.

'Albert has not been himself,' Elora said into the awkward silence. 'He misses Kenna a great deal.'

Skandar felt the words slice through his heart. He missed her too. Even after everything she'd done.

'You'd better be off,' Agatha announced to the quartet, as

– 53 –

# SKANDAR AND THE SKELETON CURSE

though sensing Skandar trying to keep it together. 'I'll walk you out.'

It took a few attempts to get Flo up on to Blade's back, but she was able to ride alongside Bobby and Mitchell as Falcon and Red led the way out of the Glowing Caves.

Agatha walked beside Scoundrel, occasionally reaching out to stroke his ebony neck. Skandar knew she must be thinking of Swan as she did it, and he could hardly bear to watch.

'The Eyrie's gone pretty weird,' he blurted.

Agatha grunted and dropped her gnarled hand. 'So I hear.'

'Training starts tomorrow, and I'm not sure what I'm going to do,' Skandar admitted. 'I chose to be classified as a spirit wielder, not a water wielder.'

'Brave boy,' Agatha said approvingly.

'I guess I'll just have to train on my own, without an instructor.'

Agatha looked up at him on Scoundrel's back, and her eyes were alight with a kind of fire Skandar hadn't seen since before Swan had died. 'Has it occurred to you that Rex might have engineered your situation? A situation that forces you to train alone?'

Skandar frowned. 'But Rex seemed surprised by Instructor O'Sullivan giving me the option to choose between water and spirit. He seemed angry about it.'

Agatha scoffed. 'Rex Manning is a good actor – I suspect he knew O'Sullivan was going to do that. And given the option, he knew *you* were always going to choose spirit – he understands how important bringing the spirit element back to the Island is to you. He made it clear on the solstice that he hates spirit wielders – of course he doesn't want you to succeed. By separating you from the other Rookies, he's keeping you weak.'

Skandar sighed. 'Say that's true, what can I do about it? I can't

# POISONED

exactly turn up to any other training sessions – I'm pretty sure the instructors will notice.'

Agatha's face was mischievous. 'Why not try it?'

'You want me to break Rex's new rules?' First Instructor O'Sullivan, now Agatha.

'I bet you're not the only rider who's unhappy. You don't have to break them alone. In fact, it would be better if you didn't.'

'You want me to start a revolt?' Skandar asked, raising an eyebrow.

'Only a little one,' Agatha said – and winked.

<u>Kenna</u>

# HAUNTED HOUSE

K enna Everhart had come home for the first time.
She looked up at the old family treehouse, the moonlight catching the stripe of white paint that coated her face. The building looked as though it had been magnificent once – a treehouse fit for the most powerful spirit wielder family on the Island. But now the Everhart mansion was a rotting shell, its former glory eroded by years of abandonment. It spanned five pine trees, but the black cedarwood arches that must once have been grand now sagged with decay, and the ladder Kenna was climbing felt brittle, like treading on old bones—

*Bones. Death. Murderer.* The imagined voice in her head was not hers but Skandar's – and she'd been running from it since the day of the Earth Festival. But as soon as she shut out her brother's phantom accusations, she would be consumed with how much she still missed him, even though he'd chosen the Island and his friends over her. Even though he'd let her suffer alone. And then the memories from June would replay. The way

## HAUNTED HOUSE

he'd stared at her when she'd told him she'd stolen the solstice stones and filled them with her power. The look in his eyes after she'd killed Arctic Swansong – the way something had been missing there.

Perhaps that was why she'd rashly flown Goshawk to Element Square on the day of the Earth Festival. Maybe she'd wanted to see her brother once more before he truly understood what she'd done. But instead, she'd only been able to laugh – laugh so she didn't cry – and hadn't been able to look at him at all.

And Skandar was back in the Eyrie now. He'd picked his side, and it wasn't hers. It would never be hers now. Especially once he found out that she'd killed again. Because one unicorn might have been an accident, but two dead? Unforgivable. That's what she was.

*Unicorn slayer. Murderer.*

Kenna's whole body trembled as she picked her way through the carcass of the Everhart treehouse, catching her boot on the corner of an overturned dining table, almost tripping over a dusty suitcase filled with musty old clothes. Mum had said her parents tried to flee when the Silver Circle came for their unicorns. But they'd been too slow and had been imprisoned like all the other spirit wielders. Like Kenna would be now if she was caught.

It was reckless to be in Fourpoint again today, but she needed to remind herself why she was doing this. Otherwise she would fall apart completely. Otherwise she might hand herself over to Rex Manning just so she could stop running. And what Kenna needed most of all right now was her mum.

Since Erika had been killed, Kenna had been raking obsessively through memories of their conversations, and the one she kept coming back to was about the Everhart treehouse.

*'It's still there,' Erika had told Kenna a few weeks before forging*

– 57 –

## SKANDAR AND THE SKELETON CURSE

her bond. 'Complete with family portraits the authorities didn't bother taking.'

Kenna had laughed in disbelief. 'I can't believe I have a family treehouse. And paintings! How fancy is that? It makes us sound like royalty or something.'

'Not royalty, Daughter. Spirit wielders.'

'Can we visit?' Kenna had asked hungrily.

'Perhaps,' her mum had said in the vague way she answered so many of Kenna's questions. 'And if we ever get separated – if you get into trouble – it's a good place to go.'

Separated. Separated didn't sound as bad as the truth, so Kenna tried to hold on to the word while she walked the length of the treehouse. She had to be careful not to put her foot through any holes, had to muffle her shout of surprise when a squirrel burst out of the moth-eaten sitting room. But just when Kenna detected a stab of Goshawk's restlessness through the bond and began to berate herself for chasing ghosts – she saw what she'd come here for. A portrait half obscured by a branch. And there she was, just like Kenna had hoped.

*Mum.* The painting was of two girls with brown hair and brown eyes. The older one had a protective arm round the younger, as though shielding her from the observer. The Everhart sisters. Kenna stared in wonder at Erika, who couldn't have been much older than thirteen. Instinctively Kenna stroked the feathers punctured round her ears and the ice spikes at her throat, as though noting the differences between them. Then her heart went cold as her gaze landed on the other sister – Agatha, her mum's murderer. And she remembered why this was all vital. She replayed what her mum had told her two years ago – before she'd forged the bond that had changed Kenna's life for ever.

'So with a destined bond, a unicorn's immortal life is compressed

– 58 –

# HAUNTED HOUSE

to the length of their rider's?' Kenna had asked. 'And when the rider dies, the unicorn dies too?'

'That's right. But with my forged bond – and the one I will forge for you – there is no such limitation. The unicorn you choose will remain immortal, even though you are joined. But I will not let your forged bond drain your strength like it has mine.'

'How?' Kenna had worried. 'You were the Commodore twice and you couldn't stop it. What chance do I have?' Kenna had thought of Dad suddenly. What if he was finally reunited with a fading Erika, drained by her forged bond, only to find out that his daughter would meet the same fate? He'd never survive grieving for both of them.

'There's a way that you can live as long as the wild unicorn you bond with.'

'But that's impossible,' Kenna had whispered. 'A person can't live for ever.'

'You can,' Erika had insisted. 'By the time I discovered how, I was too weak to carry out the steps. But you, Daughter, you will accomplish what I couldn't. You must.'

'You'll still be here to help me, though, right?' Kenna had turned to look into Erika's gaunt face, so much older than it should have been. How long does she have left? Kenna had wondered in panic. How much longer will she be able to survive her bond?

'Of course I'll help you.' Erika had tucked a stray strand of Kenna's hair behind her ear. 'But remember that you are the Weaver's successor – and you will be stronger than I have ever been. You are the wind of change, whether the Island wants it or not. And one day you will have no need of my help.'

'I'll always need you,' Kenna had said stubbornly.

But Erika hadn't replied.

Looking at her mum in the portrait now, Kenna wiped away tears. 'I won't let you down,' she promised, reaching out to trace her mum's young face.

# SKANDAR AND THE SKELETON CURSE

But as she pulled the painting from the wall, the memories billowed like the dust she'd disturbed: watching her mum's body winking out for ever, being trapped behind the elemental barrier as the sisters battled, being forced to flee from the Wanderers, being imprisoned in the Stronghold's spear, being left behind on the Mainland with no unicorn, a young Skandar being bullied at school, her dad on the sofa, absent and grief-stricken, and nothing Kenna did or said ever being enough to fix him.

With each memory Kenna felt her resolve harden. She was no longer a Smith but an Everhart. Though Skandar was still— She cut off the thought. She must not think about him. She *must* not. She was leaving her past behind and her new future wasn't just about carrying out her mum's last wishes, or stopping Goshawk from draining her strength, or even getting revenge.

It was about never feeling powerless again.

Kenna had only made it back to the hall before she felt bloodlust burst through her like a thousand flaming arrows. Goshawk's Fury was hungry. Kenna's vision blurred, and she stumbled sideways, falling through the rotting wood of a wall and into another room.

'Gos,' Kenna managed to breathe, as her knees crunched on tiny animal skeletons littered across the treehouses floor. She sent the plea down the bond, because sometimes Goshawk listened now – but today the unicorn was too distracted with the hunt to notice her rider's panic.

And Kenna was lost – all traces of humanity gone. She was destruction itself. She was immortal power. She was the ultimate predator. She could almost feel the tattered wings at her back, the horn on her head, the fury in her veins. Elemental magic burst from her palm as Goshawk's power surged. Icicles formed along rotting beams before they were melted by a burst of fire; black-flowered vines slithered like snakes across the treehouse floor.

– 60 –

# HAUNTED HOUSE

Outside, a lightning bolt hit the opposite end of the treehouse and the dry wood burst into flame.

Smoke began billowing through the rotting ribs of the remaining rooms, and something primal in Kenna, something fundamentally human, sent a message of alarm to her brain. In that brief moment of clarity, she managed to summon water to her palm and douse the flames licking at the treehouse carcass. Then she was pulled back to Goshawk's hunt, her excitement rising and focus heightening as the unicorn made the kill. It was a while before Goshawk's full presence finally retreated from her mind, as though the predator wanted privacy to savour whatever she'd caught in peace.

Kenna found herself in a kitchen. There was frost on the beam above matching the ice shining across the back of her knuckles. The Wanderers hadn't had any idea of the danger they'd been unleashing when they'd taught her to summon magic away from her unicorn. They hadn't had any idea that it would mean Goshawk could summon magic through her rider too – it seemed accidental so far, but she wasn't sure the Wanderers would approve. They wouldn't approve of much she did nowadays.

Kenna shivered and instinctively went to turn on a rusted metal tap. She felt like she had the blood of Goshawk's kill on her hands. But of course there was no running water. She supposed it didn't matter either way, though, because when Kenna looked at her hands she was always going to see the blood she'd spilled – of Arctic Swansong, of the earth unicorn and of all the others to come.

And she already knew it was never going to wash off.

Chapter Five

# RIDER REVOLT

The Rookies started training the day after Skandar, Bobby, Flo and Mitchell returned from visiting the Wanderers in the earth zone. They were subdued as they readied their unicorns – it was the first time they'd ever been separated for an elemental session. Mitchell and Red would be with Instructor Anderson on the Hatchling plateau at the bottom of the Eyrie's hill. Bobby and Falcon were assigned to the highest plateau – the one usually reserved for Preds – with Instructor Manning. And Flo and Blade headed off to the Silver Stronghold for the day, since there were no earth unicorns for them to train with.

Skandar and Scoundrel left the stables, too, although they weren't heading for training. Instead, Skandar led a belligerent Scoundrel – annoyed about being separated from his best friend, Red – through to the Divide. But the unicorn soon cheered up when they took off into the blue September sky towards one of his favourite places on the whole Island.

Skandar dismounted on the Sunset Platform to find every member of the Peregrine Society already there: Patrick and

# RIDER REVOLT

Hurricane Hoax, Fen and Eternal Hoarfrost, Liam and Coastal Crusader, Amber and Whirlwind Thief, and Squadron Leader Marcus – though there was pain in his smile of greeting. There were also two freshly recruited Nestling Grins: a fire wielder called Whitney and an air wielder called Clarence. Both looked nervous as they watched Skandar approach.

The Grins looked at Skandar expectantly, and the reality of what he'd put in motion last night made him feel a bit dizzy. All the way back from the earth zone, the quartet had discussed Skandar's chances of convincing other Eyrie riders to break Rex's rules – the revolt Agatha had suggested.

It had been Bobby who'd thought of the Peregrine Society. 'Don't they reject elemental separation? Isn't that, like, their core belief?'

And from there they'd come up with a tentative plan to test Rex's regime.

'What if you get declared a nomad, Skar?' Flo had asked. Even dozing on Blade's back, she'd still been worrying about him.

'I won't be breaking the rules alone, though. If we get as many riders as possible to break the rules, then Rex won't know who started it,' Skandar had said enthusiastically. 'He can't declare the *whole* Eyrie nomads, can he?'

'Technically he can,' Mitchell had pointed out.

'Technically, snechnically.' Bobby had stuck out her tongue. 'Ruffled Mallard wouldn't do that.'

Skandar had grinned at her newest silly name for the head of the Silver Circle, as she'd continued. 'It would look like he was doing a bad job as Commodore *and* air instructor. Think what the *Hatchery Herald* would say: *First an empty Hatchery, now an empty Eyrie. Does Rex Manning spell the end of the Island?*'

Mitchell had snorted. 'Maybe you should write for the *Herald* if you don't make it as a Chaos rider.'

– 63 –

# SKANDAR AND THE SKELETON CURSE

'How dare you,' she'd replied. 'Of *course* I'll make it as a Chaos rider!'

When Flo spoke next, she'd sounded more hopeful. 'I suppose if we all act against elemental separation, Rex might realise his mistake. Maybe he'll do more to help the earth wielders. And let us go back to our real quartets.'

So, once they'd made their excuses to the sentinels at the Eyrie's entrance, Skandar had gone in search of the remaining members of the Peregrine Society. One by one, he'd asked whether they would be willing to skip their morning training sessions to meet him on the Sunset Platform. And they hadn't needed much convincing.

Faced with the Grins now, Skandar cleared his throat nervously. 'I wanted to talk to you all because, well, I think separating riders by element is pointless and harmful. The truth is, my sister's allied to all five elements and she's equally strong in each one. Rex knows that, but he's introduced elemental separation anyway.'

The Grins were quiet, although Skandar could see Patrick nodding and it gave him confidence. 'I think this is all Rex trying to distract us from the fact he isn't really bothering to find out how to fix what's happened to the earth wielders.'

'Too right,' said Marcus, his voice low. 'He's done nothing.' There was a hard shell to the earth wielder that reminded Skandar far too much of the face Agatha wore sometimes. Having a drained bond wasn't the same as a broken one, but it wasn't far off.

Skandar tried to express the plan the quartet had come up with, bunching his fists. 'We need to send the Commodore a message and make him understand that elemental separation is not something the Eyrie is going to accept. Show him that we care about every kind of wielder – not just the ones who share

– 64 –

## RIDER REVOLT

our elements. That true riders – the riders *we* want to become – are those who learn and fight together. With *all* the elements.'

Amber flicked her chestnut hair to one side, the star mutation on her white forehead crackling. Skandar waited for her verdict.

'Despite your *deeply* chaotic energy, spirit wielder – I'm *super* on board. What do you want us to do?'

All the other Grins were murmuring their agreement, excitement and hope igniting in their eyes.

Skandar took a deep breath. 'I want the Peregrine Society to lead a revolt.'

'Epic,' Patrick declared.

'What kind of revolt?' Flight Lieutenant Fen had a hungry look on her light brown face. 'Do you want us to smash something? Perhaps we could start with Rex's treehouse?'

'No, no,' Skandar said quickly, all too aware of the water wielder's violent leanings. 'Between us we span multiple year groups – from Nestlings to Preds – and all five elements. We need to convince as many riders as possible to ignore Rex's new training regime.'

Liam pushed his wheelchair closer to Skandar, his hair sealed within its icy spikes. 'You mean we tell them to act like nothing has changed? We go back to training across all the elements?'

'Exactly. My friend Mitchell, will draw up alternative timetables for every year group. We need to knock on every treehouse door this evening, speak to every table at the Trough.'

The new Nestlings looked the most unsure. 'What if we're declared nomads?' Whitney asked, threads of fire glowing through her black braids.

'It's a risk,' Skandar admitted. 'And there's no pressure to join in. But the theory is that if we all do this, then Rex can't kick every rider out of the Eyrie.'

'So it's not true what the Commodore said?' Whitney asked.

– 65 –

# SKANDAR AND THE SKELETON CURSE

'Training in one element *won't* help us defeat Kenna? It won't help reverse what she's done?'

'It won't,' Skandar confirmed.

The truth was, he had no idea what *would* stop his sister. But he couldn't think about that right now. He could only think about one bad thing at a time, otherwise his head would explode.

'Then I'm in,' Whitney announced.

Clarence wrinkled his nose, looking sceptical. 'Isn't anyone going to point out the obvious?' He looked round at the Grins in pink-faced disbelief. 'Skandar is Kenna's brother! She uses the spirit element; *he* uses the spirit element. Why would we trust him over the Commodore?' Clarence let out a sharp laugh. 'Isn't it a bit suspicious that Skandar's trying to get us to disobey Rex's orders? What if he's on *Kenna's* side?'

There was a long silence. Skandar hardly dared to breathe.

It was Amber who broke it. She walked up to Clarence and snatched the metal peregrine feather from his black T-shirt, ripping the fabric. 'Get off our platform.'

'Amber,' Marcus warned. 'I'm fairly sure I'm the one who makes those kinds of decisions.'

The star on Amber's head was crackling furiously. 'Skandar is a member of this society, and Grins look after their own. They don't *accuse* each other.'

Flight Lieutenant Fen cracked her snowflake-covered knuckles. 'I have to say, Marcus, I agree with Amber. Clarence is clearly far too hung up on elemental allegiance to be a proper Grin.'

The squadron leader looked as though he wanted to give the new recruit a chance, but Clarence had already mounted Glorious Gale. 'I was going anyway.' He sniffed pompously. 'I don't want to be associated with a spirit wielder or a revolt against the Commodore.' He spat on to the platform before the bay unicorn rose into the air.

– 66 –

## RIDER REVOLT

Marcus stood up straighter, acting as though they hadn't just lost one of their new recruits. 'I take it the rest of us here support Skandar's plan?' Everyone nodded, and he continued. 'When it comes to the earth wielders, I'll be suggesting they attend training without their unicorns – we can still learn by watching, and we can help other riders with their earth magic. I'm also going to propose organised searches for our unicorns. It's ridiculous that we have to sneak out of the Eyrie like we're doing something wrong.'

'Umm . . . I do think we need to iron out some of the vaguer details of Skandar's plan,' Amber said, nose high. 'No offence, spirit wielder, but I suspect some of the absurd levels of drama you attract may be down to your blasé attitude towards your own safety. And I'm not risking *this* face.' She pointed to her dimpled cheeks.

Skandar grinned. 'Fair enough.'

Patrick produced a brown paper bag from behind his back with a flourish and shook it. 'Why don't we discuss it over some marshmallows? We can initiate the new Nestlings! Er . . . Nestling.' Patrick gestured to Whitney, who looked very alarmed.

'An excellent idea,' Squadron Leader Marcus said, the ghost of a smile on his lips.

'See, I bet you regret not making me your Flight Lieutenant now.'

'I am *right* here,' Fen said.

Marcus crossed his rock-mutated arm over the other and appraised Patrick. 'How about I make you captain of the revolt instead?'

Patrick's jaw dropped. 'Are you serious? I think this might be the best day of my life.' He sighed. 'Bolt, captain of the revolt.'

'The Bolt nickname is still not happening, Pat.' Marcus shook his head, laughing. And Skandar joined in, trying to forget about Clarence and his poisonous words.

– 67 –

# SKANDAR AND THE SKELETON CURSE

Over the next few days, Skandar's quartet and the Peregrine Society got to work. Patrick took his new title extremely seriously and – quite uncharacteristically – took up residence in a corner of the Eyrie's air library. Once a rider agreed to go against Rex, Patrick wrote their name on a chart colour-coded by which revolt ringleader had convinced them to join. By far the most common colour was Flo Shekoni's green. As a silver, daughter of a famous saddler *and* an all-round lovely person, Flo was having the most success persuading riders to abandon Rex's new training regime.

There were, of course, Eyrie riders who couldn't be convinced. Huddling over the chart, the Grins and the quartet would swap reports of why riders had refused to join. Most common was the fear of being declared a nomad, followed by trust in Rex's plan or mistrust in anything Skandar said because he was Kenna's brother and a spirit wielder. For some – like Clarence – it was a combination of all three.

A week after the Peregrine Society meeting, Patrick declared that the rider revolt was ready to begin. That night, Mitchell's alternative timetables were handed out secretly on treehouse platforms, along swinging bridges and behind branches high in the Trough. Mitchell had categorised training sessions by year group rather than element, as had been the case before Rex's new rules.

Skandar, Bobby, Flo and Mitchell couldn't bear to be separated that evening, so instead they slept down in the stables, leaning over the partitions and whispering their worries as their unicorns snoozed behind them.

'Do you think the other riders will do it?' This was Skandar's main fear. Riders may have agreed to put their names down, but when crunch time came, would enough of them really go against Rex?

# RIDER REVOLT

'I think so,' Mitchell said thoughtfully. 'Everyone's pretty angry about the quartets being split up.'

'What do you think Rex will say when he realises?' Flo whispered, as she picked nervously at the sleeve of her emerald jumper from the Kipper Knitters' Club.

'I don't expect he's going to like it.' Bobby sounded more pleased than concerned.

Skandar spent a while wrapped in Scoundrel's feathery wing, but when he thought he might fall asleep, he moved away across the straw. Scoundrel rumbled quietly, but there was no hurt in the bond. Unicorn and rider had come to an unspoken agreement – neither of them wanted Skandar to end up in a Mender dream with Kenna again. Though tonight they needn't have worried. Skandar barely slept at all, his mind on Rex rather than his sister.

The next morning, the wall sounded like it did on any other day. Riders called to each other in greeting, chainmail clinked and unicorns screeched for their bloody breakfast. Mitchell had cleverly taken into account Rex's timetable when making his alternative one, and the Commodore was not due to be teaching until after lunch. It meant the Rookies would be the first to face Rex at air training in the afternoon.

'It's only fair,' Mitchell had reasoned. 'We came up with the idea – I don't want to inflict an angry Commodore on the little Hatchlings.'

'Oh, I think Isa would cope,' Bobby said. 'She has – overnight – made this revolt her entire personality.'

Skandar was glad the Rookies would be first though. He wanted to see Rex's face when he realised the Eyrie riders were defying him.

There was a nervous knot in Skandar's stomach as Scoundrel flew down to the plateau where Instructor Anderson and the

– 69 –

## SKANDAR AND THE SKELETON CURSE

new silver instructor were waiting for the arrival of the fire wielders. But the knot loosened when he saw the large group of riders and unicorns already gathered on the training ground.

The Rookie fire wielders were here, of course, but as Scoundrel landed, Skandar was also greeted by Niamh on Snow Swimmer, by Zac on Yesterday's Ghost, Muhammad on Glacial Hazard and Mariam on Old Starlight. Ivan raised a hand in welcome from the back of Swift Sabotage, Benji and Cursed Whisper called hello, and they were quickly joined by Mabel on Seaborne Lament and Anoushka on Sky Pirate. According to Rex's new rules, none of these Rookies should have been at this session.

Mitchell was beaming as he landed Red next to Scoundrel; Flo looked less worried than she had last night; and Bobby had an enormous grin on her face. Skandar glanced over at the scorched red pavilion, and sitting on its steps were the Rookie earth wielders who'd remained at the Eyrie. Farooq and Freya waved hello – they were without unicorns but still ready to continue their training.

Instructor Anderson blew his whistle from Desert Firebird's back and nervous excitement pulsed through the crowd of riders as they lined up their unicorns in front of him.

'Some fire wielders from other year groups are here – ones we couldn't convince,' Bobby murmured to Mitchell, and Skandar noticed a couple of Nestlings, a Pred and a Hatchling or two scattered among the Rookies. Some looked confused, others angry. The silver fire wielder – Instructor Melville – was whispering furiously to Instructor Anderson, who wasn't paying the slightest attention.

Instead, Instructor Anderson's dark brown face stretched into an enormous smile, the flames round his ears dancing joyfully. 'Welcome to this morning's fire training!' he called gleefully. 'According to the Commodore's wishes, today all riders will start

– 70 –

## RIDER REVOLT

learning to create a new kind of magical weapon. A weapon that was banned many years ago.'

'Banned?' Mitchell mouthed at the rest of the quartet.

'At this stage, you will only be permitted to summon these magical weapons under supervision, during training. Rex Manning believes there may come a time when it will be necessary for you and your unicorn to use them to protect the Island.'

*Use them against Kenna*, Skandar thought, and he couldn't stop the cold river of fear for his sister flooding his veins.

'There are many good reasons why these magical weapons were outlawed. To be honest with you all, I was initially opposed to their reintroduction at the Eyrie.' Instructor Melville was attempting to say something, but Instructor Anderson silenced him with a look. 'And I am *still* opposed to the way the Commodore wishes to teach this magic to riders of all ages. However, I have decided to compromise by teaching it to Rookies and Preds only.'

At this, a white-faced and furious Instructor Melville gave up trying to speak over him, and galloped Silver Scorcher from the plateau.

'Instructor Anderson is rebelling too!' Bobby hissed.

'No doubt Melville will be going straight to Rex,' Mitchell muttered.

Instructor Anderson continued as though nothing had happened. 'I make this compromise because I believe that – if it becomes necessary – this particular brand of magic will prove a useful weapon against the new Weaver's wild strength.'

Skandar winced.

'Therefore, if you are not a Rookie or a Pred, please leave the plateau immediately,' Instructor Anderson boomed a little louder. The younger fire unicorns headed for the plateau gate, their riders talking in low, unhappy tones.

# SKANDAR AND THE SKELETON CURSE

Meiyi spoke up from the back of Rose-Briar's Darling. 'This is all wrong! *All* the fire wielders should be here – there's some sort of rebellion going on, Instructor. See! There are Rookies of every kind of element. Even the spirit wielder is here.'

The flames at Instructor Anderson's ears ebbed dangerously low. 'If you wish to leave, Meiyi, there is nothing stopping you. But then you will fail to learn the powerful and previously banned magic I'll be teaching.'

Skandar watched the conflict play out across Meiyi's face. He knew she would hate to miss out on magic that could make her stronger, but she'd also refused to join the revolt. Finally Meiyi pursed her glowing lips but remained. Skandar grinned at Amber, who was smirking at her former friend's predicament.

Instructor Anderson beamed. 'Excellent. Now we can get down to business. Have you ever wondered why those in their fifth year of training at the Eyrie are called "Predators"?'

'Because they're the fiercest, the top of the food chain?' Niamh called out.

'Partly –' Instructor Anderson cocked his head – 'but there is another reason, and it has everything to do with the magic I'm going to begin teaching you today. For many years, the fifth year of training was when riders learned to summon elemental predators – hence where they got the nickname Predators. Preds.'

Mitchell's eyes were wide behind his brown glasses. 'Rex wants to legalise elemental *predators*?'

'Ah, I see one of our best-read riders has heard of them.' Instructor Anderson's voice was more serious now. 'But I suspect you have never seen one in real life, only in illustrations?'

Mitchell nodded mutely.

'A demonstration then.' Instructor Anderson backed Desert Firebird up a few paces from the line. 'I want every one of you to summon the water element to your palm.' The whole line

– 72 –

# RIDER REVOLT

glowed blue as the riders obeyed. 'And now summon a water shield stretching in front and above you. Every shield should join up with the ones on either side of you. And no matter what you see now – no matter what I do – under no circumstances must you drop the shield line. Understood?'

A shimmering wall of water burst along the line seconds later, and beyond it, Instructor Anderson's palm glowed red, flames rising into the air above his bald head and gathering in a roaring cloud. As the riders watched, the cloud began to morph into a shape, legs appearing one at a time, and then a body. Finally the fire resolved itself into a great snarling dog-like creature that snapped its flaming teeth from side to side.

'It's a jackal,' Mitchell murmured. 'A Hunter, but not Marauder level, and of course not Mythical.'

The jackal prowled back and forth in the air above Instructor Anderson, and Skandar could see that the combined fire magic of the rider and his unicorn was being drawn up into the creature, almost as though the predator were feeding off them. Before their eyes, the jackal appeared to be getting stronger – more lifelike – and it started to pounce at unseen enemies with flaming claws.

The shield wall flickered slightly, as the riders watched with a combination of shock and wonder. Skandar was finding it hard to keep his palm steady because he realised he had seen elemental predators before. Back in June, on the Weaver's dark island, he had watched Erika and Agatha Everhart summon creatures of pure spirit magic. He remembered Agatha's sparkling albatross; his mum's white wolf; the way they had fought each other; the way the pieces of Agatha's albatross had reformed to create a tiger just before . . . Before she'd killed her own sister, killed his mum.

'Skar!' Flo cried from Blade's back, and he adjusted his shield upwards again, trying to focus.

– 73 –

# SKANDAR AND THE SKELETON CURSE

Then the jackal launched itself towards the line, and riders shouted in alarm.

'Hold the shields!' Instructor Anderson called, and Skandar didn't like the panic in his voice. Was he in control of the flaming jackal or not?

The riders were struggling as the jackal pounced again and again at the line with sharp, flaming claws. The unicorns were completely spooked, and only the close bonds they'd developed during the Chaos Trials kept them obeying their riders and staying in line. Skandar glanced desperately towards Instructor Anderson, who was attempting to summon another element, but his palm kept defaulting to a red glow, and now there was panic on his face as well as in his voice.

Flo whimpered as the jackal stared at Silver Blade through the haze of her water shield, with eyes as black as smouldering coals. It backed up – preparing to pounce again – but as the jackal crouched, something barrelled into it with an explosion of sparks. A cheetah.

The big cat was constructed of the air element itself – its spots sparking with electricity, its teeth bared, its speed unmatched as it collided with the jackal. The two predators rolled together on the ground in front of the riders. The cheetah was bigger than the desert dog, stronger, more solid round the edges. Within seconds, its fizzing yellow teeth had sunk into the jackal's neck and Instructor Anderson's predator flickered out, like a fire starved of oxygen.

'Do we change our shields?' Bobby hissed to the rest of the quartet. 'Earth? Water's not going to do much good if that cheetah comes for us next.'

But the cheetah was lying on its stomach in front of the line of unicorns, licking one sparking paw and looking more like a domestic cat than monster. Then, as though it had heard

– 74 –

## RIDER REVOLT

someone calling, it flicked a fizzing ear and trotted across the training ground back to its master.

'Would someone like to tell me what's going on here?'

It was Rex Manning.

CHAPTER SIX

# A COMMODORE'S REVENGE

Rex Manning rode Silver Sorceress along the line of Rookies, his sparking cheetah following at the unicorn's hooves. He stared hard at every single one of them, like he was committing their identities to memory, though the Commodore's gaze skated over Skandar like he wasn't even there.

Finally Rex turned towards Instructor Anderson with pity in his voice. 'Daniel, you really ought to have told me you can't control your elemental predators. It's nothing to be ashamed of; many cannot. But it was very irresponsible of you to unleash one – a Hunter, no less – on a group of Eyrie riders.'

'I *can* control my elemental predators,' Instructor Anderson said, working hard to keep his voice level. 'But it's been two decades since I've summoned one. Persephone and I did warn you that we should wait, that it was too soon—'

Rex turned away from him mid-sentence and Sorceress faced the line again. 'You have all just witnessed the reason elemental predators were banned. It's relatively simple to create one, but much harder to maintain control. They feed off the magic in the

## A COMMODORE'S REVENGE

bond, but if you are too weak to master them, they can gain too much power and become rogue. There were times, so I hear, when the Island was crawling with these creatures, and they would cause all kinds of chaos completely outside their riders' control.'

'Do you think he's going to say anything about us all being here?' Skandar heard Niamh murmur to Mariam further down the line. 'He's just ignoring it!'

'Maybe he's realised he was wrong?' Mariam whispered back.

Rex was still explaining. 'As I just demonstrated, rogue predators can only be destroyed by another stronger creature. They can be held off by magical attacks and defences, but not completely defeated. Of course, if a rider still has *control* of their own predator –' Rex paused, closed his glowing yellow palm, and the cheetah disintegrated to sparks on the wind – 'then they can simply make it disappear.'

'If there's such a big risk, why would you bring this magic back at all?' The question came from Skandar's right, and for a moment he couldn't believe Flo had spoken to Rex like that. Her hands were shaking on Blade's reins, and she looked both angry and disappointed.

The electricity at Rex's white cheeks spluttered to life, but he sounded calm when he spoke. 'As a future instructor, Florence, of course you have a right to ask this. Elemental predators – when controlled properly – make excellent weapons, particularly against wild unicorns. I believe introducing them to the Eyrie is the key to defeating Kenna *Smith*.'

Rex looked at Skandar for the first time that morning and the pure hatred in the Commodore's green eyes was plain to see. Scoundrel hissed, and Red squeaked out a tiny flaming fart in support. But Skandar forced himself not to flinch. He stared

– 77 –

# SKANDAR AND THE SKELETON CURSE

back at the head of the Silver Circle, trying not to think of Kenna surrounded by terrifying elemental creatures. Finally Rex broke eye contact and paraded Silver Sorceress up and down the line, her wings flicking threateningly as she went by.

'As you are all well aware, I also believe that the way to vanquish our greatest enemy is unity. It is focusing on our own elements, perfecting and growing our strengths. But there appears to be some sort of confusion this morning.' He made a show of looking down the line. 'This is supposed to be a fire session, but I see riders of all elements here. Including a silver rider who should be training in the Stronghold. Why is that the case?'

Nobody spoke. Everyone had been cautioned against giving Rex information he could use to cast blame on any one rider.

'Daniel, can you shed any light on this?' Rex asked, his voice clipped.

Instructor Anderson stuck out his chin defiantly. 'Riders turned up and I taught them. That is the Eyrie's way.'

Rex glanced along the line of Rookies, and the smile that Skandar had once read as charming now looked more like a toothy shark approaching its prey. 'I will allow you all this one misguided morning. There will be no second chances. I cannot risk the safety of the Island by allowing you to weaken the Eyrie's resolve in this way. You train in your own element or you do not train at all. I expect to see only air wielders at my session this afternoon.'

And without another word Rex and Silver Sorceress soared back up towards the Eyrie's forest. The silence they left behind them was deafening.

Instructor Anderson looked shaken and ended the session immediately, But as Skandar, Bobby, Flo and Mitchell passed the red pavilion on their unicorns, Desert Firebird caught up with them.

– 78 –

# A COMMODORE'S REVENGE

'I'm not saying this revolt is your doing,' Instructor Anderson said carefully, the flames at his ears the brightest they'd been since the session had begun. 'But what happened this morning gave me courage. Keep going. Don't let him scare you. And let's hope our actions speak to Rex in a way our words have not.'

At lunchtime the Trough was busier than Skandar had ever seen. Judging by the conversations the quartet overheard as they filled their trays, riders had gathered to chatter excitedly about the elemental predators, as well as to whisper about the possible consequences of continuing to break Rex's rules.

As Skandar passed a quartet of fire wielders, a heated argument was going on between two Rookies – Violet who rode Roaring Flame and Sarika whose unicorn was Equator's Conundrum.

'All I'm saying,' Violet insisted, her irises glowing like embers, 'is that I'm not sure we should be part of the revolt any more. He's the Commodore. He won the Chaos Cup! He has the support of the whole Council *and* he's head of the Silver Circle. Who are we to question him?'

'He only won because Nina was killed,' Sarika argued, fingernails flaring as she gestured angrily. 'And he's only head of the Circle because his father almost destroyed the Island! Training in one element is stupid.'

'It's sensible!' Violet retorted. 'Especially if that's what the Island is telling us to do!'

'It's not *the Island* telling us.' Sarika made smoking quotation marks in the air. 'It's just *him*!'

The quartet didn't talk until they reached their usual high platform, half-concealed by a branch.

Skandar was worried. 'How many riders do you think are wavering like Violet?'

'Do you think Rex turned up at all the training sessions this

– 79 –

# SKANDAR AND THE SKELETON CURSE

morning and gave that speech?' Flo asked at the same time.

'Definitely,' Bobby answered, shovelling rice into her mouth. 'I heard Nestlings and Preds talking about it on the way here. Apparently O'Sullivan and Webb did the same as Anderson – just got on with their training sessions as usual until Rex turned up.'

'I can't believe he's bringing elemental predators back,' Mitchell murmured. 'It's incredibly reckless!'

'You seem to know a lot about them,' Skandar remembered. 'How did you describe them – Hunter? Marauder?'

Mitchell looked bashful. 'My mother lent me some books on them when I was younger. They probably weren't suitable for my age category, but it was around the time my parents moved into separate treehouses, and I think she was trying to distract me. And it worked – I was obsessed with elemental predators for years.'

Flo raised an eyebrow.

'I mean, they *are* very cool,' Mitchell spluttered defensively. 'There are four levels of predator that riders are capable of creating: Hider, Hunter, Marauder and Mythical.' On the last of those words, Mitchell went a bit misty-eyed. 'The Hiders are the least powerful – think of the types of animals that eat others but aren't that big or scary, the ones that lie in wait to strike, like a snake. The Hunters are the next level up – like that jackal today. Then Marauders are even more impressive – like Rex's cheetah. He must have studied cheetahs really closely in the library. And then—'

'Wait, Rex created that cheetah based on a *book*?' Bobby interrupted.

'Riders used to spend hundreds of hours in libraries poring over ancient illustrations brought by the first people to train here,' Mitchell explained, and then he blinked rapidly. 'I've just had a thought! Maybe that's partly why elemental predators have stayed banned. After the Treaty, maybe the Island was worried

– 80 –

# A COMMODORE'S REVENGE

that Mainlander riders would be better at creating them because Mainlanders can study the predators in real life.'

'That sounds *very* likely,' Skandar said darkly.

'Anyway,' Mitchell continued, clearly wanting to finish his lecture, 'the Mythicals are the fourth level of predator and hardly *any* riders in history have been able to create those. The First Rider could, and one of the silver brothers who started the ancient war with the spirit wielders. Erm, let me think . . .'

'Mythical? As in, they take the shape of mythical creatures?' Skandar couldn't quite believe what he was hearing.

'Yes. Phoenixes, griffins, krakens, thunderbirds, dragons—'

'Dragons?!' Bobby looked very excited.

'They were made illegal for a reason,' Flo said stubbornly. 'Elemental predators used to kill a lot of people. My dad told me there was a dedicated team of riders who were tasked with destroying the predators that'd escaped their riders' control – the rogue ones.'

'And Rex thinks if he gets the whole Eyrie creating them, they'll help against my sister.' The thought terrified Skandar. Which was confusing, because he was also so angry with her, but obviously he didn't want her to get hurt.

Patrick suddenly launched himself on to the platform. The air wielder's static-sizzling hair made him look even more like an eccentric professor than usual. 'What are you lot doing sitting here gossiping? You need to be doing the rounds, reassuring the troops. Rex has freaked everyone out – we have to make sure the revolt doesn't collapse!'

Skandar stood up, his chair scraping, as he thought of Violet and Sarika's conversation. 'Right, we'll get on it.'

That afternoon Skandar's nerves were even worse than they'd been in the morning. Scoundrel launched bubbles of reassurance

– 81 –

# SKANDAR AND THE SKELETON CURSE

into the bond, but it didn't help. According to Mitchell's timetable, the Rookies were heading for an air session with Rex Manning himself.

Scoundrel, Falcon, Blade and Red landed on the highest plateau while it was still deserted. The warm September wind whipped through the unicorns' feathers as their riders waited. The same question kept repeating in Skandar's mind: *Will the other Rookies come?*

Amber and Whirlwind Thief were the next to land, and she nodded to Skandar, face serious. He was pleased to see her, but she was an air wielder – so according to Rex's new rules, she was supposed to be here anyway. More air wielders arrived: Zac and Yesterday's Ghost, Ivan and Swift Sabotage, Benji and Cursed Whisper, and a few younger riders that Skandar didn't know, who were also clearly air-allied.

'Flaming fireballs,' Mitchell cursed, looking like he might be sick.

But then there were more. Niamh's Snow Swimmer landed on the grass, followed swiftly by Art and Furious Inferno. Next were Mariam and Old Starlight and Ajay and Smouldering Menace. The remaining Rookie earth wielders marched purposefully through the plateau's gate, and Skandar's heart exploded with hope. They hadn't given up! They were here!

A silver unicorn circled above the Eyrie's hill and landed elegantly on the training ground. It was Silver Sorceress – and this time, fury flooded Rex's entire perfect face.

'There will be no training until I see only air wielders before me.' If the Commodore's words had been sparks, they would have burned.

None of the Rookies moved.

And then Rex's lips curled into a horrible simpering smile, and he spoke as if to himself. 'You did give them fair warning.'

– 82 –

## A COMMODORE'S REVENGE

He pointed at Niamh and Snow Swimmer. 'Leave the Eyrie. Now.'

Niamh cocked her head in confusion, the ice-spiked bars across her ears catching the light. 'What?'

'I did warn you. I'm declaring you a nomad.'

Rex halted Silver Sorceress opposite Snow Swimmer and stretched out a hand. 'Your water pin, please.'

'This is ridiculous,' Art said, every visible vein in their arms and neck igniting in fury as Inferno moved out of line towards Niamh.

Benji and Cursed Whisper did the same from the other end. 'You can't be serious?'

'I am deadly serious,' Rex said, balls of electricity spiralling at his cheeks. Meanwhile Farooq – the fourth member of Niamh's original quartet – had sprinted over from the pavilion. 'You can't just randomly declare Niamh a nomad! She's one of the best in our year.'

'I am the Commodore,' Rex said, and he didn't sound anything like the young instructor who'd hung out with riders in the Trough last year. He sounded older. More aloof. 'I do as I see fit for the safety of this Island.' Then he whistled loudly with his fingers, the shrill sound echoing off the Eyrie's hill.

The noise shook Niamh from her shocked silence. 'I'm not going anywhere until I speak to Instructor O'Sullivan!'

Four mounted sentinels jumped the plateau gate and galloped towards the gathered riders. Benji's and Art's palms glowed, preparing to defend Niamh, and Skandar's did the same, along with many other riders' on the training ground. Everyone liked Niamh, and she was an excellent rider – she didn't deserve this.

'Any rider who tries to fight my guards will *also* be declared a nomad,' Rex barked.

The riders' glowing palms flickered uneasily.

– 83 –

# SKANDAR AND THE SKELETON CURSE

'Don't do anything!' Niamh shouted to her quartet, though tears were pouring down her pale freckled face. 'Don't get kicked out because of me, please—' Her voice cut out as a sentinel pulled her from Swimmer's saddle. 'And that goes for the rest of you too! Stay here and fight!' Niamh managed to look back once as she was bundled off the training ground, Snow Swimmer roaring with rage as he was chained and pulled along by the other sentinels.

Once she was gone, the silence among the Rookies was absolute. Skandar felt sick with fury and guilt. He'd helped start the revolt, and now—

'Know this,' Rex said very quietly, though every word felt like a hammer blow, 'continued rebellion will result in more of you being declared nomads. In fact, I do not care if I lose the entire Rookie year if it means I keep this Island safe, do you understand?'

'That doesn't make any sense,' Mitchell muttered impulsively.

'What was that?' Rex's eyes flashed towards the quartet.

'N-n-nothing,' Mitchell stammered.

'You must understand, I don't *want* to declare anyone a nomad,' Rex said, his voice pleading. Perhaps Skandar would have believed the act last year. 'I do not make any of these changes lightly, but you saw what happened to the earth unicorns. Kenna is a danger to all of us, and building the strength of our allied elements is the only way to defeat her. I will see *all* the air wielders at my training session in the morning. And I expect you, Florence, to report to the Silver Stronghold with Blade, bright and early. Please do not test me again.'

Skandar watched Rex and Sorceress take off. Bobby was looking up too, a frown between her eyes. 'I always said Rex was too handsome. Being that attractive messes with a person, you know?'

– 84 –

## A COMMODORE'S REVENGE

And Skandar wondered how he'd ever doubted that Rex Manning was just a monster with a pretty face.

True to his word, Commodore Manning continued to declare nomads at random if they were caught in the wrong session. The other instructors didn't do the same, but it hardly mattered since Rex would turn up arbitrarily with his gang of silver-masked cronies and drag someone away. Instructors O'Sullivan and Anderson had protested when he'd done it the first time, but now they watched on, tight-lipped.

And as the instructors continued to teach the basics of creating Hiders – the simplest form of elemental predator – Skandar wondered whether Rex had threatened them. Jamie had heard rumours that sentinels were intimidating the families of some of the Council of Seven if they refused to toe the line – perhaps he was doing the same to the instructors. Even Flo – a fellow silver – was now escorted by sentinels to and from the Stronghold every day to train Blade with the rest of the Silver Circle. The sheer number of sentinels that Rex sent to fetch her each time meant she was forced to abandon the revolt, however much she didn't want to.

Rex used other tactics in his attempt to crush the revolt too. He introduced compulsory 'evening talks' at the Eyrie, where he would ask a member of his Council or an air librarian or various other experts to talk to the young riders about their work on reversing the wildness of the earth unicorns. And one evening, Tom Nazari – an incredibly famous air wielder – came to speak about elemental predators, how they were easiest to create with your allied element and how he believed they were the answer to defeating Kenna. Starstruck, Skandar tried to remind himself that Rex was doing this on purpose. But he knew others were being persuaded.

– 85 –

# SKANDAR AND THE SKELETON CURSE

'But none of it's true!' Skandar groaned after yet another talk from a historian about the benefits of single-element training and treehouses. 'Kenna is allied to all five elements! Aren't historians supposed to be clever? Why are they all going along with it?'

'Sometimes, when people are scared,' Mitchell said, rather grimly, 'they would rather believe lies than the truth. Especially when the lies get them to the answer they want.'

'And Rex is the Commodore – they can tell themselves he has information on Kenna that they don't,' Bobby said, while dolloping raspberry jam atop Marmite by Skandar's stove. Her new air quartet had banned emergency sandwiches from their treehouse within two days. 'Most people on this Island are going to take his word over a group of rebellious teenagers.'

'I've never been called a rebellious teenager before,' Flo said thoughtfully, and Skandar couldn't help grinning at her.

Consequently, as September moved into October, the revolt began to crumble. It was small fractures to begin with – fewer riders risking attending the wrong training sessions; debates in the Trough about whether Rex was right about how to defeat Kenna. Riders started to become used to their allied quartets, many realising that Tom Nazari was right – creating predators was a lot easier if the rider used their own element. And – most of all – they were afraid of being declared nomads for a cause they were no longer sure they believed in.

It was this that was causing the most division. Skandar could barely set foot on a swinging bridge or walk the line of stables without people yelling at him to abandon the revolt.

'Don't have a go at us!' Bobby shouted at Kobi one mid-October evening. 'Take it up with the Commodore – *he's* the one declaring nomads for no reason.'

'Can't you see he's just trying to show us how serious the

– 86 –

# A COMMODORE'S REVENGE

situation is? He doesn't want to declare nomads, but he has no choice.'

'That is nonsense, Kobi! He doesn't give a flying feather about the *situation*!'

But Skandar sensed riders listening to the argument and felt the tide turning.

Finally, on a chilly evening in late October, Patrick was forced to call an end to the revolt. With so few riders still involved it was no longer viable.

After a depressing gathering on the Sunset Platform – where Patrick dramatically ripped up his colourful chart of names – Skandar, Bobby, Flo and Mitchell retreated to the spirit wielder treehouse. They settled themselves on Agatha's sheepskin rug and warmed their hands at the stove while they talked.

'What I don't understand,' Skandar said, 'is why Rex hasn't declared *me* a nomad.'

'I've been thinking about that,' Mitchell mused. 'Perhaps he wants to keep an eye on you? Safer here than running about with the "Executioner" who can teach you her spirit wielder tricks.'

'But what do we do now?' Skandar asked, frustrated. 'We can't let Rex get away with this.'

Flo shifted slightly next to Skandar, and he waited for her to speak. 'I don't think we should focus on what *Rex* is doing for now.'

'What do you mean?' Bobby exploded. 'He's ruining the Eyrie! He's stopping riders from training properly, and it isn't even going to work against Kenna.'

Flo fiddled with the three bracelets on her arm. 'I know. But honestly, I think we'd be better off trying to investigate what's happened with the earth wielders.' She swallowed. 'I feel like we've all sort of forgotten about them during the revolt, but riders of my element are suffering – some are even dying looking for their unicorns.'

# SKANDAR AND THE SKELETON CURSE

A sledgehammer of guilt hit Skandar's chest. He had truly believed the revolt might work, but he also knew the distraction of it had kept the big waves of sadness at bay. He'd been too adrenaline-filled and furious at Rex to think about the promise he'd made to the earth wielders. And deep down he knew he'd been avoiding confronting Kenna's attack because it had been easier to focus on Rex as the enemy – especially when he had no idea how to fix what she'd done.

'You're right, Flo,' Mitchell said. 'Reversing what's happened to the earth wielders is what matters most.'

'But Rex is just so, so—' Bobby struggled for a word bad enough.

'Evil,' Skandar supplied flatly.

'I really do think it'll be harder for Rex to stick to his changes if the earth wielders go back to normal,' Flo said, looking a little brighter. 'My dad says everyone is in panic mode right now – with the wild unicorns destroying treehouses, and the curfews – so Islanders can hardly think about what's going on at the Eyrie.'

'Okay,' Mitchell said, sounding energised. 'We have a few details we can investigate.' He cleared his throat and used his Quartet Meeting voice, though he'd left his blackboard behind in the old treehouse. 'The earth wielders and unicorns still have bonds, but they're empty – what can that tell us? The earth silvers haven't been affected, so we believe the spirit element is responsible. Can *that* information help us in some way? The magic on the earth line that hurt Flo could be related to Kenna's attack. Can we find any magic that's similar? And that magic didn't affect Skandar – what does that mean?'

'That's a lot of questions,' Skandar said with a sigh.

'Questions are good,' Mitchell argued. 'Questions lead to answers. We can check the four Eyrie libraries, but we'll need

– 88 –

# A COMMODORE'S REVENGE

permission if we want to go to the bigger ones in Fourpoint. Or I guess we could try to sneak—'

Bobby suddenly slapped a palm against her forehead. 'I can't believe I didn't think of this before!' She pointed at Skandar. 'You used to see your sister in Mender dreams, right? Can't you spy on her now?'

Skandar found himself wrapping his arms round his knees, drawing himself in tighter.

'Yes!' Mitchell sounded just as excited. 'Couldn't you dream and see where Kenna is? Didn't you do that with the spirit wielders the Weaver recruited last year?'

'It's not the real Kenna,' Skandar mumbled into his left knee. 'I can't hear her conversations or know what she's thinking. I just get a bunch of emotions, and it's hard to see where people are in the dreams. I didn't recognise the treehouse where she was—'

'So you've tried already?' Flo asked gently, perhaps noticing more than the others that Skandar wasn't excited about this idea.

Skandar swallowed. 'A few days after my mum . . . after the Chaos Trials ended.' He looked up, his brown eyes desperate. 'It was so hard seeing her. Please don't ask me to do that again. Please don't—' His last two words were half-sobs.

Bobby, Mitchell and Flo looked at each other, stunned.

'You should have told us, spirit boy,' Bobby said quietly.

'Of course you don't have to,' Flo murmured.

'It sounds like it won't be helpful anyway, so let's forget it,' Mitchell said, finishing the matter.

And Skandar nodded shakily.

'I'll write to my mother,' Mitchell continued. 'She's a librarian at the . . . er, well, she's connected to the water library.'

Sudden sounds from elsewhere in the Eyrie reached them – bridges clanking, running footsteps on ladders.

# SKANDAR AND THE SKELETON CURSE

Flo flinched as a series of screams broke through the evening quiet.

'This can't be good,' Mitchell said ominously, as they rushed to the treehouse door.

The quartet crossed the bridge to the instructors' colourful treehouses, but they were all quiet and dark. Puzzled, they climbed down ladders, the shouts growing louder.

'I think the noise is coming from the Eyrie's entrance,' Bobby said, jumping off the last ladder halfway to the ground and breaking into a jog.

She was right. A large number of riders had gathered in the moonlight, the colourful leaves of the Wild Unicorn Queen's tree muted in the semi-darkness. Screams, shouts and hushed questions came from the crowd.

'Is it alive?'

'Don't call him an *it!*' That was definitely Mariam's voice.

'Has someone called for the Commodore?' That was Kobi.

'He's trying to say something. Be quiet!'

Skandar's quartet rushed through gaps in the crowd, attempting to get closer to whatever was causing the disturbance. But when Skandar finally saw what was in front of the Eyrie's entrance, he thought he might have fallen into a nightmare.

He understood now why the crowd had struggled to choose between *it* and *he*. The hideous shape in front of him was human-shaped but looked more dead than alive – more beast than boy. He was all skeleton and sinewy flesh – his skin rotted away in most places – and there was a death rattle in his throat as he attempted to draw enough breath to speak. In his horror, Skandar was struggling to work out what the boy reminded him of.

Mitchell solved it first. 'He's like a wild unicorn but human.'

'Don't you recognise him?' Tears were streaming freely down Flo's face.

– 90 –

# A COMMODORE'S REVENGE

Skandar tried to see beyond the gruesome image of exposed bones and missing flesh, but the realisation was even more terrible.

The skeleton was a Rookie.

The skeleton was Elias.

Skandar remembered then that Squadron Leader Marcus had been looking for Elias on the day of the Earth Festival – before any of the unicorns had gone wild. And Mariam had mentioned she hadn't seen him or Marauding Magnet for days right before Rex had disbanded the quartets.

Skandar swayed a little on his feet, his body unsure whether to throw up or pass out.

'Isn't that Marauding Magnet's rider?' Mitchell breathed, at the same time as Bobby recognised the boy they'd trained with for three years. 'Isn't that Elias?' Then suddenly Isa was there too, bleary-eyed. 'What's happening, hermana? Someone said—'

'Be quiet!' Mariam begged the crowd. She was closest to Elias, kneeling down in the gap left by the terrified riders. 'He's trying to say something.'

The hiss of failing breath emerged from between Elias's black gums, the bones of his teeth far too long without the flesh of his lips. And then he raised one skeletal finger and pointed right at . . .

Skandar.

'Your sister did this.' His words were unsettlingly quiet, but completely audible in the sudden silence. 'Kenna took my bond; she k-killed Magnet.' There were shocked gasps from the crowd, and whispers of *'dead?' 'did he say Kenna killed his unicorn?'*

Elias gestured to himself and almost stumbled, a horrible clack sounding as he saved himself and straightened. 'And then this happened to me.'

The bones in his neck creaked as he turned his head this way

– 91 –

and that, bare eyeballs taking in the crowd of riders. He pointed to Skandar again. 'You cannot trust the spirit wielder. The death element did this to me. Do you really think Kenna is going to stop at earth wielders? Not one of you is safe with her brother in the Eyrie.'

And, as though the declaration had taken a superhuman effort, Elias collapsed in a clatter of bones and lay in an exhausted heap on the ground.

Mariam screamed. Lots of people screamed. Someone was grabbing Skandar by the shoulders and shouting in his face, and Bobby was fighting them off. And then the instructors arrived in full armour on their unicorns, and Commodore Manning was ordering the riders back to bed as a team of healers swarmed the Eyrie's entrance in a whirl of elemental magic.

Bobby grabbed Skandar's hand, Mitchell took Flo's, and they fought through the angry crowd to shelter in the shadow of an armoured trunk.

The quartet looked at each other in absolute horror and Skandar knew exactly what they were all thinking.

Elias had said Kenna wouldn't stop at the earth wielders – that she was coming for every element.

Mitchell's voice was hollow. 'If Elias is right, and if Kenna continues in the pattern she started at the Earth Festival, then I'm . . . then what if Red . . .' He tailed off, the reality of it too awful to speak out loud.

The Fire Festival was less than a week away.

Chapter Seven

# SACRIFICE

In the week leading up to the Fire Festival, Mitchell went into a research frenzy, desperate to find anything about what Kenna had done to the earth unicorns. Anything that might stop the same thing happening to his fire unicorn. Skandar, Bobby and Flo helped as best they could, but after Elias's appearance at the Eyrie, Rex had introduced more rules. He was even stricter about who could enter and leave the Eyrie, he 'strongly encouraged' eating and socialising only with those of the same element, and he banned riders from any elemental library other than their own. As a result, Mitchell became increasingly frustrated with his quartet's less than adequate research abilities.

The quartet also had to sneak around a lot more. They even had to hide from their fellow riders. There wasn't a whisper of rebellion from anyone now – not after they'd seen Elias. They were too afraid for their own futures to question a Commodore who declared he was trying to help them and too terrified of the spirit element to trust anything Skandar said. Even Rookies who'd been friendly to him before wouldn't make eye contact in the Trough.

## SKANDAR AND THE SKELETON CURSE

Skandar spent a lot of time with Scoundrel down in the stables while his friends were training in their allied elements, either on the Eyrie's hill or – in Flo's case – at the Silver Stronghold. The mystery of Elias haunted him. Elias was the only earth wielder who'd turned, well, skeletal. Why had Kenna done that to him? Was it linked to Magnet's death? Or was it just out of malice?

There was plenty of gossip echoing through the stables, too – and some of the conversations had Skandar worried.

A voice echoed along the wall one day. 'So she's the Weaver's successor, right?'

'Yeah, remember that truesong from my Saddle Ceremony? *True successor of spirit's dark friend.* Everyone thinks it was about her. Also, Kenna has a white stripe down her face, wild unicorn – the whole deal.' This voice belonged to a Rookie – Sophia, who rode Monsoon's Wraith.

At that point Scoundrel attempted to bite Skandar's boot, so he missed some of the conversation.

'. . . weird that the Weaver picked a successor from the Mainland? Erika Everhart was from one of the most famous Islander families. I bet they hated that the Treaty brought Mainlanders here – although I guess the Everharts were all locked up by then.'

'Have you heard the rumour that Kenna is actually the Weaver's daughter?'

Skandar's heart thundered at those words. Nobody outside his close circle knew that. Had someone discovered it from the Secret Swappers?

But Sophia laughed. 'Yeah, I think Kobi might have made that one up to get at Skandar. You do realise that not all spirit wielders are related to each other?'

Skandar sighed with relief. It was fine. Of course nobody knew Erika had fled the Island and started a life with Robert Smith.

– 94 –

## SACRIFICE

It had been *before* the Treaty, before any open communication between the Island and Mainland. His and Kenna's secret was safe for now – Sophia and her friend were just repeating easily dismissed rumours, that was all.

Aside from overhearing gossip, most days Skandar would sketch pictures of Scoundrel for Dad and write long letters to Flat 207 about his fictional normal life at the Eyrie. Somehow this helped him keep the waves of sadness away, stopped images of the Weaver's empty shroud flashing behind his eyelids. Once or twice, Dad seemed so upset not to be hearing from Kenna that Skandar faked a few lines in her handwriting, then spent the next half-hour in tears.

After the letter-writing and long hours of waiting, Bobby, Mitchell and Flo would return for dinner. Skandar would eat with them, then fly Scoundrel to the training grounds and attempt a lonely training session without an instructor or any opponents. The rest of the quartet had offered to train with him, but Skandar wouldn't let them, insisting it was too risky with Rex's restrictions in place.

On the last night of October – the night before the Fire Festival – Skandar and Scoundrel were on the highest training plateau. Skandar could tell from Scoundrel's bewilderment in the bond that he still didn't understand why there weren't any other unicorns training with them. And there was an edge of irritation too – the black unicorn missed battling with his friends, especially Red Night's Delight.

Skandar went through all the spirit weapons Agatha had taught him last year, summoning them seamlessly from the dark abyss of the fifth element and imagining them into bright reality. He pushed himself to create illusions with them too. It wasn't exactly satisfying making daggers or javelins or arrows appear to change direction, when there was no real opponent to

– 95 –

aim at. He also managed to duplicate himself and Scoundrel – though the shining white doppelgängers winked out after only a few seconds.

Then, as it grew darker, he tried to put into practice what Mitchell, Bobby and Flo had told him about creating elemental predators. No rider had managed to create more than a Hider-level predator yet – except Bobby, of course. Amber had been spitting mad the day Bobby had moulded the sparking hyena. Skandar didn't think it had helped that Bobby had said she'd chosen to make a hyena specifically so it could laugh at Amber's slow progress. A battle had followed between the two air wielders that had been fought so fiercely it had cleared the training ground.

On that same training ground Skandar now summoned the spirit element into his palm, the magic filling his nostrils with a cinnamon sharpness, a hint of vinegar and a leathery edge. He let a cloud of spirit magic build above his head, the pearlescent magic swirling, as he tried to mould it into a Hider – a tarantula. Skandar felt his power being drawn up into the cloud but, as hard as he tried to shape it, the magic remained formless. Scoundrel began to shriek with impatience, Skandar started to sweat and his thumb ached – the one Goshawk had injured with wild magic the year before –and he was just thinking that perhaps eight was a lot of legs for a beginner when—

Something fell heavily a few feet away. Skandar glanced upwards and saw a unicorn swooping back towards the earth zone with a rider he didn't recognise on its bare chestnut back.

Skandar dismounted and felt for the object in the grass. It was a rolled-up piece of paper with a rock tied round its middle to give it weight. He unrolled it:

# SACRIFICE

*Don't go to the Fire Festival tomorrow. Too dangerous for you, especially if Kenna strikes again. Lots of rumours about the spirit element and that skeleton boy. Elora is moving zones with Wanderers and some of the wild earth unicorns and riders. Use the eagle whistle – the blacksmith bard will get you out of the Eyrie to intercept us. I want you to try something.*

Agatha didn't need to sign her name for Skandar to know she'd written the note. She sounded worried – clearly Elias's warning about more attacks had reached the Wanderers, too. But if the worst happened – if Red was turned wild – he couldn't possibly leave Mitchell to go through that alone.

Half an hour later, Skandar had just reached Mitchell's new fire treehouse, when he almost bumped into Mariam going in the other direction.

'Oh, umm, hi,' Skandar spluttered. 'I was, er . . .'

Mariam sighed and looked pointedly at the fire treehouse. 'You know we're not supposed to hang out with people outside our allied elements, right? The Commodore says it'll—'

Skandar felt his temper rise. 'And as *I* said when you agreed to join the revolt, that's complete rubbish and has nothing to do with what happened to Elias.'

Tears shone in Mariam's dark eyes and Skandar felt awful. 'Is he . . . how's he doing?'

Mariam sniffed. 'He's alive, if that's what you're asking.' And she hurried away.

Skandar knocked on the door and was relieved when Mitchell answered.

'What's happened?' He clearly hadn't been sleeping; he had that manic look he got when he'd been reading tiny print for hours on end. Skandar hated that they no longer shared a room, that he couldn't check on Mitchell in the hammock beside him.

– 97 –

# SKANDAR AND THE SKELETON CURSE

Skandar handed Mitchell Agatha's letter.

'I'm not going to the fire zone tomorrow, though,' Skandar said, as soon as Mitchell handed it back. 'I can't, not if Red—'

'You need to go,' Mitchell said forcefully. 'Agatha says she wants you to try something. That might mean she's worked out how you can fix bonds with the spirit element. So even if Red . . .' Mitchell didn't finish the sentence either. 'If it does happen, then I want Red to be with the Wanderers anyway – like the wild earth unicorns. We can meet you there.' Neither of them acknowledged that Mitchell would be unlikely to have any control over a wild Red.

'We don't even know that Kenna has any plans for tomorrow,' Skandar said stubbornly. 'That's only what Elias said, and he *also* said that *I* was involved. And we know *that* isn't true.'

Mitchell's glasses flashed in the light of a moving lantern. 'Sentinels. I'd better get inside – they shouldn't find you outside a fire treehouse.'

'I hate this,' Skandar muttered darkly.

'Me too,' Mitchell agreed, and turned away.

Getting out of the Eyrie the next morning wasn't quite as simple as Agatha's letter had suggested. It certainly involved a lot more shouting than Skandar had been expecting.

'I SAID, LET US PASS!' Jamie yelled, angry blotches blooming on his tanned cheeks.

Jamie, Skandar and Scoundrel were standing under the colourful leaves of the Eyrie's entrance. Skandar had opened the trunk to find Jamie waiting to collect him and Scoundrel, but now the sentinels guarding it were refusing to accept that the blacksmith's letter was valid – which, to be fair, it wasn't. On receiving instructions from Agatha, Jamie had copied the handwriting of the head of his forge.

– 98 –

# SACRIFICE

'I'm not letting you out, spirit wielder,' one of the sentinels said, crossing his arms. 'You do know it's compulsory for all riders to attend the Fire Festival this evening? The Commodore expects all Eyrie unicorns to travel together into Fourpoint for security reasons. I can't let you go alone.'

'The head of my forge SPECIFICALLY requested his presence,' Jamie said, and there was a desperate edge to the blacksmith that Skandar suspected was mostly to do with him worrying about Mitchell and the impending Fire Festival.

The other sentinel narrowed her eyes at Skandar behind her silver mask. 'Riders and unicorns can be fitted for their armour *inside* the Eyrie, there's no reason to travel to a forge.'

They weren't going to make any progress like this.

'Fair enough,' Skandar said, putting a hand on Jamie's back, forcing him to retreat with Scoundrel towards the entrance trunk that had now closed again.

'What are you—' Jamie protested.

But Skandar interrupted him, keeping his voice low. 'When I put my palm on the tree you get up on Scoundrel's back.'

'Absolutely not!' Jamie hissed.

'When the trunk shines with the spirit element, I'll jump on too and we'll gallop into Fourpoint.'

'You do realise I've never actually ridden a unicorn before!'

'It's the only way we're getting out of here, Jamie. Okay?'

Jamie gulped. 'No flying, you hear me?' he warned, before reluctantly taking Scoundrel's reins.

Skandar approached the gnarled trunk. Under his hand, the indentations in the bark began to glow, joining up to form a round web of blinding white light. He heard an 'Oomph' behind him, then a surprised rumble from Scoundrel. The tiny cracks blazed whiter. Skandar waited until the tree was at its brightest and then sprinted back towards Scoundrel's Luck.

– 99 –

# SKANDAR AND THE SKELETON CURSE

'Stop right there!' one of the sentinels shouted.

'Hold on tight!' Skandar vaulted up behind Jamie, summoned the spirit element as soon as he was in contact with Scoundrel and yelled spirit speech at the top of his lungs.

'ARGH!' The sentinels covered their ears, crouching over in their saddles.

Then Scoundrel was galloping at a breakneck pace down the spiralling path of the Eyrie's hill, along Fourpoint's main shopping street. Still, Skandar didn't miss the destruction that had been wrought by the wild earth unicorns – quite a few treehouses had clearly been hit by elemental blasts. As they finally screeched to a halt outside the sloping metal roof of Jamie's forge, Skandar spotted two more that had clearly been abandoned.

Jamie didn't waste any time flinging himself from Scoundrel's back. He landed heavily and then his legs immediately gave way.

'Are you all right?' Skandar asked, dismounting and helping the blacksmith up.

'What do you think?' Jamie snapped. 'I just rode a unicorn. I'm not supposed to ride unicorns. I'm a blacksmith. Or did you forget?'

Skandar fought a grin. 'So you didn't enjoy it?'

'No, I didn't! Can't for the life of me see what you riders like about it. Surprisingly uncomfortable, weirdly sweaty and downright dangerous. Though I'm sure Mitchell is going to find the whole thing totally . . .' He tailed off, his mismatched eyes pained.

Mitchell's name brought Skandar back to reality too. 'I'd better head to the fire zone.'

'Oh, you're not leaving me here,' Jamie said, tools clinking in his apron pockets. 'Non-riders aren't allowed to go to the festival.'

'Why not?'

# SACRIFICE

'For the same reason Rex wants every fire unicorn out of the Eyrie tonight, I expect.'

Skandar didn't get it.

'If Kenna strikes again, Rex doesn't want the newly wild fire unicorns causing havoc inside the Eyrie, so he's making all the riders take them to the festival. But he also doesn't want a load of non-rider casualties either. You've got unicorns to protect you; *we* haven't.'

Understanding dawned on Skandar's face.

'Got there eventually,' Jamie said. 'Take me with you. If I stay at the forge, I'm going to send everyone round the twist worrying about whether Mitchell and Red are still . . . okay.'

Jamie refused to ride Scoundrel again, so their progress into the fire zone was slower than Skandar would have liked. Still, he was glad of the blacksmith's company, although he seemed intent on distracting himself by asking Skandar awkward questions.

'So, how's Flo?' Jamie asked, as they reached the rocky terrain peppered with Joshua trees.

'She's fine. I mean, as worried as the rest of us, I suppose—'

'Oh, come on, Skandar!' Jamie cried. 'You know that's not what I mean! How are things *between* you and her?' The blacksmith wiggled an eyebrow this time, and what felt like carnivorous butterflies erupted in Skandar's stomach.

'I, er, we haven't really talked about anything to do with us. Romantically, I mean.' Forking thunderstorms, Skandar *hated* that word – why was he using it now?

'What are you scared of?' Jamie asked not unkindly.

Skandar stared resolutely down at Scoundrel's mane, the increasing temperature of the zone adding to his discomfort. 'Flo is my best friend. I mean, Bobby and Mitchell are too, but there's always been something extra between me and Flo, you

# SKANDAR AND THE SKELETON CURSE

know? Like I always find myself sitting next to her, or wanting to be near her, or . . . thinking about her when she's not around.'

'Mm-hmm,' Jamie murmured.

'But I have no idea how to tell Flo any of that – and what if she doesn't feel the same? What if it ruins our friendship? I'm so scared of losing that, but . . .'

'It's getting impossible to ignore how you feel?' Jamie said quietly. 'Like if you don't speak up, it'll just burst out of you?'

'Yes!' Skandar said, finally meeting Jamie's eye as he walked alongside Scoundrel. 'Before, I could sort of squash the feelings and tell myself our friendship was too important to risk, but now that doesn't feel possible. I keep thinking there's a lot more to worry about. My mum died in front of me –' Jamie put a comforting hand on Skandar's boot – 'my sister is turning unicorns wild, the Commodore is a power-hungry murderer, and my grief-stricken aunt is on the run. And I *am* worrying about all that stuff a lot, but somehow it doesn't stop how I'm feeling about Flo. My heart won't listen to my head – I feel a bit like a Fledgling unicorn ignoring its rider.'

'That's very romantic, Skandar,' Jamie said playfully.

'Oh, don't!' he groaned, his stomach squirming. 'And please don't tell Flo!'

Jamie scoffed. 'Obviously I'm not going to do that. But *you* should. That's exactly how I felt with Mitchell. I honestly had no idea whether he liked me or not for ages – I knew I liked him, but I worried he was only really interested in borrowing my books about armour.'

Skandar chuckled.

'It took Mitchell asking me to the dance to show me how he felt – *he* was the brave one for both of us. I think you can be brave too.' Jamie rushed on. 'And we never know how long we've got to tell people how we feel. The Island is in flux, can't you sense

– 102 –

# SACRIFICE

it? It doesn't feel stable or safe – and it isn't just Kenna; it's the people in charge.'

'Rex,' Skandar said darkly, and he blew the eagle whistle as they tracked the fault line.

Skandar, Scoundrel and Jamie had only just entered the desert proper when Silver Soldier came galloping towards them across the sand dunes. The Pathfinder barely glanced at Jamie before she spoke. 'Skandar, I need you to come with me. The Wanderers have found something – someone – on the line. Come. Quickly.'

Fear flooded Skandar's body. He'd never seen Elora so bewildered and afraid.

Jamie made a sound of resignation in his throat, and Skandar helped him up on to Scoundrel's back.

'Who's she?' Jamie whispered to Skandar.

'The head of the Wanderers,' Skandar replied. 'Their Pathfinder.'

'Oh, right, Mitchell told me about them. They sound class,' Jamie murmured, before his arms tightened round Skandar as Scoundrel increased his speed.

After a few minutes, their destination was obvious. Wanderers – some mounted, others on foot – were clustered near the fault line a little way ahead. Scoundrel halted sharply. His horn was high in the air, magic crackling round his wingtips. He started to bellow then shriek and backed away.

'Scoundrel, what are you—' Skandar tried to make the black unicorn go forward again, but he'd planted his hooves in the sand, refusing to move. The bond was full of Scoundrel's fear. 'We'd better get off.'

Jamie slid gratefully down to the ground.

'What is it, boy?' Skandar walked round to Scoundrel's head and stroked the unicorn's white spirit blaze. 'It's all right. I'm here. What's got into you?'

– 103 –

# SKANDAR AND THE SKELETON CURSE

Agatha appeared at Skandar's shoulder, dressed in a deep mauve tunic. 'Scoundrel's right to be afraid. But we could do with the spirit element to know what you see. Can you try to get him closer?'

'What's going on?' Skandar pleaded. 'Is this what you meant in your letter?'

Agatha shook her head. 'No, this just happened. The Wanderers only found them minutes ago. Come on.'

Skandar managed to lead Scoundrel forward, though mainly because the unicorn seemed scared to be separated from his rider and blacksmith. He kept making tiny squeaking noises like he had when he'd hatched, the bond vibrating with his terror. The emotion was so strong that Skandar felt his own hands shaking, even though he had no idea why Scoundrel was afraid.

The Wanderers parted for the spirit wielder to approach the fault line, familiar faces nodding grimly in greeting. And Skandar finally understood why Scoundrel was so distressed.

A scarlet unicorn lay across the fault line. And, like a nightmarish Grim Reaper, a skeletal man crouched alongside her, his ribcage rattling with sobs. A faint red glow surrounded them, as though sealing them in with their misery.

Skandar recognised both unicorn and rider almost immediately. Growing up, he'd watched them race, collected their Chaos Cards, marvelled at the strength of their wildfire attacks – hadn't they qualified for the Chaos Cup last year? It was Federico Jones and Sunset's Blood.

Agatha touched Skandar gently on the shoulder. 'Can you summon the spirit element to see if their bond is completely gone? Some of the Wanderers tried to reach Federico, but it's the same magic you faced with Flo. They can't get close enough to tell if . . .' Agatha couldn't finish the sentence, but Skandar knew what she was trying to say. The Wanderers couldn't get close

– 104 –

# SACRIFICE

enough to check if Sunset's Blood was still alive.

Skandar summoned the spirit element into his palm, and forced himself to look at the mighty Chaos rider and unicorn. He wished with all his might for a shining red bond to burst into his vision. But there was only empty space. The bond was broken.

'Sunset's Blood is dead,' Skandar whispered to Agatha, who passed the message on. Heads bowed.

'We need to get Federico out of there,' Elora said. 'If he's experiencing the same poisonous level of magic as Flo did, then I don't know how long he'll survive if he stays on the fault line.'

'I'll get him,' Skandar volunteered.

'If it feels any different from last time, you turn back. Okay?' Agatha said forcefully, as he stepped towards Federico and Sunset. But the only discomfort he experienced was the overpowering smell of the fire magic – bonfires, and lit matches and toast burnt to a cinder – and the sound of Scoundrel's anxious shrieks.

Even from behind, it was clear that Federico was in grave danger. Tendrils of flame tethered his skeletal body in place like chains, charring the exposed bones at his shoulders.

'Federico?' Skandar tried to get his attention. 'What happened, Federico?'

The rider turned his head, surprisingly quickly, and Skandar's heart jumped to his throat as he was faced with more skeleton than man.

'Don't you understand?' Federico's eyes were wild in their deep sockets. 'Sunset's Blood was the sacrifice – that's what she said, the wild girl. Sacrificing Sunset – like this, in this place, on this day – so that all the other fire unicorns would turn wild. But why us? Why did she choose us?'

'I'm sorry. I'm so sorry,' Skandar said. *All the other fire unicorns?*

– 105 –

## SKANDAR AND THE SKELETON CURSE

'She came for us in the night. Used magic – some sort of elemental cage – to get us out to the zone. We fought her off as best we could,' Federico continued, his voice a little stronger than Elias's had been. 'I injured her a little, I think, and then she fled when the Wanderers came.' Skandar couldn't help the panic bubbling up: was Kenna okay? He squashed it. Smoke started to billow up from the fault line in black plumes and, although Skandar was immune, he could still see it curling between Federico's ribs.

'She used something,' Federico wheezed. 'It looked like a piece of bone.'

*Bone? Why had she needed a piece of—*

All of a sudden, a unicorn shrieked so loudly that Skandar thought he'd been wrong about Sunset. But no – the fire unicorn lay still. Maybe Scoundrel had made it through the fire barrier? But he remained beyond the red glow.

Then there were more shrieks and bellows and a storming of hooves. Skandar looked this way and that, certain that the stampede would reach them any moment.

But nothing came. No unicorns. No hooves. No destruction.

Skandar had no idea where the sounds were coming from, but some primal instinct was screaming at him to get away from the fault line. It didn't feel safe. 'Please, Federico, we need to get to the healers.'

'But Sunset's Blood!' The rider's voice was a gurgling wail.

'I know,' Skandar choked out. 'I'm so sorry.'

As though defeated, the legendary Chaos rider let Skandar take his skeletal arm and lead him off the line. He didn't even react as the fire magic rose up and attempted to ravage what was left of his body – his grief seemed vast enough to eclipse any physical pain.

Within seconds, a team of Wanderers had Federico on a

– 106 –

## SACRIFICE

stretcher and were riding in the direction of Fourpoint.

Skandar watched numbly as other Wanderers covered the body of Sunset's Blood with a large blanket, carefully lowering the corners without entering the red glow over the fault line. Elora, Agatha and Jamie approached Skandar.

'Tell us,' Agatha urged, trying to read her nephew's face.

'Federico described this as a sacrifice site.' Skandar's voice came out strange and monotone. 'Apparently my ... apparently Kenna killed Sunset's Blood here. She said that Sunset's death would affect the other fire unicorns. Turn them—'

'No,' Jamie breathed.

'A sacrifice site?' Elora checked, her violet eyes intense. 'But I don't understand how breaking one bond would affect them all. How is it possible?'

Skandar swallowed. 'Federico said Kenna had a piece of bone with her – that she was using it to help her somehow ...'

Understanding filled Agatha's eyes. 'Kenna's got the First Rider's staff,' she said ominously.

Skandar nodded heavily. 'I think so. She was there on the Divide two years ago when it went missing. She must have stolen the pieces from the Eyrie and kept them with her.' *She had them the whole time she was with me in the Eyrie,* Skandar thought wildly. *The whole time she was with the Wanderers.* When he spoke again, he tried to keep the hurt out of his voice. 'She must be using the bones somehow – to help her do this to the bonds.'

Then chills swept down Skandar's spine at another awful thought. Had Kenna broken the bone staff on purpose when they'd saved the Island together? Had she known *then* that she was going to do this terrible thing? The depth of his sister's betrayal, the planning that must have gone into it, took away his voice; he had no words to speak the realisation aloud.

Elora looked very troubled. 'The elemental glow on this part

– 107 –

# SKANDAR AND THE SKELETON CURSE

of the fault line matches the one Flo encountered in the earth zone. It's almost like the leftover fire magic is shielding the sacrifice. When Flo stumbled across the site, Marauding Magnet was already gone – perhaps the poor earth wielder boy buried him – but the aftershocks of whatever she'd done remained.' Elora gestured to the line, to the blanket covering Sunset's body. 'There's an extraordinary amount of power at play here – magic as old as the bone staff itself.'

*But why didn't it harm me?* Skandar wondered.

'Sacrifices and empty bonds, and riders rotting away like wild unicorns.' Agatha actually sounded afraid. 'This is much darker than anything Erika ever would have—'

There was a shrieking sound in the air above like a bird of prey. Everyone looked up to see Goshawk's Fury soaring over the fire zone, perhaps a victory lap before carrying Kenna back towards the Wilderness.

A wave of rage broke over Skandar and he mounted Scoundrel. He needed to catch Kenna, to stop her, to get her to reverse what she'd done. To ask her *why, why, why—*

But Scoundrel made a chirruping noise that distracted Skandar – the noise he used when he was greeting a very specific unicorn.

A red unicorn was blazing across the sand towards the Wanderers. Skandar could feel Scoundrel's excitement in the bond – he'd had a horrible morning, but now his best friend was coming to make everything better.

Skandar allowed Scoundrel to trot towards the rapidly approaching fire unicorn. But then the spirit unicorn stopped short, his confusion vibrating all the way to Skandar's heart.

It was Red Night's Delight. Yet it wasn't her at all. Skandar noticed her horn first – always so solidly blood red but now colourless and ghostly. The muscles she had built up over years

– 108 –

## SACRIFICE

of Eyrie training were wasting away – ribs visible, Red's skeleton poking through.

Scoundrel took another step, but Red bellowed angrily – a sound Skandar had never heard her make. Scoundrel shrieked softly and pawed the sand with his hoof. Red sent a warning blast of smoky, rancid magic, and Skandar was forced to throw up a water shield. The bond twanged with Scoundrel's hurt. Why was his best friend acting like this?

A thundering of hooves suddenly filled the air, and Skandar looked over to see Silver Blade and Falcon's Wrath galloping over the nearest sand dune. Red skittered a little way onwards, although she still kept one burning eye on Scoundrel.

Skandar saw Flo's face first, the tears streaming silently down her cheeks. Bobby's features were a mask, hiding her worry. And Mitchell . . . Mitchell was sitting behind Bobby on Falcon's back, his eyes desperately tracking Red as she sent an angry fireball at the sky.

Everyone dismounted, and just as Mitchell's black boots hit the sand, someone came barrelling towards him.

'Jamie,' Mitchell whimpered, as the blacksmith took him in his arms. 'Red, she's— I can't feel the bond. I can't—'

'I know, I know.' Jamie stroked Mitchell's flaming hair. 'But we're going to fix this, aren't we?' Jamie looked up then, right at Skandar. 'You're a Mender. You *can* fix this, can't you? Spirit wielders are all about bonds!'

'I-I don't know.' Skandar looked between Red – about two hundred metres away across the sand – and Mitchell. Holding Scoundrel's reins against his neck with one hand, Skandar summoned the spirit element into his palm with the other.

Red and Mitchell's bond stretched out over the sand but – just like those of the earth wielders – it was completely empty of colour.

– 109 –

# SKANDAR AND THE SKELETON CURSE

'It's still there,' Skandar confirmed.

Mitchell gulped, looking longingly over the sand at Red.

Agatha and Elora arrived to join them, their faces solemn. And Skandar suddenly remembered why he'd come to meet Agatha in the first place. He practically shouted at her in his desperation. 'What was the idea you had, Agatha? You said you wanted me to try something!'

She looked reluctant to speak. 'Just a theory – I have no idea if it'll work.' Her eyes flicked between Mitchell and Red. 'I don't want anyone to get their hopes up.'

'Well, things can't exactly get much worse, can they?' Bobby snapped, her olive skin unusually pale.

Agatha sighed and addressed Skandar. 'I thought perhaps you could use a combination of the spirit element and the fire element to . . . refuel the bond. I don't think mending magic will work – since the connection still exists. But the spirit element will let you enter the bond itself, and then you'd be trying to refill it. In Henderson's case – with fire magic.'

'That would be brilliant,' Flo said overly brightly.

'Try it,' Jamie insisted, running a hand anxiously through his sandy hair.

'Ideally, Red would be closer to you,' Skandar told Mitchell, hope and nerves mixing in his stomach. He wanted so badly to be able to fix this.

Mitchell wiped tears from his cheeks, trying to sound businesslike. 'Red only seems to be paying attention to Scoundrel at the moment. She might let *him* closer?'

Skandar remounted Scoundrel and Mitchell scrambled up to sit in front of him.

'Be careful,' Elora warned, anxiously tucking her white hair behind both ears.

Scoundrel didn't need any persuading to get closer to his

– 110 –

# SACRIFICE

best friend. As they crossed the sand at a hurried pace, Skandar summoned a mixture of the spirit and fire elements into the bond. Seeing them approach, Red startled and shied away to the left. Scoundrel shrieked at her, no doubt trying to get her to stay still.

'That's it, boy,' Skandar breathed, as he felt Scoundrel's confusion and hurt spiralling in the bond. 'Red's still in there somewhere. Try to get her to listen.'

Scoundrel shrieked, and when that didn't work, he switched to low bellows – a sound he had made before around wild unicorns. Red stopped in her tracks – staring at Scoundrel, rancid smoke rising from her nostrils. Skandar couldn't help his intake of breath at the sight of Red's head, the outline of her skull visible where her blood-red coat had rotted away.

*Please work, please work,* Skandar begged silently, as he reached out for Mitchell's bond with tendrils of the spirit element.

'Is it working?' Mitchell whispered, unable to see his own bond.

'Give me a minute,' Skandar grunted, focusing.

Once he'd wrapped the spirit magic round the ghostly bond, he switched his palm to fire and sent a single flaming jet right at the thread between Mitchell and Red. The connection between their hearts flared scarlet, glowing just like it had before.

And for a moment Skandar thought he'd fixed it. 'Can you feel anything?'

Mitchell shook his head quickly, the flames in his hair billowing wildly.

Skandar sent another jet of fire into the bond, and this time Red bellowed at it suspiciously. The connection glowed red, and Skandar shut his palm, desperately hoping that the colour would stay.

It didn't. Almost immediately the bond returned to a transparent shimmering cord.

– 111 –

# SKANDAR AND THE SKELETON CURSE

Mitchell turned to look at Skandar and the two boys didn't need to speak to understand each other. Mitchell had known Skandar a long time now – had seen him win and lose, had seen him sad and happy, had seen him afraid and fearless. He could tell that Skandar had failed. And Skandar couldn't find the words to tell Mitchell that everything would be okay. Couldn't summon the feelings to tell Scoundrel he would bring his best friend back.

Because, right now, he didn't know how.

Kenna

## OLD FRIENDS, NEW TRICKS

Kenna Everhart had not been expecting company.

She was living so far into the Wilderness she hadn't even bothered hiding herself and Goshawk's Fury. Anyway, they could defeat any lone rider stupid enough to attack them. And when it came to those hunting her, Kenna was pretty confident she could take out an entire battalion of masked sentinels without breaking a sweat.

Kenna had discovered thickets and groves peppered across the Wilderness's outer edges. Not long after the events on her mother's island, she'd been exercising Goshawk and passed through a spinney of tall, gaunt pines. They barely looked as though they were the same species as the ones that grew inside the Eyrie's walls. But their fresh smell, in the middle of the barren Wilderness, had made her pause.

That was when she'd spotted the treehouse. Unlike the old Everhart family home, it had been constructed from metal not wood, and, though rusted, was incredibly well preserved. Kenna had loved it immediately because it reminded her of her

# SKANDAR AND THE SKELETON CURSE

bond with Goshawk – so similar yet completely different from anything at the Eyrie. The metal had clearly been scavenged from multiple treehouses at different times. Some parts were dull silver, others coppery; the roof was constructed from corrugated black sheets. Large patches of metal in the walls were oxidised or warped, and none of it slotted together exactly how you'd expect. It was like an experimental sculpture, a collage – a scrapyard treehouse.

Kenna had explored it cautiously at first – checking for signs of human life – but had soon been climbing the rusted spikes that punctured the treehouse's central trunk and led to the upper floor. There she'd found a small enclosed space at the end of the landing, with a large square window that had a view off the Island and out to sea. It had reminded Kenna of where she'd grown up. She hadn't very often loved Margate, but she did love the sea – the sight of it, the sound, the idea that she could sail away on a boat and see things she'd never dreamed of. As she'd stared out of that window, Kenna had let a tiny spark of happiness into her heart at the thought that perhaps her mum had built this treehouse. Somehow it suited Erika more than the grand Everhart building had done. Perhaps her mum had been standing there when she'd decided to flee to the Mainland, where she'd end up falling in love with a man called Robert Smith who lived by the sea.

As Kenna had settled into the Scrapyard Treehouse, whenever she had started doubting whether she'd be able to do what was required, she'd found herself talking to her dad. It wasn't like she'd thought he was talking back to her – despite what the Island thought, she wasn't losing her mind to Goshawk. Not most days.

But out loud she'd told Robert Smith how Erika had believed she was strong enough to live for ever like Goshawk. Cried to him about the idea of letting her mum down – letting them both

– 114 –

## OLD FRIENDS, NEW TRICKS

down really – because she wasn't sure Dad could deal with more grief if the forged bond killed her. He'd loved her enough to let her go to the Island even though it made him sad. But there was a different grief in losing someone to death. Its shadowy claws had dug into Kenna's shoulders her whole childhood. She couldn't put Dad through that again, could she?

And she'd confessed the big, scary things too. The things she'd never be brave enough to say to him. She'd told him how she had felt so useless growing up because she'd never been able to make him happy – not truly. She'd told him about Skandar's bullies and how she hadn't been able to stop them, even though she'd tried so hard. She'd told him how the events in her own life had always felt like a string of consequences for other people's actions. She'd tried to convince him that she needed to do these terrible things so that she could take control of her future in the way she had always wished she could.

'I don't want to just disappear from the world like Mum. I don't want my body to wink out like stars, as though I never existed. As though I never mattered. I've spent so much of my life feeling powerless – and I never want to feel like that again, Dad.'

And that thought had won.

And now Sunset's Blood was dead.

Kenna stood in the very same spot – at the window of the smallest room in the Scrapyard Treehouse – watching the afternoon sunbeams dance down the portrait of the Everhart sisters she'd taken from the family treehouse. Well, it was just one sister now – Kenna had burned the canvas with her shadow-edged fire magic, obliterating any trace of Agatha.

Suddenly there was the sound of knuckles on metal. Had they found her? Kenna sent a blast of alarm into the bond to Goshawk, who'd gone out hunting. She could use elemental magic to protect herself, but the further away Goshawk was, the

# SKANDAR AND THE SKELETON CURSE

harder Kenna had to work to summon the power.

The knock came again, and this time Kenna realised how polite it sounded – what kind of sentinel knocks like that? Curiosity replaced her unease, and, listening all the time, she climbed down the iron spikes of the trunk, wincing at the burn Federico and Sunset's Blood had managed to land on her elbow.

As Kenna reached the front door, she heard a soft voice.

'Hello? Are you in there?'

Kenna's breath hitched in surprise. She knew that voice. And she also knew that – no matter what she'd done – the person it belonged to would never harm her.

She opened the door.

And standing with his fist raised to knock again, the coals of his knuckles smouldering, was a friend she'd assumed was lost to her for ever.

'Hello, Kenna,' Albert said, smiling. 'I thought you might want some company.'

But Albert hadn't arrived alone. Kenna noticed Eagle's Dawn on the ground below. The fire unicorn's newly transparent horn was ghostly among the pine trunks, and Kenna felt a twinge of guilt. Then hurt. So Albert had not come to her out of friendship, but because he was going to beg Kenna to make Eagle a bonded unicorn again.

'I can't reverse it,' Kenna said immediately, retreating towards her misshapen door. 'If that's what you want, I can't help you.'

But Albert shook his head.

Kenna listened as he explained that he wanted her advice and guidance, and, most of all, for them to be friends again. Out on the rusted platform, he laid everything before her like an offering to a goddess. He raged about the Wanderers doing nothing to stop the silver tyrant increasing his power, lamented that they were never going to fight for the Island they loved. He

– 116 –

## OLD FRIENDS, NEW TRICKS

spoke with disappointment about their attitude towards those whose unicorns had been turned wild – welcoming them but not embracing them, accepting the change but refusing to talk about their futures as wild unicorn riders.

'The Wanderers have looked after wild unicorn foals for generations, but they can't cope with what's happening now,' he raved. 'They pretend to be all progressive, but the Wanderers are othering those of us whose bonded unicorns have turned wild. Just like the Island has always rejected those who don't fit its mould.'

'You do know *I'm* the one responsible for turning them wild, don't you?' Kenna said finally.

'And I wish it hadn't been necessary, but I see now what you're trying to do, Kenn.' Her skin went cold at the nickname, *that* name that had belonged only to Skandar for so long. *Don't think about Skandar.*

'What do you think I'm trying to do?' Kenna asked. Because the truth was that the idea of her immortality had been planted by Erika years ago, and she had hung on to it like a lifeline after her mother's murder. The pieces of the bone staff were her revenge, her inheritance and her grief – most of all they gave her power over both her life and her death. But perhaps – to Albert – they were something else.

'You're . . .' Albert stumbled. 'You're resetting the Island. This is how it was, wasn't it? In the beginning, before the Chaos Cup and the Eyrie and the Silver Circle. It was a fisherman who washed up on a strange land and befriended a unicorn. *All* unicorns were wild then. There was no hierarchy, no difference between bonded and wild – just this Island and the power of elemental magic hanging in the air, radiating from its earth. And a connection between a lost boy and a curious foal. You're taking us back to that, you're helping us fix our mistakes,

– 117 –

you're helping us start over. And I want you to teach me how to connect with Eagle's Dawn as she is now – a wild unicorn, an original – so I can ride into that future with you.'

And Kenna suddenly recognised in Albert's serious blue eyes something that she had seen in Skandar when they were growing up.

Belief. An unshakable, fanatical belief in *her*.

Just as Skandar had once trusted that Kenna could vanquish the monsters that lived under his bed, Albert now believed she was bringing about a new beginning for the Island. That she could show him – and everyone – a new way to live.

It was nice to listen to him praising her like she didn't have unicorn blood on her hands. Like her crimes were necessary for her great, selfless plan. As though perhaps she wasn't the broken one, after all. So Kenna invited Albert inside. She nodded knowingly when he told her why her actions were going to make the Island a better place. She showed him the pieces of the broken bone staff – the two pieces she'd already fused together, as well as those still waiting to be added. He took the partially repaired staff in his hands, marvelling at the elemental veins that had appeared there – green vines pulsing against the white bone, fire smouldering in a thin snaking line. He stared reverently at her then, talking about how the First Rider must be guiding her down this path, how the magic of the bone staff only proved that it was what the founder and his Wild Unicorn Queen would have wanted for the Island.

Kenna realised something else important in that moment. Albert *needed* to believe in her. He wanted to believe in her goodness so badly that he was willing to overlook, to embellish, to misremember some fundamental truths – about her present *and* her past.

And Kenna didn't hate that. She didn't hate that at all.

CHAPTER EIGHT

# THE SKELETON CURSE

The quartet left Red Night's Delight in the desert with Jamie – who'd insisted on staying with the unicorn until Mitchell returned – and rode back to the Eyrie for the fire wielder's belongings. Each of them had offered to go for him, but Mitchell had said that they'd bring the wrong armour or spare reins or research books he needed to try to help Red. They hadn't argued or discussed what was going to happen *after* Mitchell collected his possessions, but the unspoken horror of it hung between them on the ride back to Fourpoint, like one of Red's flaming farts.

News of Federico Jones and Sunset's Blood had already reached the Eyrie. The number of sentinels outside had doubled, though now they were only made up of water and air wielders. Luckily the guards assumed that the quartet were simply returning from the Fire Festival and didn't even bother to look up from their whispered conversations as Scoundrel, Falcon and Blade passed under the colourful leaves.

Just then, Fen and Eternal Hoarfrost melted out of the trees and blocked their way. Fen's cropped black hair was unusually dishevelled, her face full of worry. 'You weren't at the Fire Festival, were you?' she puffed, without any kind of greeting.

'No, we . . . er—' Skandar answered haltingly.

'It doesn't matter,' Fen said quickly, cracking a frozen knuckle. 'Rex is about to start another speech at the Divide. We're all supposed to be there, and—'

'Got it,' Skandar said, and – with Mitchell still on Scoundrel's back behind Skandar – the quartet rode after Hoarfrost towards the clearing.

Skandar didn't care about getting in trouble with Rex, but he wanted to hear what the Commodore was going to say. Now there was clearly a pattern, surely Rex was going to stop messing around with the Eyrie and actually start trying to reverse what Kenna had done.

The clearing wasn't nearly as packed as it had been after the Earth Festival, and many water and air wielders had chosen to bring their unicorns with them – perhaps afraid to be separated. Many earth wielders were missing, but now fire wielders were absent too – Skandar couldn't see Art and Furious Inferno or Sarika and Equator's Conundrum or the new Grin, Whitney, with Brimstone's Chorus.

When the quartet arrived, Rex was already on his raised platform, flanked by the other instructors. In the glow of the lantern-light, Skandar desperately tried to read their faces to work out whether there was more bad news coming, but their expressions were carefully neutral. All except Instructor Anderson, who was clenching his hands to stop them from shaking with anger or grief – maybe both.

'Desert Firebird must be wild too,' Flo murmured quietly, and Mitchell let out a choked sob from behind Skandar on Scoundrel's back. Skandar took his friend's hand, and from

# THE SKELETON CURSE

Falcon's back Bobby managed a comforting squeeze on the fire wielder's shoulder.

Rex raised a palm for silence and the effect was immediate. 'It is with the greatest sadness that I am forced to call a meeting of the whole Eyrie again in light of the Wild Rider's attack on the fire wielders tonight. And I think it's right that we stop calling Kenna by the name she was known to us when she was our friend. From now on she is the *Wild Rider*, our enemy, who has unleashed the Skeleton Curse upon the Island through her mastery of the spirit element.'

Bobby and Flo looked sharply at Skandar, who had a hand knotted in Scoundrel's black mane. Rex hadn't mentioned the spirit element in relation to Kenna before, and attaching a name to what she was doing – the Skeleton Curse – made it sound more like it was something that all spirit wielders could do. Sure enough, eyes flicked towards Skandar, riders shifting their unicorns away from Scoundrel.

Rex's voice rang out with authority. 'As a result of this evening's attack, I will be introducing more rules here at the Eyrie. And just as my previous changes sought to protect you all, these go further in keeping you safe – the protection of the Island's young riders is of the utmost importance to me.'

'Here we go again,' Bobby muttered.

But she clearly wasn't the only one who was feeling dissatisfied with Rex tonight.

'What about our unicorns?' It was Ajay. 'Smouldering Menace is wild – shouldn't turning our unicorns back to normal be *of the utmost importance* to you?'

'Yeah!' Meiyi practically shrieked. 'What use are new rules at the Eyrie when only half the riders have unicorns they can actually train?'

'And how are you going to stop this Skeleton Curse affecting

– 121 –

# SKANDAR AND THE SKELETON CURSE

the water and air wielders, too? It's obviously a pattern! What are you doing to stop Kenna? Apart from giving her a spooky new name?' This last question from Fen elicited amused support across the crowd.

'Silence!' Rex shouted, and his cheeks sparked silver. Despite the clear unrest among the riders, they obeyed, still wary after he'd declared so many nomads. 'If you would do me the courtesy of *listening* for one moment,' Rex continued, regaining his composure. 'My team of researchers is very close to reversing the Skeleton Curse – it may only be a few weeks until every unicorn is back to normal. I'll be inviting my experts back to the Eyrie to share their progress.'

A bubble of excitement went through the clearing – nobody had reported such a big breakthrough. Not even the *Hatchery Herald*.

'I don't believe him,' Mitchell said flatly, speaking for the first time in hours. 'He's been saying that for months.'

'In the meantime,' Rex continued, 'I wish to keep you all safe – *as I said* – so I will bring in the following changes. First, any fire or earth wielder who leaves the Eyrie after tonight will be declared a nomad immediately. It is extremely important to me that riders are not harmed out in the Wilderness searching for their unicorns. Earth and fire riders will continue their studies in their allied libraries while my research team perfects the cure for the curse. Understood?'

'I can't be away from Red,' Mitchell was muttering feverishly along with many of the other fire wielders. 'I can't just leave her out in the zones, in the Wilderness!'

'Secondly, any fire or earth wielder who is currently outside the Eyrie will be given twenty-four hours to return. I will send out sentinels to spread the word that if they aren't here by sunset tomorrow, they will also be declared nomads.' Skandar thought

– 122 –

# THE SKELETON CURSE

of his fellow Rookies, Gabriel and Aisha – who'd fought so hard to pass the Chaos Trials last year – living in tents by the Glowing Caves. How dare Rex declare them nomads just for wanting to stay with their unicorns?

'And finally.' Rex paused for a long time, going for maximum effect. 'In light of the findings made by my research team about the Skeleton Curse –' Rex looked right at Skandar – 'the spirit element will once again be entirely banned at the Eyrie. We cannot have the same dark magic that is harming our earth and fire wielders being used inside the Eyrie walls.' Every syllable he spoke was measured, reasonable. 'Especially by the sibling of the very person who is wielding that element for evil. It would be unfair of me to let his spirit training continue in the place you should all feel safest.'

'You can't do that!' The words were out of Skandar's mouth before he could stop himself.

There was a great shuffling and whispering as riders turned to stare at him. He heard Bobby's curse, Flo's intake of shocked breath, Mitchell's groan. But there was no going back now.

'In my Hatchling year I made a deal with Aspen McGrath. She made an exception to Island law so that I could train in the spirit element here.'

Rex smiled. 'Well, I'm the Commodore now. The death element has always been dangerous, and it was foolish of us to forget that. While it's not technically *illegal* for you to use the spirit element, I will no longer allow you to bring its danger into the Eyrie.'

Though some riders looked unsure, many others were nodding in agreement. They believed Rex that the spirit element was to blame for the unicorns going wild, for the riders turned to skeletons. Wild unicorns and spirit wielders always were linked, after all.

– 123 –

# SKANDAR AND THE SKELETON CURSE

'But I'm not declaring you a nomad, Skandar,' Rex shouted to him. 'Instead, you will join a water treehouse and hereafter be treated entirely as a water wielder. Is that not generous? More than fair?' Rex spread his hands, Nina's ring glinting on his finger, and there was a smattering of applause.

Skandar's horrified stare slipped to Instructor O'Sullivan standing behind Rex. Why wasn't she saying anything? Surely she didn't agree with this? Then he noticed three sentinels behind the platform, half concealed by the shadows of the trees. The instructors were bent over slightly, as though fearful.

But Skandar was not afraid. He was furious.

And he was done.

This was not the Eyrie he loved. This was not the Island he had dreamed of. It didn't exist any more – perhaps it never had. Hoping for change was no longer enough; Skandar would have to *bring* the change. Because he didn't want others to suffer the way he had, to be forced to hide themselves away. He knew how hard it was to be yourself, when the world refused you a place to belong. Because belonging came from the outside as well as the inside. It came from seeing yourself *and* it came from others affirming what they saw. And Rex was never going to make a spirit wielder welcome.

So if taking a stand meant Skandar would forfeit his bargain with Aspen McGrath, then so be it – Rex was never going to honour it anyway. And if Skandar ever managed to bring spirit wielders back to this Island, he would make sure the bright lights they ignited on the Divide were celebrated not dimmed. Skandar couldn't fight for that from behind these poisoned Eyrie walls any longer. This present had to become his past if that future was ever going to stand a chance.

'I can't stay here any more,' Skandar whispered to his quartet while Rex droned on about the new clearance process for Eyrie

– 124 –

# THE SKELETON CURSE

visitors. 'I'm going to declare myself a nomad. Now.'

'Skar, are you serious?'

'Spirit boy, are you sure?'

'Skandar, are you absolutely certain?'

Three versions of his name were whispered by his three best friends – each form full of shock and warning and worry. But none of them tried to talk him out of it. They had heard the resolve in his voice. After all, they knew him better than anyone else.

'I don't expect you to come with me. Rex is dangerous,' Skandar said, swallowing down his panic. 'This is my choice, my—'

But Bobby interrupted him. 'Yep. I think I'm about finished with Right Muppet too.'

'No, Bobby – you don't have to. What about Isa?'

'She's tougher than I am – and I'll be more use to her trying to stop this Skeleton Curse before it reaches the water wielders than trapped here with a power-hungry fella with fizzing cheekbones. Don't argue with me – you know you'll lose.'

But Skandar was going to try. 'What about becoming Commodore, Bobby? What about your dreams? You're good enough to go all the way, but if you leave . . .'

Bobby stuck out her chin. 'There's no rule against nomads entering the Chaos Cup, is there?' She glanced at Mitchell for confirmation.

'That's right,' he whispered. 'Thus far a nomad has never won it, I suspect because they miss out on a lot of training, can't get into yards but –' pride shone through his grief-stricken eyes – 'there's never been a Bobby Bruna before either, has there?'

Bobby grinned. 'Exactly. New ambition unlocked – become the first nomad to win the Chaos Cup. It's decided.'

'I'll be declaring myself a nomad with you too, Skandar,' Mitchell said. 'There's no way I'm leaving Red out there on her

# SKANDAR AND THE SKELETON CURSE

own. She might be wild but she needs me.'

'What about your dad?' Bobby whispered. 'I know he's been more understanding lately, but leaving the Eyrie, Mitchell – that's the biggest deal to someone like him.'

Mitchell shrugged. 'My father will either accept it or he won't. I don't need his approval – not if I believe it's the right thing to do. I'm leaving with Skandar.'

'We're a quartet,' Flo said, her voice sure and steady. 'We leave together.'

Skandar felt completely torn – he was desperate for Flo to come with them, but the risk for her was much greater . . .

'You're not like the rest of us, Flo,' said Bobby, her face solemn under her fringe. 'You know the Silver Circle will lock you and Blade in the Stronghold if they find you. You're a silver, you can't just declare yourself a nomad.'

'Watch me,' Flo said, and she'd never sounded more determined. 'If Elora and Silver Soldier left the Circle, so can we.'

'You do realise you'll be on the run, indefinitely,' Mitchell said seriously.

'Then I guess I'll have to make sure they don't catch me.'

'Flo—' Skandar attempted to speak, but her name came out as a plea.

She turned in her Martina saddle to look him right in the eye and there was a secret intensity to her gaze that was only for him. 'There is no world in which I stay here without you, Skar.'

'What's going on over there?' Rex's voice lashed like a whip across the clearing. 'Did one of you have a question?'

Bobby stuck out her chin. 'I have a question, *Commodore*. Did you feel bad when you killed Nina Kazama?'

'Bobby . . .' Flo warned.

'Well, since we're going anyway,' Mitchell muttered, then raised his voice. 'I have a question! Why are you pretending

– 126 –

# THE SKELETON CURSE

you've made progress on the Skeleton Curse? Is it because you want all our unicorns wild so the Silver Circle will reign supreme?'

The clearing was abuzz with loud chatter now.

Skandar was grinning. 'I also have a question!' he yelled over the unsettled crowd. 'Why did you take credit for the Weaver's death, when Agatha Everhart killed her?'

Gasps and more loud talking from the crowd.

'Now listen here!' Rex practically screeched, pointing at the quartet.

'No, YOU listen!' Skandar shouted, adrenaline and rage pulsing through him. 'I am a spirit wielder and I am a good person. Those two things can go together, and I won't stay here pretending to be someone I'm not.' Skandar ripped the spirit and water pins from his red jacket and held them in one fist, high in the air. 'I am declaring *myself* a nomad.'

'I am declaring *myself* a nomad,' Bobby echoed from Scoundrel's right, air pin clutched in her hand.

'I am declaring *myself* a nomad,' Mitchell shouted, ripping away his fire pin, arm raised.

'And I am declaring *myself* a nomad,' Flo cried and removed her earth pin with shaking fingers.

Instructors O'Sullivan, Anderson and Webb raised their fists in solidarity, unseen by Rex standing in front of them. They would stay at the Eyrie, Skandar knew, to protect the riders who remained, but they were silently cheering the quartet on. And he spotted a few remaining Grins cheering them on, too. Isa gave Bobby a huge thumbs up.

Then Rex made his next move. 'Skandar Smith, Bobby Bruna and Mitchell Henderson, you are perfectly entitled to declare yourselves nomads. Florence Shekoni, however, you are a silver and therefore must spend the remainder of your training years

– 127 –

inside the Stronghold. Sentinels, please escort—'

'GO!' Bobby yelled. The crowd scattered as Falcon moved towards Rex's platform, wings already pumping. Bobby threw her gold pin right at the Commodore's head, before managing to take off practically from a standstill. Rex ducked and shouted furious orders for Sorceress to be fetched for him. Sentinels swarmed towards Scoundrel and Blade on foot, but were suddenly distracted as a large bird – a falcon, made entirely of electricity – dive-bombed the clearing over and over, forcing riders into the trees. Skandar looked up – the elemental predator belonged to Bobby, who was still circling above the trees.

Flo and Blade took advantage of the crowd dispersing and managed to increase their speed for take-off. As Blade rose into the air, Flo threw down her earth pin and it clanged against the mask of a sentinel who'd been hot on their heels. Skandar could no longer see Rex.

'Hold on tight!' Skandar shouted to Mitchell, and Scoundrel careered through the gap left by Silver Blade. They took off in four strides, and Skandar and Mitchell pelted their elemental pins at the sentinels who were in disarray down below.

Satisfied that the whole quartet were now airborne, Bobby's predator fizzled out and she swooped Falcon round so the unicorn's slate-grey horn pointed towards Fourpoint.

'Well, that was rather intense,' Mitchell said, as they flew onwards.

'D'you remember what I said to you, Skandar? When you were a Hatchling?' Bobby yelled over the beating of unicorn wings. 'I said being friends with you was going to keep things interesting.'

'I remember!' Skandar cried, unsure whether he was feeling euphoria or terror. 'Is this interesting enough for you?'

And despite everything – despite the fact that they had no

– 128 –

## THE SKELETON CURSE

idea how to stop the Skeleton Curse, that they had just declared themselves nomads, and Flo was now on the run from the Silver Circle – the whole quartet burst out laughing as they flew up towards the stars.

For a while Skandar and the rest of his quartet just flew as far and fast from the Eyrie as they could. They soon realised they didn't have much of a plan beyond fleeing. Scoundrel kept trying to swing out toward the fire zone, back to Red, his distress for his friend spiralling in the bond. But Flo eventually suggested circling back to Wildflower Hill, insisting that her parents would be worried when they heard she'd left the Eyrie. And more practically, the Shekonis would at least be able to provide the quartet with some supplies for their onward journey.

'It isn't fair to rely on the Wanderers for everything,' Flo said. 'They're going to have a whole new influx of fire wielders – we have to be self-sufficient.'

Skandar knew Flo was right, but as they approached the base of Wildflower Hill on foot, he couldn't help worrying that this was the first place the Silver Circle would look for her.

As it turned out, a silver rider had already paid Wildflower Hill a visit. She, along with a few sentinels, had checked everywhere for Flo, and then declared that they'd wait to see if she turned up. Sara – worried that her daughter would indeed arrive – had invited the silver rider and accompanying sentinels into the Shekoni treehouse for a cup of fire zone tea and taken matters into her own hands.

'What do you mean you poisoned them?' Flo was demanding.

Mismatched candles were lit along the yellow table of the Shekonis' kitchen, and mugs of hot chocolate and fire zone tea were warming the quartet's freezing hands. Olu and Ebb Shekoni were in their pyjamas, though completely wide awake.

– 129 –

# SKANDAR AND THE SKELETON CURSE

'"Poison" is a strong word, sweetie,' Sara said innocently. 'I just added some special healing herbs to their tea, and it sent them into a nice restful sleep.'

'What if they wake up?' Skandar glanced at Flo.

'Oh, we've got a good ten hours before they even start stirring,' Sara said, sipping her hot chocolate. 'The plant I used is generally for anaesthetising unicorns, so . . .'

Flo put her head in her hands. 'What if they realise you drugged them? You could get into serious trouble, Mum!'

Sara shrugged. 'They'll have no proof. And honestly, I doubt any of them will admit to falling asleep on the job. Rex wouldn't exactly be happy to hear they've been snoozing rather than searching for you.'

Bobby cackled but Flo groaned, still uneasy. 'Where have you put them?'

'My healer apprentices are watching over them. And your dad's saddler apprentices have put their unicorns in our recovery stables. Don't worry, it's all under control.'

'Please tell me it wasn't Rex who came looking for me?' Flo asked. 'Please tell me you haven't knocked out the Commodore.'

Flo's dad answered this time. 'No. The silver was Ayana who rides Silver Phoenix – and then a bunch of sentinels.'

Flo looked horrified. 'Ayana is Rex's second in command!'

Olu looked a little stern. 'And if it hadn't been for your mum's quick thinking, Ayana would be carting you off to the Stronghold as we speak.'

Flo looked between her parents and then sank down on to the bench next to her dad. 'I know. I'm sorry, thank you. Tonight has just been . . .'

'You don't have to thank us,' Sara said, leaning over and putting her arms round Flo's shoulders. 'Ayana told us about you declaring yourself a nomad. We're proud of you – all of you.'

– 130 –

# THE SKELETON CURSE

Olu put an arm round Flo too, so she was cocooned by them both. 'Honestly, doesn't Commodore Manning have more important things to focus on than a teenage runaway?'

'I suppose silvers are more precious than ever now.' Mitchell sounded exhausted. 'They're the only ones unaffected by what Kenna is doing.'

'The silver slimeball can't be sure it's going to stay that way, though, can he?' Bobby said, picking aggressively at her purple nail varnish. 'I don't get why he isn't making more effort, even for the sake of saving his own skin. For all he knows, the silvers *will* be affected by the Skeleton Curse at some point. Then he's going to look like even more of an idiot.'

'Is that what they're calling it? The Skeleton Curse?' Ebb asked.

'Rex called it that tonight,' Skandar confirmed. 'I think he was trying to scare everyone.'

Flo's mum sighed. 'Unfortunately it seems a fitting name. I have healer friends who've been caring for the earth wielder Elias. They've never seen anything like it. He's alive but he's dying at the same time. As a healer, what do you do with a case like that?'

'Federico described Sunset's Blood as a sacrifice,' Skandar said quietly. 'It seems that whatever Kenna did to Federico and Sunset's bond affected the bonds of all the fire wielders.'

Mitchell made a small sad noise in his throat, and Ebb put a gentle hand on his shoulder.

'And I think the bone staff has something to do with it,' Skandar murmured.

'It had elemental pieces, didn't it?' Flo frowned as she tried to remember. 'We each held our allied bone on the Divide. Do you think the piece of the staff she used today was the fire one?'

'I think it's likely,' Skandar murmured.

– 131 –

# SKANDAR AND THE SKELETON CURSE

'Do you reckon Kenna can choose any rider she wants for the Skeleton Curse? Or is there something about Elias and Federico that's special?' Bobby wondered out loud.

'I suppose they have to match the elemental season the Island is entering,' Mitchell said hoarsely. 'Elias is an earth wielder, and Magnet was sacrificed on the Earth Festival. Federico is a fire wielder, and Sunset was sacrificed on the Fire Festival. That implies that it'll be a water wielder and an air wielder next.'

'You've bored me to tears on thousands of occasions about how the festivals symbolise the new season's magic overcoming the old.' Bobby grinned at Mitchell. 'Well, it's your lucky day – that knowledge has actually come in useful. It has to be why Kenna's using those specific festival days, hasn't it?'

Skandar smiled to himself. Bobby was clearly trying to distract Mitchell by being rude to him.

It worked. Mitchell looked a bit stunned, as though he was unsure whether Bobby was insulting him or complimenting him, but he looked a bit more animated as he said, 'I agree. I doubt the festivals are just for show.'

'The bone staff had a spirit piece, though,' Flo said, looking at Skandar. 'Do you think spirit will be included in the pattern?'

It was Olu who answered. 'The Spirit Festival was always on the summer solstice. It used to be the most exciting day of the year because the Chaos Cup was traditionally held that day too – before the Treaty, at least.' He smiled. 'That's where Sara and I first met – we were both apprentices at our first-ever Cup, and as soon as our eyes met across—'

'Well, I don't think we should be worrying as far ahead as June,' Bobby interrupted, sounding alarmed by the romantic reminiscing. 'Ideally we'd work out who Kenna's going to choose next, in time for the Water Festival.'

'Yes, if we work that out, then maybe we could stop the rider

– 132 –

# THE SKELETON CURSE

and unicorn being taken,' Skandar said, feeling a little less hopeless. It felt good to be free of the Eyrie and planning their next move. And as long as he was problem-solving, Skandar could avoid thinking about the fact that it was his sister who'd done this to the Island. To Mitchell.

Their discussions jumped between reversing the Skeleton Curse and where the quartet were going to stay. The Wanderers seemed the obvious choice – especially as Mitchell was desperate to be reunited with Red. After an hour or so, Flo's mum stood up abruptly, opened a drawer and brandished a fistful of spoons at everyone. 'I'm calling an end to worrying tonight. *And* planning.'

Mitchell made a disappointed face.

'And I don't think any one of us is likely to sleep so, entirely selfishly, we are going to play my favourite game.'

Olu found a pack of element cards and started dealing them. Flo and Ebb grinned at each other across the table as Sara arranged six spoons in a diamond at its centre.

'Spoons?' Bobby blew her fringe out of her eyes, looking between the cutlery and Sara.

'That's the name of the game,' she smiled. 'One of the Mainlander tavern owners taught it to me years back. All you have to do is pass the element cards to your right, and when you've got five of the same in your hand, you must grab a spoon from the table. Once one person takes a spoon, everyone else has to get one too.'

'But that won't work,' Mitchell argued. 'There are six spoons and seven of us.'

'Exactly,' Sara said, rubbing her hands together gleefully. 'If you're left without a spoon, you lose. So keep an eye on how many spoons are on the table.'

'Then what?' Skandar asked eagerly. He'd not had many opportunities for games like this growing up. They weren't

– 133 –

# SKANDAR AND THE SKELETON CURSE

as fun with two people – and Dad had barely ever been up to joining in with him and Kenna.

'When you lose, you get a letter,' Ebb explained. '"S", then "P", then "O" and so on. Once you can spell *spoons* – you're out of the game.'

Within fifteen minutes, all thoughts of the Skeleton Curse or Rex Manning or the Eyrie had disappeared completely from everyone's minds. Skandar already had an 'S' because he'd been distracted by the cards which depicted the spirit element symbol – Sara explained mid-game that the cards were pre-Treaty and probably illegal. Bobby had managed to give both Ebb and Mitchell minor injuries in her violent attempts to grab spoons. Flo had only picked up a couple of letters so far – she was very sneaky at taking a spoon without anyone noticing, whereas Olu struggled not to crow with glee when he completed an elemental card set.

Sara Shekoni was the best, though. They played game after game, and somehow, hours later, she had still only picked up one single letter. And that was only because Ebb had pretended to have something in his eye to distract her.

'No, no, no! I'm not a SPOON! I'm a SPOO!' Bobby protested sometime in the early hours – she was having a particularly bad round. It might have been sleep deprivation, but the way she said it sent everyone into laughing fits. But even as he was chuckling with everyone else, there was something in that moment that pulled Skandar outside of it all. It was like he was watching the game from a distance, watching himself laughing – and it sickened him. His mum was dead. Kenna hated him. Dad was so far away. How could he possibly be having fun when all those things were true?

The next thing Skandar knew, he was up from the table. 'I'll be back in a second. I just need a minute.' He fled through

– 134 –

# THE SKELETON CURSE

the Shekonis' floral-patterned door and found he needed great lungfuls of air. It was like there wasn't enough air in the world. A wheezing noise started in his throat, and he was horribly reminded of Elias at the Eyrie gate. He doubled over by Sara's elemental herbs. Was he dying?

'Hey, spirit boy. It's okay. Take my hand.'

And suddenly Bobby was with him on the colourful treehouse platform, and she looked so calm that he managed to speak. 'What's happening to me?'

Unbelievably, Bobby rolled her eyes. 'Not the cleverest cat in the alley, are you? How many times have you helped me through mine?'

'A panic attack?' Skandar wheezed. 'But I don't – I've never . . .'

'Anyone can have a panic attack. They're not *Copyright Bobby Bruna 2009, All Rights Reserved* – I just have them more than most people. They can be brought on by stress, pressure or fear. So it's not exactly surprising, given the year you're having.' She didn't say anything more – just held Skandar's hand until his breathing and heartrate returned to normal.

Eventually he cleared his throat. 'Sorry.'

Bobby cocked her head. 'What for?'

'Not sure,' Skandar mumbled. 'I just – in there we were all laughing, and I felt happy for the first time in ages and I forgot. I forgot for a minute that . . .'

Bobby looked at him very seriously from under her fringe. 'Your mum died, Skandar. And you've lost your sister to the wild side. It's okay to feel sad about that, but it's also okay *not* to feel sad all the time.'

'But I'm not supposed to miss her – miss them – am I? Erika was the Weaver and Kenna is . . . Did she plan this Skeleton Curse from the beginning? Was it the Weaver's plan or hers? Kenna stole the pieces of the bone staff when we were *Nestlings*,

– 135 –

Bobby! She's turned Red wild – Scoundrel's distraught. How can that be true and yet I still miss—'

'I don't think we decide who we get to miss and who we don't. So be sad, be happy, be angry – nobody is going to judge you, all right? You've always accepted me for who I am.'

'And me.' Skandar looked up to see Mitchell, hair blazing in the doorway. 'Even right at the beginning when I was all mixed up about spirit wielders.'

'And me.' Flo was beside him. 'Even though I'm a silver who took an oath to hunt you down.'

Skandar let himself smile. Let himself feel grateful for them, allowed himself the joy. And something in his chest loosened for the first time in a while.

As the beginnings of sunrise turned the wildflower meadow pink, one of Sara's healer apprentices reported that Ayana was starting to stir. Quickly the quartet gathered whatever supplies they could carry – hammocks, blankets, food, water and clothes discarded by former apprentices. They'd left the Eyrie so suddenly that everything they owned was still there.

Just before they were about to leave, Skandar found himself standing next to Sara at the top of the steep plank that connected the grass of the square to the main entrance of the Shekoni treehouse. He breathed in deeply and found his nose tickled by the elemental herbs growing in colourful pots outside the family's front door.

'How are you holding up, Skandar?' Sara asked kindly.

He thought about saying he was fine, but there was something about the openness in Sara's face that made him want to tell her the truth. 'I don't really know how I am.'

'That's understandable,' she murmured, her gaze fixed on her unicorn patients dotted across the hill, rather than on him. Almost like she knew he wouldn't want to make eye contact

# THE SKELETON CURSE

when he asked his next question:

'Why do you think Kenna is doing this?' It was the thing that haunted him the most. 'I thought I knew her, and I never would've believed she'd be capable of doing something so . . . so cruel.'

Sara turned to look at him. 'I don't know your sister, but I do know people. And do you know what makes them do the strangest things?'

Skandar shook his head, trying to keep his emotions in check.

'Loneliness. And I reckon your sister is pretty lonely right now, don't you?'

'She didn't have to be lonely!' Skandar choked out. 'I was going to leave the Eyrie. I *chose* her over the Eyrie, over my friends.'

'Skandar,' Sara said gravely, 'Kenna is now the only person on the Island with a forged bond. Nobody can understand what she's going through. Can you imagine how isolated she must feel?'

Skandar remembered something the Weaver had said back in June. *You will see your sister gain a whole new family, with bonds just like hers.*

'You think Kenna is inflicting the Skeleton Curse on the whole Island because she feels alone? She's making bonded unicorns wild so more people will be like her?'

'Perhaps she just wants to be understood,' Sara said sagely. 'I think you know how good that feels. The four of you, your quartet, you give that to each other. Not everyone is that lucky.'

Skandar thought of last night. 'Yeah, I don't know what I'd do without them.'

Flo appeared in the treehouse square then, attaching supply bags to Blade's saddle. Skandar's heart skipped a beat when she waved over at them, and he felt Sara's eyes on him.

– 137 –

'She's braver than she appears, my Florence, but I wouldn't say she's temperamentally suited to being on the run.'

'Um, no.' Skandar cleared his throat. 'Breaking the rules doesn't come naturally to her.'

Sara fixed Skandar with a penetrating stare. 'I know you'll all look out for each other, but mind you take care of my daughter's heart too, all right?'

'I, er, of course,' Skandar stumbled, feeling his face turn the shade of the fire fern by his leg.

Sara smiled knowingly. 'That's what I thought.'

CHAPTER NINE

# SAPPHIRE

As always, the Wanderers welcomed Skandar, Bobby, Flo and Mitchell without question or hesitation after they'd fled the Eyrie. For a few days they stayed at the Desert Oasis with Jamie, who'd managed to keep Red there by gifting her stinking animal carcasses. But given Flo's outlaw status, Elora didn't think the Wanderers' fire zone base would be secure enough for the quartet long-term. And unfortunately, the Glowing Caves and overflow tents in the earth zone were full; and their air zone home – hidden within the Terraced Valleys – was too difficult to reach during the fire season due to the strength of the sylph-led winds.

That left the Ambling Archipelago – a network of small islands known only to the Wanderers, that moved round the outer edge of the water zone in a fixed cluster. A few of the newly wild fire unicorns had already ventured to the archipelago's islands, following their distraught riders – along with a team of Wanderers sent to help them. Elora said she suspected Albert might have chased a wild Eagle's Dawn that way, and asked them to send word if they crossed paths with him. Nobody had seen him since the Fire Festival.

So, a week after their visit to Wildflower Hill, the quartet, Agatha and a Wanderer guide called Jordan set out for the water zone. Skandar had been hoping that Jamie could come with them too, but with a sombre expression the blacksmith declared he'd be more use to them back in Fourpoint. And although Mitchell agreed, Skandar could tell that leaving Jamie was another blow he could hardly take.

The group's progress was slow, mainly because of Red Night's Delight. She clearly didn't want to be too far from Mitchell, but she often got distracted by attacking anything she believed to be a threat. The only unicorn who could really help when this happened was Scoundrel – but then everyone had to stop while Skandar tried to herd her back on to one of the Wanderers' secret paths.

'Don't scare her!' 'Be careful!' 'Make sure she doesn't hurt herself!' These were Mitchell's constant cries from behind Bobby on Falcon's back, as they looped across the fire zone and into the water zone, giving the Silver Stronghold on the edge of Fourpoint a very wide berth.

'Henderson does realise that Red Night's Delight is a *wild* unicorn now, doesn't he? Wild as in immortal, bloodthirsty, deadly. I think she can look after herself,' Agatha grumbled from behind Skandar. She was struggling with riding a unicorn that wasn't her own.

Over the course of the long journey, Jordan, who'd been shy at first, started to tell them about his time at the Eyrie. He was only four years older than Skandar's quartet, and they found that not much had changed since Jordan had been declared a nomad.

'The joust ended it all for me and Surfer's Demise,' he said, gesturing to his dark grey unicorn after a quick stop one evening. 'We were terrible at moulding weapons. Surfer isn't subtle with

– 140 –

# SAPPHIRE

his magic, and I'm not very patient. Not a good combination for Nestling year.'

'I'm sorry,' Flo said.

'Don't be.' Jordan had a warm smile that made dimples in his light brown cheeks. 'Half my quartet went out after the Training Trial – last and second-to-last place.' The corners of his mouth drooped at the memory. 'The only thing I was sad to leave behind was the Peregrine Society.'

'You were a Grin?' Skandar was delighted.

'Still have my metal feather,' Jordan said proudly. 'Maybe we can race Scoundrel and Surfer one day? For old times' sake?'

'Yeah,' Skandar said, although all the joy suddenly rushed out of him. Like Jordan, Skandar was no longer a Grin – he was a nomad now. He felt an ache for nights spent on the Sunset Platform, eating marshmallows and perfecting daring dives.

At dawn three days later, they had almost crossed the whole of the water zone's delta, when they finally reached the Ambling Archipelago's current location. Jordan warned that this crossing was the most likely point at which they'd lose Red Night's Delight. To get the unicorns on to one of the archipelago's islands, they had to fly or swim the length of about five swimming pools. Given that it was November and freezing, everyone had opted for flying. But Red's wings were far weaker than before, with bald patches already showing where she'd previously had full crimson feathers. It was possible she wouldn't attempt to fly, but would she really choose to dive into the cold water just to follow them?

Jordan and Surfer's Demise took off first to guide the way, his grey wings pink-edged in the morning light. Scoundrel – carrying Skandar and Agatha – went next, and from the air it was very difficult to make out the archipelago's islands. Thick mist hung over them, something Skandar suspected the Wanderers

– 141 –

had made sure of. Scoundrel and Surfer, then Silver Blade joined them, and finally—

There was a loud splash.

'MITCHELL! You absolute idiot!' Bobby shouted, as Falcon soared up to join the others in the misty sky.

'He jumped off Falcon!' Bobby called over the wind. 'Red trotted along the bank and Mitchell thought she was going to bolt – he's in the water!'

'Floundering floods!' Jordan cursed, and Surfer, Falcon, Scoundrel and Blade all swooped down, the water churning under the beats of their wings.

'Red's swimming behind Mitchell!' Flo cried joyfully.

Mitchell was doing a strong front crawl – perhaps swimming had been an activity encouraged by his water wielder father. Red was following a little distance behind, her newly transparent horn sticking up out of the water while her legs pumped clumsily beneath her.

'Let's land on the nearest island and help Mitchell out of the water once he gets there,' Jordan ordered, his black hair damp from the water's spray.

Once on the shore, the riders dismounted, cheering Mitchell on loudly – even Agatha joined in. The water looked freezing; it made Skandar shudder just watching his friend. But within a few minutes Mitchell reached the shallows and waded towards the beach, his clothes dripping wet and a broad shivery grin fixed across his face. Red splashed out behind him, but something changed as soon as her hooves found solid ground.

Scoundrel noticed first, the bond twanging with alarm. Then Red let off a rancid blast of fire right at Mitchell's back.

'Watch out!' Skandar yelled.

Mitchell threw himself face forward into the shallows just in time, but something had clearly angered Red. She began to

– 142 –

## SAPPHIRE

bellow loudly, ice blasts freezing the water round her hooves and acrid smoke billowing from her red nostrils.

'Get out of the water!' But Bobby didn't need to tell Mitchell. He was already sprinting up the beach, Red giving chase – not playing but hunting.

Scoundrel's Luck decided to intervene. As soon as Mitchell sprinted past him on the water's edge, Scoundrel reared up and blocked Red's path.

Red bellowed loudly, also rearing, so that the red and black legs of the unicorns kicked the air over the water. Scoundrel let the spirit element spread round his wings, the white glow flickering across his black feathers. But Red was not calming down; she kept up her bellowing and sent a fire blast towards Scoundrel. It caught his left hoof.

Skandar felt the shock and hurt of the injury slice through the bond. Scoundrel let out a noise that was somewhere between a growl and a wail and that – more than anything – seemed to stop Red's attack. She turned her flaming tail and galloped away along the stretch of beach.

Skandar rushed to Scoundrel and saw immediately that there was a thin crack down the front of his hoof. Scoundrel was holding it gingerly off the ground, but with Skandar's encouragement put it back down on the sand. Skandar breathed a sigh of relief – he could stand on it at least.

'It's okay, boy. I know she's your friend. And you don't understand, do you?' Skandar whispered into Scoundrel's neck as he hugged it. 'Thank you for helping Mitchell.'

Skandar led a hobbling Scoundrel towards the others further up the bank. Mitchell looked distraught. 'I need to go after Red! What if we lose her?'

'I doubt she'll leave this island now,' Jordan said reassuringly. 'The other unicorns who've made it to Cerulean – in the same

## SKANDAR AND THE SKELETON CURSE

situation as you and Red – have stayed. She'll just gallop round a bit and let off steam.'

Mitchell spotted Skandar approaching and rushed to him. 'I'm so sorry she did that. Is Scoundrel okay?'

Skandar pulled his friend into a hug. 'He'll be fine – just a war wound he can boast about to Red when she's back to normal.'

'My mum gave me some herbs,' Flo said, coming over. 'They might ease Scoundrel's pain a little, even if . . .' She tailed off before stating the obvious. Even if the damage would never heal.

'Ey up! There's someone coming.' Bobby was staring inland at a unicorn and rider emerging from a small forest beyond the beach.

'What is your business on Cerulean? It isn't safe here,' the rider called from a small distance away. And although Skandar was worried and wet and downright overwhelmed by practically everything in his life right now, he grinned.

'Rickesh!' Skandar stumbled up the sand to the former squadron leader of the Peregrine Society, the water wielder's wave of hair catching the morning sun.

'Skandar? Gushing geysers! What are you lot doing out here?' Rickesh's expression was a mixture of confusion and delight as he dismounted from Tidal Warrior and took in the slightly damp, very sorry-looking group. 'Oh, hello, Instructor Everhart. What distinguished new arrivals.'

Agatha inclined her head regally.

'So what happened?' Rickesh looked eagerly round at the newcomers. 'Why aren't you at the Eyrie? I thought Rex had stopped letting riders out.'

'We declared ourselves nomads,' Skandar answered, the words still feeling impossible in his mouth.

Rickesh's eyes widened. 'Can you even do that? Well, clearly you have. Tell me everything – actually, wait until we see Prim. This'll cheer her up for sure.'

– 144 –

## SAPPHIRE

'Prim's here too?' Skandar looked over Rickesh's shoulder for the fire wielder who'd been flight lieutenant of the Grins. Then he realised *why* Prim might be here. 'Winter Wildfire, she must be—'

'Yes,' Rickesh confirmed, the smile dropping from his mouth. 'The night of the Fire Festival, Prim asked me to help her track Wildfire across the zones. The two of us have been on the Ambling Archipelago ever since. As you can see, the Wanderers looped me into their patrols. Was I scary enough?'

'Terrifying,' Skandar said, beaming. 'We definitely would've run away screaming if we hadn't recognised you.'

'Stop it, you spirit wielding flatterer,' Rickesh chuckled, before turning to Jordan. 'Did Elora say which of the islands we should house them on?'

'We need to stay together,' Flo said quickly, shivering despite her red jacket.

'Wait a moment.' Rickesh held up a hand. 'You're Florence Shekoni, and *that* is a silver unicorn.' He pointed at Blade. 'If you've declared yourself a nomad, then why aren't you locked in the Silver Stronghold?'

Flo stuck out her chin, a gesture she'd picked up from Bobby. 'I'm on the run.'

Rickesh raised a black eyebrow. 'The plot thickens.'

Jordan was getting impatient with Rickesh's light-hearted chitchat. 'We need to get them off Cerulean as quickly as we can.'

'I'm not leaving Red,' Mitchell protested, crossing his arms.

'It's not safe to be here at night,' Rickesh said gently. 'The fire unicorns here are far too volatile. I do understand – Mitchell, is it?'

Mitchell nodded and Rickesh continued.

'Prim was the same at first, but the smaller islands are very close by, and you can come over here whenever you like. To see Red, to build up a connection, just like the other fire and earth wielders. But we have to assign you another island of the

– 145 –

# SKANDAR AND THE SKELETON CURSE

archipelago, at least to sleep and eat on. You have to be careful – there have already been some casualties.' There was a haunted edge to the water wielder's eyes.

'What about Sapphire?' Jordan suggested. 'Nobody else is occupying it yet.'

'Perfect!' Rickesh clapped his hands together. 'Sapphire is one of the more tropical islands – sand, a smattering of palm trees, warm climate – you'll love it,' he told the quartet. 'And it's only a short swim from Navy – where Prim and I are staying with a few of the other Eyrie riders.' Noticing their horrified faces, he added. 'Or boat ride – there are boats! But the inner islands have warmer waters, I promise. Cerulean is an anomaly because it forms a barrier to the rest of the archipelago – a chilly entry point, if you will.'

'I think I'll head to Indigo,' Agatha said thoughtfully. 'That's where I used to stay when I lived with the Wanderers. I wouldn't mind seeing it again. As long as you four can be trusted not to do anything . . . well, *anything* at all.'

Skandar promised they would stay put, and as Agatha hugged him goodbye – they were getting better at it – she whispered, 'You did the right thing, you know. It was brave. I'm proud of you, and I would have paid good money to see Rex's face when you all started throwing your element pins.'

Skandar hugged his aunt tighter before watching her mount Surfer's Demise with Jordan and fly off.

Moments later, Scoundrel, Falcon and Blade took off after Tidal Warrior, Rickesh leading them right over Cerulean and in towards the island of Sapphire. Skandar was worried about Scoundrel's hoof, but thankfully he didn't struggle with the take-off and it looked like the damage was only superficial. The hairline crack would stay for ever, but while it didn't seem to be affecting Scoundrel physically, the bond was still full of

– 146 –

# SAPPHIRE

his hurt and confusion about Red.

Mitchell was riding on Warrior, and Rickesh was attempting to distract the fire wielder with random snippets about the Ambling Archipelago. 'Well, Mitch – can I call you Mitch?'

'No. Only Bobby's allowed to call me Mitch, and very rarely,' he answered, still looking for Red over his shoulder.

'Fair enough. Mitchell, did you know that the Ambling Archipelago is made up of over a dozen islands, each of them named after a different shade of blue?'

'I guessed as much. We've had Cerulean – the entry island, Navy, Indigo, Sapphire . . .'

Skandar smiled – Rickesh was doing an excellent job of reeling Mitchell in with facts. He looked down over Scoundrel's wing joint at the constellation of islands below. If Skandar concentrated long enough, he could see them moving– inch by inch – in perfect unison.

Rickesh laughed. 'Okay, genius, but do you know *why* the islands are named after shades of blue?'

'Because it's the water zone,' Mitchell said sarcastically.

'Wrong!' Rickesh crowed. 'Because the water round each island is supposedly the colour of its name. You see Sapphire down there? Take a look at its waters!'

Skandar craned further over Scoundrel's wing as they started to descend and saw what Rickesh was describing. The tiny green island was surrounded by sparkling sapphire water that – further out from its shore – swirled and combined with the waters of the neighbouring island, which were a slightly darker shade of—

'Navy! That water is more navy-coloured!' Mitchell cried, and Rickesh winked at Skandar over his shoulder, looking very pleased with himself as he pointed out the islands of Cobalt and Teal.

The result of all the different blues encircling the islands of

– 147 –

# SKANDAR AND THE SKELETON CURSE

the archipelago was a beautiful patchwork quilt effect.

The unicorns landed on Sapphire's white sand and the riders dismounted. It was a tiny island, appearing to consist only of a jungle-like tangle of trees circled by a beach. It was the kind of island a young child might draw. Skandar's heart sank a little – he'd left his sketchbook at the Eyrie.

'It's warmer here,' Flo said, removing her jacket – the outermost of her multiple layers.

'It's weird, isn't it?' Rickesh puffed, as he dragged a large sapphire-coloured chest out of the miniature jungle. Skandar and Bobby rushed to help him. 'I've only been here a week or so, but the inner islands seem to have their own climate. Milder.'

'What is *in* this thing?' Bobby moaned, as they heaved the blue chest further on to the beach.

Rickesh stopped pushing and perched on the lid. 'There's a chest like this on every island. Inside you'll find tents, water, some dried food to get you started, fishing rods, nets, firewood, blankets. Usually the Wanderers are only here during the water season, but they leave these supplies for any of them making unexpected stops or long journeys through the zone. Honestly, I was a bit disappointed it wasn't treasure – I was ready to enter my pirate era.'

Skandar chuckled and simultaneously fought off a yawn – the talk of tents and blankets had made him realise just how exhausted he was.

'I'd better check on Prim. Get some sleep and watch out for carnivorous crabs.' Rickesh moved towards Tidal Warrior. 'Joking!' He was still chuckling at the looks on their faces, when Warrior took off for Navy.

It was only mid-morning, but the quartet were in desperate need of sleep. They decided to pitch one tent and, predictably, Bobby pronounced herself in charge of the operation. She set

# SAPPHIRE

Mitchell and Flo the task of preparing a campfire, while she ordered Skandar around with ropes and pegs, saying she'd been camping loads of times with her family in Spain and knew everything about tents. Skandar, whose family had never been on a holiday of any kind, trusted her completely – right up until the supposedly 'finished' tent sagged horribly in the middle.

'Is it supposed to do that?' Mitchell asked, as he placed pebbles round the fire pit he'd dug with Flo.

'Island tents must be different,' Bobby said through gritted teeth. And they started all over again. The unicorns were fascinated by their riders' antics and kept coming over to sniff the tent's blue tarpaulin or paw at the sand.

After three more failed attempts the tent looked sturdy enough to sleep in. The quartet crawled inside, removing their sandy black boots at the entrance on Mitchell's insistence. They set out the roll mats, blankets and cushions – all sapphire-coloured – attempting not to elbow each other in the process. Finally they lay down in a row – Mitchell, then Skandar, then Flo, then Bobby.

Mitchell fidgeted uncomfortably. 'It's odd not sleeping in a hammock.'

'On the Mainland people sleep in tents for fun,' Bobby said, yawning loudly.

'It's sort of cosy,' Flo said, wriggling further under her blanket.

'Can you believe we've left the Eyrie?' Skandar murmured. He'd been wanting to have this conversation for days, but he'd swallowed the words each time. He felt like it was his fault; he was the first one who'd said he couldn't stay there any longer. He knew that if they didn't talk about being nomads properly, the guilt might eat him in his sleep.

'I was over the Eyrie,' Bobby said breezily, and by the dip of the blankets he could tell that she'd shrugged.

– 149 –

# SKANDAR AND THE SKELETON CURSE

'It wasn't a sustainable option any more,' Mitchell said. 'How could Rex possibly expect us riders with wild unicorns not to go after them? I think more riders will leave.'

'Can you believe our Flo's a fugitive?' Bobby said, yawning again.

'It's not that bad so far,' Flo murmured, smiling sleepily. 'And at least we don't have to worry about the den dances this year.'

Bobby barked out a laugh. 'Is that why you're okay with being a criminal? Because it got you out of going to a *dance*?'

'It definitely factored into my decision,' Flo said mock seriously, making everyone laugh. Though Skandar couldn't help imagining a different reality – one where they were still at the Eyrie for the dances, and he and Flo went together.

'I've been thinking,' Mitchell said, leaning up on one elbow. 'We need to go back to Fourpoint.'

Bobby scoffed. 'We're not risking Flo getting arrested just so you can see your boyfriend.'

'That is *not* why,' Mitchell said crossly. 'I think we should pay my mother a visit. We need information on the Skeleton Curse – we can't just wait for Kenna to attack the water wielders. And Rex clearly isn't going to do anything.'

'I thought you'd already checked the water library?' Skandar said.

'I'm not talking about the water library.'

'Not the Secret Swappers?' Flo breathed.

'No,' Mitchell said slowly. 'I haven't told you this yet, because well . . . there were other things to talk about after the summer solstice last year.' He glanced Skandar's way. 'But my mother is now a Keeper of the Vaults.' There was immense pride in Mitchell's voice.

The announcement didn't have quite the effect he seemed to have been expecting.

– 150 –

# SAPPHIRE

'Come again?' Bobby asked.

It didn't mean anything to Skandar either.

But Flo's face was full of wonder. 'Leaping landslides, Mitchell!'

'Can one of you please explain?' Bobby asked irritably.

Mitchell switched to knowledge-dump mode. 'The Vaults are a network of underground libraries. If you want access to any of the books down there, you have to go through a whole interview process – it takes ages, and Eyrie riders are never approved.'

Bobby frowned. 'Why? They're just books – why do you have to interview for them?'

Mitchell looked affronted. 'They're not *just* books. Many of the texts are really old, so that's why they're not in the main Fourpoint libraries; others contain banned magic – I expect there's loads on elemental predators. And some have dangerous content – the kind of information that could be a disaster for everyone if it got into the wrong hands.'

'So the Keepers control who's allowed in?' Skandar checked.

'Yes, and there are only four Keepers at any time. Four Keepers, four entrances – one for each element. They each have a special interest in one particular element. My mother's is water. There used to be five Keepers, of course –' he winced apologetically at Skandar – 'but, you can guess what happened there. Not even the Commodore is allowed down to the Vaults without a Keeper's permission.'

'But surely they couldn't refuse a *Commodore*?' Skandar struggled to imagine Rex accepting this.

'My mother said it depends what they're asking for,' Mitchell said, shrugging. 'But I was thinking . . . Erika Everhart was a Commodore twice, wasn't she? What if she found out about the Skeleton Curse down in the Vaults – or at least the components for it? Maybe *she* was the one who told Kenna about it? Maybe it was even *her* plan originally?'

– 151 –

'That makes sense,' Skandar said. Somehow it felt better to think that Kenna had learned about the curse from the Weaver rather than coming up with it herself.

'Let me get this straight,' Bobby said. 'You're saying your mum is some kind of ninja-spy-librarian. Does she even *work* at the water library?'

Mitchell looked sheepish. 'Technically yes, because that's where the water entrance to the Vaults is. But she's a Keeper not a librarian, so also technically, erm, no.'

Skandar was frowning. 'Is there lots on the spirit element down in the Vaults?' He was beginning to feel like their investigations over the years could have been a lot easier if they had known about the Vaults. Couldn't Mitchell have asked his mum for information on the spirit element when Skandar had needed it as a Hatchling? And what about when he was forced to give up his biggest secret to the sinister Secret Swappers – that he was the son of the Weaver – in return for information about the First Rider? Already Islanders had dubbed Kenna the next Weaver, but Skandar could do without them finding out he and Kenna were actually Erika Everhart's children.

'My mother only became a Keeper this year,' Mitchell said quickly, guessing Skandar's thoughts. 'I found out after the Air Trial. The last Keeper died just before the summer solstice. And, truthfully, I don't know how much there'll be on the spirit element. It's possible the Silver Circle destroyed anything spirit-related when they got rid of the Spirit Keeper.'

'But you think there might be something on the Skeleton Curse?' Skandar said.

'It's worth a try, isn't it?' And Skandar knew Mitchell was thinking of Red back on Cerulean – wild and angry and alone.

## Chapter Ten

# THE WATER KEEPER

Before they set out for the Vaults, the quartet spent the next few days settling in on the Ambling Archipelago, mainly shuttling between the islands of Sapphire and Navy. Navy was much bigger than Sapphire and was currently home to an assortment of riders who'd followed their wild unicorns to the water zone and been taken in by the Wanderers. Skandar recognised a few of them as they sat round their large campfire in the evenings: two fellow Rookies – Art, who rode Furious Inferno, and Sarika with Equator's Conundrum; as well as Walker, rider of Savage Salamander, and Chiyo, rider of Burning Star, who'd both been made nomads when they'd failed the Chaos Trials.

The mood was not a happy one. The earth and fire wielders, including Mitchell, spent most of their days trekking across Cerulean, attempting to rebuild some kind of connection with their unicorns. Scoundrel would watch them gloomily, as they left in the boats. The black unicorn didn't try to fly to the outer island – he seemed to know it was too dangerous – but that

# SKANDAR AND THE SKELETON CURSE

didn't stop him from missing his best friend.

As with Gabriel and Queen's Price, the fire unicorns *did* recognise their own riders, but only fleetingly. At night, the crying of those whose bonds had been drained could even be heard across the water between islands. The sound made Skandar clutch his heart as though checking his own bond with Scoundrel was still wrapped round it.

Mitchell didn't cry for Red at night, but his reaction was almost more worrying. He would spend hours trying to approach Red, much longer than any of the other riders. One day he got close enough to stroke her nose. But on his triumphant return to Sapphire, it'd taken Flo only seconds to notice the hole singed into the shoulder of his red jacket. Mitchell had brushed off their concern, but they all knew the wound – though small – would never heal, and Skandar began to worry about how little regard Mitchell had for his own safety.

Five days later, Skandar, Mitchell and Bobby set off for Fourpoint to meet Ruth Henderson – and hopefully visit the Vaults. Flo had tried to come up with all kinds of ways she and Blade might be able to join them, but eventually they all had to accept it wasn't worth the risk.

A few riders came to wave them off, including Agatha, who'd given their mission her blessing. She seemed more relaxed on the archipelago and had started wearing what could only be described as beachwear – today a flowery skirt and a loose cotton shirt. She insisted they were the only clothes she'd been able to find on Indigo, but Skandar suspected his aunt might actually be enjoying herself. The spectral look she'd borne since Erika and Swan's deaths was – if not absent – at least less obvious under her suntan.

Skirt swishing, Agatha approached Skandar once he'd mounted Scoundrel.

# THE WATER KEEPER

'Can you make sure Flo's okay?' Skandar asked once they were out of earshot.

'She looks fine to me.' Agatha glanced over at Flo laughing at something Walker had said. Skandar suddenly felt a stab of dislike towards the boy – with his honey-coloured curls and his flatteringly deep tan and his ridiculously white teeth. Then he felt immediately bad about it. Walker had lived in a treehouse with Elias. Elias who was now—

'Are you even listening to me?' Agatha whacked him on the boot.

'Oh, er . . . sorry.'

'I was saying,' Agatha continued, rubbing her fading cheeks in frustration, 'I know you're not quite as *on the run* as the Shekoni girl, but you need to keep a low profile in Fourpoint. Go straight to the Vaults if Henderson's mother clears you, and then come right back here. Don't go making a nuisance of yourself to any sentinels.'

'I won't—'

'Rex will be looking for any opportunity to arrest you for something now you're outside the Eyrie's protection. Don't give him an excuse.'

'Are you worried about me, Aunty Agatha?' Skandar teased.

'Don't call me that,' Agatha growled, but there was a tiny smile hiding in her scowl.

The unicorns made quick work of the flight to Fourpoint, despite Falcon carrying Mitchell's extra weight. Skandar felt a crushing sadness as they passed over the Eyrie, knowing that as a nomad he'd never be allowed back inside. Then hot anger flared in his chest to replace it. Rex had taken his quartet. Taken his element. Taken his home.

Skandar tried to shake off his thoughts of the Commodore as

– 155 –

# SKANDAR AND THE SKELETON CURSE

they landed in a field beyond Fourpoint. Kenna was responsible for the Skeleton Curse, not Rex. She was turning the unicorns wild, was *sacrificing* unicorns on the fault lines. Rex might hate spirit wielders, want to change the Eyrie, and be trying to hoard all the power for himself, but he was just a tiny part of the Island's problems right now. *That* was a whole lot more complicated to think about, but was exactly why they'd risked this trip.

Scoundrel pushed a bubble of concern for his rider into the bond but it was half-hearted. The soft ebb of sadness that had been present since Red turned wild was detectable in all Scoundrel's emotions.

'Let's walk to the Library Quarter from here,' Mitchell declared, looking relieved to dismount from Falcon. 'It'll draw less attention. Who knows what anti-spirit wielder feelings Rex has been stirring up since we left, and Scoundrel's blaze isn't exactly subtle.'

'Great, walking. My absolute *favourite* activity,' Bobby grumbled as she thumped to the ground. 'Also, it's freezing! Take me back to the archipelago already.'

'Anything else you want to moan about before we set off?' Mitchell said impatiently, rolling his shoulder. The injury Red had inflicted was clearly bothering him.

Skandar followed Mitchell and Bobby. Most of the time he was sure they argued for their own entertainment – it was easier to let them get on with it.

Mitchell avoided the main streets of Fourpoint and they passed through residential areas with their mix of red, blue, yellow and green treehouses, though a few had recently been destroyed, presumably by the new wild unicorns. Only the occasional person hurried about their business, and Skandar wondered whether, alongside curfews at night, Rex was encouraging the residents to stay inside during the day too.

– 156 –

## THE WATER KEEPER

The Library Quarter was different from the organised layout of the nearby Council Square. The four library treehouses were spread across the quarter and dwarfed everything else in both size and splendour. It was immediately obvious to Skandar that the Eyrie libraries were tiny copies of these giants, each with a roof shaped like a book splayed open across the top. Mitchell had stopped a few metres ahead of Skandar and was pointing out the shining blue spine of the water library.

As he hurried to catch up, Skandar heard an unfamiliar voice ring out from near the fire library. 'Are you sure? There are a lot of fire wielders in my family.' The voice came from a treehouse with a sign swinging from its platform that said VAL'S VOLCANO CHILLI.

Then he heard a younger voice. 'But I *can't* be a spirit wielder – please let me try, and if I am—'

*Spirit wielder?* Skandar couldn't help himself. He darted under the scarlet-painted buildings until he was close enough to eavesdrop from the shadow of a treehouse boasting a flaming pizza oven.

'. . . as Island protocol dictates, three different riders have now tested you and come to the same conclusion. Just like they did, I sensed the spirit element in the unfinished bond round your heart. If you bond with a unicorn, we are almost certain you'll be a spirit wielder.'

The boy started sobbing. And Skandar realised that he was witnessing the Island's version of the Hatchery exam. A rider had never shaken Skandar's hand to test if they could detect an allegiance to the spirit element – he'd never made it to the exam thanks to Agatha. But this poor Islander boy had been identified as a potential spirit wielder in his own home and would now be barred from the life for which he was destined.

The first adult spoke again, and Skandar thought it might

– 157 –

# SKANDAR AND THE SKELETON CURSE

be Val herself. 'Come on, JJ. If three riders have sensed it, then I think you're going to have to accept—'

'It's not fair!' JJ yelled, and Skandar's heart squeezed at the crack in his voice. 'Skandar Smith is a spirit wielder and he got to try the Hatchery door. *He* got a unicorn!'

'Skandar Smith was a mistake,' the person delivering the bad news said forcefully. 'A mistake we do not intend to make again.'

*We?* Skandar felt fury building in his veins and he craned his head to try to see the speaker. Was it a silver? Was he talking about the Silver Circle ensuring spirit wielders wouldn't return?

But there was a sudden slam and the conversation became more muffled. Skandar realised the matter had been settled, the boy's future shattered in the shake of a hand. Anger pulsing through him, Skandar made his way back to the others.

'Where did you go? We've got an appointment to keep!' Mitchell said, as Skandar reached his friends near the water library.

'What's wrong?' Bobby asked, seeing his face.

'I heard . . . a potential spirit wielder. A boy who was being told he wouldn't be allowed to try the Hatchery door.'

'Oh Skandar, I'm so sorry,' Mitchell switched from scolding to sympathetic. 'I forgot that they do that around this time of year.'

'They just took away his future. He was so upset! He was . . .' Skandar couldn't say anything more. He was overwhelmed by memories of Kenna after she'd failed her Hatchery exam.

Suddenly he was surrounded by the smell of fresh bread and the citrus fizz of air magic. 'It won't be like this for ever,' Bobby promised as she hugged him. 'We're going to change things; we are. I'm going to be Commodore for a start. That should help.'

Mitchell snorted, and Skandar felt a smile tug at his lips, though it didn't quite settle.

– 158 –

# THE WATER KEEPER

He distracted himself by studying the library in front of them. Skandar couldn't even count the trees it spanned or the number of cables supporting its bulk like the ropes of a circus tent. Each library was like a planet with orbiting satellites peppered around them – shops, cafes, restaurants, all themed to their closest element.

Skandar and Bobby headed for the stairs that led up to the library's arched entrance. From a distance they looked like glass, though on closer inspection every step was filled with water, brightly coloured fish swimming within.

'No, over here!' Mitchell dragged them towards Ike's Imaginative Ices instead.

'Ooh! Are we getting ice pops?' Bobby had already climbed three rungs of the shop's ladder.

Mitchell tugged her back down again. 'Obviously not. I asked my mum to meet us here. I don't know what the rules say about nomads our age entering the Vaults and I didn't want to draw attention to Skan—'

There was a blur of coppery brown hair and a cry. 'Mitchell! Thank the elements!'

Ruth Henderson couldn't have looked more different from Mitchell's father. Where Ira was all sharp lines, stern looks and straight hair, Ruth was soft curves, open smiles and bouncy curls. There was a warmth to her that Skandar had seen in Mitchell more and more often over the years – when he'd turned back for Skandar in the Training Trial, when he'd insisted on facing the fire unicorn on the path to the tomb, whenever he talked about Jamie. It made Skandar like Ruth immediately.

'Red's wild.' Mitchell's voice was muffled against his mum's shoulder.

Skandar had never seen Mitchell let anyone hug him for this long.

– 159 –

# SKANDAR AND THE SKELETON CURSE

'I know, I know. And I heard you'd declared yourself a nomad and left the Eyrie . . . I've been so worried about you.' Ruth's eyes were wide behind her wire-framed glasses.

'How did you know we'd declared ourselves nomads?' Mitchell pulled back to look at her. 'Was it in the *Herald*?'

'No chance of that – Rex tried to keep it very hush hush.' Ruth grinned mischievously. 'But it's not every day an entire quartet declare themselves nomads to protest against the Commodore – people have been talking.'

'Have you spoken to Father?' Mitchell swallowed. 'Is he angry?'

'*He* will get over it.' Mitchell jumped about a foot in the air, as Ira Henderson climbed down from the ice cream shop. 'In fact, he's rather proud of you. It takes real bravery to stand up for what you believe in.' Then, with a formal nod, Ira handed his son a red ice lolly.

'Are you really?' Mitchell asked, the lolly starting to melt over his hand.

'We both are,' Ruth said, firmly. 'Truthfully, I never thought you'd turn out to be a rebel, Mitchell – I thought you'd be more of a conformist like your father. I must say, I'm very pleased to be proved wrong.'

'There's no need to be discourteous, Ruth,' Ira growled, and Skandar thought he might be getting a glimpse into Mitchell's childhood before his parents had decided they were better off in separate treehouses.

'I had rather a lot of help on the rebellion front,' Mitchell said quickly, clearly sensing the tension too and he gestured to Skandar and Bobby, waiting awkwardly by Ike's tree trunk.

Ruth beamed at them. 'Mitchell has written to me so often about you – I'm sorry we've never met. Library hours are always unpredictable, and we've had some rather unusual events over

– 160 –

# THE WATER KEEPER

the last few years.' She raised an eyebrow at Skandar, then frowned. 'Where's Florence?'

'The Silver Circle are looking for her,' Mitchell explained. 'She and Blade have to stay hidden.'

'I think I'd better be heading back to Council Square before I hear anything I shouldn't,' Ira announced suddenly. 'It's very good to see that you're all safe.' And with that, Ira pulled Mitchell into an awkward hug and rushed away, watery braid flashing.

'Flaming fireballs!' Mitchell murmured, staring open-mouthed after his father.

'He's been pestering me daily for news about you,' Ruth said. 'He really does love you, you know – I'm glad he's starting to learn how to show it.'

Mitchell beamed.

'But I think it's about time you all tell me why you're here,' Ruth continued briskly. 'I'm assuming you haven't just come for a half-melted ice lolly?'

Mitchell shook his head. 'I didn't want to put it in writing.' He took a deep breath. 'We want to go down to the Vaults.'

Ruth gave her son a searching look. 'I think we should talk about this *inside*.'

She herded them round the back of the huge structure of the library and soon had them climbing a ladder into the rear of the building. Once inside, they followed Ruth along one of the most beautiful corridors Skandar had ever seen. Books filled every possible space on the walls and every single spine was a different shade of—

'They're all blue,' Bobby said, gawping.

'Just in this private corridor,' Ruth said, running her hands down a couple of spines. 'It plays havoc with the library catalogue system.' She paused, then crowed triumphantly. 'Aha, that's the one!' Then she pulled out a copy of a book called *Diary*

– 161 –

# SKANDAR AND THE SKELETON CURSE

*of a Water-Allied Nomad.* Skandar's mouth fell open as an entire section of books lining the corridor swung back to reveal a room beyond.

'Pretty nifty, isn't it?' Mitchell said, grinning at him. 'As a Keeper, my mother is the only one who can find the door to this room. It's a different book every time.'

'When I leave my office, I choose a title at random for when I return,' Ruth explained, shepherding them through the book door. 'That way nobody can crack the code. Although admittedly even *I* sometimes forget which book I chose.'

Ruth's office reminded Skandar of the quartet's treehouse back at the Eyrie, with its stove, overflowing bookshelves and beanbags. But the main feature of the room was an enormous tree stump at its centre that was being used as a coffee table. Yesterday's *Hatchery Herald* lay open at a page advertising The Brilliant Boot Company, and a mug of abandoned tea was balanced on a stack of ancient-looking books.

Ruth gestured to a squashy sofa with cushions embroidered with forget-me-nots and sank into the fluffy beanbag opposite. 'And why do you want to go to the Vaults?'

'Information on the Skeleton Curse,' Mitchell said without missing a beat. '*Any*thing that could help us understand how it works, maybe even reverse it. Or at least stop Kenna doing the same to the water wielders in a couple of months.'

'Darling, do you really think you're the first rider who has come to the Keepers?' Ruth said gently. 'I've got interviews backed up for weeks with earth and fire wielders searching for information on the curse.'

'Has anyone found anything?' Bobby asked hopefully.

Ruth shook her head, curls bouncing. 'I even went to search for myself after the Fire Festival. I just don't think the Vaults have an answer. Although . . .' Ruth's eyes swept over Skandar's

– 162 –

# THE WATER KEEPER

arm, his spirit mutation just visible. 'Perhaps a spirit wielder might get different results – the Vaults *are* technically within the spirit zone.'

Skandar's jaw dropped. 'I thought there were only four zones!'

'Ah, of course. You've never seen an old map of the Island, I expect. When they banned the spirit element, they changed the name of the capital from Fivepoint to Fourpoint.'

Skandar nodded; he knew this already.

'They also destroyed the majority of the old maps. Have you noticed on current maps how the four zones skirt round Fourpoint – leaving a kind of circular gap where you find the Eyrie, the graveyard, Element Square . . . all the capital's landmarks?'

'Whoa,' Bobby breathed.

Mitchell was nodding as though this all made sense, but Skandar couldn't believe it. 'So the spirit zone is Fourpoint?'

'The capital plus its outskirts,' Ruth confirmed. 'And that includes everything underground, like the Vaults. The spirit element's influence is strongest close to the Divide, where all the elements are held in balance. That's why I think it's possible a key might lead a spirit wielder somewhere unexpected. You might have more luck than the riders who've visited so far.'

'What do you mean, a *key*?' Mitchell spluttered. 'Aren't *you* taking us?'

'Only to the entrance chamber. The Vaults are complicated,' Ruth said vaguely. 'The keys are the reason for the interviews. They're very old – I suspect they're imbued with elemental magic. There are only twenty of them – five for each Keeper. That means a maximum of twenty people can safely enter the Vaults at any one time.'

'Safely?' Skandar asked warily.

– 163 –

## SKANDAR AND THE SKELETON CURSE

'The Vaults are vast. They stretch for miles under Fourpoint, reaching as far as the inner edges of the fire, water, air and earth zones, the outer edges of the spirit zone. The only way to be guided is by a key. Without one you could be wandering around down there for ever.'

'So are there skeletons down there?' Bobby asked ghoulishly.

'A few,' Ruth murmured. 'Bypassing the Keepers is never a good idea. Are you sure you want to do this?'

Skandar, Bobby and Mitchell nodded decisively. They hadn't come all this way to turn round and leave empty-handed.

Ruth started to move objects off the tree stump. She spoke at lightning speed, in the same way Mitchell did when he wanted to convey information quickly. 'Obviously we don't have time to do a full interview with each of you, but I think I can tell you each have a settled intention. Without that a key can lead you astray.'

Bobby looked puzzled. 'What's a settled intention?'

'It means you have to be really focused on the information you want to find out, otherwise you could get lost down there.'

'We all want to find information on the Skeleton Curse. Right?' Mitchell asked. But Bobby and Skandar were distracted by the tree stump hingeing open like a lid. Ruth must have pressed a hidden button.

'Ninja-spy-librarian,' Bobby whispered, as Mitchell's mum opened three of five concealed compartments in the underside of the wooden lid and removed three identical keys.

Ruth waved the friends over and dropped a key into each of their outstretched hands. Skandar's had the word KNOWLEDGE engraved along its long side. The key was made of a heavy transparent material and was intricately carved with the symbols of all five elements. He was still trying to work out what the key reminded him of when Bobby beat him to it.

– 164 –

# THE WATER KEEPER

'It looks like a wild unicorn horn.'

'The Keepers do believe that might be their origin.' Ruth looked troubled. 'Thankfully we now have laws against that kind of thing.'

Mitchell squinted over at the keys Skandar and Bobby were holding. '*Knowledge. Expertise.* And mine says *Wisdom.*'

Ruth nodded. 'The other two are *Inspiration* and *Insight.* Keep hold of them at all times. I mean it – if you lose them in the Vaults, you won't be able to find your way back to the entrance chamber.' Then she stepped inside the tree stump. 'Last one in, shut the lid behind you. It's a long way down.'

'As an entrance to a load of fabulously dangerous information, this isn't very impressive,' Bobby mumbled, as she climbed in after the Keeper.

'That's the idea,' Ruth said, her voice floating upwards.

Mitchell's mum wasn't joking. Skandar felt like he must have climbed down hundreds of metal rungs by the time his feet finally landed in the entrance chamber to the Vaults.

Torches burned in brackets and the dark rock reminded Skandar a little of the inside of the Hatchery. It was a rectangular space, but where he'd been expecting to see shelves of books, there were a dozen blue glass doors. Their colour and material matched the solstice stones from the Water Trial last year.

'There are four – originally five – entrance chambers spread out under Fourpoint. The water doors are mine to guard,' Ruth said proudly. 'Any second, your keys should— Ah. There you go.'

Skandar felt a slight weight in his hand, a gentle pull that reminded him of the way the bond tugged on his chest during a Mender dream. He looked down and the transparent key now glowed ghostly white in his hand. Bobby's and Mitchell's were doing the same.

– 165 –

# SKANDAR AND THE SKELETON CURSE

'Feel it pulling you?' Ruth asked, voice hushed. 'The key acts like a magnet, trying to connect with the part of the Vaults that will help you the most. Never ignore its pull. Let the key guide you. And *do not* try to remove anything from the Vaults, otherwise the key will go dark and refuse to guide you to the exit.'

Skandar found himself following the tug of the key in his hand towards a door on the right-hand side of the chamber. It was an unsettling feeling – not quite like he would drop the key, but more that it could slip between his fingers if he didn't go the way it wanted. He stood in front of the frosted blue glass and looked over his shoulder to see Mitchell and Bobby at two different doors on the other side of the room.

'Can't we go together?' Mitchell called to his mum, but she shook her head.

'The keys may wish to show you different things – and not only books.'

'What else is in here?' Skandar asked, unnerved. Mitchell also looked surprised.

'Don't worry – you'll all meet up here afterwards. It's often through sharing what we've learned that we make our greatest discoveries.'

'How long are we going to be inside the Vaults?' Bobby sounded less sure of herself than usual.

'As long as the keys keep you there,' Ruth answered cryptically.

Skandar's key glowed brighter in his hand and after another tug towards the door, he slipped it into the lock and left the Water Keeper and his friends behind.

Chapter Eleven

# THE VAULTS

The silence of the Vaults pressed down on Skandar as he moved onwards, and he immediately realised why the keys were so necessary. This was not an ordinary library. Okay, so there were tables and chairs set out every few metres – and book stands, paper and pencils for taking notes – but that was where the similarities ended.

Everywhere he looked, hanging glass boxes swung gently above his head, though there was no breeze. There had to be thousands of the illuminated boxes lighting the underground treasury of knowledge. Some were up so high that they looked like stars twinkling in a distant sky. Meanwhile, down by his feet, there were keyholes every few steps, but his key did not pull towards them.

At first Skandar thought each box contained a book, but he soon realised that other *things* were suspended in the glass prisons too. Looking up, he could see that quite a few contained jars full of liquid with specimens floating inside. His stomach turned over when he spotted something that looked like a

# SKANDAR AND THE SKELETON CURSE

preserved animal brain. Others were more like display cases with objects presented on velvet cushions – one very low box Skandar passed held a bloody knife. And, creepiest of all, some of the higher boxes seemed as though they held items that were . . . alive. Occasionally a box would swing more violently than its neighbours, as though moved by its own contents, and its light would dance eerily across the floor. Skandar was sure he could hear scrabbling noises or tiny thumps.

It wasn't long before he lost track of time, with no idea which direction he had come from. The only reassuring thing was the gentle magnetic pull of the key in his hand, which had to be taking him somewhere . . . right? The silence was somehow deafening, though it was worse when the noises punctured it. Skandar tried to be rational, telling himself that the other Keepers had entrances, so it was perfectly normal for others to be down here too. But every scrape, knock or cough was amplified, as though the sounds belonged to a monster lying in wait or looming in the glass boxes above.

It was equally bad trying to fight off the demons in his own head that tended to descend when he was alone with his own thoughts. He tried to picture Sapphire – the tiny, perfect island felt a thousand miles away from an empty black shroud in the middle of a scorched circle of grass – but then the ghosts of conversations started to pop into Skandar's head, things he wished he'd been able to ask Erika Everhart before she'd died. *Why did you leave us on the Mainland? Were you ever planning on coming back for me? Are you sorry for all the suffering you caused?*

Skandar had just started desperately hoping he might bump into Mitchell or Bobby, when his key began to glow brighter. It felt suddenly heavy, as though pulling him downwards. He followed the feeling and crouched, noticing a keyhole right by his foot. Heart racing, he slotted in his key and turned it,

– 168 –

## THE VAULTS

then watched awestruck as a single glass box descended on its transparent thread like a spider from a web. The box stopped right in front of him so that he was almost holding it. Relieved it contained only a book, Skandar reached inside hungrily and took it to one of the nearby tables.

It was an old book. The paper was crisp and yellowing, the print faded, the pages encased in burgundy leather. It didn't appear to have a title, but as Skandar flicked through he recognised drawings of the Mainland coastline. Had someone brought it from the Mainland a long time ago? One of the people inspired to come to the Island by the First Rider? As far as he could tell, there was nothing about elemental magic at all. Disappointed, he returned the book to the glass box and it rose gracefully back into the air.

Almost immediately Skandar's key glowed brightly again and it led him to another keyhole. He went through the same process and a glass box floated down to him from an even higher space. This time the book did have a title: *Mainland Fortifications: A Comprehensive History.* Skandar searched painstakingly through the book this time, thinking perhaps he was missing some link between the Mainland and the Skeleton Curse – but there was nothing.

Skandar became increasingly frustrated as the same process happened three more times. He flipped through the dusty pages of *My Life as a Mainlander*, studied a tome called *Weather & Flight: Volume II* – which contained very detailed explanations about weather patterns across the Mainland for pilots in training – and finally flicked through something that looked suspiciously like a secondary-school history textbook.

'What is going on?' Skandar murmured, his voice loud in the oppressive silence.

And then it wasn't silent any more.

Footsteps. Skandar had just sent the textbook back up in its

– 169 –

# SKANDAR AND THE SKELETON CURSE

glass box and he froze, listening intently. Was it Bobby? Mitchell?

A distant conversation now accompanied the footfalls. It sounded like two men. Should he hide? The thought of coming across strangers in this endless labyrinth of knowledge sent him scurrying under the nearest desk.

Two people emerged only seconds later, and he had never been gladder to have listened to his gut. Although the first person was a rider Skandar didn't recognise, the other was Commodore Rex Manning.

'. . . always hated this place,' Rex was saying. 'The Keepers behave like they're the curators of all this knowledge, but in truth they're just glorified security. I really should look at getting everything transferred above ground. It's a ridiculously antiquated system.'

'That Keeper didn't like you bringing me with you,' the rider said nervously. 'Said I shouldn't be down here without a key.'

'Oh, stop babbling on, Bradley. You're a silver – don't listen to these people.' Rex looked down at his palm, and Skandar spotted a key glowing there.

'It's Brad,' Skandar heard the man mutter. Peering out from under the desk, Skandar could see that Brad's hair was entirely mutated into long tendrils of seaweed.

'Have you seen this?' Rex seethed. 'The keys to the Vaults still have a spirit symbol carved into them – the law-breaking here really is unacceptable.' He sighed. 'But for our purposes today . . . useful.'

'I still don't understand why we had to come *here*,' Brad whined, eyes roving to a box displaying a Chaos rider's race jersey that had been ripped to shreds by something with a lot of teeth. Skandar shrank further under the desk. 'A lot of the information you're seeking—'

'I'm aware,' Rex cut him off. 'But I need the privacy of the

– 170 –

## THE VAULTS

Vaults. There's no record of the books I've studied down here. No overzealous librarian peering over my shoulder. I'm the Commodore – my every move is watched.'

'I suppose,' Brad grumbled. 'What's the key doing?'

In answer, Rex held up a finger, cocked his head, crouched down like Skandar had, and then turned his key in the floor. A glass box lowered itself on transparent thread and Rex took out—

'*Weather & Flight: Volume II*,' Brad read, as Rex held the very same book Skandar had returned just moments before. 'Useful?'

Rex thrust the green leather book into his fellow silver's hands. 'Hold this. The key is taking me to another one.'

From his hiding place, Skandar watched with utter astonishment as Rex's key led him to the exact five books as his own had. Rex seemed to be particularly pleased with *Mainland Fortifications: A Comprehensive History*, and threw it on to the stack that was teetering unsteadily in Brad's arms.

'Is this everything?' he puffed, trotting to keep up with the Commodore.

Rex barked out a laugh. 'Of course not! I need to read everything about the Mainland I can possibly lay my hands on. We might even be down here all night. Preparation will be key to success. I'm going to be making *history*, Bradley, not a cup of fire zone tea.' Skandar had never seen Rex Manning like this. His cheeks buzzed with electricity, his green eyes alive with excitement. And it was perhaps the scariest he had ever been.

Skandar stayed under the desk long after the sound of the silvers' footsteps had been swallowed up by silence, questions thundering through his mind. Why had Skandar's key taken him to the same books as Rex? What was Rex's settled intention? And *why* didn't the Commodore want anyone knowing what he was reading?

There was an insistent tug from Skandar's key that he could

– 171 –

# SKANDAR AND THE SKELETON CURSE

no longer ignore, and finally he crawled out from his hiding place. The key pulsed, leading him on. Skandar was wary at first, praying that the key wouldn't take him towards Rex again, but after a while he relaxed. The only sounds were his own footsteps and his steady breathing. And as Skandar walked on below the constellations of boxes, his mind began to slot the pieces of the overheard conversation together.

Rex was looking for information on the Mainland. Books about its history, its coastline, its fortifications, its people, its weather. From his own lessons at school on the Mainland, Skandar could make a fair guess why a leader might be interested in those things. And a dark dread settled over Skandar as he remembered the words Rex had spoken.

*I'm going to be making history.*

He was so caught up in his thoughts that he barely registered turning the wild bone of his key in a frosted door and leaving the Vaults at last.

'You took your time!' Bobby cried, getting up from her cross-legged position on the floor. 'I would've bet three hundred emergency sandwiches on Mitchell being the last one back from a never-ending library.'

Mitchell marched up to Skandar. 'What did you find out? It must have been good! My key took me to some *horribly* gruesome volumes on elemental curses – and a few specimen jars showcasing their effects, which I'd rather not have seen.' He looked a bit green. 'But I think I've identified that the Skeleton Curse is most likely a cyclical curse.'

Skandar's brain was still fixed on Rex. 'Cyclical. Like circular?'

'Yes. According to what I read, these types of curses reverse if any of the stages are left incomplete. I think that's something, isn't it? And I—'

'Mitchell, take a breath and give someone else a turn,' Bobby

– 172 –

# THE VAULTS

interrupted. 'My key took me to records made after riders walk the fault lines and are officially in the Eyrie. Who knew they kept records? Anyway, it was *very* boring – not a cursed body part or dead animal in sight. They just had name, place of birth, date of birth, unicorn colour, allied element. We were all in there.'

'But you wrote down notes on Elias and Federico, didn't you? Every detail, like I asked you to?' Mitchell prompted.

'Anything useful?' Skandar managed to ask.

'Not that I could tell,' Bobby shrugged. 'But they're worth having, I suppose. Can't say I fancy a return visit to these Vaults. Creepy, boring, dusty.'

'So, Skandar,' Mitchell asked feverishly, 'what did you find out?'

Skandar hesitated. Part of him really didn't want to tell his friends about his suspicion. He wanted to shield them from the knowledge, let them carry on their day without the weight that was now sitting heavily on his shoulders. Once he told them, that would be it. Once he told them, nothing would be the same.

'What is it, spirit boy?' Bobby's dark eyebrows knitted together.

Skandar took a deep breath. He wouldn't leave his quartet behind again. He'd promised them that, after he'd returned from the Weaver's dark island last year. They would face this together. They would fight him together.

'My key didn't take me to any books on the Skeleton Curse,' Skandar said quietly. 'It took me to information on the Mainland.'

'The Mainland? Why—'

Skandar held up his hand to stop Mitchell's questioning. 'My key led me to five books on the Mainland. And then Rex Manning came.'

'What?' Bobby and Mitchell said together.

'I hid. But I saw what he was doing, heard what he was saying. Rex's key took him to the same books as mine. Books on the Mainland. It can't be a coincidence.'

– 173 –

# SKANDAR AND THE SKELETON CURSE

'I don't believe in coincidences,' Mitchell murmured almost automatically.

'I think my key led me to those books on purpose,' Skandar said, his voice stronger. 'I think it was trying to show me what Rex is up to. To warn me.'

'Warn you about what?' Bobby asked.

It was hard to get the words out – speaking them would make it real. Irreversible.

'I think Rex Manning wants to invade the Mainland.'

---

After leaving the Vaults, Skandar, Bobby and Mitchell flew back to the Ambling Archipelago. They found Flo on Navy, sitting between Walker and Prim on a long piece of driftwood, with Rickesh and Art cooking skewers of fish over a sizeable campfire. When Flo spotted her friends, she got up immediately, relief washing over her face. The reunited quartet walked along the beach a little way, so their words would be muffled by the lapping of the waves.

'Well?' Flo asked eagerly. 'Did you find anything helpful?'

Mitchell started with the good news. The Vaults had shown him various books that pointed to the Skeleton Curse being of a cyclical nature. This kind of curse, he explained, had to have all its component parts completed perfectly for it to remain effective. He handed out the notes he'd taken, which were filled with hastily scrawled diagrams and tiny writing.

'All the curses the Vaults showed me required the spirit element, which explains why they're no longer common on the Island,' he said.

Bobby was peering at a page of the notes. 'Does this say seaso*ning* or season*al*? Because if there's a curse that could give our food more flavour out here, then I am ready to kill anything to make that happen.'

– 174 –

# THE VAULTS

Mitchell snatched it from her. 'Seaso*nal*. This was a cyclical curse where a rider made every elemental season the fire season.'

Bobby snorted. 'Why would you choose the fire season all year round? It's dark and cold and depressing.'

'Maybe the rider liked warm jumpers and cosy fires,' Flo said a bit defensively.

Skandar also peered at the piece of paper. 'It says this fire season curse failed on the Air Festival because the spirit fires they were burning got rained on. What's a *spirit fire*?'

'I have no idea,' Mitchell said. 'But that's beside the point. What's helpful to us is that there wasn't a permanent change in the seasons because the cycle was broken by the rain before the curse was completed.'

'So if we stop Kenna turning the water unicorns wild, then that might mean all the others would go back to normal?' Flo asked hopefully. '*We* have to be the rain!'

'That's the theory,' Mitchell said. 'Although there's still so much we can't be sure of. We don't know, for example, if the spirit element is included in the cycle. So far, it seems like Skandar being a spirit wielder has protected him from the curse. Remember how the magic on the fault lines didn't affect him?'

'We don't know the reason for that for sure, though,' Skandar mumbled. But he had his own unspoken theory about it – a tiny beacon of hope. Maybe the glow of elemental magic on the line didn't affect him because Kenna didn't want him to get hurt.

Mitchell ploughed on. 'And we also don't know when the cycle of the Skeleton Curse will be complete.'

'It's got to be the summer solstice.' Bobby rolled her eyes. 'I swear, with villains it's *always* the solstice. They're not very original.'

'It's not about originality,' Mitchell snapped. 'The summer solstice is a sacred day on the Island – when all elemental magic is at its most powerful.'

– 175 –

# SKANDAR AND THE SKELETON CURSE

*And,* Skandar thought, *it also used to be the Spirit Festival.*

'We *know,*' Bobby said dismissively. 'But if we can't work out what links Kenna's sacrifices, then it's going to be impossible to stop her carrying out the next steps in the Skeleton Curse. And what if there is no link? What if they're random riders and unicorns?'

'Either way,' Flo said, looking stricken, 'Skandar and Scoundrel are the only spirit pair left. If there's a spirit sacrifice, they'd be her only possible target!'

'She wouldn't hurt me,' Skandar said immediately. The idea had been creeping up on him too, but there was no way Kenna would do that. She loved him still, like he loved her. He had to believe that.

'Skar,' Flo protested, 'you can't know that. She's done some really terrible—'

'Not to me,' Skandar insisted. 'She had every chance to hurt me on the Weaver's island last year – but she lashed me to a tree, out of harm's way.'

'Maybe she was just waiting to kill you at the right time!' Bobby exploded. 'Don't be so naive!'

Skandar held up a hand. 'Please. Let's concentrate on the water wielder, okay? That must be the next stage of the cycle. Could we maybe tell all the water-allied riders to hide on the festival day or something?' He threw the idea out there, trying to distract them from his sister.

Mitchell sighed deeply. 'You're Kenna's brother, Skandar, and we're all linked to you – most people aren't going to listen to anything we have to say.'

They were all silent for a moment, though the air was charged with frustration.

Finally Flo asked, 'Did *you* find anything in the Vaults, Skar?'

Skandar swallowed. 'I, er, sort of overheard Rex and another silver. Brad? Down in the Vaults. And it seemed as though Rex

– 176 –

## THE VAULTS

might be planning to do something with the Mainland.'

'What do you mean *do something*?'

'Invade,' Skandar blurted. 'That's what it sounded like anyway. He was taking down books on Mainland fortifications, defences, weather, coastline, history. Things you'd want to know if you were planning an attack.'

'But that's ridiculous!' Flo was half laughing. 'He's already Commodore, head of the Silver Circle and practically running the Eyrie. Why would he want the Mainland as well?'

'Power,' Skandar said, repeating the words Nina Kazama had spoken on the Sunset Platform just weeks before she'd been killed. 'Nobody ever thinks they have enough.'

'Could you tell what he was planning?' Mitchell asked tentatively. 'From the books you saw?'

Skandar shook his head, unable to believe they were even having this conversation.

'If he takes unicorns there . . . if he takes silvers,' Bobby murmured frantically. 'What if he wants to destroy it? To kill everyone? The man's evil! He killed our Commodore, his own friend!' Skandar noticed she didn't call Rex a silly name this time.

'I don't think—' Flo started, but at that moment Rickesh called them.

'Come and have something to eat, you lot!'

'He's right,' Mitchell announced. 'It's been a long day and we could go round in circles about sacrifices and invasions all night. We need to strategise when we're less exhausted.'

'Yes,' Flo agreed quickly. 'There's nothing we can do about Kenna or Rex right now.'

But Bobby caught Skandar's eye, and he saw his fear reflected in her gaze. The Mainland was their home – it was where their families were, where they'd grown up – and that meant the other half of their quartet couldn't quite understand how they were feeling.

– 177 –

# SKANDAR AND THE SKELETON CURSE

Still subdued, they perched by the fire on a piece of driftwood. Rickesh came to sit with them, and Prim brought over some of the freshly cooked fish. Skandar hadn't talked to her much since they'd arrived on the archipelago – she spent a lot of time on Cerulean, attempting to rebuild her connection with Winter Wildfire. In the flicker of the firelight, Skandar could see a dark red wound on her knuckle from wild magic.

The two older riders were mid-discussion and Skandar felt like he was back at a Peregrine Society meeting.

'You're entering, Ricki, and that's that,' Prim declared. 'When you left the Eyrie last year, Instructor O'Sullivan said you had a chance of qualifying.'

'Are you thinking of entering the Chaos Cup?' Skandar asked, immediately imagining the shining possibility of Rickesh as Commodore instead of Rex.

'Don't get too excited,' Rickesh warned nervously. 'O'Sullivan didn't say I had a *good* chance of qualifying. And I'm nowhere near as good as Prim.' He turned to the fire wielder. 'I didn't get into the water yard, remember?'

'How *do* you get into a yard?' Bobby asked hungrily, always interested in anything that would advance her rider career.

Prim answered, her voice muted. 'It's quite rare to be admitted to one of the four elemental yards. They're reserved for the brightest and best riders of each generation – the ones the coaches believe have a real prospect of winning a Chaos Cup one day.'

'Prim was accepted into the fire yard straight out of the Eyrie,' Rickesh told them proudly. 'The yards have all the best training facilities, the best coaches for your element, the best riders to compete against. I wasn't accepted into the water yard, so I'm not sure if I should even enter the Qualifiers this year. Especially with all the rumours about the whole Silver Circle entering.'

'Rubbish!' Prim said, jumping up so vigorously that her

– 178 –

# THE VAULTS

insulin pump fell out of her pocket. 'You're doing it. Imagine: you could race against one of the greats.' She sighed. 'Alodie Birch or Ema Templeton or Tom Nazari! How awesome would that be?'

'The whole Silver Circle might be entering?' Skandar murmured to Flo, who looked as surprised as him.

'It would be awesome for a moment,' Rickesh accepted, 'and then I'd lose. Look, I'm probably not even going to make it to the last day of the Qualifiers. In fact, let's be honest, Kenna is probably going to turn the water unicorns wild before I even get to the *first* day.'

'Don't say that! You've got to do it for both of us. Did I tell you the coaches at the fire yard said they thought I was ready, but . . .' Prim's eyes were haunted as she looked towards Cerulean.

'Next year,' Rickesh said firmly. 'We'll enter together – and I'm sure you and Winter Wildfire will absolutely annihilate us.'

Prim chuckled. 'Oh, you can bet on that.'

'There won't be any earth or fire wielders trying to qualify this year,' Mitchell told Rickesh bluntly. 'If you enter, you're likely to do better than in any other year – purely on numbers.'

Rickesh wasn't offended. 'It's going to be a Cup for the history books – especially if the whole Silver Circle is entering. I suppose I might as well be there for the excitement. Something to tell the grandchildren, eh?'

An idea was forming in Skandar's mind. An idea that was spun from everything they'd learned down in the Vaults and the words he'd just heard. Because even if Rickesh qualified, he *wouldn't* make it into the Cup. Not if Kenna carried out the full cycle of the Skeleton Curse. By the time the Chaos Cup came round in June, the water and air unicorns would be wild too. The race would be entirely made up of silvers. Unless . . .

'I could enter the Qualifiers,' Skandar blurted.

### Kenna

# ORIGINALS

Kenna Everhart had never imagined herself a teacher.

A week after Albert's arrival, Kenna rode Goshawk out into the scarred landscape of the Wilderness beyond the spindly pine trees. She made sure Eagle's Dawn followed them, summoning the spirit element to her palm to capture the wild unicorn's attention. Albert walked a safe distance behind, before standing by Goshawk, watching his own white unicorn closely.

'With Goshawk,' Kenna explained in a low voice, taking care not to startle Eagle's Dawn, 'at the beginning it was about showing her she could trust me. Proving I wouldn't hurt her. You can't expect Eagle to be the same as she was before – she's immortal now, and it's weighing on her. It's hurting her too. You have to understand it's going to be different for both of you.'

Albert nodded.

'Take a step towards her and keep your hands where she can see them,' Kenna instructed.

Eagle's skeletal head jerked upwards, her eyes blazing red.

# ORIGINALS

Rancid smoke rings swirled round her rotting nose as she snorted in warning.

'Stop,' Kenna ordered Albert. 'Wait for her to adjust. And squash your fear – she'll smell it on you and she'll run. Wild unicorns are afraid of everything and nothing, because they see the world for what it is – a place of suffering. It hurts them, but never enough to release them into death.' The explanation came easily to Kenna – it was a desolation she lived whenever she couldn't block Goshawk's emotions out.

'Wow.' Albert let out a low chuckle. 'That's not depressing at all.'

Eagle let out a low rumble. 'Is, er, that a good sound?' Albert asked, looking up at Kenna on Goshawk.

'Yes! I think she liked your laugh. Take a few more steps.'

Albert walked more quickly, wanting to take advantage of Eagle's good mood. The unicorn watched him closely, eyes flattening to glowing coals that matched her rider's knuckles.

'What now?' Albert breathed, frozen in Eagle's smouldering stare.

'Stroke her neck; keep talking – it helps,' Kenna whispered, also transfixed.

'Hello, my gorgeous girl,' Albert said, his voice barely audible over the winter wind ripping through the Wilderness. 'I see you, okay? I see you and it's all right and I love you like this. It's more honest. It's who you really are – who you really were all along.'

Kenna knew the words were tumbling out of Albert as a way to reassure Eagle, but she felt her eyes stinging with unfallen tears.

Eagle's Dawn was clearly listening too. She was alert but didn't move away. Didn't set off any elemental blasts. Albert lifted his Hatchery-scarred palm and stroked her neck, flaked with the blood of a seeping wound.

– 181 –

# SKANDAR AND THE SKELETON CURSE

'We're going to be just fine, you and me,' Albert crooned. 'Kenna and Goshawk are going to show us the ropes, eh?'

And Eagle's Dawn bowed her head slightly, her transparent horn catching the light of the low-hanging sun.

Albert heard Kenna's intake of breath. 'What does that mean?' he asked without moving.

'I think she'd be okay with you riding her,' Kenna translated.

'What? Now?' Albert sounded suddenly nervous.

'Don't show her you're afraid,' Kenna ordered firmly.

More gently than Kenna could have imagined for a boy of Albert's height and strength, he pulled himself up on to Eagle's back. And the unicorn stayed still while he did it.

'Holy hailstones,' Albert breathed, in a mixture of Mainland and Island curses. 'Can you believe this?' He looked over at Kenna on Goshawk.

'Turns out I'm a good teacher.'

And Kenna found the words made her feel strong in a different way. Not because she had taken power but because she had empowered someone else. She was smiling for the first time in months.

---

Weeks passed, a month. Kenna and Goshawk taught Albert and Eagle every day, and slowly the boy and wild unicorn began to build a new connection. The only interruptions to their daily routine came from a dapple-grey unicorn.

Kenna had felt Goshawk's Fury sense something the day Albert had first ridden Eagle. Afterwards Goshawk had pummelled rage and bitterness into the forged bond, and Kenna had been unable to sleep or eat. During these long hours, Kenna had sent Albert out on to the treehouse platform, not wanting to strike out at him – verbally or physically – while she was trapped in Goshawk's emotional turmoil. Raging flames had

– 182 –

# ORIGINALS

exploded from Kenna's palm as she'd snarled and thrown them at prey she could not see. Afterwards she'd marvelled at how undamaged her room was – as though the Scrapyard Treehouse had been built for someone exactly like her. Another time she'd somehow frozen herself to the wall and been forced to use the earth element to chisel herself off once Goshawk relented. But after a while Kenna began to learn how to retain a little more of herself during these outbursts – building elemental shields in her mind – and recently she'd successfully delayed the arrival of a tornado to her palm for long enough to throw it a safe distance from the treehouse before letting rip.

It was a month later, when Goshawk had gone off to hunt, that Kenna finally realised what had upset her wild unicorn so much. She was collecting wood for that evening's campfire, when she noticed her hand was glowing. Alarmed, Kenna dropped the wood and gazed at her finger bones shining through her skin.

'Soul-shine,' Kenna breathed, remembering that boy, Tyler Thomson and his bones blazing white for Goshawk back on her mum's island, her brother trying to tell her—

Just then, there was a movement between the skeletal pines and Kenna looked up to see the shimmering outline of a wild unicorn, its bones shining to match hers.

The dapple-grey had found her. The unicorn Skandar had insisted she'd been destined for.

It was too much for Kenna. She sprinted back to the treehouse. Goshawk would never forgive her for getting close to this unicorn. The price of their forged bond was Kenna turning her back on her destiny. That was the deal.

But even now – as Kenna and Albert sat on a log, side by side, warming their hands by the fire – Kenna could sense the dapple-grey somewhere close by, watching them. She glanced anxiously over at Goshawk's Fury, but she and Eagle's Dawn

– 183 –

# SKANDAR AND THE SKELETON CURSE

were snoozing peacefully on the other side of the fire, their rotting wings lightly touching. Goshawk was either ignoring the presence of the dapple-grey or getting used to it. But Kenna could do neither.

'I mean, I *can* live without chocolate,' Albert was saying. 'But I just don't want to.'

Kenna sighed. 'If you go into Fourpoint, I'm worried someone will follow you back here. Wait, what's Eagle doing?'

Eagle's Dawn had walked over to where they were sitting and was staring with red smouldering eyes at Albert's right palm. Specifically she seemed to be staring at his Hatchery wound; it was facing upwards as he warmed his knuckles over the fire.

Albert rose from the log as if in a trance, Eagle letting out a low bellow. Then she nudged the fingers on Albert's right hand open so his Hatchery wound was more exposed. Impossibly gently Eagle touched the tip of her horn to Albert's palm. And the wound began to glow. First red, then blue, then yellow, then green and finally bright white – the five lines snaking up his fingers and lighting up like the fault lines.

The blond boy and his white unicorn looked at each other, as though for the first time. Kenna wasn't sure how much time passed like this – it could have been seconds or minutes. Until eventually, slowly, Albert lowered his palm and Eagle lowered her horn, shrieking softly.

'Should I?' Albert asked Kenna.

'Try,' Kenna breathed, scared of startling Eagle.

Albert mounted Eagle's Dawn, and at the same time – trying not to distract them – Kenna summoned the spirit element to her palm.

The bond between Albert and Eagle had been a transparent cord until now – empty of the magic that had filled it before, just like all the other earth and fire wielders. But now she saw that

– 184 –

# ORIGINALS

same bond light up, elemental colours flickering in and out of it at random.

Albert must have felt the change she could see and he summoned elemental magic to his palm, flames erupting like fireworks from his hand and illuminating the trees above.

And then there were tears. From Albert mostly – but also from Kenna. Because she hadn't believed in the story of the First Rider and the Wild Unicorn Queen. Even after Skandar's supposed encounter with that phantom rider, she had thought it was a fairy tale he'd made up to explain the origins of the Island. She hadn't truly believed that this, *this* was how it had all started, a wild unicorn gifting magic to a person they had grown to love.

When Albert finally dismounted and sat on the log again, he asked. 'Could you see my bond? Is it back to normal?'

Kenna answered honestly. 'There was colour coming in and out of the transparent bond – but it wasn't only red. Whatever your bond is, I don't think it's stable yet. I think it's going to take some time. Your magic could be unpredictable.'

'But do you think one day I might be allied to five elements?' Albert asked, ignoring Kenna's uncertainty. 'Like you?'

'Maybe one day, if it stabilises,' she said. And for the first time in a *long* time, Kenna Everhart didn't feel quite so alone.

'We have to recruit more riders, tell them what you're going to achieve with the Skeleton Curse,' Albert said determinedly.

Kenna raised an eyebrow. 'Is that what Rex is calling it? The Skeleton Curse?'

But Albert was too excited to answer. 'We'll tell people that you're rebuilding the bone staff. That they can have magic again if they join you – be allied to all five elements, be even more powerful than before. They can be like the original rider – the First Rider!'

– 185 –

'You think there are others who'd want to learn like this? Who'd feel the way you do?' Kenna asked. She hadn't considered this. She hadn't considered others.

Albert laughed, and then stopped himself as Eagle let out a warning bellow at his shoulder. 'Kenn, there are riders all across the Island with wild unicorns and they have no idea what to do with them. They're wandering the Wilderness, or trapped in the Eyrie, or sheltering with the Wanderers – and they need help. Don't you see? The Commodore has abandoned them. They need *you* to help them. Help them become originals too. Your Originals.'

And Kenna didn't hate that idea at all.

Chapter Twelve

# THE LIONESS AND THE PUPPY

Everyone around Navy's campfire stared at Skandar, and somehow he found himself repeating the idea. '*I* could enter the Qualifiers, couldn't I?'

'What do you mean?' Mitchell asked, the flames in his hair mirroring the fire.

But the more Skandar thought about it, the more he became absolutely convinced this was the only way. 'Don't you see?' he said feverishly. 'Obviously we're hoping that we can work out the pattern of the Skeleton Curse before Kenna attacks the water and air wielders, but what if we can't? The Chaos Cup is going to be made up *entirely* of silvers, who are probably already supporting Rex's Mainland plan.'

Rickesh and Prim looked at each other in confusion at this, but Skandar didn't pause to explain. 'I have no idea if I'm good enough. I mean, I would *definitely* not be good enough in a normal year, but this year is different. Silver magic can be unpredictable, can't it?' He swallowed. 'And someone has to stop Rex or one of his silver cronies becoming Commodore.'

# SKANDAR AND THE SKELETON CURSE

'Wholeheartedly agree with that,' Rickesh said gravely. 'The Qualifiers will be carnage. Silver unicorns are notoriously difficult to control during a race, but odds are that with that many entering a fair few will still make it through to the Cup.'

'Exactly,' Skandar continued. 'And if the Skeleton Curse carries on until the Chaos Cup itself, then the only *non*-silver rider who won't have their unicorn turned wild yet is . . .'

'You,' Mitchell finished, nodding. 'That makes sense. It really does. The Cup is always *before* the summer solstice now so it can be broadcast to the Mainland before the new riders set off for the Hatchery.'

'But, Skar, you can't enter the Chaos Cup,' Flo cried. 'It's too dangerous!'

'He's Rookie age,' Rickesh said evenly. 'And, even as a nomad, technically Skandar's allowed to enter. Qualifying will be your biggest obstacle. The earth and fire wielders might be missing, but you'll still be up against the best air and water combinations on the Island.'

'Do you really think they'll let a spirit wielder enter?' Prim asked Skandar.

'I guess all I can do is try.'

'If *you're* entering, spirit boy, then so am I,' Bobby said, all the feathers along her arms standing up. 'There's every possibility we'll stop Kenna before the Air Festival, and – no offence – Falcon and I have a far better chance of qualifying than you and Scoundrel.'

'She's right,' Mitchell said. 'Bobby and Falcon's Wrath outperformed you and Scoundrel at the Eyrie. *And* she's an air wielder – statistically air-allied riders have won more Chaos Cups than anyone else.'

Skandar wasn't deflated by Mitchell's words. Instead, the idea of Bobby doing this *terrifying* thing with him made him

– 188 –

## THE LIONESS AND THE PUPPY

feel much better. He thought of the spirit wielder boy he'd heard that morning, being automatically disqualified from trying the Hatchery door. Bobby had joked about becoming Commodore and changing all that, but if either of them won the Cup, then it wouldn't just be the Mainland they'd be protecting. They could bring spirit wielders back to the Island too. They really could change things.

'How about it?' Skandar grinned. 'Two Mainlanders protecting our home from Rex?'

Bobby barked out a laugh. 'Forking thunderstorms, Agatha is going to be absolutely furious about this.' But Skandar wasn't so sure. *Don't you dare let him win, Skandar Smith.* That's what Agatha had written to him after Swan's death. And wasn't that exactly why he wanted to enter the Chaos Cup?

'We're not too late to enter, are we?' Skandar asked Rickesh urgently. 'Wait, how *do* we enter?' He'd loved the Cup his whole life, but he'd never seen riders registering for it on TV or even the Qualifiers themselves – the Island kept all of that to itself.

'Don't stress, you're fine for time. Registration is a few weeks away on the winter solstice. To be honest, the whole registration process is quite the spectacle.'

Skandar glanced at Flo as Rickesh embarked on an elaborate explanation about registration for the Qualifiers. She hadn't said a word for ages.

When they returned to Sapphire later that night, Skandar caught Flo's hand before she crawled into the tent behind the others. 'Are you all right?' The waves lapped gently on the shore behind them, the sapphire water sparkling in the light of the moon.

Flo shrugged. 'I just feel useless, that's all. I'm a silver and I'm supposed to be powerful, but I can't enter the Qualifiers like you and Bobby, or the rest of the Circle, because I'm hiding. I'm

# SKANDAR AND THE SKELETON CURSE

a coward, like I have been since the beginning.'

'You've never been a coward!' Skandar argued, thinking of her throwing herself between him and the Weaver as a Hatchling, of her rescuing the wild unicorn from the Stronghold as a Nestling, of her swimming for the solstice stone as a Fledgling. Even after all that, she didn't believe she was one of the bravest people he knew. 'You declared yourself a nomad, Flo. You risked being locked in the Stronghold because you wanted to stand up for what's right, to stay with your friends, to stay with . . .' He tailed off before he said 'me', though he still hadn't let go of her hand.

'Yes, but what use is any of that if I'm just going to stay here on this ridiculously beautiful island and wait for you and Bobby to fix everything? Silver Blade has the most powerful magic of any of our unicorns, and while you and Scoundrel are racing to save the Island, what are we going to do? Sunbathe?'

'You can't enter the Qualifiers, though,' Skandar said tentatively. 'As soon as you turn up to register, the Silver Circle will cart you off to the Stronghold.'

'I know that, Skar.' Flo dropped his hand and turned towards the tent. 'I know.'

As Skandar had predicted, Agatha was very enthusiastic about their plan to enter the Qualifiers. She exchanged her beachwear for a white linen suit – perhaps to imitate the white instructor's cloak she no longer had – and threw herself wholeheartedly into the idea. She even included Rickesh in her plans, who she'd decided was a 'nice, though exhaustingly flamboyant, young man'.

'I never entered the Chaos Cup myself – being Commodore always seemed like a lot of paperwork,' Agatha explained. 'But I did have quite a few friends who ended up qualifying and they used to go on *endlessly* about it. I'll see what I can remember.'

– 190 –

## THE LIONESS AND THE PUPPY

Skandar noticed she avoided mentioning Erika, who'd won the Chaos Cup twice.

The process of devising a training regime created one of the most unlikely friendships Skandar had encountered so far: Agatha and Mitchell. The two of them spent a whole week together on Indigo and declared they would use it for training due to its abundance of open space. They seemed to enjoy planning every detail of the training – from feed schedules to elemental magic drills and fitness routines. But the inclusion of Jordan and Surfer's Demise in some of the training sessions led to one of the only arguments Skandar had ever witnessed between Mitchell and Flo.

Flo had been spending more and more time alone with Blade. At night she was the first into the tent and was almost always asleep – or pretending to be – by the time the rest of the quartet returned from eating on Navy. Skandar had tried to talk to her, but she had brushed him off. Then the night Mitchell and Agatha's schedules were handed to Skandar, Bobby and Rickesh round the campfire, Flo lost her temper.

'Why is Jordan's name on the schedule?' she demanded, reading over Skandar's shoulder.

'He was a Grin,' Mitchell explained cheerfully. 'We thought Surfer's Demise could help with speed training.'

Flo scanned the schedule more closely. 'But I'm not on here. Blade's a silver unicorn!' She was practically shouting now. 'Don't you think it might be helpful for everyone entering the Qualifiers to train against *us*?'

'Of course we're going to train against you,' Skandar said quickly, alarmed by Flo's reaction. 'Right, Mitchell?'

Mitchell's hair burned very brightly. 'I, well, yes, I suppose—'

'You forgot about us, didn't you?' Flo said accusingly. 'You actually forgot!'

– 191 –

# SKANDAR AND THE SKELETON CURSE

Unusually it was Bobby who tried to play peacekeeper. 'C'mon, Florence! Give him a break, can't you? He's been working on these schedules non-stop for a week.'

'I just thought,' Mitchell said, hurt in his voice, 'that we shouldn't draw attention to Blade being here. You're on the run, Flo. You have to be careful.'

'I'm SICK of being careful!' Flo cried and jogged away towards the sea. 'And don't follow me, Skar!' she added, before he'd even taken a whole step towards her.

Agatha, who had kept out of the argument but clearly overheard the whole thing, sauntered over. 'Add Flo and Silver Blade to all the predator sessions,' she said. 'She's right – Blade is a silver, and you all need to prepare for what that means.'

This was how – two days before the winter solstice – Skandar found himself face to face with one of Bobby's elemental predators in front of Rickesh, Agatha, Mitchell and Flo. They were watching from a driftwood platform hanging from one of the taller trees a few metres in from the vast beach. Mitchell had asked Jordan to help him rig it up so that they could watch the riders training in the air from a safe vantage point. Silver Blade and Tidal Warrior waited in its shade for their turn, watching the black and grey unicorns soaring above the sand.

Although Scoundrel almost always beat Falcon in a straight race around Indigo, Bobby was still absolutely wiping the floor with Skandar during sky battle training. Today she had managed to create a Hunter-level predator, a flaming fox that bared its glowing teeth as it pounced towards Scoundrel through the air.

'Don't just *look* at the predator, Skandar!' Agatha yelled from the platform. '*Do* something about it!'

'I'm trying!' Skandar shouted, as he was forced to raise a water shield to block the creature from swiping at Scoundrel's right wing.

– 192 –

## THE LIONESS AND THE PUPPY

The trouble was, Skandar had essentially had no elemental predator training at the Eyrie. He'd listened to countless stories about it, he'd been to a couple of training sessions on the theory of summoning one, but he hadn't ever created a predator himself. So now he was hopelessly behind and unable to conjure up anything bigger than the smallest of Hiders.

Skandar turned Scoundrel in mid-air, managing to drop his water shield long enough to send a cloud of spirit magic above his head, just as he'd seen both Agatha and his mum doing, before she—

'Concentrate, Skandar!' Agatha cried, as the cloud dispersed to join the real ones above his head.

He tried again. And this time he felt the magic building – the same feeling that filled his hands as when he was moulding a weapon in his mind. There was a strange tingling sensation in his chest as the power was drawn up into the silvery-white cloud and something began to take shape. He looked up, hoping to see the creature he'd imagined in his head and—

Bobby's howling laughter filled the sky. 'Is that a puppy?'

It was not at all what Skandar had hoped for. He wasn't sure the elemental predator he'd summoned was a puppy exactly, but the pearly white spirit magic had indeed formed into something resembling a *very* small dog. It looked suspiciously like a Yorkshire Terrier.

'What are you going to call it?' Bobby jeered.

'Oh, be quiet!' Skandar said, but even he couldn't help laughing as the dog bounded through the air, tumbling around as though trying to play with its own tail.

Then, out of nowhere, an enormous elemental predator raced through the sky between Falcon and Scoundrel. It was a lioness with a body constructed from a tangle of plants, its every claw the sharpest of thorns. A Marauder. First, it barrelled towards

– 193 –

# SKANDAR AND THE SKELETON CURSE

Bobby's creature, a blur of green that immediately extinguished the fox's glow as it pounced and clawed at the weaker predator in mid-air. The last embers of the fox rose up above Falcon, as Bobby shouted out in shock.

'Who does it belong—' Skandar began, but before he knew it, the lioness was heading in his direction and Scoundrel had no choice but to swerve sideways as the great creature caught Skandar's little dog in its thorned paws.

Flo and Silver Blade came soaring towards them. At first Skandar couldn't understand why they were flying right into danger, but then he spotted the concentration on Flo's face and the emerald-green glow of her palm.

'Wait for your turn!' Bobby called to Flo, as Blade flapped his wings, suspending her in the air between Scoundrel and Falcon. Then understanding dawned. 'Wait, is that Marauder yours?'

Flo nodded seriously. 'I've been holding back; I didn't want you to worry about your progress. But we were separated for most of our Eyrie training before we declared ourselves nomads, remember? I was forced to go to the Silver Stronghold every day – and learned to do *this*. I've been capable of making Marauders for a while now.'

Skandar glanced at his little dog trapped between the great lioness's paws.

'That's why you have to take predator training more seriously – both of you,' Flo scolded. 'You're up here laughing because all Skandar can create is a tiny Hider, but do you know why I can summon a Marauder?'

Bobby and Skandar both shook their heads, mute with shock and a sprinkling of shame.

'Because Blade is a silver. Making a predator is all about the amount of power you can summon in that first burst of raw magic – before you've even started to shape the creature. And

– 194 –

# THE LIONESS AND THE PUPPY

although it's hard to control sometimes, the natural power of silvers is greater than other unicorns. To create that lioness –' she pointed at it – 'all I had to do was keep control and concentration for the split second I summoned Blade's raw power.'

'But what about after you've made it? Aren't Marauders really powerful? Isn't that lioness leeching magic from you right now?' Skandar worried.

'Yes, that can be a danger,' Flo said more patiently, even as her power was being drawn up towards the lioness, 'but when I was training at the Stronghold, they were already teaching us tactics to prevent our predators from getting too powerful and breaking free. They have centuries of knowledge. Because elemental predators are what silvers do best.'

'And that's why Rex legalised them this year?' Skandar guessed. 'To give silvers an even greater chance of dominating the Chaos Cup.'

'I expect so,' Flo accepted. 'But if you want to qualify, you have to stop worrying about Rex and start focusing on yourself, Skar. It's not a joke, okay?'

'I-I'm sorry,' Skandar said, feeling a mixture of hurt and guilt. 'I didn't realise you cared so much about it. You've barely spoken to me since the Vaults.'

'It's just been difficult – not feeling like I can help you,' Flo said vaguely. 'But I *know* about predators and I can help with this, all right? I'm not going to hold back any more. And I'm sorry if that makes you feel worried but . . . worried is better than injured, isn't it?' She finished anxiously, as though trying to convince herself she'd done the right thing.

'We hear you, Flo,' Bobby said, matching her friend's serious tone. 'Teach us everything you know about these pesky pets.'

Skandar nodded solemnly too. If silvers were the best at predators, what if Rex planned to use them for his invasion of

– 195 –

# SKANDAR AND THE SKELETON CURSE

the Mainland? He and Bobby *had* to qualify; they had to stop him.

Flo looked slightly happier. 'There's quite a bit of theory I can tell you about on the flight to Fourpoint.'

'Wait, what?'

'I'm coming with you to Fourpoint when you register for the Qualifiers,' Flo said, stubbornly. 'I've already talked to Jordan, and he thinks we can dull Blade's colour with a mud paste he's made. I'll keep a low profile, probably land in the graveyard. I've got it all planned.'

'But what if Rex sees you?' Skandar was horrified. 'He'll be registering for the Qualifiers, won't he?

'I'm not staying behind again,' Flo said stubbornly. 'I'm part of this quartet – and if Mitchell's coming along to help you, then so am I.'

Skandar opened his mouth to argue back, but Bobby shook her head at him. 'Just leave it. She's made up her mind. I wouldn't want to be left behind either.' Bobby raised a sharp brown eyebrow and looked at Flo. 'And I'm sure you'll stay hidden. Won't you?'

'I'm coming with you,' Flo murmured again. And as she said it, Skandar's dog splintered into a thousand glowing pieces between her lioness's claws.

Chapter Thirteen

# REGISTRATION

Once they reached Fourpoint on the winter solstice, Rickesh went to meet Warrior's saddler, while Flo and Blade disappeared to find a place where they could listen to the registration commentary without being seen. Skandar, Bobby and Mitchell's first stop was at the communal post trees, and the Mainlanders rented canisters from the nearby kiosk that would allow them to send letters back and forth to the Mainland. Luckily they still had access to their unspent Eyrie rider allowances.

'I think we'll get a different kind of allowance from the Rider Liaison Office if we qualify for the Cup,' Bobby explained, juggling her canister from hand to hand. 'There are a lot of expenses obviously – with new saddles, new armour, rider jerseys, healer fees. If we were members of a yard, apparently we'd get money from them, but . . .' Bobby shrugged.

Skandar hadn't thought about *any* of that, though he felt uncomfortable about how much they'd been relying on the generosity of the Wanderers since they'd left the Eyrie.

It took Bobby about two seconds to scrawl her note, but

# SKANDAR AND THE SKELETON CURSE

Skandar struggled – and it ended up being an odd mix of shocking news, empty reassurances and Christmas wishes.

Hi Dad! Sorry I haven't written for a while. I'm fine, but also I'm no longer training at the Eyrie – don't send letters there any more. Kenna isn't either. We'll write as often as we can – send your replies to Fourpoint, canister no. 207 (get it!?).

I'm registering for the Chaos Cup Qualifiers today, so hopefully my name will be in the Mainland papers this March – I know you always read the Qualifier lists. I'll try to write before then. Love you and Merry Christmas!
Skandar x

Once Skandar had placed his letter inside the canister and left it in its hollow in the tree trunk, Bobby set off to buy second-hand rider jackets from Battle Bargains. For registration, riders were required to wear the colour of their allied element, although Skandar was certain that the shop wouldn't have anything resembling a spirit jacket. Meanwhile Skandar and Mitchell's next stop was the blacksmith forges.

When the sloping metal roof of Jamie's forge came into view, Mitchell quickened his pace, almost breaking into a jog. Jamie and Mitchell had been separated for weeks now – the longest since they'd first met. Skandar could tell how much his friend had been missing Jamie. Not because Mitchell talked about him all the time, but because he didn't. Whenever the question of armour for the Qualifiers had come up, Mitchell had stayed quiet, staring into the distance.

'I'll go inside and find him,' Mitchell said breathlessly.

But there was no need. A sandy-haired figure burst so quickly from the forge that Scoundrel shrieked in warning and Skandar

– 198 –

# REGISTRATION

barely registered who it was until he'd thrown his ash-streaked arms round Mitchell.

'You're here,' Jamie breathed into Mitchell's flaming hair. 'You're okay.'

'Didn't you get my letters? About registration? About the armour?'

'I haven't had *any* letters. I was worried that maybe Red had injured you or—'

'I'm okay,' Mitchell murmured against Jamie's ear – the fiery tendrils of his hair eclipsing the billowing furnaces behind them.

'You're here,' Jamie repeated, pushing Mitchell's glasses gently back up his nose.

The two boys stared into each other's eyes, and then – at almost exactly the same moment – they leaned in for a kiss. Hammers banged behind them, metal flashed, and steam hissed, almost like the forge itself was applauding. In their eagerness, they accidentally bumped noses at first, both laughing. But then their lips met in a kiss of relief, and of love, and of hope for a future where they no longer had to be apart.

Skandar thought perhaps Mitchell and Jamie had completely forgotten that he was standing there. He didn't want to interrupt but he also knew that they had to register for the Qualifiers by midday. Luckily Scoundrel had clearly had enough of waiting and – with something he could only have learned from Red – ignited an extremely loud belch.

'Oh, hi, Skandar,' Jamie said casually, although the tips of his ears were pink.

Skandar raised an eyebrow but couldn't help smiling at the expression of pure happiness on Mitchell's face.

'So, er, obviously I'm really happy to see you . . . both,' Jamie said, rubbing his neck a bit sheepishly. 'But what are you doing in Fourpoint?'

– 199 –

# SKANDAR AND THE SKELETON CURSE

Mitchell finally found his words, although there was still a glow to his tawny cheeks. 'Skandar and Bobby are registering for the Qualifiers.'

Jamie's mouth fell open. 'As in . . . the Chaos Cup Qualifiers?'

Skandar grinned. 'I think I'm going to need some new armour.'

There was a moment of silence. Then—

'Thank the five elements!' Jamie crowed. 'I've been so *bored* since you left the Eyrie! There's only so much spying on sentinels I can do to keep myself entertained.'

Mitchell checked the time and gasped. 'Jamie, we have to go now – you need to be present at the registration. I'm hoping Olu Shekoni got my letters, although he's bound to have loads of other riders registering, I suppose.'

'Registration! Me! Registering my unicorn and rider for the Qualifiers!' Jamie looked like all his festivals had come at once. 'This really is fast becoming the best day *ever*.' He winked at Mitchell, who blushed more deeply.

'Don't get too excited,' Skandar warned. 'We have no idea whether the Commodore will actually allow a spirit wielder to enter.'

Jamie waved away this significant detail. 'Don't worry – if we can get your name into the Chaos Register, then everything will be grand.'

Skandar highly doubted this, but he was here now. He had to try.

'Wait.' Jamie paused. 'What's the rush to enter this year? Not that I'm complaining, but—'

'Rex may have some Mainland plans,' Mitchell answered cryptically. 'We'll explain on the way.'

Fourpoint was usually quiet in December, but Skandar had never visited it on the winter solstice before. Everywhere

– 200 –

# REGISTRATION

Skandar looked, there were nervous-looking riders being tailed by excited friends and family. Many were having animated conversations with their blacksmiths or saddlers – both had to be in attendance for a rider's registration to be accepted. And there were no signs of wild unicorns loose in the streets – perhaps they'd been spooked by all the activity – and Skandar could almost imagine the Skeleton Curse was just a horrible nightmare.

They met Bobby and Falcon on the corner near Sally's Succulent Sandwiches. Bobby had insisted on an emergency sandwich before registering – Sally had, inexplicably, decided to include Bobby's Marmite, cheese and jam concoction on her regular menu. Bobby said eating one would bring her good luck, though Skandar suspected it was really to calm the nerves she'd never admit to having. Flo was nowhere to be seen and Skandar was relieved she was keeping hidden.

As Bobby chatted away to Jamie – along with Reece, her own blacksmith – Mitchell dropped back to walk with Skandar and Scoundrel.

'Did you see that?' Mitchell whispered feverishly to Skandar. 'We kissed! I kissed him. He kissed me.'

'It was sort of a bit hard *not* to see it,' Skandar said, half grinning. 'Have you, er, not done that before then?'

'No!' Mitchell's eyes were wide with awe.

Skandar chuckled. 'And you decided to do it right in front of me? I'm honoured.'

Mitchell spluttered. 'I mean, we didn't *decide*, it just sort of happened – we haven't exactly got a lot of opportunities for kissing at the moment. You really should try it, Skandar. It's excellent.'

'Kissing Jamie?'

'Don't be obtuse – you know *who* I'm talking about.'

'What does "obtuse" mean?' Skandar asked, deliberately missing Mitchell's point.

– 201 –

## SKANDAR AND THE SKELETON CURSE

Mitchell rolled his eyes in a perfect imitation of Bobby.

As they neared the arena, black-clad stewards guided the group towards the Chaos Compound. This enclosure was tucked right behind the main arena, where they'd waited to be called for their Nestling jousts two years before. At the entrance Mitchell wished Skandar and Bobby good luck and went to find a seat in the stands. Unlike for the Qualifiers or the Chaos Cup, the arena wasn't packed with spectators, but there were still quite a few who'd come out to see that year's crop of hopefuls.

As Skandar led Scoundrel into the Compound, all he could see was silver – silver horns, silver tails, silver manes. The riders were wearing jackets in different elemental colours and Skandar immediately felt self-conscious in his plain black hoodie.

Jamie whistled, taking in the shining throng.

'The rumours were true.' Bobby's eyes tracked the nearest unicorn. 'The whole Silver Circle really are registering.'

Suddenly there was cheering from the arena and a booming voice came over the loudspeaker.

'Good morning! I'm Declan Dashwood – and it's registration time on the winter solstice. You may remember me from last year, the year before that and . . . well, you get the picture – clearly nobody else wants this job. But I promise if you stick with me, I'll always speak my mind, no matter what the folks in charge say. Aaaand, speaking of the folks in charge, we are underway with defending Commodore Rex Manning and Silver Sorceress registering first – as per Island tradition. A truly thrilling moment that means today really is the start of this year's Chaos Cup cycle.'

'I guess we're doing this,' Bobby said, the feathers on Falcon's wings sparking with electricity as they headed for the arena. The air wielder's purple-sashed saddler, Lucy Henning-Dove, and blacksmith, Reece, rushed after her.

– 202 –

# REGISTRATION

Nerves hit Skandar like an ice attack as he watched Bobby go, and he was still shaking when a black-clad steward called him forward. Was he – a spirit wielder – really going to be allowed to register? And even if Skandar was permitted to compete, did he actually have any chance of qualifying? He hadn't even finished his training. He didn't feel all that different from the boy who used to watch the Chaos Cup at home in Margate with his dad and . . . his sister. How he wished suddenly for *that* Kenna to be here and tell him he was doing the right thing.

'Hey!' Jamie was tapping urgently on Skandar's boot. 'Have you seen Olu anywhere? He needs to present you for registration too – they won't accept just a blacksmith.'

'Where's your saddler? No saddler – no registration.' The steward echoed Jamie's words. He raised an arm to stop them passing into the arena, and waved a different unicorn through instead – a bay unicorn Skandar recognised.

'Shekoni's just coming,' Rickesh called over his shoulder from Tidal Warrior, flanked by his saddler, Max Holder, and blacksmith, Lixin Zhang.

Skandar felt a wave of nausea, unsure whether it was relief or terror. But in a matter of moments Olu Shekoni arrived at Scoundrel's side, sweat pouring down his forehead.

'I'm sorry, Skandar, I—' He broke off, panting. 'Have you spoken to Flo? Have you seen her?'

'No, why—'

'Skandar!' He turned in the saddle to see Craig from Chapters of Chaos weaving between the waiting unicorns. He had something draped over his arm – something white – and the bookseller handed it up to Skandar.

'A little present from me.' He lowered his voice. 'And some of my spirit wielder friends.'

It was a spirit jacket – battered and stained in multiple places

– 203 –

# SKANDAR AND THE SKELETON CURSE

with a mixture of grass, mud and what Skandar suspected was blood. But it looked well loved too, with patches of fabric and chainmail sewn over scorches and rips from long-forgotten battles.

As Skandar shrugged it over his shoulders, he felt a lump rise in his throat. He felt better wearing this. Calmer. 'Thank you,' he croaked to Craig. 'Where—'

But Craig was talking to Olu. 'And remember to use the exact wording we discussed.'

Olu nodded seriously and Craig dashed away without another word.

'Are you registering or not?' the steward shouted, eyeballing Skandar in his spirit jacket.

'Let's go,' Jamie said firmly. He had a hand on Scoundrel's left rein, Olu took the right rein, and – as one – they entered the arena.

Skandar's nerves quickly returned when Scoundrel walked out on to the sand. Why did registration have to be in the arena? He hadn't exactly had a brilliant time when he'd last been in here. He'd been possessed by Scoundrel, come over all bloodthirsty and thrown a load of spirit daggers at Instructor Saylor.

There were only a few people dotted around the stands, though that emphasised to Skandar just how *big* it was. The raked seating surrounded him on all sides, so high he could barely see the top seats, and the arena itself was far larger than any of the training grounds on the Eyrie's hill. Then he spotted – under the famous finishing arch – a man standing at an ornate iron lectern that looked so ancient it might have belonged to the First Rider. As Scoundrel approached, Skandar recognised the tall serious man as a member of Rex's Council of Seven.

'He's the race representative,' Jamie whispered.

The towering air wielder did such a big double-take when

– 204 –

## REGISTRATION

Scoundrel halted under the finishing arch that it was almost funny.

'You can't wear a spirit . . . He can't seriously be . . .' The race representative looked at Olu.

'Interestingly there's nothing in the rules that prohibits a spirit wielder from entering the Chaos Cup,' Olu said casually, as though they were discussing an innovation in saddle design. 'There wasn't any need, you see, because the Silver Circle locked them all up.'

'But he can't possibly *use* the spirit element,' the race representative spluttered.

'*Training* in the spirit element has been banned from the Eyrie, that's right, but Skandar's a nomad now. And although *using* the element is illegal on the Island, an exception was made by Aspen McGrath three years ago – specifically for Skandar Smith – and it's still written into Island law. So, outside the Eyrie, there is nothing stopping him from using his element if he wishes.'

The race representative looked appalled at the oversight, his eyes raking Skandar's white jacket as though he'd seen a ghost.

'Would it make you feel better if Skandar took *off* the jacket, Linton?' Olu said pleasantly. 'Though of course he *will* still be allied to the spirit element without it.'

'I need to discuss this with the justice representative,' the race representative declared. He looked up towards the stands, his face so white he looked like he might faint, where Skandar noticed the yellow cloaks of some of Rex's Council of Seven.

'Come on now, Linton,' Olu said firmly. '*You* are the race representative. You make the decisions today. Don't go running to her. You know the law and you know I'm right.'

'But I'm sure the Commodore will *change*—'

'He hasn't changed the law yet, though, has he? I'm reliably informed by a learned friend of mine that the Commodore is

– 205 –

# SKANDAR AND THE SKELETON CURSE

prevented from making a law that could directly affect the outcome of the Chaos Cup – if they themselves have entered, that is.'

Olu went to stand beside Linton and peered at the Chaos Register. 'Ah yes, there he is – Rex Manning, first rider to register. So unless the Commodore wishes to withdraw, then he's too late. If it's legal today for a spirit wielder to be entered into your Chaos Register, then they *are* entitled to compete in the Cup – and it's your sacred duty to register them. And it will be legal for Skandar to use the spirit element – as the current law permits – until the Chaos Cup is complete.'

If he'd had more than a tuft of hair, Skandar was sure Linton would be tearing it out. 'Yes, thank you, Shekoni. I am quite aware of the sacred nature of my task.' He squinted up at Skandar on Scoundrel's back. 'Very well, spirit wielder.'

As quick as a flash, Olu produced a pen from his pocket and wrote in the large book that lay open on the lectern. Jamie rushed forward as soon as the saddler was finished, an excited noise escaping from his throat, and did the same.

There was a commotion in the stands and Rex Manning settled himself in a seat right in Skandar's eyeline. His heart thundered, wondering if this was the moment Rex would stop him registering – of course he would want it to be in front of a crowd. Olu had relied on Island law and the sacred nature of the Chaos Cup to get Skandar this far, but Rex did what he pleased most of the time – just look at what he'd done to the Eyrie. Look at what he was planning to do to the Mainland. There was no way Rex Manning would let Skandar and Scoundrel race in the Qualifiers.

'Approach, Skandar Smith,' the race representative said, his voice full of gloom. Skandar glanced at Rex one more time, but the Commodore looked relaxed, cheerful even. Olu took

– 206 –

# REGISTRATION

Scoundrel's reins and Jamie handed over the heavy fountain pen, as Skandar approached the lectern.

Whispers buzzed around the stands like angry bees, but Skandar made himself focus on the open Chaos Register, the words swimming in front of his eyes. The first five columns on the page were titled: RIDER, UNICORN, ELEMENT, SADDLER, BLACKSMITH. The sixth and seventh columns were still empty for every single rider who'd registered so far – one said CHAOS NUMBER and the second said CUP POSITION. Right at the top Skandar could see Rex Manning and Silver Sorceress's entry, with their saddler listed as Taiting, and blacksmith as Radcliffe. Skandar ran his hand down the page until he spotted – underneath Rickesh's entry – where Olu and Jamie had signed their names.

SADDLER: *Shekoni*. BLACKSMITH: Middleditch.

Skandar quickly scribbled his and Scoundrel's names, but lingered over writing the word *spirit* in the element column. He thought of Erika Everhart – and this time it didn't make him sad or angry or confused. When Erika had first registered for the Cup, she hadn't been the Weaver – she'd been a rider just like him, riding for her chance at glory. If things had been different, she might have been proud of him today. Adrenaline filled his veins; it had been an awfully long time since a spirit wielder had registered for the Chaos Cup.

Skandar's thoughts were echoed by the commentator. 'A historic moment here, as Skandar Smith registers himself and Scoundrel's Luck for the Chaos Cup. The spirit wielder is supported by his blacksmith, Jamie Middleditch, and saddler, Olu Shekoni. I know there may be some who question the legality of his registration, but I'm reliably informed that he is well within his rights. Congratulations, Skandar. No doubt he'll be bringing some drama to the competition this year and, as you all know, Declan Dashwood *lives* for the drama.'

– 207 –

# SKANDAR AND THE SKELETON CURSE

Skandar's moment of satisfaction was cut short by some booing from the crowd. He looked up, still hardly believing Rex was allowing this to happen, but the race representative blocked his view. 'I suppose we'll see you at the Qualifiers. What a spectacle that will be,' Linton said.

Although his voice was dripping with sarcasm, Jamie either didn't notice or didn't care. The blacksmith practically skipped across the sand towards the arena's main exit, listing all the things he would need to start making at the forge. 'Two new sets obviously, but probably three. Then we'll need to start thinking about . . .'

Skandar realised Olu was no longer at Scoundrel's side. Instead, he was watching a silver unicorn and rider approach the race representative, flanked by saddler Gerri Martina – in her iconic bright blue sash – and a familiar-looking blacksmith.

Olu was murmuring to himself. 'I told her not to do this. He could easily kill her in the race. It's too dangerous.'

But Skandar was no longer listening, because he'd realised who was at the lectern, registering for the Chaos Cup Qualifiers.

Florence Shekoni and Silver Blade.

Skandar tried to run towards Flo, her pen hovering over the Chaos Register, but Jamie grabbed his arm and Olu blocked the way, putting his large hands on Skandar's shoulders.

'It's too late, Skandar.' Olu's voice was heavy, resigned.

Skandar struggled anyway, pulling his arm out of Jamie's grip, trying to see past Olu. Sure enough, Flo was handing the pen back to the race representative, an expression of grim determination on her face.

Skandar didn't care that it was too late. There had to be something he could do. They could fly – now – right out of the arena and back to the Ambling Archipelago. And if that wasn't safe enough, they could even hide Flo and Blade in the

– 208 –

# REGISTRATION

Wilderness. The whole quartet could go, couldn't they? They didn't need anyone else.

Skandar managed to free himself from Olu and sprinted towards Flo, who was leading Blade away from the lectern.

'Flo!' Skandar yelled, and there was such sorrow in her eyes when she saw him that he couldn't bear it.

He reached her, Blade shimmering beside them. 'We have to go,' he urged, a hand on the shoulder of her green jacket. 'The Silver Circle will be here any minute. They'll drag you to the Stronghold; they won't let you—'

'I know,' Flo said sadly. 'But I'm not running, Skar.'

'Why are you doing this? We decided—'

'*You* all decided,' Flo said slightly more loudly. 'But I don't want to be the one everyone has to shield from danger. Not any more.'

'But—'

Flo took Skandar's hands in hers, speaking very fast. 'It makes just as much sense for me to try to qualify for the Chaos Cup as it does for you and Bobby. More, even. I'm a silver, I haven't been affected by the Skeleton Curse, and Blade is strong – we've actually got a good chance. And if I'm living inside the Stronghold, just imagine what I'll be able to find out about Rex's plans for the Mainland. I know you're trying to protect me, but how about I protect *you* for once? That's what I'm doing. That's what I *want* to do, okay?'

Skandar's eyes were beginning to sting. 'But you won't be able to come back with us to the archipelago; I won't be able to see you—'

'We'll see each other at the Qualifiers in March,' Flo said, though her voice shook. 'And if I don't qualify, then you can bust me out of the Stronghold. It's not as though we haven't done it before. I give you my full permission to break every law you can find.'

– 209 –

# SKANDAR AND THE SKELETON CURSE

At this Skandar half sobbed, half laughed. Then he took a deep breath. 'Flo . . . I don't know if I can do this without you.'

'Do what?' She squeezed his hands.

'Any of it,' Skandar breathed. 'The Qualifiers. Stopping Kenna. Fighting Rex. Protecting the Mainland. Life in general.'

There was a glint in the corner of Skandar's eye that was getting brighter. Four silver unicorns were making their way across the sand towards them. Ice-cold panic crept down his spine.

*Please, not yet.* He needed to say something. He needed to tell Flo—

Flo glanced over her shoulder and dropped Skandar's hands so she could take hold of Blade's reins. 'They're coming. You have to go, Skar. Don't give them an excuse to arrest you too.'

The first Silver Circle member was almost upon them now – Skandar recognised him as the fire instructor from the Eyrie, Eric Melville. He dismounted, his freckles igniting with tiny silver flames.

Flo's breath hitched as the rider cuffed her right wrist. 'Go, Skar!' she begged. 'Please, just keep safe. And if you ever need to make sense of things, go to the Secret Swappers.'

'The Secret—' Skandar tried to say, but Flo shook her head violently, as the second silver rider cuffed her other wrist.

'Go!'

It went against every instinct Skandar had to turn away from Flo at that moment. How could he leave her to be imprisoned in the Stronghold? How could he let the Silver Circle take her and break up the quartet they'd worked so hard to keep whole? How could he let her go? But as he left the arena – and was met by a frantic Mitchell, a confused Jamie, a ranting Bobby and a stricken Olu Shekoni – Skandar looked over his shoulder.

Flo had her head held high as the Silver Circle led her away,

– 210 –

# REGISTRATION

the precious metal in her Afro glinting defiantly in the December sun. And although Skandar was completely horrified at what she had done – at what it meant for her, for Blade, for their quartet . . . for him – he was also deeply proud. He wished he could go back and show this moment to that girl in the Hatchery, the one who'd been so terrified of her silver unicorn that she'd screamed loud enough for Skandar to leave his hatching cell.

He wished he could tell her that one day she would decide to enter herself into the Chaos Cup, and choose imprisonment over freedom, because she wanted to save them all.

CHAPTER FOURTEEN

# BATTLE LINES

As December moved into January, life on the Ambling Archipelago was nothing short of miserable. Skandar, Mitchell and Bobby missed Flo terribly. It took them a good fortnight to stop wondering where she was or turning to ask her a question. Each of them tried to deal with their sadness in different – and largely ineffective – ways. Bobby wrote multiple letters to her sister, wanting news of the Eyrie and accosted any visiting Wanderer, begging them to deliver the notes. Mitchell threw himself into researching the Skeleton Curse, sometimes hitching lifts into Fourpoint to spend the whole day at the libraries there – or even in the Vaults if Ruth allowed. But much of the time he would head to Cerulean for hours, desperate to connect with Red again. Other fire wielders started coming to him for advice about what to try with their wild unicorns next. His bravery with Red was whispered about reverently most evenings until the campfires had turned to cinders.

And Skandar – who'd taken Flo's absence worst of all – threw himself into beating Rex and protecting the Mainland,

## BATTLE LINES

into helping Mitchell research the curse, into anything that would dull the emptiness he felt. Every night he went to bed exhausted – yet when he still couldn't sleep, he flew. He and Scoundrel would fly for hours over the archipelago, trying to outpace the ever-growing tidal wave of sadness – Mum, then Kenna, now Flo – that could crash over him without warning. A couple of times, when he felt like he might break in two, Skandar had considered trying a Mender dream again. Once upon a time, his sister would have known exactly how to comfort him. But he couldn't bring himself to sit beside her, not really being able to talk. And the more he thought about being in the dream, the more he replayed the image of the Weaver's glowing body and Arctic Swansong hitting the ground.

Skandar and Bobby were forced to put their misery aside for training. Agatha simply didn't allow them to 'wallow' and constantly reminded them that Rex wanted to attack their Mainland home. When Elora visited the archipelago to help with predator training – staying with Agatha on Indigo – she had the same mindset. She said they must focus on qualifying, on their ultimate aim. But it wasn't always easy.

During weapons training in mid-January, Skandar accidentally ignited one of the bracelets Flo had made for Bobby. Bobby completely lost her temper, hurling three lightning-threaded javelins, two ice-frosted axes and four flaming daggers at Skandar's head before Agatha managed to get her to calm down.

'By the five elements, what has got into you, Bruna?' Agatha yelled furiously from her vantage platform.

'He burned my bracelet!' Bobby shouted angrily, as Skandar raised a spirit shield – its white light knitting together to protect him from the air wielder's next bombardment.

Agatha looked confused. 'It's a sky battle. These things tend to happen!'

– 213 –

# SKANDAR AND THE SKELETON CURSE

Skandar dropped his shield, realising what he'd done. 'I'm sorry!' He flew Scoundrel closer. 'I'm sorry, Bobby. I didn't mean to.'

Bobby's sparking mace fizzled out in her hand, as Scoundrel hovered level with Falcon. 'It's just – she's not here to fix it, you know?' Her breath whistled through her mouth, a panic attack taking hold.

'It's not for ever,' Skandar said, trying to convince himself too.

'It *feels* like for ever,' Bobby wheezed.

Agatha had no patience for any of this. 'You do realise that you've officially registered for the Qualifiers? This isn't the Training Trial – you're going up against some of the best riders on the Island. I'm doing my best to coach you – with no elemental yard, no fancy facilities and no proper racecourse. I suggest you stop wasting my time or we can just forget this. Because guess what? Sometimes *I* don't feel like training you either. Some days I wake up and doubt I'll be able to get through another day without Swan.' Her voice broke over the unicorn's name. She took a deep breath, steadying herself. 'I know you both miss your friend. But this is bigger than Flo being in the Stronghold or Swan being gone. This isn't just about us.'

'I'm sorry,' Skandar said immediately. With Agatha's strictness and sharp edges when training them, it was easy to forget how much she'd lost.

'I don't want an apology,' Agatha snapped. 'I just want one of you to win the Chaos Cup.'

One afternoon a couple of weeks later, after Bobby had just beaten Rickesh in yet another sky battle, the three riders landed on Navy. Bobby immediately went to the campfire in search of food. Skandar started to follow her, but—

'Can I talk to you?' Rickesh put a hand on Skandar's armoured

– 214 –

# BATTLE LINES

shoulder. Jamie had sent some new armour over with a team of Wanderers a few weeks before – so they could get used to it before the Qualifiers.

'What's up?' Skandar asked, joining Rickesh in pulling off his boots and sweaty socks so the waves could lap over their sore feet.

The water wielder ran a hand through his wave of hair to its frothy tips, worry in his voice. 'How are you and Mitchell getting on with researching the Skeleton Curse? It's almost February, Skandar. Almost—'

'The Water Festival,' Skandar realised. He'd been in such a frenzy of training, research and missing Flo that he'd lost track of how quickly the fire season was passing. And they still didn't have a clue what linked Elias and Federico, or why their unicorns had been sacrificed by Kenna. How could Skandar tell Rickesh that all his training for the Qualifiers could very well have been in vain? But he couldn't lie to him.

'We haven't found out much more,' Skandar answered, watching a navy wave darken the sand by his toes. 'But it's possible that Rex—'

Rickesh shook his head. 'I got my hands on yesterday's *Hatchery Herald*. Rex is still saying the same thing as he did after the Earth Festival. That his researchers are –' he made quote marks in the air – '*working round the clock to reverse what has happened to your unicorns.*' I don't think the Commodore has any idea how to stop Kenna attacking the water wielders. I mean, it's like he's not even trying to fight her.'

*Fight.* Skandar wasn't sure whether it was the hopelessness on the face of his old squadron leader or the memory of Flo holding her head high as the silvers led her away, or the horror of another unicorn dead – but quite suddenly he'd had enough. Flo was facing the two things she'd always feared – being locked

– 215 –

# SKANDAR AND THE SKELETON CURSE

in the Stronghold and riding in the Chaos Cup. But *he'd* been a coward. *He* had been hiding from the thing that scared him most – the one person he felt terrified to face.

'I think it's time I do something about my sister,' he said.

Skandar's plan started with writing letters. To the Pathfinder, to riders still in the Eyrie, to saddlers, to blacksmiths, to healers, to the bards, to Craig the bookseller, to anyone who might be able to convince riders to defend the water zone. It had evolved from that original nugget of an idea to hide all the water wielders – but it was now active, not passive. Riders would assemble on the Ambling Archipelago, then guard the water line to stop Kenna making the third sacrifice. This would *hopefully* break the cycle of the curse. They couldn't use official channels for the letters – Skandar was too wary of Rex interfering, and the last time they'd tried to communicate with Jamie that way, the letters had never arrived. But the Wanderers had networks that would make sure the letters found their way into friendly hands.

'Well, nobody's here yet,' Bobby huffed once they crawled into their tent that night.

'You are the most impatient person I've ever met.' Mitchell shook his head, trying to scrub ink from his hands. 'The Wanderers only left with the letters *three hours* ago!'

'But what *are* we going to do if nobody helps us guard the line?'

'We face Kenna on our own,' Skandar said, already under his blanket. Nobody coming to help them was his main worry too – would anyone want to follow a spirit wielder's plan? But it was the only idea he could see working. He was determined to make Kenna see reason, to warn her that her curse would ultimately make it easier for Rex to invade the Mainland. They were siblings, after all – if she was going to listen to anyone, it would be him.

# BATTLE LINES

Mitchell looked worried. 'But even I can't help you out there, not with Red the way she is. None of the earth or fire wielders can.'

'Rickesh and Tidal Warrior will help, and some of the Wanderers here like Jordan and Surfer's Demise.'

'The Wanderers won't use elemental magic in battle, though,' Mitchell protested, sitting up in agitation. 'You know they won't break their vow.'

'Chill, Mitchell, okay?' Bobby said, pushing him flat again. 'There's only one of her. We can do this.'

Mitchell didn't look convinced, and, honestly, Skandar wasn't either. On the Weaver's island last summer, Kenna's immense power had been unlike anything he'd ever seen. And now she'd managed to take down Marauding Magnet, as well as Sunset's Blood – one of the most successful Chaos unicorns in history.

As Skandar lay awake that night, he imagined Wanderers delivering letters in secret and willed the recipients to believe the honest words written there. The letters had been clear about Kenna's extraordinary magic, the danger they would face on the fault line, the risks they would be taking. Skandar had been truthful about being her brother, too, about how he thought that meant he could stop her – but only if he wasn't acting alone. *Please help us*, he'd begged the riders of the Island. And he fell asleep with those same words on his lips.

Two days later, it was as if Skandar's words had echoed through the Island's dreams. The population of the Ambling Archipelago had swelled to near unmanageable numbers. Sick of the Commodore's lack of interest in the Skeleton Curse and tired of sitting around waiting for their own time to come, many air and water wielders had jumped at the chance to guard the fault line on the day of the festival. Some riders were suspicious of Skandar at first, because he was both a spirit wielder and Kenna's brother. But with Pathfinder Elora to vouch for him,

– 217 –

not to mention Mitchell – whose own unicorn had been turned wild – they were persuaded that he was on their side.

As Mitchell had guessed, those riders who'd officially joined the Wanderers would not break their vow against using elemental magic for battle. Though, after the attack on the oasis last year, Skandar knew that they could cause a lot of disruption using the natural landscape. The rest of them – the nomads, the runaways, the rebels – agreed to guard the line from Kenna by fighting her off. But when a small group of Hatchlings arrived from the Eyrie offering their help, Elora, Agatha *and* Skandar had gently turned them down. Most of them accepted this without argument – perhaps even with relief – but there was one Hatchling in particular who was fury personified.

'I don't *care* if it's dangerous – it's up to me and Tsunami's Herald if we want to fight her! If you don't let us help, I'll hate you for ever!' Isa Bruna screamed at her sister on Sapphire's beach. Mitchell and Skandar had retreated to the tent; the fire wielder had his hands over his ears. Skandar kept an eye on the sisters through the canvas flap, worried they might come to blows. For the millionth time, he wished for Flo – she always knew what to say to Bobby about Isa.

'I am completely fine with you hating me for ever if it keeps you alive,' Bobby retorted.

'It's my life! If I want to risk it, that's up to me!'

'No, it is not!' Bobby roared, unable to keep her temper.

'WHAT DO YOU CARE?' Isa screeched back, and even her perfectly neat plaits looked frayed.

'I LOVE YOU, YOU STUPID IDIOT!' Bobby shouted so loudly that Falcon looked up in alarm from where she'd settled on the sand next to Herald. Both unicorns were keeping out of it.

'GAAAAHHHH!' Isa threw herself down and sat moodily on the sand.

# BATTLE LINES

Bobby did the same and reached for her sister's hands. She took a deep breath. 'I know you want to help. I'm really grateful that you do, but please,' she begged, as their fingers entwined, 'stay here for me, okay?'

Skandar found himself needing to turn away. The sight of the two siblings by the water reminded him too much of a Skandar and Kenna that no longer existed, the ones who'd sat on Margate beach – or outside the door of Flat 207 – trying to cheer each other up.

*Kenna*. Would he be able to convince her? Stop her?

'Please, Isa?'

Skandar thought he'd heard Bobby say 'please' more times in this conversation than in the entire time he'd known her.

'All right, hermana.' Isa sighed and then dumped a load of sand over Bobby's head.

Mitchell removed his hands from his ears. 'Skandar?' he said quietly.

'Mmm?' Skandar was watching Bobby attempting to drag Isa into the sapphire waves by her ankle.

'Will you come to Cerulean with me?'

'Now?' Skandar turned from the sisters. He hadn't been to Cerulean since they'd arrived on the archipelago.

'I want to show you something.' There was a note in Mitchell's voice that stopped Skandar from asking about the Bruna sisters coming too.

Mitchell didn't say much as he rowed the wooden boat across to Cerulean. Skandar had offered to help, but the fire wielder had brushed him off. 'I'm used to it.' And the muscles in Mitchell's arms had indeed grown bigger, his chest broader.

Eventually, when the two friends were standing on the beach of the outer island, the stars the only punctures in the absolute darkness, Skandar had to say something. 'Isn't this a bit

– 219 –

# SKANDAR AND THE SKELETON CURSE

dangerous in the dark? The wild unicorns . . .'

'Shhh,' Mitchell warned. 'She's coming. Stay back. Watch.'

And, sure enough, Red Night's Delight was walking along the beach towards Mitchell, the starlight illuminating the bones of her newly skeletal form. Dread filled Skandar's chest. She looked wilder than ever, the weight of immortality bearing down on her decaying body.

'Shouldn't we move? She's coming right for us!'

But Mitchell was moving *towards* Red. Skandar watched as boy and unicorn faced each other, and – very gently – Red nudged her rotting nose against Mitchell's permanently wounded shoulder as though saying sorry for injuring it all those weeks ago.

'It's okay,' Mitchell whispered to her, though he didn't reach out to touch her blood-red neck. 'Goodnight, Red. I'll see you tomorrow.'

And, as if that was what she'd been waiting for, Red turned from Mitchell and made her way back along the beach.

'She seems so calm around you,' Skandar said, amazed.

'I've been coming here a lot.' Mitchell shrugged. 'It's not a big deal but I think she notices. And I think it's helped that I've tried to stop thinking of her as wild and just think of her as *Red* again – my unicorn who loves getting dirty and being silly *and* getting into trouble.' Mitchell's hair flared, lighting up his face. 'I was looking at her like a monster and, well, I think she knew that.' He glanced shyly at Skandar. 'I wanted to show you first – I thought you'd understand.'

Skandar did. He had experienced first-hand the complex natures of wild unicorns, as well as the dark and light of the spirit element. When he'd first met Mitchell, it had felt impossible that Ira Henderson's son would ever feel comfortable in those grey areas that didn't fit within the Island's mould. Yet here he was.

Fierce pride bubbled out of Skandar. 'I think it's more than

– 220 –

# BATTLE LINES

just you thinking of Red differently. After she turned wild, you were brave enough to hope. You've never given up on her – I'm sure she knows. They're cleverer than us, after all.'

Mitchell frowned as he watched Red walk away. 'You know, sometimes I wish I could talk to your sister.'

Skandar frowned. 'Why?'

'I'm operating on instinct with Red, but Kenna has experience, doesn't she? With Goshawk. I'm afraid to try to touch Red in case she really hurts me. I know that if I could learn her signals, how a wild unicorn really thinks . . .' Mitchell tailed off. 'But of course it isn't possible.'

Skandar swallowed. 'I'm sorry. For all of this. Everything is so messed up.'

Mitchell attempted a smile that was more of a grimace. 'We've got a plan. Stop the water sacrifice to break the curse. We've got to believe it's going to work.'

And as though she could sense they both needed cheering up, Red let out an almighty fart that echoed across the beach, igniting her rotting back hoof for good measure. The explosion lit up the dark shore.

The boys burst out laughing – part relief, part joy, part disgust. And Skandar wished Scoundrel had been there to see his best friend galloping off through the fart light. There was something hopeful in it.

On the eve of the Water Festival, Scoundrel's Luck stood on the fault line that carved the water zone in two. The moonlight illuminated Elora and Silver Soldier further down, then the distinctive silhouette of Rickesh astride Tidal Warrior just the other side of a river tributary. Marissa and Demonic Nymph were nearby too – they'd been declared nomads after the Chaos Trials and arrived from Fourpoint just last night. A little further

– 221 –

up Skandar could see the outline of Falcon's perfectly plaited mane, then Zac and Yesterday's Ghost – who'd joined them from the Eyrie – and Niamh and Snow Swimmer, who'd been with the Wanderers since the revolt against Rex's rules.

More riders had come than Skandar ever expected. Under the light of the stars, a rider and unicorn stood every few metres, waiting for the attack that would surely come once the first of February arrived. He felt immense gratitude and pride. They were from all four zones, from the Wilderness, and even from the Eyrie – knowing full well that Rex would not let them back in.

The hours of darkness bled into each other until there was a faint glow in the sky – the promise of dawn. Skandar was aware that they could be waiting the entire day for Kenna to arrive, but adrenaline still filled his veins when he glimpsed the sun beginning to rise. Elora glanced sideways at him, perhaps sensing the sudden anticipation along the line of riders. She nodded, her white bob shining. Skandar nodded back, feeling like he might be sick.

Every guarding rider had been given a tiny whistle that let out a shrill alert call. If anyone set eyes on Kenna, the whistles would summon the other riders. At Skandar's insistence, every single rider had agreed that Kenna was to be captured not killed. He'd told them they needed her alive so they could get her to reverse the Skeleton Curse. Only Bobby and Mitchell knew this was a lie. Skandar wanted Kenna stopped. But he also wanted her safe.

By the middle of the afternoon, the unicorns began to fidget along the line, pawing the ground or setting off elemental blasts like they were in a Hatchling training session. Bobby started singing a medley of songs that made the Mainlanders join in and the Islanders ask questions about the unfamiliar lyrics like – 'What's a submarine? Why do we have to choose between being

– 222 –

## BATTLE LINES

humans or dancers? Why aren't they ever getting back together?' Eventually they were shushed by Elora who was worried about the sound of whistles being drowned out by their giggling. Skandar couldn't join in no matter how glad he was that Bobby was keeping up morale. Scoundrel too remained perfectly still, the bond full of his focus. Perhaps he sensed that if this went well, he might get his fiery best friend back.

At five o'clock in the afternoon, the first whistle sounded.

Heart hammering, Skandar grabbed Scoundrel's reins and started up the line, Bobby and Falcon thundering ahead of them.

Then there was a second whistle – from the opposite direction. Silver Soldier charged after it, Elora's face grim with determination.

The same happened with the third and fourth whistles.

Bobby pulled Falcon up. 'I'll take this lot down towards Fourpoint,' she shouted to Skandar, as more riders hesitated in confusion. 'You go towards the Wilderness.'

'Got it,' Skandar called, waving to Zac and Niamh to come with him.

'Be careful, spirit boy,' Bobby warned, and then she launched Falcon along the line, raising a shield in a spray of sparks.

The shrill sound of the whistles was now constant and seemed to be coming from all directions. Skandar, Zac and Niamh had only galloped a few paces before they realised their plan had been doomed to fail.

Kenna had not come to the fault line alone.

At least twenty riders in black shrouds were attacking Skandar's fighters and they were all riding wild unicorns. Skandar didn't have time to dwell on how sick the reappearance of the black shrouds made him feel or the questions that burst into his mind – who were these people? how were they riding wild unicorns? – because all across the water zone, elemental

– 223 –

## SKANDAR AND THE SKELETON CURSE

blasts exploded into the darkening sky, their putrid stench filling the air. Skandar looked frantically for Kenna, horribly aware that she could be anywhere, carrying out the sacrifice they were trying to—

Scoundrel roared in warning as a wild unicorn with a shrouded rider galloped right for them. Its skeletal jaw opened in a bone-chilling bellow, blood dripping from broken teeth. The rider's palm glowed red, and Skandar froze – feeling sure this had to be Kenna if they were wielding elemental magic. He raised a water shield just as the unicorn set off an elemental blast, and the rider's fireball missed Skandar's armoured shoulder by inches.

Skandar's eyes watered as acrid smoke billowed around him. Somehow, he managed to summon his favourite spirit sabre into his palm and raise it over his head for an attack. But the rider was suddenly having a problem controlling their unicorn. And as the wild unicorn reared, the shroud fell back.

'Albert?'

There was no answer. Eagle's Dawn was already careering away up the fault line, and Skandar let Scoundrel chase after her. Skandar knew that Albert had been close with Kenna when she'd lived with the Wanderers. Perhaps Albert and Eagle's Dawn would lead him to her.

Skandar's own fighters shouted out to him as Scoundrel passed by and he caught snippets of their words.

'Skandar, they're with Kenna!'

'They're fighting *for* her!'

'Have you seen her?'

'Their unicorns are wild!'

'I *know* some of them!'

Fighting his way up the fault line, trying not to lose sight of Eagle's white tail, Skandar realised that he recognised a lot of Kenna's other fighters too. There was a flash of Adela's smoking

– 224 –

# BATTLE LINES

ringlets as a wild Smoke-Eyed Saviour attacked Niamh and Snow Swimmer. Earth-allied Mateo and Hell's Diamond were hurtling towards Silver Soldier, Elora manipulating the nearest water source to try to protect herself. And, most shocking of all, a Chaos rider Skandar had first watched on TV back in Margate – Hilary Winters – on a wild Sharp-Edged Lily.

*BOOM.*

The almighty sound was accompanied by a blinding flash of blue light as the entire fault line lit up. It was the Walk magnified by a thousand – tidal waves rose up from the crack in the earth and crashed over the battling unicorns; riptides dragged fallen riders towards the bright blue light of the line; parts of the ground froze over unicorns' hooves and caught them in its icy grip. Like many of the unicorns, Scoundrel panicked – hurling himself sideways, half taking off in an attempt to get away from the active fault line. Everything happened so fast that, despite Skandar's trusty Shekoni saddle, he flew from Scoundrel's back and hit the ground only to be soaked by a crashing wave.

Thankfully Scoundrel's fierce protectiveness of Skandar overrode his fear. He trotted to his rider on the ground, sniffing his soaked brown hair. Skandar managed to struggle to his feet – ignoring a searing pain in his shoulder – and remounted Scoundrel.

Back in the saddle, Skandar saw that the elemental activity had calmed. The shrouded riders were galloping off towards the Wilderness, while Skandar's fighters were scattered across the water-logged zone. Some had remounted like him, but others—

*No.*

The water unicorns had collapsed on to the sodden ground. They looked almost like toys abandoned mid-game. Skandar spotted Rickesh nearby, his wave-mutated head in his hands, rocking feverishly by Tidal Warrior's side. Niamh was

– 225 –

## SKANDAR AND THE SKELETON CURSE

desperately trying to rouse Snow Swimmer, whose white mane was bedraggled and tangled. Marissa was screaming Demonic Nymph's name over and over.

But Skandar knew what was going to happen next. And if it was anything like the Earth Festival, the riders had only seconds. 'MOVE!' he yelled. 'I'm so sorry, but they're going to wake up wild! You need to MOVE!'

A few water wielders turned to look up at Skandar, though none moved away. The air-allied fighters began to zigzag between the motionless unicorns, calling at their riders to get out of the way. Some let themselves be lifted up on to air unicorns' backs; others point-blank refused.

Then the water unicorns began to rise from the ground. And the sight of them – their transparent horns, their rotting skin, their red eyes – was no less shocking than it had been the first time.

Rickesh's shout of alarm punctured the air. Tidal Warrior had risen and was snarling at her rider with bared yellowing teeth. Scoundrel was there in seconds, and Rickesh reached for Skandar's hanging hand so he could pull himself up on to the spirit unicorn's back.

They galloped a safe distance away, the old squadron leader of the Grins sitting limp and defeated behind Skandar. A flash of the spirit element in Skandar's palm told him Rickesh and Warrior's bond was empty. Skandar felt a surge of guilt. He'd failed. Failed to protect them all from Kenna.

'I don't understand,' Rickesh kept murmuring. 'There were so many of them. Why have they joined her?'

But Skandar thought he knew. As soon as he'd seen Albert on a wild Eagle's Dawn, he'd remembered something Sara Shekoni had said: *Perhaps she just wants to be understood.* Was that what the riders who'd joined Kenna wanted, too? Their unicorns had been turned wild; their Commodore had abandoned them; the

– 226 –

## BATTLE LINES

Eyrie had thrown them out; the Island had shunned them. And nobody understood that better than Kenna, even if she was also the one responsible for their misery.

'Skandar!' Elora was waving frantically at him further up the fault line. 'Skandar, it's Bobby!'

Pure fear shot through Skandar's entire body. He seized Scoundrel's reins, urging him towards the Pathfinder. *Not Bobby. Please.* Had she been hit by wild unicorn magic? Had Kenna . . .?

Skandar saw the blue glow first – a different colour, but otherwise identical to the magic he'd witnessed at the earth and fire sacrifice sites. Ignoring Elora, he threw himself from Scoundrel's back, leaving Rickesh calling after him.

*Bobby isn't a water wielder,* he repeated over and over to himself as he approached the fault line. *Bobby and Falcon can't be the sacrifice – she's air-allied. She isn't—*

Then he saw the bodies. Two – just beyond the blue glow of the line, as though someone had dragged them away from it. They were clearly riders, both dressed in black clothes and elemental jackets.

Skandar looked down at the face of Bobby Bruna. Her olive skin was pale, her wet fringe plastered to her forehead, her eyes glazed. Skandar fell to his knees, tears already streaming down his face.

*Not Bobby. Please, not Bobby.*

Random memories of her came unbidden to his mind. The first time they'd met, when she'd told him she'd throw him over the Mirror Cliffs if he ever called her Roberta. Inside the Hatchery, saying, 'I don't like popular people, they're overrated.' Saving him and Mitchell from the wild unicorns even after she'd 'branched out' with other friends. The emergency sandwich with added Jelly Babies she'd made for his birthday last year. Skating to the music at the Well Dance. *Spirit boy,* she called him – would

– 227 –

# SKANDAR AND THE SKELETON CURSE

he never hear her say that again?

'Skandar, it's all right,' Elora said, placing a light hand on his back. 'Look.' And Skandar realised she was holding the reins of a unicorn – a unicorn with a perfectly plaited yet extremely damp mane. Falcon's Wrath.

Skandar's heart thundered with hope. 'But if Falcon's okay, that means—'

'Bobby's alive,' Elora confirmed, yet her amethyst eyes were very troubled and her explanation was disjointed and hard to follow. 'But she'll need the Fourpoint healers – the magic on the line trapped them both before Bobby managed to drag them off it. I tried to stop her, but she wouldn't listen. It was one of the bravest things I've ever seen.'

Skandar nodded shakily. As a general rule, it was impossible to stop Bobby doing what she wanted. Even if it was going to almost kill her. 'So who—'

Skandar finally looked down at the second rider, the rise and fall of her chest the only sign that she was alive. Because – just like Elias and Federico – she was more corpse than girl, more bone than flesh, more dead than alive. A living skeleton.

At that moment, Bobby startled them all by rolling on to her side and coughing up a lungful of water.

'Bobby!' Skandar crawled towards her. 'Are you—'

But she ignored him, instead dragging her soaked frame over to the girl lying next to her and sobbed. 'Isa, please. Wake up.'

Skandar hadn't worked it out from the girl's skeletal face. He hadn't made the connection, because Isa wasn't supposed to be fighting with them. Horror filled him as he looked more closely at the bright blue glow of the line, bracing himself for the sight of Tsunami's Herald within it.

But Isabel Bruna's unicorn wasn't there.

### Kenna

# BORN TO LEAD

Kenna Everhart had failed her mother.

She didn't know if her fellow Originals had seen the tears streaming down her face out on the fault line. Didn't know if they'd heard her sobs as the group had ridden back to the Wilderness. She didn't care. She locked herself in her room at the Scrapyard Treehouse and tore Erika Everhart's portrait from the wall in shame. Then she let Goshawk's true nature fill her heart, her head, and pummelled furious magic into the room. She surrounded herself with columns of fire, covered the walls in sheets of ice, shot lightning bolts at the ceiling, and fired sharp flints at the metal, watching the tiny dents spread like a disease. Anything, *anything* to keep her own thoughts from her head, the flashes of images from the fault line—

The fear on Isabel Bruna's face as Kenna and Goshawk had attacked.

The way she had thrown herself from Herald and shielded the powerful predator with her fragile mortal body.

*No. Stop thinking about it.*

# SKANDAR AND THE SKELETON CURSE

The roar from Bobby's throat like a rumble of thunder as she'd seen her sister in danger. A sound like Kenna had made when she'd first confronted Skandar's bullies.

*No. Stop. Don't think—*

Kenna had taken Falcon and Herald down first, immobilised them with a pulse of her dark-edged magic. But even then, Bobby hadn't stopped. Half-conscious and dragging the leg she'd injured when she was thrown from Falcon's back, she'd crawled across the water-logged ground and shoved her trembling sister behind her. 'You want Isa?' Bobby had rasped out. 'You'll have to kill me first.'

*Don't think about it. Please.*

There was a surge of power from Goshawk: a lick of anger edged with vengeance. Bigger rocks exploded against the wall, the protests of the metal ringing out. The portrait of the Everhart sisters burned in a ball of flame. Electricity danced in Kenna's palm, preparing to explode the whole treehouse if she could only make the memories stop—

'Kenna! Let me in! You're going to hurt yourself!' Albert's voice floated through the fog of emotions and magic, but the images from the fault line were too strong for anything else.

With the sisters unconscious, Kenna had thrust the water-carved piece of the bone staff into the fault line and summoned the spirit element to her palm. She had drained Isabel and Herald's bond: watching the blue magic snaking round the bone – decorating it – before seeping into the ground, the water rising up from the earth as though to claim it. She had watched the water unicorns fall to the ground, watched Isabel's body twitch as she became more skeleton than skin.

But as she'd prepared for the part of the ritual that belonged only to her – directing her white glowing palm towards Herald to break the bond with her rider entirely and snuff out the unicorn's

– 230 –

# BORN TO LEAD

life – Bobby had whispered, her eyes still shut, 'Please don't take this from her. Herald was all she ever wanted.' And then the air wielder had passed out again as though Kenna had imagined it.

Kenna didn't know if it was the familiarity of those words, so similar to the ones she'd screamed at Skandar the night he'd left for the Island – *I've always wanted this* – or the way Bobby had somehow raised herself from unconsciousness to speak for her sibling. But for the first time since Erika had died, Kenna hadn't felt rage at the world; no, she'd felt anger at her mum for leaving her this bloody inheritance. She'd closed her fingers over her shining palm and relief had blazed through her chest. Then – once the last drop of magic had drained from Isabel and Herald's bond – she'd left the unicorn alive and fled.

Back in the Scrapyard Treehouse, Kenna roared again and icicles snaked up her arms, soothing the magma pulsing on one, freezing the thorns of the other.

*Coward. What have I done?*

The door of the room burst open, and Kenna prepared to strike.

It was Albert, breathing hard, blond ponytail tangled. His blue eyes scanned her, looking for damage, and then widened as he took in the destruction she'd inflicted on the room.

'Get out,' Kenna warned, her voice a bite.

Albert met her hollow gaze and raised his shoulders. 'No.'

'It's not safe for you to be in here right now.'

Albert shrugged again. 'I don't care. I'm not leaving you in this state.' And he sat down on the wet metal floor, tracing the flames the Wanderers had inked around his Hatchery wound, and waited.

Something in Kenna's chest eased a fraction at the sight of him sitting there stubbornly, the melted ice soaking into his trousers. She kneeled next to him in the pool of water. They sat

– 231 –

in silence for a while until he said, 'You didn't kill the water unicorn.' It wasn't a question.

'No.'

Albert turned to look at her, but Kenna stared straight ahead. 'Why not? You killed the first two, right?'

'I don't want to talk about it.'

Albert took her hand, still trying to meet her eye. 'The others are asking whether it means the Skeleton Curse won't work past the summer solstice.'

'It'll still work,' Kenna said, voice monotone. 'I used the bone staff, I drained the bond, all the water unicorns are wild. It's fine.'

Albert shifted to sit right in front of her, the glow of his knuckles bright in the dark room. 'So the curse works without you killing the target unicorn?'

'Yes.'

He hesitated, and she knew what he was grappling with.

'Killing the unicorns is for something else,' she answered, before he could ask the question. 'For me.'

She wasn't sure then whether he looked afraid *of* her or *for* her, though he didn't drop her hand.

'It's so I can survive the forged bond. So it doesn't kill me.'

Albert looked confused. 'But the Weaver was much older than you when her forged bond started to weaken her, and it didn't actually kill her in the end, did it? I thought you said her sister, Agatha—'

Kenna shook her head jerkily. She hadn't told anyone this, but she was so scared, so tired, so lonely. 'The forged bond is different for me. Erika Everhart's forged bond came *after* her destined bond – for a long time they balanced each other out but I-I've never had a destined bond to slow the effects of the forged one, so . . .'

– 232 –

# BORN TO LEAD

'So it's killing you faster?' Albert's voice was so quiet it was hardly a whisper.

The truth then, at last. Kenna had told someone the secret that weighed on her heavier than all the others.

'How long do you have?'

'I don't know,' Kenna admitted.

'How could the Weaver do this to you? Did she know when she forged it?' Albert demanded.

Kenna immediately jumped to her mum's defence. 'Erika always had a plan. *This* plan. When I kill a bonded unicorn, I take something from it at the point the bond breaks. The curse gives me the opportunity to get what I need. It helps me survive.'

'Then why didn't you kill Tsunami's Herald?' Albert asked, and Kenna was appalled for a moment by how much he'd changed for her. By how much he was willing to forgive. She wondered whether deep down the good boy was still in there – the one who loved his brother and dreamed of chocolate. She hoped he was, because Kenna wasn't sure what *she* was deep down any more – she was too afraid to look.

'I c-couldn't do it,' Kenna stumbled over the word. 'Bobby was there, and they're sisters, and I couldn't take the unicorn away from Isabel. And now I don't know, Albert! I don't know whether I can save myself. Erika told me the unicorn killings were supposed to happen at the same time as the Skeleton Curse and in the same order. And there's nobody to ask, nobody to help me. I wasn't able to save Erika, and now I don't even know if I can save myself.'

Before her tears even began, Albert had taken Kenna in his arms.

'I won't let Goshawk kill you. I won't.' He said the words over and over, and even though they both knew he could do nothing to stop an immortal wild unicorn, Kenna let the rumble of his

## SKANDAR AND THE SKELETON CURSE

voice against her skeletal cheek soothe her.

They stayed like that, talking in whispers, spilling secrets, and both agreed that Kenna must kill the next two unicorns. Perhaps then she would be safe, Albert said in that optimistic way of his. Perhaps then she'd have taken what she needed to survive the forged bond. And the more Albert talked, the more Kenna was desperate to believe him.

'Spirit links all the elements,' she said, wiping the tears from her cheeks. 'If I kill the air and spirit unicorns, surely missing water won't matter? Surely four unicorns is enough?'

Albert smiled at her. 'Exactly.'

When they finally stood up, Kenna saw concern cross his face. 'What is it?'

Albert hesitated as though unsure whether she could take it. 'Albert . . .'

'It's the other Originals.' The words burst out of him. 'They saw how upset you were in the water zone. They know you didn't kill Tsunami's Herald. They're worried. They need reassurance from you as their leader. You need to show them the staff. I'm worried they'll leave us, otherwise.'

'Then gather them,' Kenna said, her voice steadier now.

And relief washed over Albert's face.

The following morning, Kenna Everhart appeared like a queen on the platform of the treehouse, its fractured form rising behind her like a monstrous palace. Albert, her second in command, joined her at the rusted rail, his face an unreadable mask. He was the only other person she trusted with the secret of the unicorn murders. The terrible truth of her forged bond. The only one allowed to stand at her side.

There were three others behind Kenna up on the platform – and, along with Albert, they made up her generals. The first was

– 234 –

# BORN TO LEAD

outspoken Adela, rider of Smoke-Eyed Saviour – a fire wielder and former member of Skandar's beloved Peregrine Society. The second was Mateo – an earth wielder whose unicorn was Hell's Diamond. He'd already been declared a nomad by the time the Skeleton Curse had hit and was a quick, quiet learner. The final general was Finneas – an air wielder who'd been a coach at the air yard. When he'd joined the other Originals, he'd caused quite the stir. His unicorn – Vulture's Voltage – was not yet wild, so many of the other riders had mistrusted him. But all Finneas said was that Vulture's time to be wild would come, and since then he'd proved his loyalty to the new Island they were building over and over again.

The generals had been briefed earlier that morning so none of them stared at the partial bone staff Kenna held. She'd now fused three pieces together, their elemental veins snaking across the bone from green vines at the base to smouldering fire and the eerie flow of a thin river. The change happened when Kenna used each bone to help her siphon the magic from the draining bonds, as though the staff was soaking it up. As though its original purpose – the way it had restored elemental balance back on the Divide – had been warped. Reversed. It felt right to rebuild it piece by piece, sacrifice by sacrifice.

Kenna's generals smiled as their jubilant leader addressed the crowd gathered below the platform. She had learned very young how to pretend everything was okay – to teachers, to social workers, to concerned neighbours – even when Dad was falling apart. 'The water unicorns are wild! The next stage of the Skeleton Curse is complete, and the future we have dreamed for the Island remains secure.'

A couple of people cheered, but others murmured uncertainly. Hilary Winters – the former Chaos rider – shouted up to Kenna, 'But the girl's unicorn lives. Surely that means—'

– 235 –

# SKANDAR AND THE SKELETON CURSE

'Are you questioning me?' Kenna's voice was like a whip. She cast her eyes across the crowd below.

A pulse of expectant, fearful silence.

'So everything is going according to plan then?' A boy called Fawwaz called up bravely.

'It is,' Kenna confirmed. 'But this is an important moment for us all to remind ourselves what we're fighting for. Why we call ourselves Originals.'

Kenna raised the partially rebuilt bone staff so her Originals could see it over the platform. 'I am the wind of change. The First Rider entrusted me with this task and gifted me the pieces of his broken staff so that I may rebuild it. So that I may rebuild this Island that has become rotten to its roots.'

She heard their gasps, saw their hands pointing at the staff, the reverence in their lowered voices.

'Know this,' Kenna almost whispered, making them co-conspirators, 'Rex Manning is a poison. That's why many of you have joined me, isn't it?'

There were nods, some louder murmurs from the riders who'd fled the Eyrie.

'But Rex is only part of the disease that has been allowed to spread on this Island. The First Rider who wielded this staff was allied to all five elements – like I am, like Albert is becoming, like I hope all of you will be when you reconnect with your unicorns.'

There were excited whispers at this – at their own magic being compared to that of the First Rider.

'By joining me, you are walking in his footsteps. By assisting me with the Skeleton Curse you are founding your own future. You are helping to reset this Island. To start again. We will be the new generation of first riders, rediscovering the life he wanted us to live. The Island he wanted us to care for. The magic he wanted

– 236 –

# BORN TO LEAD

us to wield. And in so doing, our power will be unmatched, even by the likes of a silver Commodore. And we will triumph!'

There were cheers then and fists punching the air. Kenna could have sworn she felt the tension leave Albert's shoulders as he stood beside her, and she wondered how close they'd come to a mutiny.

Kenna held a hand up for silence. Hopeful eyes gazed up at her like they'd suddenly remembered who she was. Their leader. Their saviour. The second coming of the First Rider.

'There are many who don't yet know about our cause. Others who may be willing to join us. Quietly, carefully, I want you to spread the word to those you trust.'

Their chorus of enthusiasm rang out through the spindly copse.

But there was a question – from Hilary again, though her voice was full of hope rather than scepticism now. 'Where are we going to put new recruits? One semi-waterproof treehouse and a few tents isn't going to be enough. Where will we all live? Where will we train in all five elements once we can wield them?'

And an idea entered Kenna's mind. An idea so outlandish, so impossible that she was immediately obsessed with it. It was an idea Erika Everhart would have adored. An idea that was chaos itself.

'How about the Eyrie?'

And the cheer that answered her echoed endlessly across the Wilderness.

CHAPTER FIFTEEN

# THE QUALIFIERS

After the Water Festival, the Island was in turmoil. Word had spread about Kenna's supporters, and people were becoming mistrustful and even fearful of each other, especially those with cursed unicorns. Rumours about an evacuation of the Island were rife. However, the *Hatchery Herald* was unyielding in its support for Rex Manning and damning in its judgement of the original Wild Rider, Kenna Smith. It declared that her capture by the Commodore was imminent, though clearly no progress was being made since it reported it every other day.

The newspaper had also started to refer to Kenna as 'the Wild Rider from the Mainland' and in the weeks that followed, Mitchell's mum wrote to him about attacks on Mainlander-led businesses. The *Herald* published lists of missing Mainlander riders, implying they had joined Kenna. Gabriel's and Zac's names were published, even though Skandar knew air-allied Zac had joined the Wanderers and poor earth-allied Gabriel was still living in a tent beside the Glowing Caves.

Many people assumed that the Qualifiers would be cancelled

## THE QUALIFIERS

now three of the elements had been affected by the Skeleton Curse. But Rex did nothing. This didn't surprise Skandar. Having fewer riders in the Cup suited Rex, as every single member of the Silver Circle had entered. If anything, the Skeleton Curse was making everything easier for him.

But the quartet were throwing everything into making life *harder* for him. Once Bobby's leg had recovered after her fall, she and Skandar started training more intensely than ever for the Qualifiers. Flo was doing the same inside the Silver Stronghold – Skandar was sure of it – and although they hadn't heard from her, they hoped that when they did, she might be able to give them more information about Rex's plans for the Mainland.

Alongside their training, Bobby searched for the newly wild Tsunami's Herald. Eventually she found the young unicorn terrorising the undine living in the Lake of Shoals. With a reckless determination only Bobby Bruna could muster, she managed to half herd, half chase Isa's unicorn all the way to the archipelago.

'You'd think Herald would be grateful,' Bobby complained in their tent that night. 'But no – the little idiot tried to blast me and Falcon to pieces.'

'What did you expect?' Mitchell said. 'She *is* a wild unicorn.'

Bobby scowled at him from under her fringe. 'Well, now you and Red can babysit her.'

'I bet you can't wait to tell Isa you've found her,' Skandar said, attempting to head off an argument.

Softness warmed Bobby's flinty eyes. 'I'll go to Fourpoint first thing tomorrow and see if she's awake.' Isa was so frail she could barely open her eyes most days, and although Herald wasn't dead, their bond was still drained. Bobby said that sometimes it was easier for Isa to sleep and forget.

'Why did Kenna leave Tsunami's Herald alive, though?' Mitchell mused.

– 239 –

# SKANDAR AND THE SKELETON CURSE

They'd been having the same conversation all the way through February.

'Because I asked her to – remember?' Bobby murmured sleepily. 'I can be very persuasive.'

'But that doesn't make sense!' Mitchell hated mysteries he couldn't solve. 'Kenna killed Marauding Magnet on the Earth Festival, then Sunset's Blood on the Fire Festival – surely killing the unicorns is part of the curse?'

'The water unicorns are definitely all wild – same as before,' Bobby pointed out, and Skandar felt a tug at his heart for Rickesh and Tidal Warrior – all the training they'd put in, now useless. 'Maybe Kenna doesn't have to kill the sacrifice for it to work?'

Skandar kept quiet, like he had every other time they'd reached this point in the conversation. He was thankful beyond belief that Isa's unicorn was still alive, but what about Magnet and Sunset? On her visits to Isa, Bobby had overheard the healers talking about how broken Elias and Federico were, how they mourned their unicorns through wasted throats. And the idea that Kenna had *chosen* to make those two riders suffer, when she could have left their unicorns alive, haunted Skandar.

The night before the Qualifiers – towards the end of March – Skandar, Mitchell and Bobby were sitting around Isa's hammock in a Healer Hut along one of Fourpoint's quieter streets. Unlike other treehouses, healer huts were round, with roofs of cone-shaped thatch. There was a respectful hush here that was missing from the livelier parts of the capital. The Bruna sisters, however, were not respecting that hush.

'I want to watch you race,' Isa was insisting. The words rattled in her throat as the sinewy muscles in her larynx visibly spasmed. Bobby had come to visit Isa regularly over the last few weeks, but this was the boys' first time. Skandar could tell Mitchell was trying very hard not to look horrified at the

– 240 –

# THE QUALIFIERS

skeletal girl lying in her hammock – he kept swallowing and checking the scribbled notes on his lap.

'The healers are never going to let you out for the Qualifiers,' Bobby said firmly. 'I've asked them already.'

'We'll come straight back here and tell you the results, Isa,' Skandar promised, having been prepped for this argument by Bobby. Isa might be a skeleton, but she was still very demanding.

'Since when did you all get so old and boring?' Isa muttered, though it came out mostly as a hiss.

'I shield you with my own precious body, find your grouchy unicorn in the Wilderness, fly miles to visit you every time I can – some gratitude, hermana, wouldn't go amiss,' Bobby ranted, though it was good-natured.

'You know I'd do the same for you,' Isa said, and her large bright eyes were solemn. Then: 'Can you replait my hair?'

Bobby pretended to grumble but was gentle as she weaved Isa's hair strands together, being careful not to pull them from her rotting scalp. By the time she had finished, her sister had fallen asleep.

Bobby let out an enormous sigh. 'She turns fourteen in April. Fourteen but looks four hundred. I know all that matters is that she's alive, and that Herald is alive, but if we can't stop the curse, Isa's going to be stuck like this . . . for ever.'

Skandar kept opening his mouth to say something reassuring, but what could he say? His own sister had done this. Bobby didn't blame *him* – at least it didn't seem like she did – but it was there, hanging in the air between them.

He changed the subject to something he'd been obsessing over since the Water Festival. 'I still don't understand how Albert was wielding elemental magic. Did Kenna somehow fix his bond?' The idea made Skandar feel guilty, like he should be trying harder to help the others.

– 241 –

# SKANDAR AND THE SKELETON CURSE

'Never would have put Albert down for a traitor,' Bobby said when she looked up from Isa's face. 'It's always the quiet ones you have to worry about.'

'But could Kenna be a Mender, like me?' Skandar wondered, not for the first time. 'We don't know the limit of her powers – especially when it comes to the spirit element.'

'When she took me down,' Bobby said seriously, 'she was using magic I didn't recognise, something I couldn't fight. She must have done the same with the others – Federico was a Chaos rider, for lightning's sake. We can't rule out anything when it comes to her.'

Mitchell, who had been examining the towering pile of notes on his lap, finally spoke. '*When* did you say Isa's birthday is?'

'Mitchell, we've moved on from that now,' Bobby said irritably. 'Keep up!'

'Roberta,' Mitchell insisted, 'I need to know when your sister was born. Now!' Skandar's heart spluttered in his chest – that was Mitchell's *I'm having a breakthrough* voice.

'April,' Bobby snapped, then her mouth twitched. 'Same month as me, but I always used to tease her because she was born on the first – April Fools' Day on the Mainland. Like her being born was some sort of practical joke.'

'I don't know what a *Fools' Day* is,' Mitchell said dismissively. 'But that means Isabel was born in the water season.'

'Is that important?' Skandar asked, trying to understand.

'Yes! It's vital! Flaming fireballs, at last!' Mitchell rifled feverishly through his notes and pulled out a crumpled page in Bobby's handwriting. He adjusted his glasses, scanning it quickly and then waving it triumphantly at her. 'Double elementals!'

Skandar thought he'd heard the term before, but he knew that with Mitchell it was best to wait for an explanation. Bobby had an impatient hand on her hip.

– 242 –

# THE QUALIFIERS

Mitchell spoke very quickly. 'On the Island we don't celebrate birthdays, as you know. But we do have this concept of double elementals. It's a rider who is born in the season of their allied element. So Isabel was born in April – and the water season runs from the first of February until the thirtieth of April, then it changes to air on the first of May.'

Bobby growled in frustration. 'Mitchell, get to the—'

'These notes you made in the Vaults.' Mitchell shoved the paper towards her. 'You included Elias and Federico's birthdays. Because you're a weird Mainlander who thinks it's normal to celebrate surviving another year of life.'

Bobby arched an eyebrow at him.

But Mitchell was beside himself with excitement. 'Elias is an earth wielder, and he was born on the eighth of September – slap bang in the earth season, which runs from the first of August until the thirty-first of October. See? He's a double elemental. Then Federico—'

'Federico's birthday is the fifteenth of November,' Bobby cried. 'And he's fire-allied. He's a double elemental too. Forking thunderstorms!'

'There's a *pattern*.' Mitchell sounded happier than he had in months. 'And if there's a pattern, we can protect the unicorns and riders Kenna might choose next.'

'It all makes sense!' Bobby agreed. 'Kenna is sacrificing on the festival days – the days when the new season's elemental magic overpowers the old season's. And *maybe* double elementals have some kind of enhanced magic running through the bond too.'

'Exactly what I was thinking!' Mitchell crowed. 'It all fits perfectly with the curse magic I read about in the Vaults – coincidences, overlaps, synergies. It's old magic but it's powerful stuff.'

'So if we break the cycle,' Skandar said breathlessly, 'you

– 243 –

# SKANDAR AND THE SKELETON CURSE

think Isa, Elias and Federico will go back to normal, and the unicorns will change back from wild to bonded?'

Mitchell nodded. 'Come the summer solstice, the magic should reset. That's what happened with all the failed cyclical curses I found in my research.' His eyes shone with hope. 'I'll get my bond with Red back!'

'What if spirit is part of the cycle?' Bobby looked between the two boys. 'When's the spirit season?'

'It doesn't matter!' Skandar said. 'Because right now, we're in the middle of the water season. And my birthday's this week. I'm the only spirit wielder left for Kenna to sacrifice and I'm *not* a double elemental!'

Skandar had insisted to his quartet that Kenna would never sacrifice Scoundrel. That she would *never* turn her brother into a living skeleton. But judging by how relieved Skandar felt knowing that he wasn't a double elemental, it seemed that – until this moment – he hadn't been quite as confident about that as he'd thought.

The morning of the Qualifiers dawned, bright and chilly. Scoundrel and Falcon had spent the night stabled at the Shekoni Saddles workshop in the centre of Fourpoint. Skandar and Bobby had slept there too – wrapped in blankets and surrounded by saddle pieces – while Mitchell had slept at his mum's treehouse. Skandar woke up at first light, nervous and shivering, and there was still frost on the ground when Jamie arrived to make final adjustments to Scoundrel's armour.

The Qualifiers usually took place over five days, but this year – with the Skeleton Curse drastically reducing the number of entrants – it was only taking place on one. With no need to whittle down the competitors, the race representative had decided to do away with the early heats. Therefore there would only be four

– 244 –

# THE QUALIFIERS

qualifying races, with up to twenty-five riders in each – just like the Chaos Cup itself – and they would all take place around the course that Skandar had seen on television growing up.

'You need to finish top six in your heat,' Jamie was saying, fastening the last of Scoundrel's metal knee guards. 'Four heats, top six riders, that's twenty-four qualifying for the Chaos Cup. And then there'll be one Wildcard— Oh, stop that, you silly thing.'

Scoundrel was stamping his hooves on the stone floor of the workshop, sending sparks flying. The black unicorn could sense the excitement – he could feel Skandar's nerves in the bond – but there was also something different in the air today, a feverish anticipation. People were desperate for a distraction from the Skeleton Curse – and what better than the best riders on the Island battling it out for a place in the Chaos Cup?

Olu, Mitchell and Reece – Bobby's blacksmith – were huddled over a single copy of that morning's *Hatchery Herald*. As was tradition, the newspaper printed which Qualifier heats the riders were competing in, listing them all by name. Bobby wanted to keep the paper as a souvenir; Skandar's nerves were so bad, he was more likely to throw up over it.

'Who am I up against?' Bobby called to Reece, a needle and thread in her hands. She was replaiting Falcon's slate-grey mane. The unicorn had been unhappy with her first attempt. 'Please tell me it's Random Meerkat, I'd just *love* to take him down.'

Despite the stress of the day, Skandar couldn't help laughing at the confusion on Jamie's face at Bobby's latest nickname for the Commodore.

'I've not heard of that unicorn.' Reece stroked his pointy grey beard thoughtfully, looking like a grumpy wizard. 'You're in the first heat – that can be an advantage. There'll be less time for Falcon to wind herself up, and the crowd won't be too rowdy yet. I hate crowds,' he added gruffly.

– 245 –

# SKANDAR AND THE SKELETON CURSE

'Florence is in the first heat with you, Bobby,' Olu said, and the worry in his voice made Skandar's stomach roll over. Ever since Flo had registered for the Cup, it was like her parents carried heavy weights on their shoulders – their raucous game of Spoons felt like a thousand years ago.

'You still haven't heard anything from her?' Skandar tried not to get his hopes up.

'Not a word. Locking a young silver in the Stronghold appears to mean a complete communications shutdown. The Silver Circle clearly didn't like her running away.' Olu sighed. 'But she's a strong one, my Flo. She'll be all right.'

'I'll look after her, Mr Shekoni,' Bobby promised Olu, and glanced over at Skandar. 'I won't let her *beat* me, but I'll make sure she gets over the finishing line safely. Who else are we up against?'

Reece read the rest of the names in the first heat out loud for Bobby, but Skandar only recognised a couple of air wielders – the others were all silvers. 'I think Tristan Macfarlane and Acidic Archangel are probably your biggest threat – along with Lori Fusano and Silver Rhapsody, the strongest water-allied pair in the heat.'

Mitchell practically snatched the newspaper out of Reece's hands as soon as he'd finished reading the names. 'Skandar Smith, Skandar Smith,' he murmured, running his finger down the list of riders. Jamie, unable to bear the suspense, abandoned the saddle buckle that would hold Scoundrel's chainmail in place and went to read over his boyfriend's shoulder.

'You're in the second heat,' he called out. 'Rex is in the fourth.' A collective sigh of relief went through the workshop. Then silence as they read the rest of the names.

Skandar tried to make himself *feel* the good news. He wouldn't be racing head-to-head against the man who clearly hated his guts. Not yet anyway.

– 246 –

## THE QUALIFIERS

'I'm not going to lie to you, Skandar, it's a tough heat,' Olu said, coming over to check the saddle he'd made for Skandar two years before. Scoundrel had grown a lot since then – the original model had been repaired and adjusted so often there was practically none of it left – but the design remained the same, with its five element symbols stitched in white thread. 'Quite a few of the riders you're up against have raced in several Chaos Cups – the most experienced are probably Ema Templeton and Tom Nazari. There's also Eric Melville and Silver Scorcher – he teaches alongside Daniel Anderson at the Eyrie now.'

'*The* Ema Templeton?' Skandar squeaked. He was suddenly back on the sofa in Margate watching the Chaos Cup before his Hatchery exam. Kenna was next to him with a bowl of cereal balanced in her hand, Skandar asking her who she thought would win.

*Ema Templeton and Mountain's Fear. Tenth last year, air wielder, high stamina, brave, intelligent. She's the kind of rider I would've been.* And it didn't feel long enough ago for that same Skandar to be racing Ema today. For that same Kenna to be out in the Wilderness, planning crime after terrible crime.

'Remember you have an advantage,' Jamie insisted, sensing the fear radiating off Skandar. 'It's a young field. Very few of the riders in your heat have ever faced a spirit wielder in a race before. You've got the element of surprise.'

'But *they* have the advantage of being Chaos riders, who actually know what they're doing,' Skandar said, feeling hopeless.

'Stop that nonsense,' Bobby scolded, as she took Falcon's reins from Reece. 'This is exactly what the Eyrie has trained us for. Okay, so we're a bit younger than we might have expected – *and* we're nomads – but it's not unheard of for Rookie-age riders to enter. Anoushka and Sky Pirate are in your heat, and you and Scoundrel are way better than them. I was always going to enter

– 247 –

# SKANDAR AND THE SKELETON CURSE

the Qualifiers as a Pred – we can do this, okay? Last year we faced raging stalignomes and stinking salamanders to pass the Chaos Trials – and that's not including all the times we've had to fight off wild unicorns. Of course we can get through one silly little race. Plus, we get to see Flo – so that should cheer you up, eh?' She winked at him.

'How are you always so confident?' Skandar moaned, taking Scoundrel's reins so they could head to the arena together.

'If you pretend confidence for long enough, you forget it's not real,' Bobby said, and her voice was so serious that Skandar knew she'd revealed a truth about herself that few would ever know.

'You coming or what?' she asked, as Falcon moved towards the workshop door, and Skandar was pretty sure those were the exact words Bobby had used the day they'd left the Hatchery.

Riding through Fourpoint was like nothing Skandar and Scoundrel had experienced before. Unicorns in full armour jostled each other on the way to the Chaos Compound for their heats; riders shouting for space or trying to psych each other out before the races began. The most common jacket colour under their armour was air-element yellow, but there were earth, fire and water wielders among the silver riders. And of course there was the lone spirit wielder in his second-hand white. When Skandar passed, the crowd was divided between hurling insults at him – for being a wielder of the death element, Kenna's brother, or simply *Mainlander scum* – and cheering him on at the top of their voices.

'Well, at least you spark debate,' Bobby shouted over her shoulder.

Closer to the arena, it was even noisier. On almost every corner there was a different chorus of bards singing competing songs, as well as food sellers yelling about their special Qualifier prices and journalists shouting questions at the more famous riders as they passed. Black-clad stewards added to the din, rushing

– 248 –

# THE QUALIFIERS

about and directing riders when to enter the Chaos Compound. Skandar stood up in his stirrups, trying to spot Flo and Blade amid the sea of silver unicorns. Either side of Scoundrel, Olu and Jamie were looking around, too, although they kept getting barged by other blacksmiths, saddlers and unicorns as they made their way onwards through the narrow streets.

'Bobby!' Lucy Henning-Dove – Bobby's saddler – pushed through the crowd to get to Falcon, her purple sash falling off one shoulder in her haste. 'You're in the first heat! You're supposed to be at the arena's east entrance. Like five minutes ago!'

'Right you are, Lucy!' Bobby did a salute, and then turned Falcon, completely ignoring the absolute chaos they were causing by blocking the road.

'I'll come with you!' Mitchell cried. 'I want to get a good seat.'

'I'm happy with your saddle, Skandar,' Olu said, turning too. 'I want to try to see Florence before she goes into the arena.'

'Say hi from me,' Skandar said, aware he sounded a bit tragic, as his friends wished him luck and disappeared into the crowd.

The only one left was Jamie. 'I'll stay with you as long as they'll let me.'

Skandar was so grateful he thought he might cry. 'Thank you, Jamie. You're the best.'

Jamie shrugged. 'Well, I've been here since the beginning, haven't I? I'm not giving up on you now.'

They were directed towards the Chaos Compound with the other riders and unicorns who would be competing in the second heat. Skandar tried to keep his cool as Ema Templeton rode past him. Her hair was a white blonde that almost matched her unicorn's tail, and – as she gave him a curt nod – he could see the threads of electricity running through it.

'Did you see that?' Jamie stared after her. 'Ema Templeton nodded at you!'

– 249 –

# SKANDAR AND THE SKELETON CURSE

Skandar grinned, and imagined telling Kenna. Until he remembered—

'Look, there's Flo!' Jamie cried. Sure enough, on the big screens around the arena, the camera was zooming in on Silver Blade in his shining armour. It rested on Flo's face for a moment, and Skandar's stomach flipped the same way it did when Scoundrel launched himself into the air. He barely heard the commentator reporting that she was the youngest silver competing and had been declared a nomad a few months earlier.

'Declared *herself* a nomad,' Jamie said irritably. 'Bet Rex doesn't want that getting around.'

Skandar was desperately trying to read Flo's face and work out whether she was okay, whether she . . . missed him as much as he missed her. But then she pulled down the gleaming visor of her helmet and the camera moved on.

Jamie smirked. 'You still haven't told her, have you?'

'She's locked inside the Silver Stronghold!' Skandar snapped, unable to cope with Jamie's teasing right now. 'There hasn't exactly been a good time.'

'Excuses, excuses,' Jamie muttered good-naturedly, and Skandar suspected the blacksmith was trying to distract him.

On-screen, the race stewards began to line up the unicorns behind a starting bar that had been wheeled in. The camera kept panning to Bobby and Falcon; it was unsurprising that the camera loved them: Bobby looked every inch the Chaos rider – yellow jacket bright in the sunshine, Falcon's perfectly brushed coat shining. Skandar thought of Bobby's parents suddenly – of how sad it was that the Island hadn't ever allowed the Qualifiers to be televised. He was sure they would have been so proud, just as he was as he watched his friends on the big screen.

Then there were some shouts from the arena, a loud crash, and the familiar bang of the starting bar.

– 250 –

# THE QUALIFIERS

'And they're off,' the commentator's voice boomed over the loudspeaker. 'It's heat one on this first and, well, *only* day of the Chaos Cup Qualifiers. As is the case across all four races, the competitors are almost exclusively made up of air wielders and silvers – since the Commodore decided it was somehow justifiable to press ahead with the Cup even as the Skeleton Curse ravages our—'

There was a scrape and a 'hey!' as the microphone was clearly removed from the commentator.

Jamie chuckled. 'Sounds like Declan isn't a fan of Rex.'

'Declan? Isn't he the one who was commentating at registration?'

'Obviously! There's only one Declan Dashwood. Sometimes he has assistant commentators with him, but everyone knows *he's* the voice of the Chaos Cup!'

'The Mainland has different commentators for the Cup, I think,' Skandar said, trying to remember their names, as Declan regained control of the microphone.

'Now we've got a couple of very young riders in this first heat – here's Bobby Bruna riding Falcon's Wrath, recently nomads but holding their own on the first third of the course.'

Skandar craned his neck to look up at the screen, and – although it was quite far away – he could clearly see a lightning bow sitting comfortably in Bobby's hands. She was firing sideways at Lori Fusano and Silver Rhapsody, and the water wielder was forced back behind Falcon, her frustrated shouts audible over the speakers.

'What's interesting about the two young Rookies in this first qualifier is that there's a rumour – which I personally choose to believe – that they declared *themselves* nomads in support of another member of their quartet,' Declan continued. 'You might have heard of him – Skandar Smith, the only rider permitted to

– 251 –

# SKANDAR AND THE SKELETON CURSE

wield the spirit element on the Island. He'll be competing in our second heat today, so stay tuned, folks – these are going to be some Qualifiers we'll never forget—'

'*Flaming Fireballs*,' Declan interrupted himself. 'That's the other Rookie – Florence Shekoni riding Silver Blade – and her elemental predator is one of the most impressive I've seen in this race so far. For those who need a reminder after all those years when they were sensibly illegal – the predator levels are Hider for the most basic, Hunter, then Marauder and finally Mythical. Coincidentally there has been much controversy over the legalisation of elemental predators both at the Eyrie and at this year's Chaos Cup . . .'

Skandar focused his attention on the screen. The camera was following a sand-beast so large it was hard to capture it all at once, Flo and Blade soaring along beside it in the air. Then, Acidic Archangel's white wings were filling the screen, gaining on Blade from behind. Tristan's palm glowed yellow, an almighty lightning hammer sparking into his hand. Skandar almost shouted out in warning.

Then, with a flick of Flo's hand – without even turning to look over her shoulder – the elemental predator twisted in mid-air, grains of sand pouring from its jaws in a snarl.

'And if my eyes do not deceive me . . . Yes! That is a *Marauder*-level predator from the youngest silver,' Declan was saying, his voice awed. 'A grizzly bear – Shekoni must have been doing some serious training in the Stronghold. Tristan is going to have to think of something— OOF!'

The camera had a direct shot as the full weight of the bear's sandy body collided with Tristan's armoured torso and knocked him clean out of the saddle. Archangel roared with rage as he chased his rider's falling body through the sky to scoop him up just before he hit the ground. Flo didn't even look down, but

– 252 –

# THE QUALIFIERS

Silver Blade increased his speed and went up two more places – into eighth.

There was a ragged cheer from the crowd lining the course, as Tristan signalled that he was all right and healers streamed towards him.

'I'm glad Flo's doing well,' Jamie said. 'But I can see why those creatures were outlawed. They're brutal!'

Skandar nodded shakily, thinking about heading into his heat where at least half the competitors were silvers. He remembered Flo's words: *Elemental predators are what silvers do best.*

Declan's voice came back over the speakers as the camera panned out to show as many unicorns as possible flying along the course. 'EEESH! There is absolute carnage at the back of the field right now – at least three of the silvers have taken each other out and another injured its own rider. And watch out for that rogue – it's some kind of snake, I think – if you're down on the west side of the course, folks. But as they start on the home straight, Lori Fusano is in the lead with Silver Rhapsody, followed by Bobby Bruna on Falcon's Wrath, and behind them there's a battle going on between—'

'They're in second!' Skandar cried. 'Bobby and Falcon are in second!'

'She might actually do it!' Jamie was hopping from foot to foot with excitement. Scoundrel watched him warily out of the corner of his black eye.

'And bringing up the rear we have Akis and Silver Pine. It's possible the water wielder is playing it safe – many of the silver riders in this qualifier have been dangerously out of control. That's no surprise given that the entire Silver Circle have entered, even if they can't tell a horn from a tail.'

'Did you hear what position Flo is in?' Skandar asked Jamie desperately. Part of him was wishing she wouldn't qualify. That

– 253 –

# SKANDAR AND THE SKELETON CURSE

way they could get her out of the Stronghold somehow and the quartet could be together again.

'No, I didn't catch it,' Jamie said, glued to the images of the unicorns flying across the screen. 'There's magic blasting everywhere, and there are so many silvers it's impossible to tell...' The noise of the crowd crescendoed as the unicorns approached the arena stands. And a chant started up: 'BRUNA! BRUNA!'

'Well, this crowd seems very set on the winner they want,' Declan said, chuckling. 'And I can't say I disagree with them. Bobby Bruna and Falcon's Wrath are flying an absolute blinder of a race. But as they fly over the stands now, Lori Fusano and Silver Rhapsody are still about half a metre ahead.'

Along with everyone else, Skandar turned his face to the sky as Falcon and Rhapsody soared overhead. Bobby was up in her stirrups, her body turned towards Lori and flinging every single weapon Skandar had ever seen her mould at the silver rider. Ice dagger. Rock mace. Flaming javelin. Lightning sword.

Lori had clearly given up on moulding anything, and was pushing Rhapsody hard towards the sand of the arena, throwing up a different shield as soon as she saw Bobby's palm glow with whatever element she was about to use.

'She's already qualified,' Jamie said. 'She doesn't actually need to win! She knows that, right?'

Skandar grinned. 'Oh, she knows – but that won't make any difference. Bobby *always* fights to win.'

There was an almighty roar from the crowd as Rhapsody and Falcon landed on the sand of the arena neck and neck, hurtling towards the finishing arch. There was a flash of green from Bobby's palm – Lori glanced at it, threw up a lightning shield, then turned back towards the arch, sure of her victory. But in a split-second Bobby's palm turned from green to blue and she hurled three water daggers right at the sparking shield.

– 254 –

## THE QUALIFIERS

Lori yelled in shock, the electrocuted water hitting her shoulder. It slowed Rhapsody just for a moment – but it was enough.

The crowd were screaming now. 'BRUNA! BRUNA! BRUNA!' And Skandar joined in at the top of his lungs. Bobby was going to do it. She was actually going to win her Chaos Cup Qualifier.

'And that's Bobby Bruna and Falcon's Wrath in first position in the first Qualifier for this year's Cup.' Declan took a deep breath, and his words blurred as more unicorns landed in the arena. 'And in second it's Lori Fusano and Silver Rhapsody. Our third qualifier, just passing under the arch now, is Oliver Parton and Fearless Comrade – the ex-air council member has done himself proud today. Then, qualifying in fourth, we have Aerial Destruction, ridden by veteran air wielder, Dorina Zachariou, out of retirement on account of the Skeleton Curse. Yes, that's right, folks, the Cup is *still* going ahead despite this unprecedented crisis. And qualifying in fifth and sixth, we have two silvers – water wielder Brad McBryde, riding Silver Pirate and earth wielder Florence Shekoni, on Silver Blade—'

Skandar froze. Even as he watched Flo passing under the finishing arch, he couldn't believe it. Flo had qualified for the Chaos Cup. He was so proud of her. Yet he was also devastated. It was brilliant to have two of the quartet competing to oust Rex, but he was terrified for them. For all of them.

'CLEAR A PATH!' the black-clad officials were shouting. 'FINISHERS COMING THROUGH!'

Bobby still had her fist raised in triumph as she entered first, dismounting from Falcon and giving her the most enormous hug. Then Bobby's eyes landed on Skandar, and – ignoring the stewards who were attempting to get her out of the Compound and towards the waiting reporters – she dashed over to him, Falcon trotting behind.

She hugged him tight.

– 255 –

# SKANDAR AND THE SKELETON CURSE

'Bobby! Well done! That was—' Skandar started to say into her armoured shoulder, but she shushed him.

'Don't get complacent,' she hissed into his ear. 'The Skeleton Curse might get us air wielders too. There's no guarantee Falcon won't be wild by then. You need to qualify – just as much as before. The Mainland, remember?'

Skandar nodded and she released him.

'Let's meet at Sally's, okay? After your Qualifier. I'll see if Flo can meet us there before they take her back to the Stronghold. Hey! Don't touch my unicorn! She *will* bite you!' One of the stewards had grabbed Falcon's left rein and was attempting to move the winning unicorn out of the small space.

'Those racing in the second qualifier, this is your five-minute warning!' The shout echoed around the Compound like a siren.

There was a surge of movement as Skandar's opponents crushed towards the arena.

'All right, Skandar. This is it,' Jamie said. 'Don't think of it as a qualifier – it's just another race. And you and Scoundrel are good at racing. Remember the Air Trial? And *that* had windmills and screaming sylphs. You're fast. You're a Grin. You've got this.'

'Just another race. Fast. Grin. Got this,' Skandar repeated, tracing the white element symbols stitched into his saddle to try to keep calm. Until this moment Skandar hadn't really believed this was going to happen. He'd been half expecting Rex to arrest him in the Compound. But there was no sign of the Commodore anywhere.

'Look after him, old boy,' Jamie said, patting Scoundrel, before dashing to get a seat in the stands. Scoundrel stared after him, as though confused at being called *old*.

Skandar looked over his shoulder just once before crossing through into the arena. And that was when he saw Flo. Her helmet was off and she was smiling as silver rider after silver

– 256 –

# THE QUALIFIERS

rider came to congratulate her – some shaking her hand, others even pulling her into hugs. Skandar knew she had to be pretending – she couldn't possibly feel at home among the very people who hated his element, who were taking advantage of the Skeleton Curse to seize power, who wanted to invade the Mainland. But the sight unsettled him all the same, and he couldn't get the image out of his head, even as Scoundrel jostled for a place behind the starting bar.

Finally, Skandar managed to slot Scoundrel in beside a unicorn with a bone-white tail, and all thoughts flew from his head when Ema Templeton raised her helmet, and spoke to him.

'I'll watch your left side, spirit wielder,' she murmured, as the swirling debris of the elemental blasts rose from the excited unicorns.

'Y-you don't have to,' Skandar said, tipping his helmet back up.

A ghost of a smile passed over Ema's lips. 'You didn't have to help Aspen and New-Age Frost, either, but you still did.'

'No, I—'

'And neither did you have to win the bone staff from the First Rider, and yet you did.'

'Well, if I hadn't—'

'And you didn't have to carry on searching for the eggs last year when the rest of us had given up.'

Skandar was stunned to silence.

'Some of us have not forgotten the debt we owe you, Skandar Smith. I'll watch your left side – you just concentrate on your right. Got it?'

Then, with a crash and a bang, the starting bar rose. And twenty-five unicorns exploded forward – Scoundrel's Luck and Mountain's Fear side by side.

CHAPTER SIXTEEN

# VANISHING ACT

As the unicorns launched themselves into the air, Skandar could tell that Scoundrel was nervous. He was by far the smallest unicorn in their qualifier – in both sheer size and muscle-mass. And Scoundrel knew it. He swung his black horn from side to side as they soared upwards, taking in his opponents, and the bond filled with his lack of self-confidence.

Skandar put a hand on Scoundrel's neck to reassure him, and repeated Jamie's advice. 'It's just another race.' The unicorns began to level out after take-off, and Scoundrel settled, slotting into the middle group of fliers. As they soared away from the arena, Skandar caught snippets of Declan's commentary from the loudspeakers below:

'And that's Billy Bridport and Wicked Thunder quickly asserting their lead over fire-allied Ayana Magoro and Silver Phoenix. Word is that this silver rider is our Commodore's closest confidante, so she will be desperate to qualify for the Cup this year. Behind Phoenix, in fifth position, we have Silver— Forking thunderstorms! Look at that predator from the leader!'

## VANISHING ACT

Skandar tried to block out the words and concentrate on the race itself. So far, nobody had tried to attack him – all the riders in the middle group seemed intent on catching up with the leading five unicorns. Skandar glanced to his left and saw Mountain's Fear sticking to Scoundrel's side like glue. Ema was staying true to her word.

A ferocious sky battle suddenly raged out of nowhere. The silver ahead of Scoundrel launched a flamethrower that burned brightly in the sky and blasted right through the ice shield thrown up by the air wielder she'd challenged. Elemental debris flew everywhere, the smell of fire magic like burnt toast in Skandar's throat. But as it disbursed, he spotted an opening – clear blue sky and a chance to gain on the leading group.

'Come on, boy – we can go faster than this,' Skandar murmured through his helmet. But the unicorn was already increasing the speed of his wingbeats, the hum of the wind rising in pitch as it skimmed the tips of his feathers.

Scoundrel's nose inched ahead of the rest of the group, and there was an almighty crash of weapon on armour from Skandar's left. The impact reverberated through the air, accompanied by a strangled yell of surprise and anger.

Alarmed, Skandar looked over his shoulder to see Ema Templeton battling two silvers at once. One silver had summoned an elemental predator. It was only a Hunter – an Arctic fox – but, combined with a furious tornado attack from the second silver, it was impossible for Ema and Mountain's Fear to keep their position. Skandar forced himself to look forward again, the rush of air stinging his eyes. Ema had been protecting him – he had to make it count; he had to qualify.

Scoundrel reached the back of the leading group as they passed the floating halfway marker. Skandar counted five silvers

– 259 –

# SKANDAR AND THE SKELETON CURSE

ahead, as well as two non-silver air wielders: Wicked Thunder, ridden by Billy Bridport, and Electric Kestrel, ridden by Sadie Lang, who'd crashed out of the Chaos Cup the year of Kenna's Hatchery exam. The two air unicorns were in first and third, so if Skandar was going to get himself into a qualifying position, he'd need to take down at least two of the silvers.

Noticing that the silver at the rear was slowing ever so slightly, Skandar summoned the spirit element to his palm to mould a ghostly dagger. And when Scoundrel had brought them level with the unicorn – Silver Phoenix – he threw it towards her rider's shoulder and began moulding another. Ayana's reaction was much faster than Skandar had expected. Instead of throwing up an elemental shield to block the dagger, the rider unleashed a predator – impossibly fast – in the shape of a hawk, its body a flaming inferno. It swiped the dagger off course with a sparking wing, then began circling above Scoundrel as though looking for prey.

Trying not to panic, Skandar threw his second dagger and concentrated hard on creating a spirit illusion. As the weapon soared forward, it looked as though it was heading for the silver rider's chest, but Skandar had, in fact, aimed for the same shoulder as before. The hawk swooped in again, kicking out its smoking talons to deflect the dagger, but it flapped in confusion when it was met with thin air. Ayana cried out as the spirit dagger connected with her armoured shoulder, and storm clouds rolled off Phoenix's wings in fury. Skandar couldn't bring himself to feel bad – this was the silver rider who had hunted Flo to Wildflower Hill.

'Steady, girl,' Skandar heard Ayana calling to the raging unicorn, and there was fear in her voice. Was she worried about losing control? Thunder clapped overhead, the sky darkening, and the flaming hawk soared further and further away from

– 260 –

# VANISHING ACT

its maker. Ayana slumped a little in the saddle, and Skandar realised the predator was leeching enough of the rider's magic to break free. If he and Scoundrel didn't want to be chased by a rogue elemental bird or get trapped in the fire silver's storm, they needed to move.

Understanding flooded the bond, as Skandar summoned the water element alongside spirit. Almost like a tidal wave had broken over him, Scoundrel's neck, then his body, then his legs transformed to sparkling blue. The unicorn was pure water and salt-spray as the pair dodged the tempest and sped forward, stealing the silver's position.

Free of the storm, Skandar could make out the distant rumble of the crowd below, but he had no idea if they were cheering or booing. Bursts of commentary reached him as the wind rushed past his ears:

'Oh, this is really very exciting. Skandar and Scoundrel's Luck *overtake* Ayana and Silver Phoenix with that aqua-batic display – did you see what I did there? – as they inch a little closer to those coveted qualifying positions. Behind them, Silver Cyclone has just taken out Silver Scorcher with a frost-tipped wave that I'm not sure was entirely on purpose, but either way that *will* be a disappointment for Eric Melville. Perhaps standards at the Eyrie really are slipping – in my day it was a requirement that instructors had competed in at least three Chaos Cups.'

Skandar counted the unicorns ahead of Scoundrel from his new position. He was in seventh – one place away from qualifying – and he could see the arena looming in the distance.

'Faster, boy!' Skandar bent low, putting a palm on Scoundrel's neck and pouring confidence into the bond. 'We're faster than all these unicorns. We're Grins. So let's fly!'

Scoundrel screeched happily – flying fast was his favourite thing to do – and Skandar felt the shift as the unicorn lowered

– 261 –

# SKANDAR AND THE SKELETON CURSE

his black horn in concentration, his muscles straining, his wingbeats increasing again.

'Yes!' Skandar cried. 'Yes, that's— ARGH!'

Skandar's vision blurred with pain, as three flashes of elemental magic – blue, red, green – hit him simultaneously. Fire seared his arm, the chainmail glowing with heat – just as a rock hammer hit him squarely in the chest and winded him as it clanged and fell. Most painful of all, an ice shard pierced his hip and imbedded itself between the joins in his armour.

Scoundrel was roaring in anger, spraying columns of fire from his mouth at the attacking silvers. But the sound was distant to Skandar, who was fighting to stay conscious through the agony of the injury. He had only one thought in his head as the arena came fully into view: *Get to the finishing arch, and then you can pass out.*

The loudspeaker was blaring as Scoundrel swooped down over the upturned faces in the stands. Skandar knew his unicorn was worried – Scoundrel could sense how much pain his rider was in, but he also knew they needed to finish. And – whether it was a training session, the Air Trial, or a Chaos Cup Qualifier – Scoundrel never liked to lose a race.

Declan Dashwood's voice filled the arena: 'You can say what you like about Skandar Smith, but there's no denying his absolute *determination* to qualify. Judging by his awkward position in the saddle, it's clear he suffered a severe injury from that co-ordinated attack. I can't say I approve of the way those silvers . . .' Declan's voice shifted gear. 'And they're landing in the arena now. Wicked Thunder is under the arch first, comfortably qualifying for the Chaos Cup after leading the field the whole way round. Silver Cyclone is in second, Silver Warlock in third, Electric Kestrel in fourth . . .'

Darkness started to pull at the corners of Skandar's vision,

– 262 –

# VANISHING ACT

but he was jolted back to himself as Scoundrel landed to gallop towards the finish. There were unicorns in front of him, but he couldn't tell how many. Distantly, as though slipping into a dream, Skandar thought he heard the crowd chanting his name. But as Scoundrel passed under the arch, Skandar's body finally gave in. He slipped from the saddle, unconscious before he even hit the sand.

When Skandar's eyes opened again, he could smell freshly baked bread.

'Oh, Skar, you're awake!' Skandar barely had time to register Flo's voice before she was hugging him for the first time in three months.

'Nice to have you back, spirit boy.' Bobby grinned from the other side of— Wait, what *was* he lying on?

Mitchell read Skandar's thoughts. 'You're at Sally's Succulent Sandwiches.'

'The counter was the only thing long enough for you to lie on during the operation,' Flo added, her voice choked. Skandar tried to look at her to make sure she was okay. But Sally's shop swam before his eyes, and he had to put his head back down.

'I argued it was highly unhygienic for an operation to be carried out in a *sandwich* shop,' Mitchell said haughtily.

'A sandwich shop is probably one of the *most* hygienic places, Mitchell. People eat here!' Bobby argued.

Skandar tried to sit up – slowly this time – and managed to stay upright. He noticed a fresh bandage on his hip, and flashes of the race came back to him.

'The ice shard?' he asked weakly.

'It's out,' Flo confirmed. 'My mum did the operation – there wasn't a lot of time. You were losing so much blood.'

'Wait,' Skandar croaked. 'Why did a unicorn healer do my

– 263 –

# SKANDAR AND THE SKELETON CURSE

operation . . . in a sandwich shop?' None of this made sense.

Mitchell took a deep breath. 'Somehow you finished the race, even though you were bleeding heavily. But when you passed out on the sand, none of the healers on duty came over to help – it was bizarre. No stretchers, nothing. Scoundrel was going berserk. It was Ema Templeton who moved you, and then Jamie and the three of us managed to get you to Fourpoint. Jamie was devastated about the ice shard getting through your armour – I've never seen him so upset.'

'Obviously we headed for the Healer Huts.' Bobby took over. 'You were bleeding everywhere; you looked worse than after that sleepsong disaster last year. But none of the healers would take you in.'

'What?' Skandar breathed.

'They told us they'd lose their jobs if they helped you,' Bobby said darkly.

'There was a lot of shouting,' Mitchell said stiffly. 'Mostly from Bobby. But I also got very irate.'

Bobby inclined her head proudly. 'Then Flo had the genius idea of asking her mum. At that point we would have settled for a mediocre seamstress with a needle and thread, so a unicorn healer seemed like a much better bet. And Sally agreed to shut up shop for the operation.'

'None of the healers would help me?' Skandar's voice felt too loud in his ears.

'No,' Mitchell said. 'Not one.'

Skandar turned to Flo. 'I'm assuming Rex did this? He couldn't stop me registering for the Cup, but he *could* stop people helping me if I was injured.' Saying it out loud made it sound even worse.

Flo's eyes filled with tears. 'I don't know, Skar. Rex might not be behind it. I didn't hear anything about it at the Stronghold.'

– 264 –

# VANISHING ACT

Skandar sighed. 'I'm guessing I didn't qualify?'

'You were seventh,' Flo answered quietly. 'Ayana and Phoenix regained enough speed to overtake once you were hurt.'

'Honestly, I don't know how you did that well,' Bobby said, sounding genuinely impressed. 'Those attacks were brutal, and *then* you were bleeding out. Even finishing at all showed some serious guts. Literally – ha! – they were practically falling out of you. We really did think you were a goner there for a minute.'

Skandar felt three hands land on him. Flo's on his left shoulder. Mitchell's on his right. Bobby's ruffling his hair. Despite having been stabbed by an ice shard, Skandar felt happier than he had in months. They were all together again – like they should be. A tear escaped the corner of his eye.

'We are all extremely proud of you,' Mitchell said formally, though his eyes were also glistening.

'Skar, I—' Flo broke off, and Skandar looked at her properly for the first time. It wasn't that he'd forgotten what she looked like, but it was as though his brain had filled in some of the gaps slightly wrong and this moment was putting everything right again.

'Mitchell, didn't you say Jamie was going to meet us here? Let's see if he's outside,' Bobby said.

'I'll go,' Mitchell replied. '*You* don't need to—'

'Oh, I think I do.' Bobby looked pointedly between Skandar sitting on the counter and Flo hovering by his side. Comprehension dawned on Mitchell's face as Bobby steered him out.

Now they were alone, Skandar's heart started to beat faster, and for some reason he couldn't think of a thing to say. There was *too* much. So of course he asked the most boring question imaginable. 'How's it been in the Stronghold?'

'I've missed you . . . all. So much,' Flo said jerkily, easing

– 265 –

herself up on to the counter beside Skandar, her legs dangling next to his. 'But it hasn't been as bad as I expected. The other silvers have looked after me, helped me with training.'

'You qualified,' Skandar said, suddenly remembering. 'You're going to be in the Chaos Cup, Flo!' And he was relieved to find that he was happy for her; there was no stab of jealousy underneath.

She laughed nervously. 'Yeah, I wasn't exactly planning on that, to be honest.'

'Your predator – the bear. Terrifying!'

'Who would have thought I'd be good at illegal magic?' Flo chuckled. 'Well, not illegal any more but still dangerous. I'm sort of proud of myself, I think. When I first hatched Blade, I'd pretty much decided he was going to kill me off and now—'

'You're a Chaos rider!'

Flo sighed. 'I wish you were, too, Skar.'

There was something in the way she said his name that Skandar had missed so much. And before he could stop himself, he'd seized her hand, blood thundering in his ears. 'Please don't go back to the Stronghold, Flo. Come back with us to Sapphire. The Wanderers can hide you – we can run from here right now!'

But Flo was already shaking her head. 'I can't. Not now I've qualified – there's something I haven't told you yet. Something bad.'

Skandar felt a wave of nausea pass over him.

'I overheard Rex and Ayana talking. They *know*, Skar. The Silver Circle know that Kenna's curse is cyclical, and they . . . they've decided not to stop it before the Chaos Cup.'

Skandar wished he was surprised, but at this point he'd believe anything of Rex Manning. 'So we were right. Rex is trying to guarantee his victory in the Cup – or at least victory

– 266 –

# VANISHING ACT

by a silver. Which will mean no one can stop him attacking the Mainland.'

Flo swallowed. 'I think he definitely wants to be Commodore again, but I've not heard him say anything about the Main—'

'And he's not going to worry about *me* stopping him,' Skandar continued feverishly. 'I'm the only spirit wielder left. He's probably hoping I'll end up a skeleton.'

'But Kenna won't come for you and Scoundrel, will she?' Flo asked desperately. 'Bobby and Mitchell told me you'd have to be a double elemental, and your birthday's in the water season – it's the day after tomorrow!'

'Exactly,' Skandar confirmed. 'But Rex doesn't know that.'

'This is exactly why I have to stay in the Stronghold,' Flo said, fighting off tears. 'I need to keep an eye on Rex. If he's doing nothing to stop Kenna, there's a big chance the air wielders who've qualified for the Cup – like Bobby – might not actually end up racing. And now *you're* not racing . . . I need to keep training with the silvers – you never know, I might even win. I am *really* good at predators.'

Skandar couldn't help but grin. 'Florence Shekoni, Commodore of Chaos. Now *that's* something to look forward to.'

'I do wish I could stay with you instead, Skar. You know that, right?'

Somehow the two of them had inched towards each other, and as Skandar turned to answer Flo's question, he found himself so close to her face that he could see the scar on her cheek – the one from their Stronghold break-in two years ago. Something made him reach out to touch the faint line, his fingers brushing her jawbone. Flo's intake of breath made his heart beat impossibly fast, faster even than when Scoundrel went into a particularly ambitious dive. Now was the time. Now was the time to tell her—

'SKANDAR!' Jamie, Mitchell and Bobby burst back through

– 267 –

# SKANDAR AND THE SKELETON CURSE

the door, and Flo launched herself down from the counter in panic while Skandar desperately tried to read the expressions on his friends' faces.

Jamie spoke first, completely breathless. 'You're being considered by the Qualifier Committee. As a Wildcard. You and Scoundrel have to get to the arena right now!'

Skandar stared at him, and Mitchell went into explanation mode. 'They've finished all four qualifying races now. But the committee will choose one more rider who performed particularly well. The Wildcard. Six other riders are being considered too, but—'

'Surely the committee won't choose me?' Skandar tried to keep his excitement in check. 'Surely Rex has packed it full of his mates?'

But Flo was smiling. 'Skar, the committee is independent. It's made up of people from across Island life. My *dad's* on it!'

'That's one vote!' Bobby crowed.

'Come on,' Jamie urged. 'You need to be in the arena about five minutes ago.'

Ten minutes later, after almost blacking out twice more from the pain of remounting Scoundrel, Skandar was in the arena with the six other riders being considered for the Wildcard position. One by one, the seven members of the Qualifier Committee would enter the arena and point to the pair they thought had proved themselves worthy of racing in the Chaos Cup.

Declan Dashwood announced the first committee member – and the saddler representative, Olu Shekoni, pointed immediately at Skandar and Scoundrel with an enormous grin on his face. 'You deserve this, Skandar,' he said, approaching them. 'And it's not just because you're a Shekoni Saddles rider or because you're in my daughter's quartet. You earned this –

– 268 –

# VANISHING ACT

you and Scoundrel flew a fantastic race.'

Pride swelled in Skandar's chest. 'Thank you, Mr Shekoni.' And he let a pinprick of hope into his heart. There were six votes to go, but he'd at least got one.

Declan's voice came over the loudspeaker as Olu marched back out of the arena. 'No surprises with that vote. I've always thought Shekoni was an excellent judge of character, and he has believed in this spirit wielder since his Nestling year.' Skandar grinned, wondering how long it would be until someone tried to remove Declan's microphone again.

That was when Skandar spotted Rex, still in his armour, occupying the best seat in the stands. His expression was carefully neutral, but his jaw was tight, as though clenching his teeth.

'Next, we have the healer on the committee entering the arena to make her decision. And it looks like she's heading right for Eric and Silver Scorcher. One for Skandar, one for the Eyrie instructor so far. And now it's the turn of the committee's bard.'

The bard didn't look at Scorcher or Scoundrel, merely stopped a few metres back from the unicorns and waved vaguely in the silver's direction. 'Umm.' Declan seemed a little unsure. 'I think that's a vote for Eric, but could you please confirm?' The bard put a thumb up and rushed from the arena. 'Bards, who'd have 'em, eh? All right then – that's two for Eric, one for Skandar. On to the blacksmith committee member, please.'

At first Skandar didn't recognise the blacksmith. Her shoulders were slumped, her blonde ponytail sagging. But when she looked up there was a fierceness to the haunted eyes of Clara Matthews, who'd been blacksmith to Nina Kazama and Lightning's Mistake. She walked right up to Scoundrel, arm outstretched to indicate he was her chosen Wildcard. 'Nina trusted you,' she murmured, stroking the spirit unicorn's ebony neck. 'I do too.'

– 269 –

# SKANDAR AND THE SKELETON CURSE

'Leaping landslides!' Declan exclaimed. 'She's only gone for the spirit wielder!' He dropped his voice theatrically. 'Well, this is getting very exciting. We have two clear favourites so far – two votes for Eric and Scorcher and two for Skandar and Scoundrel. With three more votes to go, we'll be hearing from the merchant on the Qualifier Committee – Katherine from the Brilliant Boot Company!'

Katherine was a short plump woman with grey curly hair and glasses perched on the end of her nose. The arena was almost completely silent as she marched purposefully out on to the sand in a pair of her very own boots that were shined to perfection. Skandar swallowed, his heart thundering. He didn't know Katherine, but he did remember that she'd closed her shop to him after the truesong-fuelled rumour he was the Weaver's successor. And, sure enough, the bootmaker pointed at Eric and Silver Scorcher.

'Well, folks, that's three votes for Eric and still only two for Skandar.' There was a note of disappointment in Declan's voice, which made perfect sense when he called the next member of the Qualifier Committee. 'Next to cast their Wildcard vote, we've got the silver representative – Brad McBryde.'

Skandar's heart sank as he watched Brad walk out on to the sand and flick his seaweed hair over his shoulder. It seemed incredibly unfair that he would be allowed to vote when he'd just been racing, though he supposed the Circle never fought fair. And Skandar had seen this silver with Rex down in the Vaults – there was no way he was going to vote for a spirit wielder.

But then he did. Brad pointed right at Scoundrel, and Skandar was so surprised he almost fell off.

'I . . . I don't believe it, I—' Declan cleared his throat, trying to regain composure. 'The silver representative has voted for

– 270 –

# VANISHING ACT

Skandar and Scoundrel. Yes, he's confirming now. That is three votes each for Skandar and Eric!'

Skandar's heart thundered, and his gaze slid towards Rex Manning – but the head of the Silver Circle had gone. His thoughts whirled. Had Brad broken ranks and voted for Skandar against Rex's wishes? He remembered how horrible Rex had been to the silver down in the Vaults – ordering him about, intentionally calling him by the wrong name. Had Brad voted out of spite? Or maybe Flo had managed to convince her fellow silver to vote for Skandar?

'Unbelievable scenes!' Declan was clearly enjoying himself an enormous amount. 'Everything rides – excuse the pun – on the final member of the Qualifier Committee, always a former Commodore. Will it be the silver or the spirit wielder?'

There was a flash of plaited red hair as the final member of the committee walked out into the arena.

Skandar could hardly believe his luck. It was Aspen McGrath, and she was heading right for Scoundrel.

With a flourish the water wielder – whose bond with New-Age Frost Skandar had repaired three years before – pointed at him. Though parts of the crowd descended into jeering, others exploded with cheers. Skandar spotted Instructors O'Sullivan, Anderson and Webb sitting together, whistling and whooping in support – and he gave them a quick wave.

Declan Dashwood was beside himself with excitement. 'A spirit wielder, a Mainlander, a self-declared nomad and – dare I say it – a radical rebel, is chosen as the Wildcard this year. Skandar Smith and Scoundrel's Luck *will* be racing in the Chaos Cup this coming June. I, for one, will be cheering him on all the . . .'

But Skandar had stopped listening. Aspen McGrath – the rider he'd admired so much growing up on the Mainland – was speaking to him, one hand resting on Scoundrel's withers.

– 271 –

'Congratulations, Wildcard. That was one hell of a race you just flew.'

'Th-thank you,' Skandar stuttered, trying not to wince at the pain in his injured side.

'Just make sure you win, all right?' Aspen winked and walked away.

Skandar let himself feel the joy of the moment. He wished he could go back in time and tell the little boy from Margate – who'd loved unicorns more than anything, who'd worried about everything – that one day, Robert Smith was going to turn on his television and watch his son race in the Chaos Cup.

That was when Skandar sensed a change in the crowd. People were peering upwards, turning in their seats, standing up. There was confusion at first, then shouts of terror, screams . . . And as Skandar looked over the top of the raised seats of the arena, he realised exactly why.

There was a landmark missing from Fourpoint's skyline.

The Eyrie had vanished.

Kenna

# NO PLACE LIKE HOME

Kenna Everhart had returned to the Eyrie.

Well, almost. All the riders and wild unicorns who'd joined her were currently scattered across the lower plateaus cut into the Eyrie's hill. Only Kenna's four generals – the most trustworthy of her Originals – accompanied her to the highest training ground.

Kenna wanted riders she trusted around her. There had been a couple of recent incidents of riders pretending to believe in her cause and then attempting to get her arrested. And she knew there were still Originals who had joined her but didn't fully forgive her for what she'd done to their unicorns, even though they had been lured in by the promise of being allied to all five elements and the promise of an island without Rex Manning in charge.

But she couldn't worry about that – not today.

Attacking – no, *reclaiming* – the Eyrie during the Qualifiers had been Albert's idea, and so far they'd had no trouble. Since the Water Festival, seeing a distraught rider attempting to corral their wild unicorn was such a common sight that the

# SKANDAR AND THE SKELETON CURSE

few Islanders *not* watching the Qualifiers hadn't even raised an eyebrow.

'Two sentinels at the Eyrie's entrance,' Mateo reported. 'Aside from that, the place looks deserted. I expect Rex wanted everyone to watch the silvers competing – and I reckon the whole Island will want to see if Skandar—'

Finneas shook his head sharply, and Mateo's tanned skin went blotchy with the awkwardness of having mentioned Kenna's brother. 'So, erm, we won't meet much resistance up there,' he finished clumsily.

Kenna knew that Skandar had entered the Qualifiers alongside Bobby and Flo. But it was the rumour that her brother's quartet had declared themselves nomads that caused her the most disquiet. Was Skandar rebelling at last? Perhaps he'd realised she'd been right all along? That the Island was never going to accept him? For a moment, she dared to wonder whether he might join her. She hadn't killed Tsunami's Herald; she had shown mercy to Bobby's sister.

But then Kenna shut that thought down with a grimace. Skandar would never join her now. Never forgive her. Not after the Skeleton Curse killings – not after Mitchell and Red Night's Delight, not after she'd turned Isabel Bruna into a skeleton. But she didn't need Skandar, did she? Even if he *had* finally realised his mistake in trusting an Island that hated difference.

The truth was, Kenna didn't need anyone. She could have taken the Eyrie all by herself. But Albert had told her that it was important for their *cause* that everyone felt involved, that they worked towards their new future together. And Kenna knew he was right. Erika had always sought out followers. Being alone for ever was no fun. Even the Weaver had known that.

'What's the situation with the sentinels?' Albert asked Mateo, bringing Kenna back to the moment.

– 274 –

## NO PLACE LIKE HOME

'Two air wielders.' Mateo blew a brown curl out of his eye. 'They're young – I guess they drew the short straw.'

Kenna snapped into action, Goshawk feeling the shift in the bond and flapping her tattered wings. 'Here's the plan. Gos and I take down the sentinels. Finneas, you flank me with Vulture's Voltage just in case one escapes. Adela, you and Smoke-Eyed Saviour keep a lookout for any unwelcome riders on the hill. Once the sentinels are distracted, Albert, you get the entrance open – and keep it that way. Mateo, as soon as you see daylight through the trunk, ride Hell's Diamond as fast as you can down the hill and signal to the others.'

The four generals nodded seriously – even though they already knew the plan inside out.

Just before Kenna gave the first signal, Albert approached her, his pale jaw clenched. Eagle's white wing collided gently with Goshawk's honey-coloured one. 'You're not going to kill them, are you?'

'Who?' Kenna frowned, the adrenaline already singing through her veins. She was going back to the Eyrie, and nobody was going to tell her she didn't belong.

'Anyone,' Albert said emphatically.

'Of course not, Al,' Kenna said dismissively. 'What would be the point?'

Kenna watched as the tension left Albert's face. He understood her on a much deeper level than her other generals. Understood her personal stake in the Skeleton Curse. And she'd let him witness some of her darkest moments– where she was more monster than human. Just last week, she'd punched clean through her treehouse window because Gos had been angry with another unicorn. Albert had bandaged up her fingers without saying a word.

As it turned out, Kenna never got the chance to kill the

– 275 –

# SKANDAR AND THE SKELETON CURSE

sentinels – even if she'd wanted to. The two air wielders were barely older than her, and as soon as they saw the Wild Rider crest the Eyrie's hill – half her head a skull, ice spikes at her throat, white stripe down her face – they didn't even bother to summon elemental magic. They dropped from their unicorns' backs and on to their knees, masks glinting as they pleaded.

'Please don't kill us!'

Kenna rolled her eyes. 'Why does everyone keep *saying* that? I actually haven't *ever* killed a person. Adela, Finneas, can you bind their hands and cover their mouths? Don't let them get away – we're taking them inside for now.'

Adela's smoky black ringlets crackled as she purred, 'Of course, darling. I'll keep them quiet.' Finneas just nodded, following the command. Kenna had borrowed enough adventure books from Margate library to know that it was better to keep the guards hostage than let them go running off to raise the alarm. It gave her more time.

With the sentinels secure, Albert approached the Eyrie's colourful entrance tree. He smiled at Kenna just before he placed a shaking hand on the trunk. 'This is the Wild Unicorn Queen's tree; you know that, right? This is the tree that grew over her body. It feels right that we're reclaiming the Eyrie – don't you think, Kenn? For wild unicorns. For us.'

Kenna could practically taste the desperation in his voice. Albert seized upon any sign or symbol that the Skeleton Curse was necessary, that it was right for the Island, that their band of Originals was being guided by the spirit of the First Rider. Anything that meant Kenna hadn't taken away their bonded unicorns for nothing. Anything that meant she wasn't a monster. And Kenna always let him. She let them all do that.

The entrance in the great gnarled trunk opened in a roar of flames.

## NO PLACE LIKE HOME

'Now, Mateo,' Kenna commanded, and Hell's Diamond jumped over the plateau's gate, thundering down to summon the rest of the wild Originals to the Eyrie.

'I'm going through first,' Kenna told her remaining three generals. 'There might be others inside I need to deal with. Don't follow until I tell you.'

Kenna blinked as she rode Goshawk into the Eyrie, the glint of an armoured trunk catching her eye. The fragrant pines filled her lungs, the gentle clinking of the swinging bridges reached her ears. Being here was going to make her feel better . . . less alone.

But she *was* alone. There were no shouts of alarm. No thundering of hooves. Nobody running towards or away from her. Kenna summoned the spirit element and let Goshawk's presence fill the whole bond – it was something she'd been practising alone in the Wilderness. In the past, Kenna had shared Goshawk's heightened senses occasionally – hearing the heartbeat of her prey or experiencing the overwhelming detail of her sense of smell – but now she was able to channel it at will. Like at this moment, when she needed to know if there were any living beings inside the Eyrie.

Kenna listened with a stillness she'd learned over many lonely days. There. Yes. The beating hearts of unicorns in the stables – first-year air unicorns, perhaps not trusted to be down in Fourpoint just yet. She would let them loose – it wouldn't be long until they were wild, too, and then they might return of their own free will.

A bird. One. Two. Chicks in a nest. A frog. A rabbit. A surge of bloodlust went through the bond and Kenna swallowed down a desire that did not belong to her.

She listened again, the spirit element bright in her palm. But there was nothing human in any of the treehouses above her. Every single Eyrie rider was watching the Qualifiers – probably

– 277 –

# SKANDAR AND THE SKELETON CURSE

summoned by the Commodore, to watch him qualify for the Cup. Their great leader, victorious again.

Kenna wanted to laugh at the arrogance of it. The arrogance that had allowed her so easily to take the Eyrie for herself. But it angered her too. Had Rex thought her so little a threat that he only needed two teenage sentinels guarding the Eyrie's entrance? Even after the Skeleton Curse, after everything she had achieved? Even after everything she had *become*?

Goshawk bellowed deeply and pushed her own anger into the bond to spiral with Kenna's. The unicorn loved it when their emotions were in sync – especially the negative ones. The whole Eyrie felt like it was vibrating with their combined fury, and Kenna's vision blurred. She felt herself raising a palm and there was a thud as wild magic rebounded from an armoured trunk and the metal melted like a teardrop running down the bark. Goshawk shrieked in triumph.

'Kenna!' Albert's worried voice from outside. 'What's going on?'

Kenna took a deep breath. She couldn't lose control now. Not today. *Please, Gos*, she begged. *Just let it go.* And unusually Goshawk quietened.

Kenna found her voice. 'There's nobody here!'

Eagle's Dawn crashed through the entrance, as the sound of bellowing wild unicorns came up the hill behind them.

'We did it!' Kenna crowed.

But there was a hesitance in Albert's face, a shadow under his smile.

'You're worrying already, aren't you?' Kenna said shrewdly.

'No, it's just that . . .' He paused. 'How are we going to defend it, Kenn? You're the only one of us who can actually wield elemental magic. And the Island isn't exactly going to be happy about this.'

– 278 –

## NO PLACE LIKE HOME

'Wield elemental magic *reliably*,' Kenna corrected him. 'That's why we're at the Eyrie. To work on stabilising your magic and everyone else's.' She had repeated this so many times, she didn't even know if it was a lie any more.

'Look, I know you're powerful, Kenna, but you can't hold them all off. As soon as the Qualifiers are over—'

'Calling me Kenna now?' she teased, full of adrenaline. 'This must be serious.'

'C'mon,' Albert pleaded, and Kenna relented.

'Of course I have a plan, Al. I just wanted everyone to be safely inside first, okay?'

'What are you going to do?' There was trepidation in Albert's tone.

'I'm going to hide it,' Kenna murmured, as her Originals started to pour through the Eyrie's entrance.

It had taken Kenna a while to land on the idea. After all, she had tried to forget everything that had happened on her mum's island. And then she'd needed to practise. Illusion didn't come as naturally to her as other kinds of spirit magic.

'Hide what?' Albert's blue eyes were wide.

'The Eyrie. Last year, Erika Everhart managed to shield an entire island with the spirit element. I don't see why I can't do that, too. I'm more powerful than her now. I'm stronger.'

'You're going to *hide* the entire Eyrie?' Albert's mouth was fully open now.

'And the top plateau,' Kenna said, almost to herself. 'That'll make it even harder for us to be attacked. Everyone will still know where the Eyrie is, but if they can't *see* it – or us – then they're going to have a lot of trouble taking it back.' She grinned at his shocked face. 'Did you really think I'd take the Eyrie without a plan to keep it?'

'How—'

– 279 –

# SKANDAR AND THE SKELETON CURSE

But Kenna was remounting Goshawk and pushing up her sleeves.

<hr />

Later that afternoon, Kenna climbed ladders and crossed swinging bridges, only half aware of her destination. She was exhausted. The spirit magic she'd used to create the vanishing illusion had drained her, and it hadn't worked quite as she'd intended. One of her Originals had gone out to test whether the Eyrie was still visible, but on trying to re-enter had been severely injured – as if by wild unicorn magic – reporting that there was a smoky edge to the shimmering air around the hidden Eyrie.

Albert immediately announced that this was excellent news for their defences, but Kenna had been troubled. She hadn't intended the illusion to hurt anyone. Had Goshawk introduced the wild magic? Was she already losing her strength, her independence? Perhaps leaving Tsunami's Herald alive was as catastrophic as she'd first imagined . . .?

No. She and Albert had gone through this a thousand times. She had to believe she could still achieve immortality as long as she killed the other unicorns. That four deaths would give her what she needed. There could be no room for doubt, or she would crumble.

Kenna tried to focus on one of the last pieces of advice her mother had given her: *The path to immortality will be a dark one, daughter. You must embrace it like a starless sky, and the rewards will be as infinite as galaxies.*

But the words didn't comfort her as much as they once had. Because the longer Kenna walked in darkness, the more she noticed the pinpricks of light. The pride she'd felt as Eagle's Dawn touched a horn to Albert's palm. The closeness growing between her and Goshawk. The hope at Skandar and his friends taking a stand against the Commodore. The relief as Tsunami's

– 280 –

## NO PLACE LIKE HOME

Herald galloped away wild but alive. The faith in the eyes of her Originals as she led them towards the life they'd imagined. The outline of a dapple-grey unicorn watching over her from the shadows.

Kenna stopped on a familiar metal platform, her memory summoning the ghosts of the Smith siblings sitting with their legs dangling over its edge. She turned to the door and pushed it open. And there was the central trunk splashed with five colours of elemental paint.

Kenna put a hand on the trunk – her brother's old treehouse dark and quiet around her – and she felt a wave of sadness break over her so strongly she almost stumbled.

She had thought it would feel different coming back to the Eyrie. That maybe a piece of her heart might heal on entering this familiar place. That she could start gathering up the ashes of her soul and find a tiny spark burning, ready to ignite the rest.

But all she felt was emptiness. And for the first time in a very long time, Kenna Everhart let herself mourn everything she had lost, and everything she was going to lose.

## Chapter Seventeen

# RESISTANCE

From the arena, Skandar stared up at the place the Eyrie should have been, but lifting his head caused a stretch in his injured side that immediately had him doubled over with pain. Scoundrel turned his black head to check on his rider, the bond full of concern. Skandar tried to stroke the unicorn's neck, but his vision blurred and he found himself unable to focus on one thought at a time.

*I'll be all right, Scoundrel. The Eyrie has disappeared. We've qualified for the Chaos Cup. Kenna has to be responsible for this. It must be spirit magic – illusion? I'd never be strong enough to hide a whole— My mum is dead. My hip hurts so much. Why did the silver vote for me? The Weaver hid her island last year, did Kenna learn this from her? My sister hates me. My hip hurts so much I think I'm going to be sick. I miss my dad. Is Kenna inside the Eyrie? Somebody, help me. Kenn, it really hurts—*

Skandar's whole body began to shake and he was drenched in cold sweat within seconds. Sleep . . . he wanted to sleep. The sand of the arena by Scoundrel's hooves looked so soft, so welcoming.

# RESISTANCE

'Skandar! Get it together!' Bobby was suddenly filling his vision, waving a hand in front of his face. Falcon shrieked loudly as though trying to keep Skandar conscious too.

'We need to get him out of the arena. He's too visible – there's already talk of Kenna and the spirit element. We've got to hide him until this calms down.' Olu's deep voice was urgent. 'Rex won't touch him, but he can't control other Islanders – they're angry and they want someone to blame.'

'Am-bling Arch-i-pel-ago?' Skandar managed to say.

'There's no way you can fly that distance,' Bobby snapped.

Mitchell sprinted towards them. 'Jamie said we should go to the Song School. Now. He also said something about it being *time* and that Craig would also meet us there because it was *happening*.'

Olu nodded, as though that all made sense.

Bobby wasn't convinced. 'Why's Jamie talking in code?'

Mitchell shrugged. 'I have no idea, but I trust him.'

Bobby considered their non-existent options for a moment and then sighed. 'All right. Where is this singing school? Is it safe?'

'The Song School,' Mitchell corrected her. 'It's the bard equivalent of the Eyrie. And I don't think Jamie would put any of us in danger.'

A burst of shouting reached them, along with an explosion of elemental magic. The stands were empty now but the streets of Fourpoint sounded full and frenzied.

'People have completely lost it out there,' Mitchell said nervously. 'Everyone's saying it must be Kenna who's done this. Everyone thinks she made the Eyrie dis—'

'Not now,' Bobby said, glancing at Skandar's ashen face.

'Let's go.' Olu began to lead Scoundrel from the arena. 'Hold on to the front of your saddle,' he ordered gently, as

– 283 –

Skandar groaned at the movement. Scoundrel rumbled quietly, apologetically, but followed, Falcon, Bobby and Mitchell close behind.

'Flo?' Skandar whispered suddenly, the bright colours of the saddlers' temporary tents blurring together as Scoundrel passed them.

'She's safe.' Olu took a sharp right, leading Scoundrel along a line of stalls that had been selling programmes for the Qualifiers, now abandoned. 'The Silver Circle retreated to the Stronghold as soon as they saw what happened to the Eyrie – Flo and Blade went with them.'

'I wanted to . . .' The way Flo had looked at him on the counter at Sally's flashed into Skandar's mind, stealing his breath. The way her cheek had felt under his fingers.

And then he fainted against Scoundrel's neck.

Skandar regained consciousness as Scoundrel jerked to a stop, Bobby's voice ringing in his ears.

'How do we get in there?' She was standing up in her saddle to peer over the gate at what Skandar assumed was the Song School. It was one of the most unusual gates he'd ever seen. It appeared to be made of a series of different-sized pipes: dark and light metal, like the keys of a piano. In his haze of pain, he thought he might be hallucinating.

But Mitchell was also staring at the gate, in panic rather than wonder. 'I don't know how we open it, I've only been here once and—'

'You can't get in without a songprint.'

Mitchell jumped about a foot in the air, as Jamie arrived behind them.

'Why aren't you safely inside already?' Mitchell asked frantically.

– 284 –

# RESISTANCE

Jamie grinned and kissed Mitchell quickly in greeting. 'Craig told me to move Skandar and Scoundrel's armour – and all my tools.'

'My team are doing the same,' Olu said seriously.

'Good. I've just come from Chapters of Chaos – I think Craig's already inside with Agatha.'

'Agatha?' Skandar wheezed. 'What's *she* doing here?'

'Nice of you to rejoin the party,' Bobby said, but her relief outweighed her sarcasm. It was only at that moment that Skandar realised Olu had a firm hand on his back, holding him in place.

Jamie frowned at Skandar's hip. 'Let's get you inside. Fourpoint is in complete meltdown, and you're in no state to protect yourself from angry mobs.' Then a large grin spread across the blacksmith's face. 'Congratulations, by the way. Knew you could do it.'

Then, before Skandar could say thank you, Jamie touched five of the pipes on the gate one after the other – three dark, two light – and they tipped towards him so they were at head height. Then he blew a tune through them that was so *Jamie* – that so perfectly reflected his slightly sarcastic, bluntly honest, totally dedicated nature – that once he'd finished, Mitchell was wearing the goofiest grin ever. 'It's individual to me – like a fingerprint, but in a song,' Jamie explained, as the gate started to move.

'How do I get a songprint?' Bobby asked hungrily.

The blacksmith chuckled. 'If you're nice to the bards, they might write one for you.'

'*Nice* . . .' Bobby contemplated the word like she'd never heard it before.

The Song School gate didn't creak as it opened – it sang. It was as though a whole choir was breathing into its pipes as it swung forward and then closed again in a chorus of notes.

Olu put a grateful hand on Jamie's shoulder. 'Thank you for

– 285 –

# SKANDAR AND THE SKELETON CURSE

setting this up – I know it wasn't easy. But it's the safest place for all of us right now.'

*All of us?* Skandar wondered, but he was distracted by the Song School itself. Behind a giant fountain shaped like a singing woman – water pouring from her mouth like sound – were five tall Douglas fir trees. Nestled within their branches were different-sized treehouses clad with hollow wooden pipes – making them look bulbous, like log cabins wearing puffer jackets. And when the spring breeze blew, musical notes played out from the treehouses, like the Island was breathing a melody through their walls. There was no denying it: the Song School *sang*.

With its music tinkling in his ears, Skandar took a deep breath and suddenly his heart yearned for somewhere else. Because the Song School smelled like the Eyrie.

Skandar looked to where it should have been in Fourpoint's skyline. At the enormous, impossible void. The sight brought him back to reality. The Song School was beautiful, but couldn't riders just blast their way in if they were looking for the brother of the Wild Rider? He didn't want to put the bards or his friends in danger. And in his injured state he couldn't exactly defend any of them. 'Jamie, I'm not sure if I should be here. I don't want to put everyone at risk.'

Jamie shook his head. 'Stop worrying. You won't be here for long; we just need to work out our next move with the others. Craig's called a meeting.'

'What meeting? What *others*?' Skandar demanded, and then immediately winced at the effort it had taken to speak loudly.

'You'll see,' Jamie said infuriatingly. Skandar only vaguely understood what was going on as Olu strapped him to a platform at the base of the school's trees and advised him to hold on tightly to the metal handles on either side of his thighs.

Scoundrel and Falcon went off to hunt, and Bobby, Mitchell

– 286 –

# RESISTANCE

and Olu climbed behind Jamie towards the main part of the school. Then – after a minute or so – Skandar's platform began to rise on its ropes.

As he rose higher, Skandar realised that it wasn't just the treehouse walls that were musical. Every ladder rung was a wooden block, sounding a different note as his friends' heavy black boots hit them; and with four of them climbing, they made a constantly changing tune. Hundreds of bells tinkled in the trees above their heads as the wind blew. The bridge slats clacked against each other as they crossed. Even the roofs of the treehouses played their part; they were made from metal strips which, Jamie explained as he climbed, sounded out like xylophones when it rained.

Jamie's mum was waiting for them at the school's largest treehouse. Olu helped Skandar to his feet, and she waved the group through a piped door that sighed a chord as she opened it.

'I hear things in Fourpoint have just become rather exciting,' Talia said gleefully, as though Fourpoint's most famous landmark had not just disappeared into thin air. 'Oh dear, what happened to you?' she asked, noticing Skandar wincing as he hobbled into an entrance hall filled with paintings.

'He was injured in the Qualifiers, Talia,' Olu said politely.

'Perhaps one of our bards specialising in curesong can help?' Talia said to Skandar. 'Our magic won't be able to fix the injury completely, but it might make you feel more comfortable.'

'I'll be okay, thanks,' Skandar said quickly. He hadn't quite forgiven Talia for almost letting him die in a Mender dream last year.

Bobby had stopped in front of one of the paintings. 'Forking thunderstorms,' she breathed. 'Jamie, is that *you*?'

Mitchell turned back, but the blacksmith immediately tried

– 287 –

# SKANDAR AND THE SKELETON CURSE

to cover his eyes. 'Don't look – it's terrible!'

Mitchell fought him off and stared thoughtfully at the painting. In it, Skandar guessed Jamie was supposed to be singing – his mouth in a wide O – but instead it looked a bit like he was screaming.

'It's not *so* bad,' Mitchell said unconvincingly.

'Jim-Jam finally sat for his bard portrait,' Talia announced proudly. 'Every bard who sings a truesong is honoured with a portrait in the Song School.'

'I keep telling you, Mum, I'm not a bard,' Jamie said, grinding his teeth, but she was already leading them out of the hall, and up to the first level of the treehouse. Olu glided to Skandar's side so he could help him every time there was a step, but Talia barely noticed. She kept chattering as they rushed after her along a corridor of glass cubicles – Talia called them song-rooms. Inside a few, rehearsals were going on. The mouths of the trainee bards were moving, although Skandar couldn't hear a thing.

'The glass was designed and built with earth magic,' Talia explained. 'They're completely soundproof.'

'It's also why the bards are letting everyone meet here,' Jamie murmured to Skandar in a low voice. 'Well, that, and the fact I bribed my mum by agreeing to the bard portrait.'

'Who do you mean *everyone*?' Skandar asked, but before Jamie could answer, Talia was opening the glass door to the final song-room in the corridor.

'Welcome to the first meeting of the Scoundrels' Resistance,' Olu announced.

'I'm pretty sure we didn't agree on that name,' Jamie said.

And then Skandar was greeted by a room full of people clapping and cheering. Sara Shekoni was there and Craig from Chapters of Chaos. There was Mitchell's mum, Ruth, standing alongside a woman in a healer's white apron. And barrelling

– 288 –

# RESISTANCE

towards him, almost at a run, was—

'Agatha,' Skandar breathed, as she flung her arms round him. And he found he didn't care that the hug was hurting his hip.

She withdrew first to look at him. 'You look dreadful,' she said, but then a smile tugged at her lips. 'Hell of a race, though. Congratulations, Chaos rider.'

'Hang on.' Skandar frowned. 'How did you see the race? Were you in *Fourpoint*?'

'Might have been,' Agatha said evasively.

'That was rather foolish,' Mitchell observed. 'There's a warrant out for your arrest.'

'I'm aware, thank you, Henderson. But I wasn't going to miss the Qualifiers, was I? Not with two of my riders competing.' Agatha looked the happiest she had in months as she winked at Bobby. 'Congratulations, Bruna – I reckon you might win the whole damn thing!'

'That *is* the idea,' Bobby said, and she sounded very pleased.

At that moment, the apron-clad healer gently guided Skandar over to a chair, and gave him a colourful drink. 'For the pain,' she said. 'I'm Fiona – so sorry I didn't get to you earlier. I was with a patient in the fire zone. I didn't hear the news until after your operation.'

'I'm o—' Skandar started to say.

'What do you think of my handiwork? Not bad, eh?' Sara asked Skandar.

Craig cleared his throat. 'Shall we get down to business, Jamie?'

Jamie looked nervous as he stepped into the centre of the space and addressed the room. 'As soon as Skandar registered for the Chaos Cup, I decided to set up an unofficial network of the people I knew we could trust. People I knew could help if things got . . . tricky.'

– 289 –

# SKANDAR AND THE SKELETON CURSE

'The Scoundrels' Resistance!' Olu chanted, trying to lighten the mood. Everyone chuckled and Jamie rolled his eyes.

'What?' Olu said innocently. 'It's a *great* name.'

Sara shushed him, and the atmosphere became serious again.

'None of us expected Rex to make it easy for a spirit wielder to compete in the Cup,' Jamie continued. 'And we've been waiting for something to happen. Craig?'

The bookseller nodded, taking over. 'As you know, Skandar, the healers refused to help you when you were injured today. That order did not *officially* come from the Commodore, but Olu and I have contacts in Council Square who believe it *was* Rex who gave the command.'

Agatha made a disgusted noise.

'That's not all,' Craig warned. 'Those same contacts believe that Rex is preparing to pass an emergency law tonight that makes it a crime *to assist a spirit wielder*. He claims it's necessary so the riders in the Eyrie with Kenna can be arrested, but the wording would, of course, include anyone helping you.'

Bobby looked angry. 'He's taking a leaf out of Daddy Dorian's book. This is exactly what happened after the truesong in Nestling year. I mean, it wasn't a *crime* to be associated with Skandar then—'

'Back then, the head of the Silver Circle wasn't also the Commodore,' Skandar said darkly.

'But how can this be allowed?' Mitchell sounded indignant. 'That law will affect Skandar's chances in the Chaos Cup. He couldn't have a blacksmith, saddler, coach, healer – it's illegal to affect the outcome of the Cup like that.'

'I agree,' Craig said. 'But Rex would argue it doesn't affect Skandar directly. And that could probably be challenged, though at the moment everyone is more worried about Kenna's occupation of the Eyrie than the fairness of the Cup. The Skeleton

– 290 –

# RESISTANCE

Curse has affected many people on this Island and they're angry with the person responsible for it; they want her to pay for her crimes. I'm afraid they don't really care what happens to her brother.'

'Rex can't be allowed to get away with this,' Bobby said sharply.

'That's why the Scoundrels' Resistance is here,' Olu said brightly. 'So that he doesn't.'

'That's right,' Ruth Henderson said. 'Every person in this room is one hundred per cent committed to assisting *this* spirit wielder win the Chaos Cup.' She winked at Skandar.

Skandar was filled with gratitude and horror in equal measure. 'But it's too risky. What if you go to prison because of me?'

The healer stood up, her short brown hair emphasising the determined expression on her slightly pink face. 'If we go to prison, it will not be because of you, Skandar Smith. It will be because we are standing up for an Island we believe in. I, for one, do not want to live in a place where the authorities pick and choose the people I'm allowed to heal.'

'Yeah, sorry, mate, this isn't really about you,' Jamie said, grinning. 'You're a *symbol*, you see? We want to stand up against Rex and the Silver Circle. Lots of people do. And I'm very happy that means helping you, but that's not the only reason we're doing this.'

Bobby smirked. 'Yeah, spirit boy – don't be so self-centred.'

'Now that's all out of the way,' Sara said, businesslike, 'the most important thing for this first meeting is to decide *where* we're going to set ourselves up. It's no longer viable to rely upon the Wanderers – we don't want the sentinels to go after them for helping Skandar.'

Skandar felt an ache at the loss – he'd loved living on

– 291 –

# SKANDAR AND THE SKELETON CURSE

Sapphire, especially when the quartet had all still been together. The archipelago had felt safe, though now he suspected he might not feel safe again for a long while.

'We need somewhere my team can store and adjust Scoundrel's saddles,' Olu said thoughtfully.

'It needs to have some kind of forge,' Jamie said to Skandar. 'I have to make you both new armour with an improved design – I don't want any more ice shards getting through.'

'Fiona and I will need space for our healing supplies – human and unicorn – as well as space to operate if that ever becomes necessary,' Sara added.

'And although I can't get you a *Book of Spirit*, I'll make sure you have all the other Elemental Scriptures and as many other helpful books as I can get my hands on,' Ruth added. 'I'd love some shelves for them, if at all possible.'

'The Song School isn't an option,' Olu said, glancing at Talia. 'We'll be easily spotted coming and going. The entrance is far too visible – noisy too. It won't be long before Rex works out what's going on.'

'Ideally we need somewhere that can't be accessed by anyone other than us,' Jamie said thoughtfully.

'And don't forget Skandar and Bobby need to be able to actually train their unicorns,' Mitchell added. 'That means having enough space to fly and to sky battle.'

They talked in circles for a while. Eventually a few bards brought in refreshments – including a cheerful, bearded man who Skandar recognised as Jamie's dad.

One of them was wide-eyed as she handed round biscuits. 'Apparently the sentinels that have tried to climb the Eyrie's hill since it disappeared have come back with unhealable injuries – like from wild unicorn magic. Like the Wild Rider has made the Eyrie walls into weapons themselves.'

# RESISTANCE

Skandar sipped his healing drink as the bards chattered about the rumours. He felt strange at the thought of Kenna inside the Eyrie. In many ways, he was pleased she'd managed to take it from Rex. But Skandar was perplexed about what Kenna wanted. Was she trying to start her own Eyrie, like they'd feared the Weaver might do the previous year? Were he and Kenna on opposing sides or did they want the same thing now? How could that be, when Kenna's Skeleton Curse was making it easier for Rex to seize power? Did Kenna understand that? Did she care?

It was only then that Skandar realised Agatha had disappeared. He hobbled into the corridor and found Agatha inside the song-room next door, her eyes half closed.

'Are you all right?' Skandar asked.

'Are *you* all right?' she countered, pointing to his hip.

He waited.

Finally she said, 'I don't trust bards.'

'Why not?'

'They're unsettling.'

'Because of the truesongs?'

Agatha shrugged, staring out at the green of the trees. 'The future belongs in the future. If I'd known I was going to end up killing –' Agatha hesitated – 'killing Erika and losing Arctic Swansong, it would have sent me truly mad. The future should be unknowable – anything else is dangerous. Also, bards are extremely powerful.'

'Are they?' Skandar asked, surprised.

'Why do you think they're happy harbouring fugitives in the Song School? They can defend it – no problem.'

'With *what*?'

Agatha raised an eyebrow. 'I mean, you've experienced the power of sleepsong. How did that go for you?'

'That wasn't a bard's power. It was the Mender dream.'

– 293 –

# SKANDAR AND THE SKELETON CURSE

'You were *dying* in that dream, Skandar, and you still couldn't wake yourself up. Imagine how useful that is as a weapon. Then there's memorysong – where a bard will sing you a lovely tune and dredge up your absolute worst memory to distract and torment you mid-battle. There's sirensong, where you'll follow a bard anywhere, even off the edge of the Mirror Cliffs. And Talia Middleditch might seem delightful, but she is one of the most powerful people on this Island – her battlesong is legendary.'

'What exactly *is* battlesong?' Skandar asked worriedly.

'The bards can amplify riders' elemental magic with song or deepen their feelings of courage and bravery, even recklessness.'

Skandar frowned. 'But that sounds like a good thing . . .?'

Agatha chuckled mirthlessly. 'It is – if Talia Middleditch is on your side. If she's not, it can be a death sentence. Oh, look, we might get a demonstration.'

From their vantage point Skandar spotted five air-allied sentinels riding towards the Song School's musical gate. Once they reached the gate, the sentinels started shouting between the pipes. One even seemed to be trying to force it open. Getting nowhere, another blasted it with electricity.

Agatha chuckled again. 'Fools.'

'Why are you so relaxed? They might see Scoundrel any minute. What if they find out you're all helping me? Shouldn't we tell the others?'

'They won't get through the gate,' Agatha said. 'Watch.'

Bards were suddenly climbing down the Song School's ladders in a steady stream like ants, *singing* ants. Skandar couldn't hear anything through the impenetrable wall of the song-room, but he could see the bards' mouths moving, elements starting to swirl round their bodies like colourful leaves in a storm.

The sentinels were still at the gate, but as soon as the first line

– 294 –

# RESISTANCE

of bards reached the Song School's perimeter, the silver-masked riders started to fall.

Through the magic-thick air, Skandar watched as two sentinels slipped from their unicorns' backs, fast asleep. Another two appeared to be mesmerised by ghostly white images playing out scenes over the gate. One started to sob violently, her whole body shaking, and the other simply turned, face pale, and galloped his unicorn in the opposite direction. However, the final sentinel had been clever, hanging back and keeping cocooned behind shifting elemental shields that must have muffled the music's effects.

The front line of bards joined hands at that point, then the next line, then the next – until they were five lines deep. And Skandar could see that they were all singing the same song in unison.

All of a sudden, the rider dropped her elemental shield. Then dismounted.

'What is she doing?' Skandar murmured.

'Maybe don't look,' Agatha suggested darkly.

But Skandar couldn't look away. He watched as the rider removed her helmet, approached the Song School's gate on foot, and then – quite calmly – walked right into the pipes, her head bashing against the hard metal.

The rider stopped, rubbed her head, took a few steps back – and then *ran* at the gate. She smashed right into it and dropped to the ground, before struggling shakily to her feet again and—

Agatha moved in front of Skandar so he could no longer see, and he blinked as though coming out of a trance.

'Why . . .' he tried to ask, but the words caught in his throat.

'That was sirensong – it made the sentinel want to get through the gate at any cost. And she won't stop trying until she can't try any more.'

# SKANDAR AND THE SKELETON CURSE

'They won't *kill* her?' Skandar asked, completely horrified. 'Will they?'

'Oh, surely not. They'll probably stop once she's knocked herself out.' Agatha said, keeping her tone neutral – though she didn't meet his eye. 'Riders are not *always* the most violent people on this Island, Skandar. Worth remembering when you're making friends with these bards.'

Skandar hugged his arms tightly round himself. The glass beauty of the Song School felt threatening now. He thought of Jamie – big-hearted and kind – and wondered whether it wasn't just the singing that had made him reject his parents' way of life.

'It is very kind of the bards to allow us to hold this meeting,' Agatha said, watching Skandar closely, 'but I don't think we should stay here – even tonight. I don't think you should owe the bards any more than you already do.'

Skandar shivered, thinking of the sirensong. 'But where *are* we going to go? Where is there enough space for making armour and saddles, and healing and training – all in secret?'

Agatha sighed. 'I know somewhere.'

Skandar frowned. 'Why didn't you suggest it before? In the meeting?'

'It's rather complicated,' Agatha murmured. 'But I'm beginning to think it's the only viable option – no matter how much I wish it wasn't.'

Skandar waited.

'The spirit yard,' Agatha said, as though the words burned her throat. 'I think that's the only place that will do.'

Skandar knew vaguely about the other elemental yards, but a *spirit* yard? He was just opening his mouth to ask a million questions, when Agatha changed the subject.

'Do you have any idea why the silver member of the Qualifier Committee might have voted for you as the Wildcard?'

– 296 –

# RESISTANCE

'Oh, so you saw that too, did you?' Skandar said, raising an eyebrow, but Agatha just waited for him to answer. 'I don't know. All I can think is that he's acting against Rex, or maybe Flo persuaded him?'

Agatha looked thoughtful. 'Not much surprises me these days, but that—'

She was interrupted by Mitchell hurtling into the song-room, hair blazing, glasses askew. 'You have to come! They're going to sing a truesong!'

Skandar made to follow Mitchell, but realised that Agatha hadn't moved from her position by the window.

'You don't have to listen, you know,' Agatha said. 'You can just wait until the future arrives.'

'Skandar, come on!' Mitchell urged, grabbing his hand.

And with one last look at Agatha, Skandar was pulled along towards the sound of fizzing elements.

## Chapter Eighteen

# CHILDREN'S WARNING

The Song School's corridor was crowded with bards waiting for the truesong to begin. They were all shushing each other and staring towards the other end of the long passage, where a large group of children had gathered. As Mitchell pulled Skandar towards Jamie and Talia, he realised that they were bard children – from toddlers up to about six years old.

Talia had a hand half outstretched towards the children – as though wanting to help – but every single one of them had become a vessel for the elements themselves. Lightning cracked round tiny jaws, fire sparked in innocent eyes, ice formed round pigtails, and the floor of the corridor shook beneath little feet.

Skandar had thought a truesong was sung alone – was it usual for so many to sing together? Was it normal for *children* to sing a prophetic melody? He turned to ask Mitchell, but he already had his head bent over a notebook, pen poised, and multiple bards were doing the same, ready to record the precious words of the truesong. Then every child straightened up and began to sing in haunting high-pitched unison:

## CHILDREN'S WARNING

*Where peace once reigned upon these shores,*
*The chaos now takes hold—*
*By horn and hoof and battle cry,*
*A future long foretold.*

*Where hope once reigned upon these shores,*
*Now desolation rules—*
*By war and strife and sacrifice,*
*A future rife with fools.*

*Where light once reigned upon these shores,*
*The dark days now draw near—*
*By lies and spies and treachery,*
*A future filled with fear.*

*Where love once reigned upon these shores,*
*Now friends shall turn to foes—*
*By hate and hurt and prejudice,*
*A future no one chose.*

Just like Jamie had after his truesong, the children collapsed with exhaustion as soon as they had finished. The parents of the children rushed them away to recover as Skandar, Mitchell, Jamie, Bobby and the Shekonis went back into the song-room away from the hubbub.

'Has that ever happened before?' Mitchell asked Jamie immediately. 'Children singing a truesong. Singing together?'

Jamie shook his head, seemingly unable to form words.

'Felt like a horror movie,' Bobby admitted.

'It certainly didn't feel like a good sign,' Mitchell murmured, reading over his notebook again. 'And then the song itself . . .'

# SKANDAR AND THE SKELETON CURSE

Bobby tried to be upbeat, as usual, but the lightness didn't quite ring true. 'Well, we sort of all knew we'd have a fight on our hands, I suppose.'

'It talked about war, though,' Skandar said, voice hushed. 'People always get hurt in wars.' Memories surfaced: the Weaver's lifeless form winking out, the sound of Swan's body hitting the ground. A war would bring more death, more sacrifice, more loss.

'Truesongs are not set in stone,' Olu said firmly. 'Events can change their meaning.'

'That's right,' Sara said. 'And for now I think we should focus on getting you two and my daughter finishing in first, second and third place in the Chaos Cup.' She looked between Bobby and Skandar. 'I don't care about the order, as long as none of you is Rex Manning.'

And with that the tension lifted a little.

'I think Flo would make the best Commodore,' Skandar said, cheering up at the thought.

'How dare you!' Bobby cried.

Mitchell smirked. 'You can't take it personally, Roberta. He's biased. But Flo *would* be very good, though a little too kind.'

Olu chuckled. 'There wouldn't be anyone in the prison, that's for sure.'

As they continued to talk around him, Skandar's mind drifted back to the words of the children's truesong. There were so many parts of it that scared him, that filled him with dread at their possible meanings, and he began to wish he hadn't heard it at all. Perhaps Agatha had been right. Perhaps it was better to keep the future out of the present's reach.

The rest of the Scoundrels' Resistance were very enthusiastic about the idea of the spirit yard. Craig suggested that he and Agatha take Skandar, Bobby and Mitchell there immediately,

## CHILDREN'S WARNING

and send word to the others once they were safely inside. So this was how Skandar found himself leaving the Song School, under cover of darkness, and making his way through the graveyard. It was apparently a short cut to the spirit yard.

'... and that makes total sense,' Mitchell had said ominously.

Skandar hadn't been this far into the graveyard since Hatchling year, and he didn't much like being back here. In many ways it was a striking memorial to the relationship between unicorns, riders and their allied elements. An elemental tree would grow over a unicorn once it was returned to the Island's soil, its rider buried alongside. But for Skandar the ethereal beauty was mixed with a terrible bitterness – because the first time he'd ever seen the bone-white trunk of a spirit tree, it had shown him that his mother was alive and that she had chosen to leave him and Kenna behind on the Mainland.

He tried to focus on Scoundrel putting one foot in front of the other, and the pain in his hip actually became a welcome distraction. He didn't want to see the tree that had grown over Erika Everhart's unicorn – Blood-Moon's Equinox. Not now that his mother really *was* dead too.

With Bobby and Mitchell on Falcon, and Skandar and Agatha on Scoundrel, Craig – who somehow knew the way – kept darting ahead to check for sentinels. Unusually, his hair was out of its high bun, casting his face in tendrils of shadow. As they neared an unfamiliar gate, he rushed back with a finger to his lips and made a sweeping gesture, his hand across his eyes. There were sentinels patrolling nearby.

Once Craig had checked that the coast was clear, the group eventually emerged on to a Fourpoint street that Skandar didn't recognise at all – its treehouses were rotting and abandoned, hanging like carcasses across the branches.

'This is where lots of spirit wielder families used to live,'

– 301 –

# SKANDAR AND THE SKELETON CURSE

Agatha breathed in Skandar's ear. He was about to ask which treehouse the Everharts had grown up in, when Bobby moved Falcon alongside Scoundrel.

'You do realise that if Reckless Mullet has passed that law tonight, technically Mitchell and I are *assisting a spirit wielder* right now.' Her eyes shone mischievously.

Skandar was speechless. He'd been worrying about Agatha being caught and hauled off to the prison, but he hadn't even thought about Bobby and Mitchell. He was always putting them in danger, and he was so tired of it.

'Criminals, the lot of us.' Bobby chuckled, missing his devastated expression. 'Flo would be so disappointed.'

'You – you shouldn't be with me!' Skandar managed to rasp. 'You should go back to the archipelago! I didn't think!' It was all too much – he couldn't lose anyone else. The empty black shroud flashed into his mind, then Goshawk carrying Kenna away, and Flo behind the metal shields of the Stronghold.

Bobby waved a dismissive hand in his direction. 'We've been breaking laws for you since you were a Hatchling; we're not about to stop now.'

Skandar tried to protest.

'No! That silvery idiot doesn't get to separate this quartet any more than he already has, okay? If being friends with you is a crime, then I'm *very* comfortable being a criminal.' She urged Falcon closer to Craig as he led them to an overgrown track, ending the conversation.

'How does Craig know where the spirit yard is?' Skandar finally managed to ask his aunt.

She shrugged. 'A lot of the old spirit wielders you freed from the prison trust him. Far more than they trust me, that's for sure.'

The unicorns reached a pair of oaks, blocking their way.

Craig stood between them. 'It's like the dens,' he explained.

– 302 –

## CHILDREN'S WARNING

'Takes a spirit wielder to open the entrance.'

'It's right that you do it,' Agatha murmured to Skandar and helped him down from Scoundrel's back.

*Do what?* Skandar wondered. He couldn't see anything resembling an entrance as he joined the bookseller between the two ancient-looking oak trees.

Craig pointed to one trunk and then the other. 'If you look closely, there are spirit symbols carved into the bark. You need to put your palms on both at the same time. Can you manage it?'

Thanks to the healer's pain-numbing drink, Skandar was able to stretch and touch his palms to both symbols without passing out. He stood between the twin oaks, his arms outstretched as though to push them sideways. After a few seconds, the bark began to glow under his fingers, until the light reached all the way to the roots of both trees. It flooded outwards, the ground just beyond the trees shining bright white too. The glow seared into Skandar's eyes, and then – just like at the Eyrie's entrance – the lights on the ground started to wink out, leaving a space darker than the night.

Craig put a hand on the shoulder of Skandar's spirit jacket. 'It's working – look!'

The inky black ground beyond the oaks was churning like a shadowy wave. The smell of soil was strong in the air, as the ground fell away to create a hole – a passage – right down into the earth.

'That is the creepiest thing I've ever seen,' Mitchell whispered. 'And we just watched a bunch of baby bards sing a prophecy of war.'

Skandar agreed, as Scoundrel rumbled a confused growl at the ground.

'It definitely makes me think of vampires,' Bobby said thoughtfully.

– 303 –

# SKANDAR AND THE SKELETON CURSE

'What's a vamp—' Mitchell started to ask.

But Agatha shushed everyone. 'You'll need to lead the unicorns through the passage.'

Skandar looked up at her sharply. 'We're not going *down* there, surely?' The last thing he wanted was to hide in a pitch-black underground tunnel.

'Of course we are,' Agatha snapped. 'Why else would we have gone to all this trouble?'

'Skandar, the spirit yard is unusual in that it has a single entrance – this one – and spirit wielders are the only riders who can open it,' Craig explained kindly. 'As a result, it's the ideal place for Agatha to train you and Bobby for the Cup. The only place safe enough to ensure your saddler, blacksmith, healers and friends don't get caught "assisting a spirit wielder". It's rumoured the new crime will carry a heavy prison sentence.' There wasn't much that could have convinced Skandar to lead Scoundrel underground, but Craig had identified what he cared about the most – keeping Agatha and his friends safe.

Perhaps it had been naive of Skandar to hope that the passage entrance would stay open while they were inside. After only a few moments crunching along the rotting boards lining the base of the tunnel, the soil at the entrance replaced itself. And it felt like being buried alive. The old passage seemed to disintegrate around them – earth was dropping on to their heads, covering their clothes, and coating Scoundrel's and Falcon's wings. Skandar and Bobby kept their palms glowing, but somehow the dark of the tunnel ate up most of the light.

Just when Skandar thought they might be stuck in the passage for ever, light started to filter through. Stumbling towards it, the muddy group found themselves in a vast oval atrium of bone-white marble, gold spirit symbols adorning the floor and ceiling. There were five alcoves cut into the curve of the walls, each

– 304 –

## CHILDREN'S WARNING

home to full-size replicas of unicorns and riders. Every unicorn had a white spirit blaze and a large spirit symbol on its chest.

Skandar didn't know whether to feel happy or sad. This was the first place on the Island he'd ever seen the spirit element celebrated. This had been a busy place once. A place for spirit wielders just like him. But now it was deserted, the spirit element outlawed.

Agatha's voice cut through the silence. 'Who lit those?' She was pointing to the torches burning all along the atrium's smooth walls. Was someone already down here?

Craig was untroubled. 'A couple of spirit wielders mentioned how much they'd like to help with Skandar's training. I contacted them before we left the Song School and said they could meet us here. Don't worry, they're trustworthy.'

A warm feeling filled Skandar's chest at the thought of the previously imprisoned spirit wielders wanting to help him.

But Agatha was not so happy. 'They won't exactly be pleased to see me down here.'

'That was all a long time ago, I'm sure it'll be fine,' Craig said, although there was a slight wobble in his voice.

Two of the stone unicorns began moving forward, as though about to attack. It took Skandar a few seconds to process that the statues hadn't come to life but were sliding on a mechanism in the floor. It had been a very long day.

A person stepped out from behind each unicorn – a woman about Agatha's age and an elderly man using an intricately carved walking stick.

The pale woman's grey eyes snapped straight to Agatha. 'What is the Executioner doing here?'

'Of all the people,' Agatha muttered.

Craig looked pained. 'Vivian, I did tell you there was a strong chance Agatha would accompany the young riders.'

– 305 –

# SKANDAR AND THE SKELETON CURSE

'And I told *you* that if the Executioner entered the spirit yard, there was a strong chance I'd hit her in the face.'

Bobby snorted and the sound echoed eerily through the atrium.

'You always were unnecessarily violent, Viv,' Agatha said, trying to lighten the mood.

Viv was having none of it. 'Says *you*,' she spat, 'the person who betrayed us all to save her own skin.'

'That is not—'

But Agatha was interrupted by the older man banging his walking stick on the marble floor.

'Enough!' he rasped. He had tight grey braids lining his head that shone out against his dark brown skin. 'Focusing on our past grievances will get us nowhere. We three spirit wielders –' he pointed his stick at Agatha, Vivian and then himself – 'have the chance to influence the future of the Island again. We have the opportunity to help young Skandar become a Commodore who will return the spirit element to our shores.'

'Ey up!' Bobby cried. 'What about me? Everyone keeps going on about Skandar, but I actually *won* my Qualifier. It's much more likely that I'll be Commodore.'

'It's true,' Skandar said. 'Bobby is much better—'

'But there is the matter of the Skeleton Curse,' the man pointed out. 'No matter how exceptional a rider you are, young lady –' Bobby scowled – 'I'm afraid that it is very likely there will be no air wielders competing in the Chaos Cup this year.'

'We're working on that,' Mitchell said defensively. 'We're trying to identify the rider Kenna might target next.'

The old man inclined his head. 'Well, I hope that you are successful. And we will of course train both riders. In any event, we must let old grievances lie. Don't you agree, Vivian?'

Vivian rounded on Agatha. 'We were in the same year at the

– 306 –

# CHILDREN'S WARNING

Eyrie; we were allies during our Chaos Trials – friends even,' she hissed. 'I saved your neck – and Arctic Swansong's – more than once. Yet you killed Folklore's Reaper like it was nothing. Are you even sorry?'

Agatha took a step forward, her eyes pleading. 'Viv, of course I'm sorry. Of course it wasn't nothing. In a life full of mistakes, it was one of the worst I've ever made. I thought I was killing Reaper to save you, but I know now that you would have rather gone with him.' Agatha's voice broke, but she fought through it, tears streaming. 'Now Arctic Swansong is dead, I understand how terrible that choice was. I live it over and over again.'

Viv took a breath as if to interrupt, but Agatha ploughed ahead urgently.

'But back then if the Silver Circle had given you the choice they gave me, would you have let them kill every single spirit wielder on the Island? Or would you have chosen to kill their unicorns to save them from that fate, as I did? Because I couldn't do it. I couldn't sentence you all to death – my friends, my allies. But I understand now that it wasn't my choice to make. I was a coward. I'm so, so sorry.'

And suddenly, somehow, Agatha and Viv were hugging and crying. Viv was murmuring, 'I don't know what I would have done, Agatha. And I'm sorry about Erika – I remember how close you were. Let me tell you, if Reaper was still alive, I'd take on that silver Commodore myself for what he did to her.'

Agatha pulled back. 'He didn't kill her, Viv. I – it was – me. I didn't mean to, but—'

'By the five elements,' Viv said, pure horror on her white face. 'You? I should have known *he* couldn't have beaten her. Your sister did some terrible things, with horrible consequences for all of us, but I'm still ... I'm sorry.'

Once they'd quietened, the old man spoke up. 'The Silver

– 307 –

Circle has caused harm to us for generations. A silver must not win the Chaos Cup again.'

'Rex wants to invade the Mainland too,' Skandar said quietly. 'I'm sure of it.'

Although this was no surprise to Agatha, Viv demanded an immediate explanation of how Skandar knew this. Mitchell chipped in with extra details as he explained.

When he'd finished, Viv's tears had been replaced by a deep frown. 'Well then, Skandar Smith. We'd better show you around.'

Before that, Mitchell took Skandar aside. 'I'm going to head back above ground.'

'What do you mean?'

Mitchell's flaming hair dimmed slightly. 'I won't be useful here, and we can't have too many people coming in and out – it'll draw attention. You and Bobby have the Chaos Cup to focus on – and at least one of us has to concentrate on finding the next double elemental. If I stay with my mum, I can be in the Vaults from dawn until dusk. And there's Red . . . I don't want to ruin the progress we've made by abandoning her on Cerulean for weeks.'

Skandar didn't know what to say. He knew Mitchell was right, but he didn't want him to go.

Mitchell pulled him into a hug. 'I'll be back as soon as I've worked out who the double air elemental is. Craig's leaving in a minute, too; Agatha's going to walk us out of the tunnel.'

It was decided then – his quartet would split in half. Two of them above ground, two of them below. And Skandar couldn't shake the feeling that everything was falling apart.

Chapter Nineteen

# THE SPIRIT YARD

Once Mitchell had left the spirit yard, Skandar found it very hard to concentrate on his tour of the place that had been designed to train the best wielders of his element. He knew he should feel excited and grateful to be here, but he was still raw from Mitchell's departure *and* his hip hurt. He shook himself, trying to tune back in to the old man – Konrad – who was telling them that the spirit yard was the only one located underground.

'Spirit wielders have always been a secretive lot, even before the Silver Circle started confirming all of our worst fears,' Viv added.

Konrad proudly described how the yard was for the elite of the elite, and Skandar remembered a conversation that felt like a lifetime ago about Prim being accepted to the fire yard. Agatha explained, reluctantly, that she hadn't managed to win a place at the spirit yard before her element was outlawed.

The five statues in the atrium depicted famous spirit unicorns and riders, and they also served as entrances to different areas of the yard. Konrad explained that two of the five chambers,

# SKANDAR AND THE SKELETON CURSE

marked NOURISHMENT and LEARNING, could be used by the Scoundrels' Resistance.

Nourishment was the old refectory. There was no food down here, of course, and it would be ridiculous for the small group to sit at the enormous marble tables to eat, but it did have a large fireplace that Jamie could use as a forge, and enough space for the Shekoni Saddles team to work.

Learning was an empty library. 'After the Fallen Twenty-Four, lots of us spirit wielders guessed that the Silver Circle would come for us,' Viv explained. 'There were attempts to hide the books elsewhere, as we thought the spirit yard might be compromised. It was a mistake in hindsight. Now the books are lost.'

Konrad suggested that Craig, Ruth and the healers might fill the empty bookshelves with helpful texts, as well as store medical supplies. And – in case Skandar was injured again – one of the long reading benches could be used by Fiona as an operating table.

'Not as good as the counter at Sally's Sandwiches in my opinion,' Bobby whispered mischievously.

There wasn't much else to see in Nourishment and Learning, so the tour moved on to the other three entrances. The first was labelled CHAOS, which housed a small replica of the Chaos Cup course, complete with grass, small sandy arena and a real starting bar. The ceiling of the vast chamber was painted blue, creating the illusion of open sky, and the walls had murals depicting scenery from the four zones.

'It is rather nice to be back here,' Konrad said with a nostalgic sigh.

'Konrad taught at the Eyrie as well as the spirit yard,' Agatha whispered in Skandar's ear, as they exited the Chaos chamber. She pointed to the marble statue. 'His unicorn was Soul

– 310 –

## THE SPIRIT YARD

Stealer, and they were one of the most eminent spirit training partnerships ever to grace the Island. He taught your mother down here.' Skandar recognised Konrad in the marble rider now, and he felt a searing sadness, almost envy, that the spirit coach had known a different Erika – one he'd never really met.

The entrance marked COMBAT led to a vast underground battle chamber and much moodier than Chaos, the rock so dark that even the torches couldn't brighten it completely. Bobby was beside herself with excitement. 'Look at the jousting pistes! Are those archery targets? And where do those go?' She pointed to a line of heavy-looking doors lining one wall.

'Weather chambers,' Viv answered. 'Coaches send you in there and then manipulate the atmosphere to mimic how the weather can change during a race. Of course, riders can *create* weather to be used as a weapon too – they used to teach that to Rookies at the Eyrie. The chambers prepare riders for both eventualities.'

Agatha seemed very reluctant to come with them through the third entrance: REST.

'I'll just sleep out here,' she said, backing away.

'That's ridiculous.' Viv took Agatha by the elbow. And then added more quietly, 'You're going to have to face them at some point.'

Viv placed her palm over the element symbol on the statue's chest and it moved to allow them access to the fifth and final chamber. Skandar couldn't understand why Agatha hadn't wanted to come in here – Rest was breath-taking. They'd stepped right into an underground forest of bone-white spirit trees, with grassy earth beneath their feet. The trees looked exactly like those that grew over the spirit unicorns buried in the graveyard. Though, on closer inspection, the larger ones held treehouses made of bleached white wood. Cream-coloured ladders and

– 311 –

# SKANDAR AND THE SKELETON CURSE

walkways connected the trees, just like at the Eyrie. No sun shone down here, yet their spindly white branches stretched up towards the black roof of the chamber painted with clusters of stars.

Viv had gone immediately to a white tree ahead of them and was tracing her hand over the words scratched there. Agatha, meanwhile, had gone very white.

'Are you okay?' Skandar whispered, as Konrad moved to a different tree, his head bowed. Bobby wandered further into the forest, looking around curiously.

'I never wanted to come back here,' Agatha was muttering. 'I never wanted to see them again.'

'See what?' Skandar asked gently, trying to understand the stricken look on his aunt's face.

It took Agatha a very long time to find her voice. 'Spirit wielders and their unicorns have been buried down here for centuries – many didn't trust the Island graveyard, you see. And, well, I, when I was the Executioner, after I killed the spirit unicorns, I buried them down here.'

'You what?'

Agatha's eyes were haunted. 'The Silver Circle didn't care what happened to the bodies – as long as they weren't buried in the Island's graveyard. They were going to leave them to rot, so . . . Arctic Swansong and I brought them down here.'

Skandar's mouth was dry. 'That must have taken days.'

'Weeks,' Agatha rasped. 'I suppose it was the only thing I could do to try to . . . well, I could never make up for it.'

'So the tree Viv is standing at – it grew over Folklore's Reaper? And Konrad—'

'That's Soul Stealer's tree, yes. I marked where I buried all the unicorns. That way I thought they could be reunited with their riders. One day, at least.'

– 312 –

## THE SPIRIT YARD

'I can't believe you had to do that alone,' Skandar whispered. 'I'm so sorry.'

'Come on,' Agatha said, rubbing her fading cheeks. 'Let's find the others.'

Agatha and Skandar reached Bobby just as she was asking, 'So what you're saying, is that you're expecting us to sleep in a graveyard?'

'Yes,' Konrad answered, softly. 'That is the custom.'

'Forking thunderstorms,' Bobby cursed. 'Spirit wielders are *way* creepier than I thought.'

'We don't see it that way at all,' Konrad said, almost smiling. 'Our sky-fallen comrades have gone before us to another shore, that's all. They rest, just as we will rest one day. There's nothing to be afraid of here.'

And it was one of those very rare occasions when Bobby was lost for words.

'Anyway,' Viv said, glancing at Agatha's haunted face and changing the subject, 'your unicorns will sleep in the stables over there – just at the edge of the forest.'

The stables looked beautiful. They were constructed from the same white wood as the treehouses, with large doors carved with the spirit element symbol and golden lanterns hanging above. Compared to the beach on Sapphire, it was pure luxury for Scoundrel.

'I think we should all get some sleep,' Agatha announced stiffly, her eyes flicking between different spirit trees.

Once Scoundrel and Falcon were safely in the stables, Skandar and Bobby settled in a pair of hammocks inside one of the white treehouses.

'Do you reckon there are unicorn ghosts down here?' Bobby whispered.

'Ghosts aren't real,' Skandar said forcefully. He wasn't sure

– 313 –

# SKANDAR AND THE SKELETON CURSE

if Bobby was joking, but it wasn't something he wanted to talk about in an underground spirit graveyard. Especially when his sore hip was likely to keep him awake most of the night.

'Says the boy who jousted the First Rider and then had a nice chat with him,' Bobby scoffed. 'You know what's really sad about this place?' Bobby whispered.

'The spirit yard?'

'Yeah. Everything's built on years – centuries even – of spirit wielders feeling like they need to hide themselves away. All that power and they still felt like they had to be apart in order to be safe.'

'I hadn't thought about it like that.'

'It's the way I used to feel with my panic attacks, before I met you and Flo and Mitchell,' Bobby continued quietly. 'But I can't imagine how miserable it must be having so little trust that people will accept you for who you are that – well – you build an underground bunker.'

'I think seeing the spirit yard is the first time on the Island that I've actually felt grateful for the way things turned out for me,' Skandar whispered. 'I mean, if the spirit element had been legal, then maybe I wouldn't have learned what it's like to have friends like you, Mitchell and Flo. Maybe I would have accepted less for myself, hidden away with the spirit wielders, and not seen that maybe the Island could be different, better. In that way I'm lucky.'

'You're the luckiest,' Bobby said, and he could sense her grin even in the dark. 'Not everyone gets to be friends with someone as great as me.'

And Skandar was still smiling as he drifted off to sleep.

For a few weeks after arriving at the spirit yard, Skandar's injury was not healed enough for him to restart training. And Agatha

# THE SPIRIT YARD

insisted that it wasn't a good idea for him to go above ground either – just in case Rex or his cronies tried anything. Skandar had thought he might enjoy the break, but instead he found it frustrating to focus only on theory. And the more time he had to fill, the more he was overcome with worries about Rex, Kenna and the Skeleton Curse. This wasn't helped by Bobby's frequent visits to Isa in Fourpoint, which brought news of the Island's response to Kenna's occupation of the Eyrie.

The young Eyrie riders were now living inside the Silver Stronghold instead – along with Instructors O'Sullivan, Anderson and Webb – and Rex had given a speech about a *new age of efficiency and elemental strength* overseen by the Silver Circle. As rumoured, he also passed the law against assisting a spirit wielder, which delayed the arrival of the rest of the Scoundrels' Resistance, who decided they would only risk entering the spirit yard when their help became crucial in the lead-up to the Cup.

Bobby also brought back copies of the *Hatchery Herald*, which was printing more and more anti-Mainlander articles. There was an alleged food poisoning at Fred's Frothing Fish Sticks – Fred had grown up in Cornwall before being called to the Island – and a Mainlander tavern owner was accused of overcharging. And the *Herald* was still producing lists of riders who were missing and suspected of having joined their *fellow Mainlander*, the Wild Rider.

Bobby regularly checked in with Mitchell, too – in particular his progress with identifying potential air wielders who were double elementals.

'Apparently the problem is the Mainlanders,' Bobby explained to Skandar one evening as they lay in their hammocks among the ghostly white trees. 'The Island doesn't have their birth records; the only way I know about Isa is because I was literally present when she was born.'

– 315 –

# SKANDAR AND THE SKELETON CURSE

'Can we maybe ask around?' Skandar suggested sleepily; all his healing was sapping his energy.

'What? Ask every single air-allied Mainlander on the Island when they were born?' Bobby scoffed. 'We haven't got the time, Skandar! It just feels so hopeless. What if Isa gets stuck as a skeleton? What if Falcon . . .?'

But one day, just when Skandar began to feel like he might lose his head with all the bad news, Bobby finally managed to visit the post trees in Fourpoint, and brought him a card from his canister. He tore it open.

Congratulations on your new job!

Confused, Skandar read the words inside:

DEAR SKANDAR,

I WAS GOING TO GET YOU A BIRTHDAY CARD, BUT I THOUGHT CONGRATULATIONS WAS A BETTER FIT AFTER WHAT'S HAPPENED. SAW THE TWENTY-FIVE CHAOS CUP RIDERS AND UNICORNS LISTED IN THE PAPER THIS MORNING. PROUDEST MOMENT OF MY LIFE SEEING MY SON'S NAME ON THERE. MY SON, A CHAOS RIDER. I'VE ALREADY BEEN PLANNING MY TRIP TO THE ISLAND FOR THE CUP. I WAS READING ABOUT IT AND I'M GUARANTEED A TICKET BECAUSE YOU'VE QUALIFIED. I KNOW YOU WON'T HAVE MUCH TIME TO WRITE NOW WITH ALL YOUR TRAINING SO DON'T WORRY ABOUT ME. JUST KNOW I'M PROUD AND I LOVE YOU AND I CAN'T WAIT TO SEE YOU AFTER THE BIG RACE! DAD X

PS HAPPY BIRTHDAY

Skandar wiped away his tears – he hadn't realised just how much he'd needed to see Dad's words, even in a silly card. He asked Bobby to pick him up a sketchbook next time she was in Fourpoint – that way he could draw Dad pictures of Scoundrel

– 316 –

## THE SPIRIT YARD

and Falcon training for the Cup. Even if it was a while until it was safe enough to send them.

On another memorable evening, Bobby returned to the spirit yard with unusually neat hair and new purple nail varnish.

'Don't ask,' she said to Skandar, messing up her fringe so she looked normal again.

'Oh, please let me ask!'

She sighed. 'Fine. One of the *Hatchery Herald* reporters spotted me and nabbed me for an interview. Which then turned into a video for Mainland TV, which then turned into a photo shoot. You know how these things can get.' Skandar sensed a bit of pride under her blasé attitude.

Skandar chuckled. 'Wow. How does it feel to be famous?'

Bobby yawned. 'Tiring. And anyway, you're *more* famous. You just never go above ground.'

'I don't think anyone would want to *nab* me for an interview,' Skandar said, and the thought of it made him feel a bit sick.

'Isa said she thinks Real Meany is making sure the *Hatchery Herald* interviews all the air wielders that have qualified. That way he appears confident he's going to stop the Skeleton Curse before the Chaos Cup.'

'But Flo said he doesn't even *want* to stop the Skeleton Curse!' Skandar protested.

'Exactly.' Bobby frowned. 'But me chatting to reporters – going on about how excited I am to be one of the youngest Chaos riders ever – makes it look like everything is going to be okay, doesn't it? Like I'm not petrified Falcon will be turned wild at the Air Festival.'

As soon as Skandar had recovered from his injury, he joined Bobby in the most gruelling training schedule of their lives. It was so relentless that when Jamie arrived at the spirit yard with all his tools – and the Shekoni Saddles team started lugging

– 317 –

# SKANDAR AND THE SKELETON CURSE

down their supplies – Skandar barely had a chance to say hello to them.

Even when the unicorns rested, Skandar and Bobby were subjected to theory lessons from Konrad, who wanted them to catch up on the two years of Eyrie training they hadn't had, as well as anything he could remember about silver unicorns. They ate food Craig brought for them, while trying to read practically his entire shop, as well as most of Ruth's book collection. There was no time for sadness or flickering memories of black shrouds or dead unicorns. No time for being angry at Kenna, or missing her, or wondering why she'd left Tsunami's Herald alive. No time for imagining Mainland invasions or worrying over truesongs. By the evening all Skandar was good for was sleep – until it started all over again the next day.

Skandar had spirit-specific sessions from all three instructors, which irritated Bobby when she first found out.

'Why can't I learn spirit magic as well? It would give me an edge over the other competitors.'

Agatha had sighed loudly, used to Bobby by now. 'We did consider teaching you too. But it felt like a waste of your time and energy. If you use it during the Cup, even accidentally, you'll be disqualified. It's not worth the risk. Only Skandar—'

Bobby had huffed. 'Only Skandar is allowed to use it on the whole Island. I *know*. But I'm going to learn it one day. I have no doubt I'm badass enough to deal with the death element.'

Konrad had winced; Viv had rolled her eyes.

Three days before the Air Festival, Bobby and Skandar were engaged in something that Agatha liked to call an *all-out* sky battle. They'd raced round the miniature course inside the Chaos chamber three times, and now Scoundrel and Falcon were facing each other in mid-air, tired but full of adrenaline. It was an attempt to mimic those desperate moments in a race when

– 318 –

# THE SPIRIT YARD

they had nothing to lose and everything to gain. The idea was that they could use any kind of magic they'd learned. Agatha and Viv were watching and assessing their every move.

Bobby had her favourite weapon – a lightning bow – in her hands, and was shooting her fifth electric arrow of the battle towards Skandar. Scoundrel managed to freeze it with an ice blast from his roaring mouth, so it hung between the two unicorns. Then Skandar's palm glowed blue, and he copied a move Agatha had once used on him. He summoned a huge wave towards Falcon on her right side, before using the spirit element to make it appear to be crashing towards her left. But Bobby saw the glow in his palm change from blue to white, and – instead of blocking the wave with a shield – she flew Falcon downwards, avoiding the illusion altogether.

Then, suddenly, Bobby had powered up an elemental predator from fire magic – a Marauder-level golden eagle – and it was swooping towards his helmeted head, beak wide, talons flaming. Bobby almost always favoured birds – Konrad said they were the easiest predators for air wielders – and Skandar had learned that one of the best ways to defeat them was through confusion. He summoned the spirit element to his palm and within a couple of seconds had managed to duplicate himself and Scoundrel in the air.

'PAUSE!' Viv yelled. The spirit wielder loved shouting commands, and always enjoyed herself most when there was a battle going on.

Up in the sky, the eagle and duplicate winked out; the two real unicorns hovered, their riders waiting for instructions.

'Skandar,' Agatha called up to him, 'try to do what we practised with the duplicate.'

'Hey! You're coaching him mid-sky battle!' Bobby yelled. 'No fair.'

– 319 –

# SKANDAR AND THE SKELETON CURSE

'Take it as a compliment,' Agatha grunted.

'RESET!' Viv shouted gleefully.

Bobby summoned the eagle again, this time with the air element, and Skandar tried hard to do as Agatha had asked. In his spirit training sessions he'd been trying out more complicated moves with the duplicates, learning that they didn't just have to use the spirit element. Concentrating on the bond between himself and Scoundrel, he filled it with a combination of fire and spirit. Almost immediately, the duplicate burst into the air beside him, and this time the other Skandar hurled a fireball towards Bobby's electric eagle as it swooped in to attack the other Scoundrel. The real Skandar moulded a spirit sabre for his own hand, trying to make Bobby think *he* was the copy.

Bobby hesitated, but it was only for a moment. 'Can't fool me, spirit boy!' she yelled, hurling lightning bolts at the *real* Scoundrel. Skandar had not been expecting Bobby to work it out so quickly, or to attack so effectively – especially with the power drain from the predator – and he fumbled for some sort of shield, taking too long to choose between fire and earth. The duplicate Skandar and Scoundrel winked out, and in desperation the real Skandar dive-bombed the grass.

Just before Scoundrel pulled out of the dive, Skandar exploded the grass below him, throwing up great clumps. He'd first had this idea from the Wanderers back in the oasis – using your environment as magic itself – but recently Viv had told them it would normally have been taught in the Rookie year at the Eyrie. Grass and rock were thrown upwards and he summoned the air element to swirl the debris into position, shielding Scoundrel from the eagle's talons and Bobby's relentless attacks.

Then, through the crackle of the lightning bolts thumping into the turf, Skandar became vaguely aware of somebody calling both his and Bobby's names over and over. He saw Bobby turn

– 320 –

# THE SPIRIT YARD

and look over her shoulder, dropping her yellow palm. Her air eagle disappeared, and Skandar's palm lost its green glow as the earthy chunks around him fell like enormous green hailstones.

Mitchell was sprinting on to the replica Chaos Cup course, waving up at them and shouting. Skandar's heart, already thundering from the battle, felt as though it was about to burst out of his chest. It was the first time Mitchell had been down to the spirit yard since they'd arrived – Konrad must have let him in. Was it terrible news? Kenna? Flo? The Mainland? Scoundrel landed seconds after Falcon.

Bobby was already shaking Mitchell by the shoulders. 'What's happened? Is it Isa?'

Mitchell shook his head, his flaming hair billowing wildly. 'No, no, nothing like that. I've found a double air elemental. An Islander.'

'Who is it?' Skandar asked breathlessly.

Bobby was frantic. 'We have to get them. We could bring them down here, couldn't we? Kenna probably doesn't even know about this place.'

'Well, erm, you might not be so keen on that when you hear who it is.'

Skandar and Bobby waited.

Mitchell took a deep breath. 'Amber Fairfax.'

Kenna

# IN TOO DEEP

Kenna Everhart had a serious problem.

She was pacing round the Eyrie's elemental walls, waiting for her generals. She let the sounds of the training session wash over her as she ran a hand along the seaweed of the water quadrant's wall.

Since reclaiming the Eyrie, at least half of Kenna's Originals had started accessing their unicorns' elemental magic. The Eyrie had become a training school again, with magic lighting up the place at all hours. There was even the occasional white flash of the spirit element from some of the more advanced recruits. By far the most popular training sessions were those run by Finneas – who'd been an air yard coach – with his unicorn Vulture's Voltage.

Kenna had noticed that the magic of those who'd been training the longest – like Albert – did seem to be strengthening. His colours were bolder now as they filled the shining cord between his and Eagle's hearts. But they never stayed. In truth, all the Originals' bonds were still unstable – not at all like destined or

# IN TOO DEEP

even forged connections. And there was certainly no trace of the dark power that danced at the edges of her own magic. Kenna's promise that they would one day be allied to all five elements – as she was – was feeling more like a lie.

Thoughts spiralling, Kenna reached the air-allied stretch of the Eyrie's wall and found herself beheading a few sunflowers. Then she noticed that her fingertips were glowing white. She looked up.

'You,' she breathed.

Ahead of her stood the dapple-grey unicorn.

A snort shook its skeletal nostrils and it raised its head at the sound of her voice. Kenna felt guiltily for Goshawk in the bond, but the unicorn was hunting faraway in the Wilderness.

'I didn't know you'd followed me here,' Kenna said warily.

The dapple-grey looked at her with its sad red eyes and pawed at the ground – front hooves glowing with soul-shine.

'I understand who you are,' Kenna whispered. 'But I've chosen another.'

The dapple-grey just stood there, staring, and Kenna wondered whether it could tell what she'd done, could sense the unicorn blood she'd spilled. Kenna wiped away tears of shame. There was a tug of concern in the bond – Goshawk was worried about her and had paused her hunt to check in.

'I don't have time for this today,' Kenna snapped at the dapple-grey, and the unicorn rumbled in surprise. 'I hardly have any time left at all.'

The unicorn simply watched her as though she was the only interesting thing in the world. And somehow Kenna couldn't leave that part of the wall just yet. She found herself confiding in the wild creature.

'The air-allied pair I need for the curse has vanished,' she explained to the unicorn. 'The Air Festival is tomorrow, and I'm

– 323 –

worried that the Skeleton Curse *and* my chance at immortality are going to be lost if I don't find them.'

The wild unicorn blinked, an eyelash dropping from its rotting eyelid to the ground.

'Can't you see it's too late to change my mind? All these people are counting on me now. I have to do it. I can't let my mum down and I can't let Albert down or the others.'

The wild unicorn flicked a tattered grey wing as though in sympathy, and Kenna squeezed her eyes shut. She took a deep breath. 'There is an alternative, but I don't know if I can do it,' she confessed.

The dapple-grey moved one step closer, and Kenna knew that every bone in her body must be glowing, because the wild unicorn was almost blinding now in the shade of the wall.

'Have I made a mistake?' she breathed. 'With all of it? I know you probably think I have. You'd say what's the point of being powerful if you've got nobody left to protect? What's the point in living for ever if you can't share it with the one person you love the most.'

The words surprised her. She had barely admitted them to herself these past few months.

Very gently, *far* more gently that she'd ever expected for a wild unicorn, it put its rotting nose against her hand. Kenna's heart accelerated with fear and something she couldn't quite place. 'Skandar's never going to—' She stopped herself. 'Anyway, it's too late for any of that, any of *this*.'

With the last word, she flicked her hand away from the wild unicorn's nose, and its skeletal neck jerked in surprise. It backed away almost fearfully, and then turned without looking back. As Kenna watched its straggly tail disappear over the other side of the hill, she had a horrible feeling that it had indeed understood everything she'd said, and everything she was, and everything

– 324 –

## IN TOO DEEP

she was trying to be. She was hit with a wave of self-hatred. A longing for the dapple-grey's return. A sting of remorse.

But most of all, Kenna felt her resolve harden. Skandar was lost to her. Even the dapple-grey had turned from her now. She felt for the forged bond, and its searing presence round her heart settled the storm in her mind. As long as Kenna lived, Goshawk's Fury would never leave her – and neither would the promise she made herself the day she'd watched her mother die: *I will never feel powerless again.*

And so Kenna knew what she had to do, even though she was going to hate herself for it. They were all going to hate her for it.

That evening Kenna summoned three of her generals to Skandar's old treehouse.

'Where's Finneas?' Mateo asked Adela and Albert, as they settled on the beanbags. Mateo, in typical earth-wielder fashion, was unhappy to start the meeting without the air-allied general.

Adela combed her fingers through her smoking curls. 'Maybe he wasn't asked, darling.'

Kenna cleared her throat, stroked the feathers at her ear. 'As you're aware, we had everything in place for the Air Festival. We'd identified the target, and extracting her was going to be easy enough – she was in the Stronghold and we have our flame-eyed friend there.'

'What do you mean extracting her *was* going to be easy?' Mateo asked anxiously.

'She's no longer in the Silver Stronghold. And, well, none of my contacts can find her.'

Adela and Mateo started talking at the same time, panicking, while Albert sat in silence.

'Where did she go? It's tomorrow!'

– 325 –

## SKANDAR AND THE SKELETON CURSE

'What if the unicorns return to normal? We'll never be allied to five elements!'

Kenna held up her hand and the silence was immediate. 'I have a solution.'

The generals visibly relaxed – except Albert. He looked pained, as though he already knew what Kenna was about to say.

'I have identified another target. Extraction won't be a problem.'

'Why not?' Adela asked.

'This rider and unicorn are inside the Eyrie.'

There was a beat of silence as they processed what she'd said.

A beat before they remembered that she was a monster.

Mateo was first – the cleverest. 'You mean you're going to sacrifice an *Original's* unicorn?'

'Turn one of our own riders into a skeleton?' Adela echoed.

Kenna made herself shrug, as though unbothered. 'One of our number happens to be an air wielder *and* a double elemental.'

'Finneas?' Albert breathed. 'Isn't it? That's why he's not here.'

'Kenna, you can't!' Adela cried, her cool facade gone.

'Unless you find me another sacrifice in the next twelve hours, I don't have a choice.' Kenna was getting impatient now. She felt guilty enough already; she didn't need them making her feel worse.

'Why even bother to call us here if you've already made up your mind?' Mateo demanded angrily.

Albert twitched protectively – he was still on Kenna's side, even after this. He was in too deep, just like her.

'I need you to deal with the consequences. Explain to the rest of the Originals why it is necessary to sacrifice Vulture's Voltage.'

'We have magic now,' Mateo threatened, though his voice wobbled.

– 326 –

# IN TOO DEEP

'You don't have magic like mine,' Kenna said evenly.

'We can stop you,' Adela insisted.

Kenna sighed. 'No. You can't.'

They shifted uneasily on their beanbags, their eyes flicking to Albert for support.

'What?' Kenna asked aggressively. 'Did you think this was going to be easy? We're following in the First Rider's footsteps, rebuilding his bone staff. We are reclaiming an Island by taking down a silver Commodore. Or did you think Rex would just stand aside and hand over the power he has worked so hard to build? The Skeleton Curse *must* be completed, no matter the price.'

Kenna caught Albert's eye, and she detected the shadow of a nod. Albert had promised he would not let the forged bond harm Kenna the way it had the Weaver. And he always kept his promises. They'd agreed after the Water Festival that the death of the air unicorn was vital, the spirit, too – no matter whose they were. If Kenna was to avoid the devastation inflicted on her mortal body by the forged bond, she needed more than the draining of their bonds that the Skeleton Curse required – she needed to kill both the final sacrifices to ensure her best chance at immortality. And although Albert cared for the future of the Island they were striving for, he cared more about Kenna. It was the one thing they never spoke of.

'We have work to do,' Albert said abruptly, rising from his beanbag.

Adela and Mateo looked as though they still wanted to argue.

So Kenna blasted the treehouse door from its hinges, which she thought was a clear enough signal for them to get the hell out of her sight.

### Chapter Twenty

# PARLEY

In the end, it was Flo who'd managed to get Amber to leave the Silver Stronghold. Olu was saddler to a couple of the Eyrie riders who were training inside, and although *he* was refused entry, he'd convinced a sentinel that Flo needed to check over the stitching on one of his saddles before it was handed to its rider. The stitching was bad on purpose, and because Flo knew her dad would never let a saddle out of his workshop like that, she'd easily found the note he'd hidden within it.

> *Get Amber Fairfax out of the Stronghold before the Air Festival. Tell her Whirlwind Thief's life depends on it.*

Two nights before the season changed, Amber had snuck Whirlwind Thief out of the Stronghold under cover of darkness. They'd been met with a trio of bards singing sleepsong along the silver birch avenue. Bobby had thrown a snoring Amber over her shoulder, and Mitchell had pulled a sleepy Thief along the row of trees. From there Bobby had rushed Amber to the Shekoni

# PARLEY

workshop to snooze off the effects of the song under the watchful eye of Sara Shekoni. Mitchell had met Skandar at the entrance to the spirit yard, and they'd smuggled a drowsy Whirlwind Thief safely underground. It had been Mitchell's genius idea to separate Amber from Thief – Kenna would have to find both of them if she wanted to complete the next stage of the Skeleton Curse.

The first morning of May dawned and the air season with it. But by late afternoon Skandar, Bobby, Mitchell and Amber weren't feeling very spring-like. The four of them were hiding out in a very small tack-room at the Shekoni workshop and somehow – even after hours of complaining on her part and hours of explaining on theirs – Amber was *still* talking.

'This is absolute foolishness! *Surely* we don't need to hide out in this ramshackle old place?' She gestured to the upturned saddle box she was sitting on. '*Surely* the Stronghold is safer – it's probably the most secure place on the Island after the—'

'The Eyrie? Oh yeah,' Bobby finished for her. 'The place Kenna is currently occupying.'

'*Surely* Kenna wouldn't be stupid enough to attack the Stronghold? *Surely* she's not strong enough to overpower the whole Silver Circle?'

'We think Kenna might have an ally in the Stronghold,' Skandar murmured. The flame-eyed sentinel from the oasis last year came into his mind. That had been their main worry once they'd found out Amber was in the Stronghold. If Kenna and the sentinel were still allies, he would have easy access to the double elemental she needed.

'But how do you know I'm the *right* double elemental? *Surely* I'm not the only air wielder born in the air season?'

'Don't look at me – I'm an Aries.' When Amber looked confused, Bobby sighed impatiently. 'Mainland thing – my birthday's the twenty-fifth of April. Water season.'

– 329 –

# SKANDAR AND THE SKELETON CURSE

'So not you, but *surely* there must be others?'

Bobby groaned. 'Amber, if you don't stop saying *surely*, I'm going to strangle you with that stirrup leather.'

The two girls had been going at each other for hours. It didn't help that Bobby was worrying about both Falcon *and* Isa. Mitchell tried to derail this latest argument. 'You're right, Amber. There's a possibility that other double air elementals exist. But it's *your* father, Simon Fairfax –' Amber froze – 'who was in league with the Weaver. We have a theory that the Skeleton Curse was originally the Weaver's plan, and that she *knew* you were a double elemental. And if that's true, then she may have passed your name on to Kenna.'

Amber opened and closed her mouth. 'I suppose that does make sense.' She turned to Skandar. 'Own up then, did your sister bring something from the Mainland for the curse?'

Skandar stared at her. 'What do you mean *from the Mainland*?'

Amber's forehead puckered, her electric star flickering. 'Oh, I see, you don't know everything. You're all just super obsessed with me then.'

'Nobody is obsessed with you,' Bobby growled.

'Not even you, Bruna?' Amber raised a chestnut eyebrow.

The air wielders stared fiercely at each other, a flush rising up Bobby's neck.

'Amber?' Skandar interrupted, tentatively. 'What do you mean about my sister having a Mainland object?'

Amber broke eye contact with Bobby. 'Apparently Rex's researchers have discovered that the Skeleton Curse requires some sort of object from the Mainland in order to be effective. He told the Eyrie riders last week.'

'What absolute nonsense,' Mitchell spluttered. 'There is no way a cyclical *Island* curse is going to require an object from the Mainland.'

# PARLEY

'All right, Henderson! I didn't say *I* believed it, did I? That's just what Rex said.'

'Rex is twisting everything,' Skandar said furiously. 'The curse does require an object – pieces of the bone staff! – but Rex is making out that it's all a Mainland thing because—'

'Why are you still listening to that snake anyway?' Bobby asked Amber. 'Why are you training in the Stronghold? You were part of the rider revolt back at the Eyrie. What happened to *that*, Amber? Are you too much of a coward to leave?'

'Look, Bruna, there's no need to get nasty. I'll have you know there's actually a group of us who are *not* fans of Rex, okay? But we thought it would be more useful to be *inside* the Stronghold than outside. In there we hear things. *Super*-useful things – about Mainland objects, for example. Although I suspect Rex isn't going to let me back in now – I didn't exactly ask for permission to leave the Stronghold.'

'So you're *spying* on the Commodore?' Bobby asked, actually sounding impressed.

Amber put a finger to her lips. 'On the whole Silver Circle. Ivan's in on it – remember him? He rides Swift Sabotage. Then there's Patrick and Hurricane Hoax – and a few non-air wielders who stayed at the Eyrie too. It's a whole thing. And naturally *I'm* the one who set it all up,' she finished proudly, her eyes fixed on Bobby.

'What else have you found out?' Skandar asked excitedly, thinking of Rex's invasion plans – but suddenly there were running footsteps and shouts along the road outside.

They listened, the ragged sound of their breaths filling the tiny space. Skandar had no idea what time it was. They knew that Rex was ploughing ahead with an Air Festival celebration and encouraging the whole Island to attend. Skandar wasn't entirely sure who would want to risk a trip to Element Square, given

– 331 –

# SKANDAR AND THE SKELETON CURSE

the chance of the air unicorns turning wild. But judging by the sounds outside, the Fourpoint streets were far from deserted.

'I'm sure it's just people on their way to the festival,' Mitchell insisted, when there was another loud shout from outside.

Then the door to the tack room burst open and Sara Shekoni stumbled in. And the haunted expression on her face was more terrifying than the noises outside.

She looked at Bobby first, then Amber, hands clasped together. 'I'm so sorry. It's happened. I've just come from the Air Festival. Amber wasn't the one . . . The air unicorns are wild.'

An awful sound came from Bobby's throat. Amber just stared back at Sara, blinking.

Sara's eyes landed on Skandar next. 'Rex is giving a speech in a few minutes. Flo just told me – she and Blade are at Element Square already. Skandar, I think you should hear it if you can. Go alone, then nobody is committing any crimes.'

'Falcon,' Bobby was saying, 'I need to get to Falcon.' She was half being held up by Amber, half holding Amber up.

Sara was still trying to convince Skandar to go. 'Rex won't touch you now. It's only a few weeks until the Chaos Cup and he wants everything to look legitimate. He wants to seize his power the way every Commodore has in history – right before our eyes, so we're trapped by our own laws.' Her voice shook with anger. 'He won't risk being accused of foul play, not now.'

'I can't leave Bobby!' Skandar protested.

Mitchell put a hand on his shoulder. 'Listen to the speech; it could be important. It's you now – in the Chaos Cup. You and Flo. Any information we can get is useful. I'll get Amber and Bobby down to the spirit yard. Agatha's keeping watch at the twin oaks; she can let us in. Go, Skandar. Now!'

And suddenly Sara was rushing Skandar to the door and he was running through Fourpoint, dodging newly wild air

– 332 –

# PARLEY

unicorns and their panicking riders. Many of them were air-allied sentinels who must have been on duty for the festival, the yellow smoke of their distress flares filling the streets. Then, as Skandar passed under the treehouse restaurants, he spotted Patrick running at full pelt towards a wild Hurricane Hoax. Along a row of boarded up Mainlander shops, he sprinted by Luke, who'd been declared a nomad after the Chaos Trials, yelling for High Flyer.

When Skandar emerged into a packed Element Square, it was filled with Islanders – some were clustered in tight groups; others were on the ground in tears. There were riders on unicorns too – every single one silver. Skandar tried to spot Flo, but his eyes were drawn towards a podium that had clearly been positioned for Rex Manning's speech. Six members of the Council of Seven were present, their unicorns absent and wild like the other air wielders. Linton – the race representative who'd registered Skandar for the Cup – was missing.

A hush descended on the gathered crowd as it was parted by sentinels on foot and Rex Manning entered as he had the day he'd announced the death of Nina Kazama – riding Silver Sorceress. When the silver unicorn reached the podium, it was impossible to read the Commodore's expression as he dismounted. But once he opened his mouth, his every movement, his every word, was riotous anger.

'This truly is a terrible night – one of the darkest in the Island's history. And although my silver unicorn has been spared the effects of this curse, I am an air wielder. I feel your pain. I bear your suffering. I share your *rage.*'

There were a few jeers at this – but the Silver Circle sent elemental warning shots into the sky and silence returned.

'I am sorry to say that I have new information about the Skeleton Curse that will cause you a new kind of agony –

– 333 –

the agony of betrayal. But it is my duty as Commodore to share it with you.' He paused ominously and the whole square seemed to hold its breath. 'My researchers have made a truly shocking discovery.'

Skandar felt the cold hand of dread gripping his neck. He knew Rex well enough to tell that he was building up to something big. This was why the Commodore had ordered the whole Island to attend the festival tonight – no matter the risks to their safety, he wanted everyone to hear what he had to say.

'The Skeleton Curse is Mainland-made,' Rex declared. 'It is now beyond doubt. The Mainland, whose inhabitants we have befriended for almost two decades, has turned on us. It has sent its agent to bring the Island to its very knees. For an evil as great as the Wild Rider does not work alone. She has a master – and that master is the Mainland.'

'You can't be serious,' Skandar murmured under his breath. 'Nobody is going to believ—'

But there was immediate uproar. All around Skandar people were pointing out the Mainlanders among them. Some were even confronting them, asking if they knew anything about the Mainland's plan. This time, the Silver Circle fired no elements into the air.

Skandar shrank further into the shadows, horror uncurling in the depths of his stomach. The words of the truesong played through his head: *By hate and hurt and prejudice . . .* And he realised now that he had been wrong: it wouldn't be the *silvers* going to war with the Mainland; it would be the whole Island.

He'd experienced prejudice against Mainlanders – mostly from the Threat Quartet – but he hadn't realised quite how willing the Islanders would be to turn on the Mainland itself. He remembered what Mitchell had said about Rex's experts: *Sometimes, when people are scared, they would rather believe lies than*

# PARLEY

*the truth. Especially when the lies get them to the answer they want.*

'My friends, it is time for decisive action,' Rex cried. 'The Mainland is in fundamental breach of the Treaty, and therefore this Island's agreement with the land across the sea is at an end!'

The crowd roared in agreement – now they had someone else to blame for all their suffering, someone else to blame for their unicorns being wild. And it was so easy to blame the Mainlanders across the sea, the faceless mass of people they'd never met. Much easier to point the finger at them, rather than the shining Commodore with the reassuringly strong jawline standing before them.

'There will be no Hatchery exam!' Rex declared, and the crowd cheered. 'There will be no televising of the Chaos Cup!' The crowd cheered again. 'The Island will be for Islanders once more. Our young *Islanders* will bond with their destined unicorns, and if they hatch wild with drained bonds, I will ensure this is reversed, just as I will with all our riders.'

Skandar felt angry tears springing to his eyes at the thought of the distraught thirteen-year-olds who'd been waiting all year for their chance at the Hatchery exam. Hopeless fury pulsed through him at the thought of his devasted dad stuck back at Sunset Heights, unable to watch his only son fly in the Chaos Cup. And some ember of hope he'd been fighting to keep alive . . . died. Deep down he'd believed that the Island and its people would choose peace over war, good over evil. But they were letting fear and prejudice and hatred rule them, and the crushing disappointment of it made it hard for Skandar to breathe.

Rex wasn't finished. 'The Chaos Cup will be restored to its rightful place on the summer solstice, as was tradition before the treacherous Treaty!' The crowd was going wild. 'We will defeat the Mainland, we will defend our Island – and we *will* reverse the Skeleton Curse!'

– 335 –

# SKANDAR AND THE SKELETON CURSE

'Reverse the curse! Reverse the curse!' the crowd chanted and began to writhe like a living thing. Skandar was almost sucked into the fray, but someone grabbed his arm.

'Mitchell? What are you doing here? You can't be seen with me!' The flames in the fire wielder's hair were bright, his eyes darting around in panic.

'Agatha sent me – it's Falcon and Thief. We need to get them out of the spirit yard; they're completely out of control. Bobby and Amber won't leave them, but I'm worried someone's going to get killed if we don't get them above ground. Agatha wants you to use the spirit element to lure them out – like you did with Red!'

Skandar's head was still reeling from Rex's speech. But if Bobby was in danger, everything else could wait.

'Let's get out of here,' Skandar said, pushing his way through the simmering crowd. For although the sentinels and the silvers seemed to be ignoring Skandar, the crowd wasn't. People were surging towards him, shouting that he was the brother of the Mainland's agent, that he was responsible for the Skeleton Curse.

'Forking thunderstorms, what did Rex say?' Mitchell managed to ask, as they reached the edge of Element Square.

'Later,' Skandar said, looking over his shoulder – and the two boys broke into a run.

They were almost back at the yard when there was movement up ahead. Sentinels were charging along the line of rotting treehouses ahead of them, chasing a lone figure . . .

Agatha.

Time felt as though it was collapsing inwards. Skandar blinked and the silver-masked figures were now surrounding his aunt. He kept sprinting towards her, but every step was too slow. Mitchell was yelling at him to stop because although the sentinels didn't have unicorns any more, they were armed with

– 336 –

# PARLEY

weapons – real weapons – from the Stronghold forges.

Skandar didn't care. He tried to push through to Agatha. She was on the ground, shouting something up at him as the sentinels tried to wrestle her to her feet. And suddenly Skandar was back on the Mirror Cliffs, watching Agatha fall from Swansong's back. Swansong who was now dead; Agatha whom they were taking. They were taking his aunt, his family—

Then Agatha was on her feet, straining against the sentinels who were trying to put her in handcuffs. She attempted one last enormous pull against her captors and managed to get within touching distance of Skandar. 'GO!' she shouted.

Time spluttered to life again.

'AND WIN!'

Skandar didn't need to ask what she meant. She was telling him to win the Chaos Cup. She was saying goodbye.

Skandar and Mitchell ran in opposite directions. They couldn't risk going back to the spirit yard right now, not when the sentinels must have discovered Agatha right outside. Tears of devastation and fury coated Skandar's cheeks. They had taken Agatha from him – and it felt as though in all the years he'd been on the Island, nothing had changed. Despite everything he'd tried to do, despite all the times he and his friends had risked their lives to save it, the Island was still the kind of place that would arrest someone – someone good, someone kind, someone he loved – just because she was a spirit wielder.

Skandar had been running in a blind rage and he realised that his legs had taken him to the base of the Eyrie's hill. The Eyrie that was currently invisible. Skandar had run to Kenna, like he had so many times growing up – for a grazed knee, a wasp sting, a bully's punch. He had been fighting this moment all year – shying away from it, fearing it – but there was a rightness about coming to her at his very lowest. It was time

– 337 –

# SKANDAR AND THE SKELETON CURSE

to confront Kenna. It was time to parley.

Skandar began to climb the hill very warily. He had heard reports of the injuries suffered by those who had attempted to storm the Eyrie. And he understood better than anyone that the spirit barrier Kenna had erected must have been tinged with her wild magic, that shadowy dark edge that he'd first seen at the Wanderers' oasis. Sure enough, he was beginning to feel slightly clammy by the time he reached the gate to the Fledgling plateau, as though he was getting a fever. He focused on putting one foot in front of the other, and thought about how he and Kenna had played pirates when they were younger out on Margate beach. They'd had many fierce battles out there on the sand, but they'd always – eventually – called for a parley. A talk. A discussion. And they'd always found their way to piratical peace. All he could hope was that Kenna might listen to him now, that she might still care enough about him to turn her back on the Skeleton Curse.

Skandar stopped just above the Rookie plateau, as the path disappeared into thin air ahead of him. It was disorientating not being able to see the entrance or the colourful wild unicorn trees that had grown around the wall since his Nestling year. He knew the Eyrie was above him – the shadow of it was flickering at the corner of his eye – but this was a much stronger illusion than the one the Weaver had used to hide her island.

Skandar took a deep breath and yelled for his sister.

'KENNA! IT'S SKANDAR! COME OUT AND TALK!' His voice echoed off the elemental walls he couldn't see.

No answer.

'PARLEY! PARLEY!' Skandar cried over and over, stopping occasionally to listen for any kind of movement in the invisible fortress above him.

Then he tried a narration of the events that had brought

– 338 –

# PARLEY

him here. 'REX IS GOING TO INVADE THE MAINLAND! AGATHA'S BEEN ARRESTED! CAN'T YOU SEE THAT YOU'RE MAKING THINGS WORSE? PLEASE TALK TO ME!'

Then finally: 'I'M SAD TOO, OKAY? I JUST WANT TO TALK!'

When there was still no movement, Skandar kicked at the ground in frustration.

'Argh!' His foot had entered the space where the path should have been, and the very tip of his black boot had melted.

'Flaming fireballs,' Skandar cursed, removing the boot to check for damage to his toe.

'Hello, Skandar.' He looked up from pulling off his sock to find himself face to face with Albert, who had somehow come through the barrier unscathed. 'Are you all right?' Albert pointed to Skandar's foot.

Skandar felt anger boiling up inside him. 'No, I am *not* all right, Albert!' he half shouted. 'Agatha's been arrested, Rex is planning to invade the Mainland, my sister is turning riders into skeletons and almost the entire unicorn population of the Island is wild. So, no, I am *not* okay.'

'Did you say Rex wants to invade the *Mainland*? Are you sure? My brother's there!'

'Yes, I'm pretty sure, but . . .' He wasn't here to talk about Rex. 'Look, where's Kenna? I need to speak to her right now.'

'I'm sorry. She won't be coming out here.'

'Albert!' Skandar said, furiously. 'Have you even asked her?'

The fire wielder fidgeted with the end of his blond ponytail. 'Kenna wants you to join our cause. If you agree, she said you can come to speak to her. I can take you straight inside the Eyrie! You could tell her about Rex and the Mainland. We can help.' There was hope in Albert's voice, as though he really wanted Skandar to say yes.

'And what cause would I be joining exactly?'

– 339 –

# SKANDAR AND THE SKELETON CURSE

A faraway look came into Albert's blue eyes. 'Kenna is bringing a new dawn to the Island. We've all strayed so far from where we're supposed to be, Skandar. So far from the days of the First Rider.'

'Yes, because that was centuries ago, Albert! Why would you align yourself with the person who *took away your bond*? Eagle's Dawn is wild because of Kenna.'

'Exactly!' Albert said enthusiastically. 'Kenna helped me see that Eagle is better as an *original* unicorn. Now I have magic too, the way the First Rider did. And it was all meant to be. *He* meant for Kenna to have the bone staff so she could bring about the Skeleton Curse. So we could all start again.'

There it was, the idea of *starting again* that the Weaver had been obsessed with.

'Starting again means losing the best in us, as well as the worst. We'll make the same mistakes. You do know that, right? It doesn't just fix everything!' Skandar found himself yelling again. 'The curse is hurting so many people – members of *your* old quartet, Albert, of mine. Every single rider, and for what? It's a cyclical curse – Kenna doesn't have a double elemental for the spirit sacrifice. Everything is going to reset on the summer solstice and all the unicorns will be bonded again, but by that time it'll be too late to stop Rex! I am the ONLY non-silver in the Chaos Cup – and I'm a Rookie – and it would be a hell of a lot less pressure if the Island's whole future, the Mainland's too, wasn't resting on me!'

Albert shook his head. 'Kenna will be disappointed you're not joining us. I am too. I always liked you, Skandar.' He turned to leave, but looked once over his shoulder. 'And you're wrong, by the way. Do you really think Kenna would have overlooked the last double elemental? Do you think she would have gone to all this trouble for nothing?' Then he disappeared into thin air.

– 340 –

# PARLEY

Skandar lost control. 'KENNA! KENNA!' Over and over he shouted his sister's name, until he was spluttering and crying, bent double in the dark on the Eyrie's hill.

Shivering and spent, Skandar eventually returned to the spirit yard, careful to skirt around the sentinels' patrols. He was tear-stained and caked in mud, but nobody had time to comfort him, nor did he want them to. Viv and Konrad asked – only once – where Agatha was, but all the information they needed was written in Skandar's hooded eyes. He felt guilty for wishing it had been one of them guarding the twin oaks instead of her. And he couldn't bring himself to ask why Agatha hadn't gone back inside the yard once she'd sent Mitchell to get him. Perhaps he was afraid that they'd tell him she'd been waiting to see if he was all right, that she'd been as scared as he was of losing someone else she loved. The idea broke his heart all over again.

As Agatha had suggested, Skandar and Scoundrel did eventually manage to use the spirit element to lure Falcon's Wrath and Whirlwind Thief through the tunnel and out of the spirit yard. Mercifully, Viv and Konrad had herded them into Combat and stopped them causing too much damage. With Bobby and Amber squeezed on to Scoundrel's back with Skandar, they chased after their newly wild unicorns – through Fourpoint and beyond – until they were slowed by the air zone's Sky Forest. There Bobby and Amber were greeted by the Wanderers, who reassured them that Falcon and Thief would likely stay near their riders. Bobby and Amber could watch over them from the large holes in the giant redwoods Skandar had visited last year.

Skandar never would have believed Bobby and Amber could have shared a treehouse, let alone a tree *hole*, without one of them murdering the other. But that night Skandar left them sleeping

– 341 –

# SKANDAR AND THE SKELETON CURSE

shoulder to shoulder and joined Scoundrel in one of the larger openings.

Early the next morning, Skandar was preparing Scoundrel to leave when Bobby jumped to the forest floor, startling him.

She narrowed her eyes, fringe skimming her downturned brows. 'Where do you think you're going, spirit boy?'

Skandar was confused. 'Back to the spirit yard. I need to train. The Chaos Cup is only a few weeks—'

'And how was I supposed to get back to the spirit yard? Walk? You know I detest walking.'

'I thought you'd want to stay here with Falcon.'

'And what use would that be?' Bobby put a hand on one hip. 'You need as much help as you can get to win this Chaos Cup. And I might not be riding any more –' she said, and took a shaky breath – 'but I can still be useful.'

As Bobby swung herself up behind Skandar on Scoundrel's back, he felt a tiny spark of hope. He still had Bobby. And he still had Mitchell, and – somewhere behind the shields of the Silver Stronghold – Skandar knew he could count on Flo too. He touched the bracelets stacked on his wrist. They would always be a quartet, even if they weren't always in the same place.

'I'm worried about a couple of things,' Skandar blurted as they rode.

'Only a couple? That's not bad going in the circumstances,' Bobby quipped, though her arms had tightened round his middle in a hug.

'I tried to get to the Eyrie after the Air Festival. I tried to talk to Kenna.'

'How did that go?' Bobby said, carefully neutral.

'She wouldn't come out to see me.' Skandar swallowed. 'Albert did though. He basically confirmed that Kenna is using the bone staff for the Skeleton Curse. And I guess he might have

– 342 –

## PARLEY

just been trying to be threatening, but . . .'

'Spit it out.'

'I said about how Kenna's curse was going to reset anyway, that all it was doing was making it more likely Rex would win the Chaos Cup. But Albert said something like, *Do you really think Kenna would have overlooked the last double elemental?* Bobby, I'm scared *we've* overlooked something. That she's got some way to finish the cycle.'

'Mitchell wouldn't miss something like that,' Bobby said, but there was concern in her voice as they reached the yard's twin oaks.

That night in the spirit forest, Skandar woke to anguished screeching. Unicorns in pain, unicorns alone, unicorns calling for help. This wasn't the first time it had happened since arriving at the spirit yard, either, but nobody else seemed to hear it. And frankly, hearing things was a low-priority worry right now.

Tonight, as soon as the screeching started, Skandar rushed to Scoundrel's stable – being close to the unicorn was the only thing that dulled the sounds.

Halfway there he stopped dead. Skandar knew what they'd overlooked.

He wasn't the double elemental Kenna needed, but he wasn't the only spirit wielder with a unicorn. There were so many who had been barred from the Hatchery door – like the boy in Fourpoint. Dozens of Islanders who had not been allowed to become riders in the years since the spirit element had been banned. The lost spirit wielders with unicorns calling for them out in the Wilderness. One of them could be the double elemental Kenna needed.

She had brought some from the Mainland last year for their bonds to be forged. Did she know one of them was a double elemental? Did she choose one of them on purpose because they

– 343 –

were spirit-allied and born on the summer solstice – spirit's old festival day? How long had she been planning this?

And the double elemental's wild unicorn would still be in the Wilderness.

What if Kenna was a Mender like him?

Skandar had voiced the question months ago. And Bobby's reply now clanged through his brain like a warning bell: *We can't rule out anything when it comes to her.*

Even if Kenna wasn't a true Mender, what if her immense power allowed her to join a rider and unicorn destined for each other and then drain the bond? Albert had been so certain that Kenna would succeed.

What if she could create her own spirit sacrifice?

## Chapter Twenty-One

# BLACKOUT

The weeks leading up to the Chaos Cup passed in a frenzy. The fact that there might be a double elemental to make the Skeleton Curse permanent meant Craig and Mitchell spent every waking moment seeking out lost spirit wielders or attempting to find birth records. Ira Henderson had even used his contacts at the prison to get them access to the lost spirit wielders who'd been arrested last June. Mitchell persisted until he knew every single one of their birthdates – but none of them was born on a summer solstice. Meanwhile, Amber used her network of spies within the Stronghold to extract the names from the spirit wielder records Skandar had seen in his Nestling year.

Reports came from Elora that a unicorn called Vulture's Voltage and his skeletal rider, Finneas, had been found near the Terraced Valleys. Kenna had killed the air unicorn, which meant the mystery of why she'd left Tsunami's Herald alive grew even stranger. Unrest was everywhere. The sentinels – now without their unicorns – were failing to keep the peace in Fourpoint as anti-Mainlander sentiment swept through the capital. It felt

# SKANDAR AND THE SKELETON CURSE

impossible that there was going to be a Chaos Cup at all. But every day the *Hatchery Herald* continued to count down to the big event, declaring that the shift of date back to the summer solstice was the Cup *returning to its proper roots*. Skandar and Scoundrel had to shut out everything that was going on above ground, and train harder than ever.

Bobby bravely replaced Agatha as a coach – even though she missed Falcon dreadfully, and wrestled with multiple panic attacks a day. She focused on fitness, agility and the air element. Konrad worked with Skandar on the spirit element, and Viv did everything else. Skandar still struggled the most with elemental predators, and he tried to abandon training in them altogether to concentrate on his strengths. This was quickly vetoed.

'All the silvers are going to be using them,' Bobby argued.

'You have to be able to block them with your own,' Viv added.

When they were united, Bobby and Viv were impossible to reason with.

Three weeks before the Chaos Cup, Skandar was training inside the Combat chamber with Konrad and – as Bobby might put it – was having a complete meltdown.

'ARGHHHHH!' Skandar yelled in frustration, as he lost control over the cloud of spirit magic he was attempting to shape into a Hunter. The bond was filled with Scoundrel's frustration, too – Skandar was sure the unicorn found creating predators boring and would rather be speeding around Chaos.

'Patience, young man,' Konrad murmured serenely.

The old spirit coach was leaning against the black wall of the chamber, hardly even bothering to look up.

'Patience won't win me the Chaos Cup!' The words somehow escaped his mouth, but he wasn't sorry. Why wasn't Konrad helping him more? Wasn't he supposed to be one of the best spirit riders there'd ever been?

– 346 –

# BLACKOUT

'You're never going to be able to summon a predator when you're this emotional.'

'I'M NOT EMOTIONAL; I'M BLOODY TERRIFIED!' Skandar roared, his palm still glowing white and suddenly he just wanted all the pressure, all the fear, all the *stress* of the Chaos Cup and the Skeleton Curse and his sister . . . to disappear.

And it did. Sort of.

Skandar's palm did something it had never done before. It went from glowing white to pulsing black. Scoundrel screeched as Skandar tried to shut his palm, tried to make it stop – the dark magic reminded him of the shadowy edge to Kenna's attacks. What if he hurt Konrad? Scoundrel?

The spirit coach let out a grunt of surprise as countless points of blinding light and utter darkness filled the space, dancing ever more quickly before his and Skandar's eyes. Then the entirety of Combat winked out, and all was shadow. Scoundrel screeched again and the sound echoed off the walls.

'Skandar?' Konrad's voice was calm. 'Are you still up there?'

'What's going on? Did I—'

'You can still see, correct?' Konrad asked, matter-of-fact.

And Skandar realised that although he was aware of the oppressive darkness, he could somehow still see the whole chamber – as though he was wearing night-vision goggles.

'Y-y-yes!'

'Land Scoundrel now. Get safely on the ground, please.'

'I don't know if Scoundrel can see—'

'He can,' Konrad insisted, and, sure enough, Scoundrel landed neatly on the black stone and shook out his wings.

'Dismount,' Konrad ordered. 'And step away from Scoundrel.'

Skandar obeyed without question, and – as soon as his physical contact with Scoundrel was broken – all the light rushed back into the room.

– 347 –

# SKANDAR AND THE SKELETON CURSE

The tap, tap of Konrad's walking stick sounded impossibly loud in the silence that followed. When the coach reached Skandar, he put a hand on his shoulder.

'Just breathe, lad.'

Skandar was drenched in sweat and shaking uncontrollably.

Konrad guided him to one of the black marble benches lining a wall of the chamber, Scoundrel tailing them, the bond full of worry that he'd done something wrong. Skandar tried to reassure him, but it was half-hearted. *Had* they done something wrong?

Once the spirit wielders were sitting, questions exploded out of Skandar. 'Did I do that? Am I like my sister? Was it wild magic?'

Konrad held up a hand, and Skandar noticed an unhealed wound that must have been there a very long time. 'That was *advanced* spirit magic, Skandar. I have taught a great many spirit wielders in my time and only a handful of them managed to bring darkness like that.'

'Were you able to do it?' Skandar asked feverishly.

'Yes.' Konrad nodded. 'Soul Stealer and I were capable of accessing the shadow the way you just did.'

That made Skandar feel slightly better, and he let out a bit more breath. 'Shadow?'

'Yes, Skandar – you called to it. Spirit magic operates from another plane, from negative space, from absence. You know this – you have seen it at the Eyrie's gate, at the yard's entrance. Today you brought forth the darkness from that place.'

'Brought forth . . . the darkness.' Something in Skandar's chest caved in, like a spark had winked out, smothered by the very shadow he had summoned.

Konrad noticed. 'You should be proud of this talent. In the old days you would have been the talk of the spirit yard after

– 348 –

# BLACKOUT

that display.' He smiled, as though recalling a memory.

But Skandar didn't feel proud. He felt like he'd been fighting a losing battle. He had been trying to prove he was good, trying to resist the darkness of the spirit element for years – and now suddenly he was accidentally plunging the world into shadow?

'Go on,' Konrad urged, as though he already knew what Skandar was going to say.

'How can I ever be good?' Skandar asked very quietly. 'How can a boy who brings darkness ever be seen as good?'

'Aha,' Konrad said sagely, 'those are two different questions. You asked how you can *ever be good* and then you asked how a boy like you can *ever be seen as good*. Those are very different things. The second is how you are perceived by other people. The first is who you really are. Which one matters more?'

'I suppose who I am,' Skandar mumbled. 'But I *am* a spirit wielder who can take away the light, the goodness—'

'No,' Konrad said strongly. 'Light does not equate to good. And dark does not equate to evil. There is no light without shadow, no darkness without dawn, no death without life. You have learned that from the wild unicorns, have you not?'

Skandar shrugged.

'This Island has taught you that the spirit element is bad – it has convinced you that you have to *prove* that you are good in order to be allowed to stay. But nobody else has to do that. Not Bobby or Mitchell or your silver friend – they never had to prove their goodness, just to belong.'

'They don't wield darkness,' Skandar muttered.

'They do,' Konrad said seriously. 'We *all* wield darkness in our own ways. We are all capable of it – perhaps not actual shadow but through the deeds of our lives. The Silver Circle would rather we all forget this, because there is strength in realising life is complicated – that the monsters are not always the ones who

– 349 –

# SKANDAR AND THE SKELETON CURSE

dwell in darkness, and the handsome leaders are not always the ones who should be in charge. That there are silver unicorns among the wild ones, silver riders allied to the spirit element, and heroes who look like the villains.'

'Silvers can be spirit-allied?' Skandar spluttered. 'And there are silver wild unicorns?'

'Of course, though both are rare. Just as there are air wielders who have killed for power and spirit wielders who have saved the Island on countless occasions.' Konrad raised a wiry eyebrow at Skandar.

Skandar thought about all the pieces of the Island that didn't fit into the Silver Circle's mould: the Wanderers and the wild foals; the spirit unicorns still calling out for their imprisoned riders. He thought of people like Kenna who'd been left behind on the Mainland, with no unicorn no matter how much they wished for it. He remembered the tears of potential spirit wielders as they were told they would be barred from the Hatchery door. And for the first time he could perhaps see why Erika Everhart had wanted the Island to start over. Why Kenna might want the same thing. But then he remembered Arctic Swansong's body hitting the ground, and Isa's skeletal form in her hammock, and Federico Jones clinging desperately to Sunset's Blood on the fault line – and pushed the thought from his mind. If he somehow won the Chaos Cup, he could think about all that later. He could even try to fix some of it.

'The darkness,' Skandar said, swallowing. 'Can I use it in the Cup?'

Konrad shook his head. 'Not this time. Perhaps one day you will be able to turn daylight to shadow, but it may take years. In the meantime . . . predators!'

Skandar didn't talk to Bobby about the shadow or attempt to bring the darkness again. Time suddenly sped up and became

– 350 –

# BLACKOUT

measured in increments of *before* and *after* the Cup. He would tell Bobby after the Cup. Konrad would teach him more about the darkness after the Cup. *After*, because *before* was now a very short time indeed.

Yet something about his talk with Konrad unwound a knot of shame in Skandar's chest, shame he'd been holding on to since he'd first learned he was allied to the death element. And it did wonders for his magic.

Two weeks before the Chaos Cup, Skandar finally managed his first Hunter-level predator, made from the glittering spirit element. And he managed to duplicate himself and Scoundrel not once but twice. Even though Konrad had taught him that multiple duplicates were possible, it had surprised the old spirit coach so much that he'd actually uttered a swearword. Bobby had cackled about it for hours afterwards, and her laugh was such a rare sound nowadays that Skandar found himself smiling for the rest of the day.

Then, ten days before the race, Skandar managed a Marauder – and Bobby brought him five emergency sandwiches, custom-made by Sally in the shape of the tiger he'd created. Skandar had been so happy he'd eaten all of them without complaint.

At one week to go, Skandar and Scoundrel's Chaos Cup team were working round the clock. Three team members from Shekoni Saddles had moved to the spirit yard permanently, so they could make adjustments to Scoundrel's saddle; Fiona the healer locked herself away in one of the white treehouses in Rest so she could *prepare herself*, which Skandar found alarming; Sara Shekoni spent evenings checking over Scoundrel in his stable after training; and Jamie finally emerged from Nourishment with a full set of new armour he'd designed for the most important race of Skandar and Scoundrel's life.

– 351 –

## SKANDAR AND THE SKELETON CURSE

Scoundrel blew warm air at the blacksmith in welcome as Jamie heaved the last piece of shining black metal past the unicorn statue and into the atrium.

'Yes, yes, presents for you,' Jamie murmured, stroking his hand down Scoundrel's white blaze. 'Let's see how it fits, shall we?'

'Thanks, Jamie,' Skandar said, feeling a wave of emotion hit him. The nerves, the fear, the anticipation of the Chaos Cup – all were making him feel everything more strongly.

'Are you okay, Skandar?' Jamie's mismatched eyes turned serious.

Skandar half laughed, half choked. 'No, I'm fine. It-it's just a lot of pressure. Like, if I lose to Rex there's probably going to be that war the bard children sang about, and people might die . . . And then there's my sister, and the curse, and the riders that are skeletons, and what if—'

'We're all here with you, Skandar, okay? It's not just on you. And Flo's racing, too, isn't she? She's been getting all that Stronghold training! The two of you will be out there together – a silver spy and a rebel spirit wielder – and I think you already know you make a good team.'

Skandar swallowed, trying to get a hold of himself. The thought of Flo and Blade flying beside him and Scoundrel did make him feel better. And after the Cup, Flo would be able to come back to the quartet. No matter what they had to face next.

With one last concerned look at Skandar, Jamie began to hold sheets of armour against Scoundrel, who snapped playfully at the edges, and it was all so familiar that the spiralling thoughts in Skandar's head began to calm down.

That last week, Jamie watched Skandar and Scoundrel's training sessions and adjusted their armour accordingly. Until, finally, on the eve of the Chaos Cup everything was perfect.

– 352 –

# BLACKOUT

On the morning of the summer solstice, Skandar woke early. Somehow his first thought was not about the Cup, but the young hopefuls queuing up for the Hatchery door at that very moment. Now Rex had torn up the Treaty, every single one of them would be an Islander. He felt sick at the thought, and then felt even worse when he thought of the Skeleton Curse. Would the baby unicorns hatch with drained bonds? Would the riders be able to hatch them at all? And at breakfast, Craig confirmed that there had still been no word from the Hatchery.

A little later, it all felt very formal as Skandar and Scoundrel stood – fully armoured – in the atrium of the spirit yard, and everyone queued up to wish them luck. The team from Shekoni Saddles – with several more Chaos riders to attend to – had left very early that morning, but Craig came forward first to shake Skandar's hand, then pulled him into a hug.

'Your story really is one of the most heroic tales I've come across.'

Skandar chuckled. 'I'm not sure about that, Craig. Without you, I never would have had *three* actual spirit wielders for instructors . . .' Craig dismissed the compliment with a wave of his hand, as though it was nothing. But it wasn't nothing. Craig had risked his freedom every day, and Skandar wouldn't forget it.

Next came Viv and Konrad, each giving last-minute pieces of advice.

'Don't be afraid of creating predators to fight the silvers, okay?' Viv said, squeezing his shoulder. 'Treat them like any other elemental magic, but make sure you pull back as soon as they start draining too much power. And illusion is your friend – they won't see you coming. Half of them have never even fought a spirit wielder.'

Konrad made his way over next. 'I spent years in that hanging

– 353 –

prison. And believe me when I say, you can hear the Chaos Cup commentary as clear as a bell. Make Agatha proud – I've no doubt she'll be listening.'

Skandar nodded shakily.

'Good lad. You've worked hard.'

Next was Jamie. 'I'm going to watch, of course – I'll be in the stands with Mitchell and Bobby. I'm just sorry I can't come into the Compound with you.'

'I'll miss your pre-race pep talk,' Skandar said, trying to lighten the mood.

'That's not why I want to be there,' Jamie said with a smile. 'It's because I'm so proud of both of you. No matter what happens. This is the bravest thing you've ever done, Skandar. I knew you were made of strong stuff the day I chose Scoundrel for my Hatchling, but this is beyond anything I ever expected. It is my honour to be Scoundrel's blacksmith – and yours.' And Skandar could have sworn he saw a tear escape from Jamie's green eye.

Then Skandar was enveloped in the most enormous hug from Bobby and Mitchell. And he couldn't help wishing there had been more time over the last few weeks to just be together – to hang out in a treehouse and to talk about anything other than the fact that Skandar and Flo were about to compete in the most famous race in the world, that Rex Manning was probably going to start a war, that the Skeleton Curse might keep Falcon and Red wild for ever. Might drain his bond with Scoundrel too.

'We'll be watching from the stands,' Bobby said. 'Every single second. I'll be the one shouting the loudest! Not sure if that counts as *assisting a spirit wielder* but I'd bet a hundred jars of Marmite I won't be the only one.'

'Just concentrate on the race,' Michell said firmly. 'I don't think there's a lost spirit wielder we haven't spoken to on this Island,

# BLACKOUT

and none of them was born on the solstice. Albert must have been bluffing. Kenna's not going to be able to complete the cycle.'

'By sundown we'll either have a Smith or a Shekoni as our Commodore and the unicorns will all be back to normal,' Bobby announced. 'Then we'll chuck Kenna out of the Eyrie, get our treehouse back, and everything will be fine.' And there was such certainty in her voice that Skandar felt like he wanted to breathe her words in and hold them in his lungs as he and Scoundrel made their way along the tunnel alone.

Fourpoint seemed impossibly loud and colourful after so long underground. Skandar hadn't known what to expect when such a large proportion of the Island had wild unicorns to contend with, but it seemed busier than ever. Mitchell had talked Skandar through the quietest route to the Chaos Compound, where he would have to leave Scoundrel's Luck with a steward and walk to the Hall of Competitors. There he would be checked in, sign the Chaos Register and change out of his elemental jacket and into the thinner race jersey – individually designed for each Chaos rider – then wait to be called back to the Compound for the start of the race.

Despite these being the quietest streets – past the Healer Huts, and then skirting round the Library Quarter – there were still plenty of people who pointed at Skandar when he passed. Aside from the white arms of his spirit jacket being visible, his element symbol and surname were painted across his armoured back – and Jamie had used the brightest white possible for the five connected circles. True, the armour on Scoundrel's head covered his blaze, but there was no hiding their elemental allegiance. Skandar tugged at his breastplate nervously as he heard a few jeers of 'spirit scum' and 'the silvers are coming for you', but others did wish Skandar and

– 355 –

# SKANDAR AND THE SKELETON CURSE

Scoundrel good luck, cheering as they went by.

Even so, Skandar felt very exposed on Fourpoint's narrow streets. This was one of the dangers of Rex having introduced the crime of assisting a spirit wielder – Skandar was forced to go to the race unprotected, unlike the rest of the Chaos riders who were surrounded by blacksmiths, saddlers, friends and family. And when they reached the Chaos Compound, it made leaving Scoundrel there even worse.

Thankfully, as he passed the steward his reins, she whispered in Skandar's ear: 'I'm one of Sara Shekoni's apprentices. Scoundrel is in safe hands, don't worry.' But the black unicorn still screeched as his rider turned, armour clinking, and walked back out of the Compound.

The path to the Hall of Competitors led Skandar through a fenced-off area lined with reporters calling out his name.

'Skandar Smith! Tell the *Hatchery Herald* how it feels to be the only spirit wielder in the Cup today!'

'How are your nerves today, Skandar? Our readers would love to know what you had for breakfast!'

He tried to ignore the questions. But if he'd answered, he would have said he'd eaten a fry-up – just like he had every Chaos Cup day with Dad and Kenna in Flat 207. He probably wouldn't have told them he was now regretting it, as the mayonnaise churned with the nerves in his stomach.

Another loud reporter's voice cut through: 'Do you think you're in with a chance?'

'Could you comment on the rumour that you declared *yourself* a nomad?' This reporter was leaning all the way over the fence, dangling her microphone like a fishing rod.

'As a Mainlander, what can you tell us about the Skeleton Curse? In fact, as the brother of the Wild Rider, what can you tell us?'

– 356 –

# BLACKOUT

This last question was the only one that made Skandar stop. The journalist looked absolutely delighted with himself, and waved a large fluffy microphone in Skandar's face.

Skandar kept his voice as level as he could. 'The Skeleton Curse has nothing to do with the Mainland. None of us Mainlanders came here to destroy the Island or whatever else Rex Manning is saying.'

'Why did you come here then?' The reporter pushed his microphone closer to Skandar's mouth. 'Even though the Hatchery door was closed to you, even though your element was illegal?'

'Because Scoundrel's Luck summoned me across the sea – just like a wild foal called a fisherman to these shores centuries ago.'

'You're comparing yourself to the First Rider?' The reporter's tone was incredulous.

'I . . .'

Suddenly there was a blur of a blue cloak and someone was ducking under the fence to join Skandar. 'And why shouldn't he compare himself to the First Rider?' Instructor O'Sullivan demanded. 'The Island called Skandar, and he came. That's all there is to say. Come on, Skandar, you've got a race to fly.' She put a hand on his armoured shoulder, guiding him onwards.

'Thanks,' Skandar said heavily, as they walked together through the rest of the shouts and camera clicks.

Instructor O'Sullivan didn't seem in the least bit bothered that there would be photographic evidence of her *assisting a spirit wielder*. But her blue eyes did swirl dangerously. 'When I was a Chaos rider, they never let reporters anywhere near the competitors before the race. It's disgraceful.'

'I don't know if I can do this!' Skandar blurted, the appearance of the water instructor suddenly making him feel like a Hatchling again.

– 357 –

# SKANDAR AND THE SKELETON CURSE

'Skandar.' Instructor O'Sullivan stopped just as they reached the base of the trees supporting the Hall of Competitors. 'Do you know what links the vast majority of Chaos Cup winners?'

Skandar swallowed. 'Bravery? Sky-battle ability? Flight speed? Not being nomad spirit wielders?'

'No,' Instructor O'Sullivan said, pinning him with her cerulean stare. 'It's how early they were able to share their unicorn's emotions. If you ask ex-Commodores when they started to share feelings through the bond, most of them were the first in their Eyrie year to do so.'

Skandar was reminded of a conversation he'd had with Instructor O'Sullivan as a Hatchling; her strong reaction when he'd told her he and Scoundrel were already sharing emotions. 'Are you just saying this to make me feel better?'

'Absolutely not. I started sharing emotions with Celestial Seabird at the end of my Hatchling year, and people are still talking about my Chaos Cup win.'

Skandar was speechless. 'You were *Commodore*?'

Instructor O'Sullivan winked. 'Remember, it's not all about how you fight or how you fly – it's about how much you want it in your soul, how much Scoundrel wants it for you. I told you when you were a Hatchling that I believed your magic was battle-worthy. And I believe you are worthy of *this*, Skandar Smith. You have already achieved more than many Commodores do in their whole lives. And you have done it all with kindness in your heart.'

Skandar's eyes stung, his voice too choked with emotion to say a word.

'Good luck, spirit wielder. The next time I see you, I expect to be addressing you as Commodore Smith.'

Chapter Twenty-Two

# LUCKY THIRTEEN

Instructor O'Sullivan left Skandar standing beneath the treehouse known as the Hall of Competitors. It looked very much like a Viking longhouse, though the side overlooking the Compound was made entirely of glass to provide a view of the unicorns milling around in the enclosure.

Skandar climbed an intricate golden ladder and found the main room occupied by stewards buzzing around with clipboards. A few were over by the glass, looking anxiously for riders walking up the press line from the Compound. The other three walls of the large rectangular room were covered with finishing lists from previous Cups, the winning rider and unicorn names inked in gold at the top. In the centre of the room, the Chaos Register rested on its ornate lectern, and Skandar was immediately guided over to it by a steward, handed a pen by another, and told what to do by someone different – a tall woman with a toothy smile.

'You're riding as number thirteen, Skandar Smith. There are actually only thirteen competitors in the Cup this year, because

# SKANDAR AND THE SKELETON CURSE

of what happened at the Air Festival. You just need to write your chaos number in the register – then you'll be signed in, okay?'

'Thirteen,' Skandar breathed, as he tried to stop his hand shaking. 'Unlucky for some.'

'Excuse me?' the steward asked.

'Oh, nothing,' Skandar murmured, handing back the pen. 'Mainland expression.'

The steward nodded politely, then led him across a gleaming gold bridge to a treehouse with an imposing round door. It had no handle and reminded Skandar of the Hatchery entrance. 'We call this place the Gilded Grove. Find tree thirteen, then change into your jersey. You'll be called out to the Compound one by one. All right?'

He nodded shakily and tried to concentrate on the wonderful thought that Flo was just a few footsteps away.

As soon as Skandar pushed open the door, the nervous chatter inside the Gilded Grove dropped to hostile whispers. He couldn't see Flo so he continued further into the room. Every metre or so there was an intricately carved miniature tree with a hole in its trunk large enough for a Chaos rider to sit in. None of the silver riders appeared to be making use of the seats, though – a few were talking to each other while adjusting their armour, while others were pacing up and down, the painted symbols of their allied elements shining from their backs.

The ornamental trees of the Gilded Grove were painted in glistening gold, and each had an elemental allegiance. The water trees had sapphires for leaves, the air trees had yellow peridots, the fire trees had rubies and the earth trees had emeralds and . . . as Skandar reached a tree with the brass number thirteen nailed to its trunk, he gasped. His tree was a spirit tree, and a little like the ones in the graveyard, though its leaves were white diamonds. A jersey hung from one of its branches, looking very out of place.

– 360 –

## LUCKY THIRTEEN

The Chaos Cup jerseys were a bit like football shirts, with long sleeves and light fabric so they would fit easily under the riders' armour. The base colour matched each rider's element, and there was an element symbol on the chest that matched the colour of the rider's unicorn. It seemed as though tradition had won out over prejudice in the eyes of whoever had designed Skandar's jersey, because it was dazzling white with a midnight-black spirit element symbol over his heart. Excitedly he turned the jersey over in his hands and saw SKANDAR SMITH and SCOUNDREL'S LUCK printed on the back, along with the number thirteen and the year in Roman numerals: MMXXVI.

To pull it on, Skandar hurriedly unclipped his breastplate, removed his chainmail and shrugged off his white jacket. For as long as he could remember, he'd stared at race jerseys hung up in shop windows. He had always wanted one, but the replicas were far too expensive for him to even ask his dad. Instead, he'd made do with admiring them from a distance – especially after Christmas, when other children tried to get away with wearing them under their uniforms at school. But now *he* had one. And it was truly his. A Chaos rider. He wished Dad could see this. He wished Rex was still allowing the Cup to be televised. Skandar hadn't been able to write to Dad for months – too afraid of Rex intercepting their letters – and now Robert Smith wouldn't even be able to watch his son compete on TV let alone come to the Island like he'd been planning.

There was still no sign of Flo, so Skandar retreated into the tree's trunk, his armour clanking against its golden roots. He wanted to keep away from the other riders and attempted to distract himself with the graffiti that had been carved inside the white trunk: good luck messages for future competitors, names of Chaos riders and unicorns he'd never heard of, and even some funny drawings. He traced his hand over the names, thinking of

# SKANDAR AND THE SKELETON CURSE

the other spirit wielders who had sat inside this tree before him on the biggest race of their lives.

'I'm really glad you're here, Skandar.' All the hair stood up on the back of Skandar's neck, as Rex Manning leaned against the trunk of his spirit tree. Rex's friendly tone did not match the glint in his green eyes.

'I wish I could say the same,' Skandar growled, fighting to keep his voice level as he scrambled out of the hole.

Rex ignored Skandar's venomous tone. 'It would have been *such* a great shame if you'd died during the Qualifiers,' Rex drawled, watching him. 'I see that now. It would have been a missed opportunity. Well, perhaps more than one.'

Skandar faced Rex and saw the sneer on his perfect mouth. And for the first time he recognised the Commodore for who he really was. A bully. He was just like Owen at Christchurch Secondary, just like the Threat Quartet, just like his father Dorian. Rex was making the Island into his own playground where nothing could hurt him. And Skandar knew that bullies like that *came* from somewhere – they weren't born; they were made.

'Who hurt you, to make you like this?' Skandar asked Rex quietly.

Rex did not hide the rage that broke across his face, his cheeks spitting sparks like matches had struck them. And Skandar knew that he was right.

Skandar imagined what it must have been like. A young Rex whose mother had died from the grief of losing her unicorn to the Weaver. A young Rex left to cope with an ambitious and domineering father – a father who was grieving, just as Skandar's dad had been. Then, after Dorian had been discovered killing wild unicorns, Rex had made a choice not to go down with him and kept his father locked in the prison even now. And all that

– 362 –

# LUCKY THIRTEEN

without a sister like Kenna to help him weather the storm.

Rex still hadn't spoken, so Skandar – feeling braver – pressed ahead, 'How will attacking the Mainland help? It won't take away whatever demons you're fighting. It'll only make more, I think.'

Then Rex laughed, and the sound was sharp and merciless like broken shards of glass. 'You're very *sweet* to worry about me, Skandar,' Rex crooned, 'but attacking the Mainland doesn't have anything to do with my *demons*.' Rex spoke louder, so that the other silver riders in the Grove could hear. 'For a long time, it was clear to my father – and to me – that the Treaty divided the Mainland and the Island unfairly. Here we all are on a very small piece of rock, forced to live alongside dangerous wild unicorns, when *we* are the ones destiny has chosen. *We* are the unicorn riders – the ultimate predators, the natural leaders. Why should the Mainlanders have all that land? All those resources? I'm sure they won't mind us taking over – they may even be relieved. It is time we redressed the balance for the good of all.'

'For the good of *all*?' Skandar choked. 'Sending soldiers with unicorns to a place that has no way to fight against them? Mainlanders won't stand a chance against elemental magic – it would be a massacre. And for what? A bit more *space*?'

Rex smirked at him. 'I wouldn't worry too much, spirit wielder. It's not like you're going to be there to see it.' And then he pushed off from the tree trunk and sauntered away.

Skandar tried to regain control of his temper. He had known Rex had planned to invade the Mainland, but it was different hearing him talk about the invasion with such casual brutality. As Skandar finished fastening his breastplate back over his jersey, he was hit by a fresh wave of fear. Rex Manning must not win this Chaos Cup.

He suddenly got the sense he was being watched. Flo had

– 363 –

## SKANDAR AND THE SKELETON CURSE

arrived in the changing room and was now standing in front of the earth tree to his left. His whole stomach lurched, and he opened his mouth to say hello. But Flo shook her head immediately. Instead, she pretended to be taking off her silver armour, but as she reached for her green jersey she dropped a piece of paper into the spirit trunk, just within Skandar's reach. He shrank back into the hole and unfolded the note.

*Skar – Rex is watching my every move. Riders will be called to the Compound in order. I'm number twelve, so we'll be the last two out. We can talk then. I've missed you so much x*

Skandar stuffed the note into his pocket, his heart racing as he waited. He hardly dared to look at Flo, even though he was close enough to hear the clink of her chainmail. He tried to focus on his training, all the tactics his coaches had taught him down in the spirit yard. In any other year he would have no chance in a Chaos Cup, but Mitchell had insisted that didn't matter.

'Unusual circumstances mean unusual results, Skandar. Thirteen in the Cup, not twenty-five. And we've never seen this many silvers in the race, so who says the spirit wielder can't win?'

The Chaos riders started to be called through the door at the other end of the Grove. Some, Skandar noticed, looked very excited. Others looked sick with nerves. Rex – number four – left quickly, without giving Skandar a single glance. Finally Ayana – number eleven – was called. And Flo and Skandar were alone.

Skandar left the shelter of his spirit tree, planning on a hug, but instead Flo put both of her hands on his shoulders and looked extremely serious. 'You can't go out there. Not today.'

'What do you mean?'

'*You're* the double elemental, Skar! Kenna could come for you

– 364 –

# LUCKY THIRTEEN

and Scoundrel at any time during the race. You're going to be too exposed.'

Skandar half laughed. 'But you know I'm not a double elemental, Flo. I was born in March, during the water season.'

Flo started to pace, looking distraught. 'I've been trying to get messages out of the Stronghold for weeks, but everything gets searched. I overheard the Silver Circle talking about the old spirit season – obviously I'm the only person in there who knows when you were born. But I thought Mitchell might have realised or maybe Agatha, but then she got arrested and—'

'Slow down,' Skandar said. 'The Spirit Festival is the summer solstice, isn't it? That's when the spirit season is, right?' His heart was beating very fast. He was trying to remember where they'd got that information, whether they'd checked . . .

'No! Not exactly anyway. It turns out the spirit season doesn't work like the others – it's spread throughout the year, woven into the other elemental seasons. So it's both solstices – summer and winter.'

'Okay, June and December – but that's still not my birthday!'

'It's not just the solstices. There are *four* spirit seasons, and each one is five days long, to represent the five elements. Haven't you noticed we all wear our own elemental jackets – not the colours of the seasons – to all sorts of important events. To Den Initiations, to Registration, to the Den Dances, to the Qualifiers, to the Chaos Cup? It's a hangover from before the spirit element was outlawed.' Flo's voice was shaking. 'Each spirit season used to be a five-day celebration at the heart of each of the other elemental seasons!'

'So when are the other—' Skandar asked, dread snatching at his breath.

'The equinoxes! The autumn equinox is in September, but the spring one . . . you were born on the spring equinox in 2009 –

## SKANDAR AND THE SKELETON CURSE

the twentieth of March, Skar! Right in the middle of the old spring spirit season.'

Skandar had only ever heard the word *equinox* in Blood-Moon's Equinox – the name of his mum's destined unicorn. This, and the devastation on Flo's face, was enough to make him stop questioning her, to remember Albert's words: *Do you really think Kenna would have overlooked the last double elemental?*

He wondered if Agatha or Konrad or Viv had remembered. Had they kept this from him so he would concentrate on the race? He thought of something Agatha had said when she'd been talking about Skandar trying to win the Chaos Cup: *This is bigger than Flo being in the Stronghold or Swan being gone. This isn't just about us.* Had it also been bigger than Skandar being the last double elemental?

'I'm so sorry, Skar. You can't fly in the Chaos Cup – you've got to hide! Go back down to the spirit yard. I'll race. I'll try to stop Rex winning—'

'Kenna wouldn't kill Scoundrel. She wouldn't hurt me,' Skandar insisted shakily.

'She killed Arctic Swansong!' Flo almost shouted. 'She turned Isa into a skeleton. I know she's your sister, but I don't think you can rely on that any more. And, Skar—'

'Florence Shekoni?' A steward had opened the door.

'No, please,' Flo begged. 'I need another minute, please.'

The steward shook his head. 'It's time.'

Flo still didn't move. 'Don't race, Skar! Promise me! Fourpoint is the spirit zone – and it's the summer solstice!'

The steward came through the door, and steered Flo by the elbow. 'Don't mind the nerves, you'll be fine—'

'I— Flo, I have to race!' Skandar called after her.

'Then I don't have a choice! You have to understand that, Skar. I just don't have—'

– 366 –

## LUCKY THIRTEEN

The door shut behind her. Skandar was left alone in the ringing silence, reeling from everything Flo had said. It felt absurd that Kenna would come for him, that she would sacrifice Scoundrel. And how would she do that in the middle of Fourpoint? It would be impossible even to get a clear aim in the middle of the Chaos Cup – with twelve silvers racing and the rest of the Silver Circle on high alert.

No. Kenna had done a lot of bad things since coming to the Island, but Flo didn't understand how close they'd been growing up. She didn't understand that despite it all, Skandar still loved Kenna and he truly believed she felt the same. She wouldn't hurt him.

But someone else would. A rider who had killed a Commodore in cold blood.

Alone in the Gilded Grove, everything fell into place. Back at the Eyrie, Rex had never declared Skandar a nomad – despite all the opportunities he'd had. He'd made it impossible for him to train properly with Scoundrel but kept him close, under watch. Then, after Skandar had declared himself a nomad, Rex had allowed him to register for the Chaos Cup, and then watched on as one of his own Silver Circle members had voted for the spirit wielder as that year's Wildcard. Rex had never seemed worried about the Skeleton Curse, but early on he'd found out it was cyclical – Flo had told Skandar that at Sally's.

And there had been no attempts to have Skandar arrested after the Qualifiers – not even when Kenna took the Eyrie. Rex had merely tried to restrict those who were able to assist him, making it less likely he'd do well in the Cup, making him weak. The quartet had thought it was because Skandar was protected by Island law, but Rex had broken so many laws, and surely he would have changed the Cup rules so Skandar couldn't race if . . . if there hadn't been a reason.

Rex had known Skandar was the last double elemental for a very long time.

And he had been planning on killing him all along.

He had tried to have his silvers kill Skandar already – at the Qualifiers. Skandar had been so distracted by Rex talking about the Mainland that he'd only just realised what Rex had meant in the Grove. He'd said Skandar dying in the Qualifiers would have been a *missed opportunity*. That could only mean one thing – he wanted another opportunity to kill Skandar. And where better than in the Chaos Cup where accidents always happened?

Then Skandar felt cold dread settle on his heart. Wait a second. Rex had said killing Skandar at the Qualifiers would have meant *more than one* missed opportunity. Rex had moved the Chaos Cup to the summer solstice – the day the spirit sacrifice had to be made. And if Rex knew Skandar was the last double elemental, he also knew how risky this was. Why not leave the Chaos Cup where it had always been? Why not safely kill Skandar before the solstice? There had to be another reason. The other opportunity Rex wanted.

And Skandar could see it clearly now. Rex was going to use the last spirit wielder on the Island as bait. The Wild Rider had been impossible to capture so far. But Rex was gambling that Kenna would come for her sacrifice – for Skandar and his unicorn. Rex believed he was going to reverse the curse and get rid of the last spirit rider on the Island, all while securing his place as Commodore again, ready to invade the Mainland. And the memory of Rex's words clanged through Skandar: *It's not like you're going to be there to see it.*

'Skandar Smith?'

Skandar tried to shut everything out as he left the Gilded Grove and followed the black-clad steward down a gleaming gold spiral staircase and back to the Chaos Compound. He

– 368 –

## LUCKY THIRTEEN

tried not to listen to the insults being hurled his way from the spectators lining the route. He just put one boot in front of the other, desperate to be reunited with Scoundrel.

The Compound was a hive of activity. Skandar spotted saddlers making checks on the unicorns they'd chosen back at the Eyrie – purple-sashed Henning-Dove tightening Silver Pirate's girth, blue-sashed Martina raising one of Flo's stirrup leathers by an extra hole, Holder giving Silver Rhapsody's saddle a polish. The blacksmiths were buzzing about, too – checking armour, giving last-minute advice.

Skandar rushed to Scoundrel's Luck, who stood completely alone, the silvers giving him a wide berth. Skandar buried his face into the unicorn's neck and breathed in his familiar scent. Scoundrel launched a bubble of reassurance into the bond, no doubt feeling the turmoil that was coursing through Skandar. Though the black unicorn seemed to have concerns of his own, he kept looking over at Blade, as though wondering why his silver friend didn't come over to say hello.

'Blade will be back with us soon, boy,' Skandar murmured, his gaze snagging on Rex as he talked calmly to Taiting, his saddler.

Skandar took some deep breaths as his heart thundered. *You might want to kill me, Rex Manning*, he thought. *You might want to kill my sister, too. But that doesn't mean I have to let you.* And somehow just thinking it made him feel braver. He refused to be another one of Rex's unforgivable crimes. He was not going to die today.

Skandar watched Flo lead Blade towards Rex and Sorceress, pushing through the other silver unicorns. She looked worried and she was speaking very quickly. Then Rex was shaking his head, his mouth moving, presumably trying to keep their conversation quiet.

'STARTING POSITIONS, PLEASE!' a steward ordered, and there was a wave of movement as riders mounted. Skandar scrambled into his Shekoni saddle, his whole body shaking.

When the unicorns emerged from the Compound, there was an almighty roar from the crowd. Scoundrel skittered sideways at the noise of a full arena, and Skandar could sense the unicorn's nervousness mixing with his own through the bond.

Unlike at the Qualifiers, the thirteen unicorns had plenty of space to line up when they reached the starting bar, and nobody had to jostle for position. Skandar pulled down his black metal helmet to muffle the sound of the crowd, and – as always – it made him feel calmer, the sound of his own breathing helping him regain his concentration.

'THIRTY SECONDS!' A steward shouted.

The crowd got louder.

Scoundrel suddenly shrieked happily, and Skandar looked to his right. Silver Blade had slotted in next to Scoundrel and was rumbling back in welcome. Flo looked magnificent in her shining silver armour, but she still had her helmet off, trying to say something to him.

'TEN SECONDS!'

Skandar pushed his helmet up to hear Flo better, but the crowd was deafening, and he shook his head at her. Then, giving up, Flo took his hand over their unicorns' tucked wings and squeezed it, her eyes bright with unfallen tears. Skandar squeezed back, attempting a smile.

'THREE SECONDS!'

Skandar and Flo unlinked their fingers, pulled down their helmets, tightened their reins and crouched low in their saddles. Then there was a crash and a bang, as the starting bar rose over the horns of thirteen warrior unicorns.

CHAPTER TWENTY-THREE

# THE CHAOS CUP

'Well, hello there, folks! I'm Declan Dashwood, this is the Chaos Cup, and I'm as surprised as you are that I've hung on to this job so long. But the starting bar is up, and this year's race is underway – perhaps one of the most memorable we've ever had. Only thirteen Chaos riders flying – twelve silvers and one lone spirit wielder who has defied all the odds to compete today, including it being a crime – yes, a *crime* – to assist him in any way. Though as the race gets underway, it doesn't look like he needs a lot of help. Skandar Smith and Scoundrel's Luck have got off to an absolutely stunning start!'

Scoundrel's Luck one hundred per cent knew he was racing in the Chaos Cup. Skandar could feel it in every beat of his black wings, every snort of his breath. And he didn't need a stopwatch to know that Scoundrel's take-off was the quickest they'd ever soared into the sky. Scoundrel was racing to win.

They reached the aerial quarter marker without incident, and Skandar felt his confidence growing. None of the silvers seemed to be even *attempting* to engage him in a sky battle at the moment.

# SKANDAR AND THE SKELETON CURSE

In the small leading group he could see Rex and Silver Sorceress, Lori and Silver Rhapsody and Eoin and Silver Warlock. But they weren't very far ahead – not for a unicorn as fast as Scoundrel.

Behind Skandar was a four-strong group of silvers, led by Ayana and Silver Phoenix. Flo and Silver Blade were nowhere to be seen – they must be languishing in the rearmost group.

Focusing back on the unicorns in front of him, Skandar realised that something very odd was happening.

'Yes – you heard me right,' Declan confirmed. 'It appears that Lori Fusano and Eoin Blake are slowing Rhapsody and Warlock. Surely these silvers can't be tired already? They're not even at the halfway marker! Has anyone told them it's a— OOF! I'm not sure the spirit wielder saw this coming!'

Scoundrel roared as Rhapsody and Warlock reduced their speed so much that they ended up flying far too close on either side of him.

'Move it!' Skandar shouted angrily. 'Their wings are going to collide!' But Lori and Eoin didn't appear to care, their unicorns' silver feathers mashing against Scoundrel's black ones. Scoundrel started to slow. Skandar could practically feel Ayana and Phoenix breathing down his neck at the head of the group behind. But she made no move to battle him, no move to take Scoundrel's position, no move towards Rex and . . .

Suddenly Skandar understood what the silvers were doing. The whole Chaos Cup was a setup – of course it was. The Silver Circle riders had all dropped back to ensure Rex Manning would be the clear winner. None of them wanted to take the Commodore title from him – or perhaps they had been threatened not to try. Skandar thought back to Flo's words in the Grove. 'I don't have a choice.' Was this what she'd meant? She didn't have a choice but to let Rex win today?

'Well, *we're* not taking orders from Rex, are we, boy?' Skandar

– 372 –

# THE CHAOS CUP

murmured to Scoundrel, who snapped his teeth angrily at the silver unicorns boxing him in.

Skandar summoned the spirit element into his palm, filling the bond with it, and then he switched quickly to fire, the two elements combining to change Scoundrel into flame itself. It was the fastest Scoundrel had ever achieved the transformation and the silver riders on either side had no time to throw up shields. Their unicorns screeched as their silver feathers were singed by Scoundrel's burning body.

Skandar tried to accelerate towards the tail of Silver Sorceress, keeping Scoundrel ablaze. But he found his way blocked by an enormous writhing water viper – an elemental predator created by Lori and Rhapsody.

*Don't be afraid of creating predators to fight the silvers*, Viv had told him.

He made the decision in a split-second, trusting Scoundrel to keep the viper at a distance with the barrage of sand he was kicking out from his flying hooves. Skandar let a cloud of pearly spirit magic build above his head and moulded his own predator. Perhaps he'd thought of Bobby in the crowd below, cheering him on the loudest, because the spirit magic gathered shape as a bird of prey. The ghostly peregrine falcon soared right for the viper as it spat ice shards at Scoundrel's head.

'Well, that's a particularly apt bird for this young rider, since he was a member of the Peregrine Society at the Eyrie,' Declan explained excitedly, 'which is currently being occupied by Skandar's *sister* and her band of wild riders. Gosh, you really couldn't make this stuff up. And it looks like the falcon has defeated the viper. Yes, Skandar Smith is trying to catch up with the leader, which is currently Rex Manning on Silver Sorceress.'

Skandar couldn't tell if the crowd were cheering or booing him as he pushed Scoundrel on towards Sorceress, but he had

– 373 –

# SKANDAR AND THE SKELETON CURSE

more pressing worries. Ayana – on Silver Phoenix – and Brad – on Silver Pirate – were both hurling weapons at him from behind, and he was forced to turn Scoundrel in mid-air to face them.

Skandar raised a fire shield to melt a volley of arrows from Brad's ice bow, then managed to return Pirate's water attack with a monster of a wave that he thought would have made Instructor O'Sullivan proud. In anger, a barely controlled Pirate set off three elemental attacks at once – one from his front hooves, one from his horn and another from his jaws – and Brad screamed in pain as the debris caught him across the face.

Before Skandar even had time to draw breath, Scoundrel gave out a warning shriek, as fire wielder Ayana started to mould a predator in the air above her head. Skandar summoned the spirit element and reached out for the red connection between Ayana and Phoenix, hoping to snuff out her predator attack within the bond. The cloud of fire above her disappeared and Skandar almost cheered in relief. With Ayana momentarily confused, Skandar threw a volley of spirit daggers at a recovering Brad and Pirate, trying to make them drop back for good. He manipulated them using illusion, every dagger aiming for a false place, so that Brad raised his shields in all the wrong directions. Finally the water wielder was forced downwards to avoid Skandar's relentless attacks.

But there was no time to celebrate. Ayana and Silver Phoenix had swooped back round in front of Scoundrel, and the pair unleashed the most powerful wildfire attack Skandar had ever seen. Panic filled Skandar's brain as the inferno billowed towards him, Scoundrel roared in fear, until he remembered something Aspen McGrath had done the year she became Commodore. Skandar summoned the water element to his palm, and – concentrating hard – knitted ice crystals all round himself and Scoundrel. By the time the attack hit, they were both sealed

# THE CHAOS CUP

within a frozen cocoon so thick that all the wildfire could do was rage around them.

Scoundrel burst from the shell in an explosion of ice shards, a vine-twisted bow already in Skandar's hands, and he fired a volley of thorny arrows at Ayana's chest. Silver Rhapsody was forced to bank sideways, almost colliding with the floating halfway marker – and the air in front of Scoundrel was finally clear.

Skandar felt a mixture of exhilaration and terror – catching up with Rex brought him closer to winning the Cup, but it also meant putting himself in the path of a man who wanted to kill him.

Declan Dashwood was not so conflicted and sounded giddy over the loudspeaker. 'Skandar Smith is leaving the rest of the field behind now – the other silvers can't keep up. Look at this spirit unicorn fly! He's gaining on Rex Manning and Silver Sorceress with every wingbeat.'

Skandar felt a twinge in his chest. There had been a big part of him that had wanted Flo to win the Chaos Cup. He didn't care about winning himself – he only cared that the Commodore wouldn't be someone who was going to invade the Mainland. But as he left the blurred line of silver unicorns behind him, he couldn't see Flo and Blade at all. It was down to him and Scoundrel now.

Rex Manning was still ahead as the arena materialised in the distance. At the sound of Declan's commentary, the Commodore had looked over his shoulder at Skandar – but only once. Now he was focused on the course ahead. Of course, Skandar thought – if Rex was going to kill him and play the hero, he'd want to do it in front of a crowd. From their speed, it was easy to believe that Rex and Sorceress had once been members of the Peregrine Society. And that made Skandar think of Nina Kazama and her ring on Rex's finger and—

– 375 –

# SKANDAR AND THE SKELETON CURSE

'ARGHHH!' Scoundrel roared along with his rider, increasing the speed of his wingbeats, the air rushing by so fast that it rattled his chainmail.

'Just in case you've been living in a stalignome's cave for the last fifteen minutes,' Declan was saying, 'we have two unicorns out in front, two unicorns in contention – Silver Sorceress and Scoundrel's Luck. Yes, you heard me. If Skandar plays his cards right, we could have a spirit wielder for a Commodore in a matter of minutes. Is that even legal? Who cares! It's *exciting*. And as they pass the three-quarter marker, they're nearing Fourpoint again—'

*The spirit zone*, Skandar thought. But he couldn't think about Kenna right now. About how Rex might try to kill him. He just had to race. He just had to survive.

Scoundrel drew level with Sorceress with less than a quarter of the course to go, and Rex finally reacted. The air wielder casually flung a lightning bolt sideways, which Skandar easily knocked out of the way with a diamond axe. For a moment, he wondered if Rex was tiring – it was such an obvious move – but as a cloud of lightning took shape above the Commodore's head, Skandar realised it had only been a distraction.

An elemental predator bigger than Skandar had ever seen cast a shadow over Scoundrel as he flew. And Skandar knew what it was even before Declan breathed its name into his microphone, even before he heard the gasps of the crowd in the stands, the shouts of awe.

It was a Mythical-level predator.

'A THUNDERBIRD!' And for once Declan Dashwood had no more to say.

It all made sense now. Skandar would bet his last jar of mayonnaise that Rex had always known he could summon a Mythical, that it was the whole reason he'd legalised predators

– 376 –

# THE CHAOS CUP

in the first place. Perhaps that was why he'd barely glanced at Scoundrel as he'd caught up with Sorceress. Perhaps that was why the silvers had dropped so far behind. To give Rex the space he needed.

Because Viv had taught Skandar one fundamental thing about Mythical predators – she didn't know how to beat one. And when predators had been legal, they'd been considered even more of a threat to a rider's life than a wild unicorn encounter. Rex's lightning bird was going to kill the spirit wielder right above the arena – in plain sight of the whole Island. The Commodore could claim he'd lost control. It was a Mythical; nobody would blame him. Rex would be able to murder Skandar and keep his own hands clean.

Skandar felt choking panic almost overwhelming him. Rex would become Commodore again, would reign supreme. There was a war coming – that's what the truesong had said – and Skandar was sure Rex would be the one to bring those dark days closer. There would be hate and treachery on the Island – maybe the Mainland too. Skandar didn't want to die at all. But he certainly didn't want to die *now* and leave his friends alone to fight for their futures, for the future of spirit wielders, for the future of the whole world.

The thunderbird rained down an electrical storm on Scoundrel – its wingspan so wide that it blocked Skandar's path to the finishing arch. Desperately he summoned shield after shield to try to protect them, each one weakening as more lightning bolts hit – from its talons, from its eyes, from its beak, from every single fizzing feather. Sorceress was edging ahead again, and as his latest spirit shield winked out, Skandar could feel himself giving up. He wished Flo could somehow catch up and fight by his side, wished Bobby were here to call the mythical bird a silly name, wished Mitchell was reeling off predator stats

– 377 –

## SKANDAR AND THE SKELETON CURSE

to calm him. If only his whole quartet were with him in the sky. Only then, he thought, would they have a chance of surviving a Mythical. But they weren't, and Sorceress was starting her descent towards the stands as the crowd roared with excitement.

Then there was a nudge in the bond. Scoundrel was flooding their connection with the spirit element, just like he had as a Hatchling. The smell of Skandar's element – of cinnamon and vinegar and leather – brought him to his senses. Skandar had wished for help, for his friends to fight with him – but what if he could *create* help?

The desire to duplicate was so great in both rider and unicorn that within a second there was another Scoundrel flying alongside them. The duplicate wasn't using the spirit element – the easiest for Skandar to use when he split himself – but the water element. The other Skandar's palm was already glowing blue, a wave crashing towards the thunderbird's storm. The great beast screeched in rage at having its enemies doubled, and Rex looked over his shoulder, confusion across his perfect features. But Scoundrel was still forcing the spirit element into the bond, and Skandar wondered about a second duplicate. They'd only done it once before, but he had to trust Scoundrel. Unicorns were, after all, much cleverer than their riders – the Chaos Trials had taught him that.

Rex was attempting to direct the thunderbird back towards the real Skandar and Scoundrel when they managed not one but two more duplicates. One wielded fire, his palm glowing red and hurling flaming javelins at Rex; the other wielded air and shot lightning arrows up at the crackling wings of the great bird so it was forced to dive sideways, thunder rumbling in its wake as the water duplicate sent ice spears towards its impossibly large beak.

Skandar could feel exhaustion hitting him now. Although Rex and Sorceress had stopped in mid-air just above the stands

– 378 –

# THE CHAOS CUP

to fight one of the duplicates, the thunderbird was still holding its own – and Skandar was struggling with the concentration required to control the three duplicates. But Scoundrel was insistent. He roared, he screeched, he pushed harder with the spirit element, and it was at that exact moment that Skandar spotted Bobby, Mitchell and Jamie in the stands.

They were very high up, their faces tipped to the sky as they watched the battle going on above their heads. Skandar could see Bobby's mouth moving and he imagined how loud her voice was as she shouted out his name. Mitchell and Jamie were jumping up and down – hands linked, fists in the air. In the same row were more faces he knew – Rickesh, Prim, Jordan, Sarika, Patrick, Walker, Fen, Niamh, Art, Gabriel – who must all have made the journey from the zones to watch. Just behind were the three Eyrie instructors, as well as Craig, Olu and Sara and the whole Shekoni Saddles team, everyone cheering at the top of their lungs.

And a feeling of such immense joy bloomed within Skandar's chest that the fourth duplicate felt like no effort at all. Palm glowing green, it threw a lasso of thorned vines round the thunderbird's sparking neck, and the quartet of duplicates managed to move the Mythical out of the real Skandar's path. Anger bloomed across Rex's face, and then it cleared – a decision made.

Sorceress and Scoundrel dived at exactly the same moment, shooting over the top of the stands and hurtling towards the arena, silver and black horns level. Skandar gritted his teeth, holding his nerve as the sand rushed towards them, the faces in the stands blurring.

Three metres from the ground Rex pulled up out of the dive. And Skandar knew then why Nina Kazama had been chosen as squadron leader of the Peregrine Society – Rex had never had enough nerve.

– 379 –

# SKANDAR AND THE SKELETON CURSE

The feeling of unity in Skandar and Scoundrel's bond was so strong that – a metre from the ground – they both knew exactly what they were going to do. It was a move they had seen at their first-ever Peregrine Society meeting, performed by Flight Lieutenant Prim and Winter Wildfire.

Skandar leaned sharply to the left, and Scoundrel cut down through the air with his left wing. The unicorn's black feathers skimmed the sand as he rolled over in the air just above the arena's surface. Then another roll, their velocity slowing. Then a final turn, and Scoundrel had enough control to beat them out of the roll with both wings, kicking out his front legs . . . and they were upright, Scoundrel's feet on solid ground and galloping towards the finishing arch.

'UNBELIEVABLE SCENES!' Declan yelled. 'The spirit wielder is going to do it! Skandar Smith and Scoundrel's Luck are *actually* going to win the Chaos Cup.'

And Skandar looked up just in time to see the finishing arch rising above his head – the same arch he'd seen on television every year of his life on the Mainland.

'It was all you, boy,' Skandar said, touching his palm to Scoundrel's sweat-drenched neck. The crowd went absolutely wild as they crossed the finishing line, and Skandar thought of Agatha in the prison, hearing it all happening, hearing him *win*.

'Skandar Smith is the new Commodore of Chaos – I have absolutely no idea what happens next. Is the spirit element legal now? Who does he have on his Council? Do any of us actually care?' shouted Declan. 'He's the youngest-ever winner of the Cup. A nomad, a Mainlander! The ultimate underdog. Twelve silvers in the field and number thirteen wins it . . . Wait, what the—'

Like someone had pushed a button, the crowd's cheering turned to screams.

Then the world exploded.

CHAPTER TWENTY-FOUR

# IMMORTAL SECRETS

Given the force of the explosion in the arena, Skandar had no idea how he stayed on Scoundrel's back . . . or even stayed conscious. The sound the sand made was unearthly as it was thrown up so high that it blocked out the sun. An earthquake. A sonic boom. Skandar didn't have the right word to describe it, but he was so afraid that all he could do was bury his head in Scoundrel's mane. *At least if we die, boy, we die together. At least we won't have to live without each other.*

The sound stopped. Skandar looked up and saw the sand suspended in the sky. As he watched, the grains fell like rain – but they never settled. Instead, they shifted to form ice sheets, then columns of fire, then lightning strikes, and then thorny vines that cascaded through the sky. The elemental rain blocked out the sound of the screaming crowd, obscuring the shape of the silver unicorns flying above, blurring out the terrified faces in the stands so that Skandar and Scoundrel were quite alone in the eye of the storm. Then there was a triumphant cry – half wild laugh, half predatory caw.

# SKANDAR AND THE SKELETON CURSE

And they weren't alone any more.

Goshawk's Fury stood under the finishing arch of the Chaos Cup, Kenna sitting on the wild unicorn's back as her palm flashed in the colours of the impossible rain she had summoned. The rain that was keeping the rest of the world out. Skandar noticed something strapped to Kenna's hip. The bone staff was different, but it was still recognisable, though the spirit bone was missing from the top.

'Kenna? Kenn?' Skandar said, fear flooding his veins. He tried to tell himself what he'd insisted to Flo back in the Grove – that his sister would never hurt him or Scoundrel. Tried to remember that the elemental glow she'd left on the fault lines had harmed everyone except him. But it was hard to hold on to those thoughts with that white stripe painted down her face, and half her skull gleaming through to match Goshawk's rotting body. Hard to believe with the ice spikes glinting at her throat, the feathers at her ears, the vines up her right arm, the magma along her left. She didn't look much like the Kenna he had loved all his life. She didn't look much like the Kenna that had loved *him*. But he made Scoundrel take one step towards the arch anyway. Because however it ended, it would end today.

'It's funny,' Kenna said perfectly calmly, as though they were sitting on the sofa back in Flat 207. 'One of my worst thoughts when you got to go to the Island was that you weren't special enough, Skar. Isn't that a dreadful thing to think about your own brother?'

Skandar swallowed, unsure how to answer. Instead, his gaze flicked up at the elemental rain and he noticed it had a smoky backdrop, dark shadows flitting around behind its curtain. Nobody was getting through that anytime soon. Not if they wanted to live.

'But it turns out you *are* special. You just won the Chaos Cup,

# IMMORTAL SECRETS

and you're about to become the final puzzle piece in the Island's future. In its new beginning.'

'Because I'm the double elemental,' Skandar choked out. 'Because Scoundrel's Luck is the unicorn you need for your sacrifice.'

'I am sorry, Skar, truly,' Kenna said, and she almost sounded like herself again. 'If there was anyone else, if there was any other way—'

'Why are you doing this, Kenn? And don't tell me you're doing the First Rider's bidding, or you want the Island to go back to the beginning, or whatever else Albert believes. Why are *you* doing this?'

An emotion crossed Kenna's face, but it flashed so quickly that Skandar couldn't tell what it was. 'Does it matter?'

'You're about to kill my unicorn,' Skandar said stiffly. 'The least you can do is tell me why you think you need to take Scoundrel from me so badly.'

'The cycle of the Skeleton Curse will be completed,' Kenna said formally.

'Don't lie!' Skandar cried, losing control of his voice. 'I haven't always been able to tell when you were keeping things from me, Kenn, but I know there's something else going on here. Tell me why you need Scoundrel dead to complete the curse, when you didn't kill Tsunami's Herald.'

This time Skandar saw darkness creep into Kenna's eyes and he knew he'd asked a question she didn't want to answer. Suddenly her palm was glowing white and a shadowy javelin was soaring towards Scoundrel's chest. But Skandar had just spent the last few months training solidly for the Chaos Cup. He reacted at lightning speed and sent a crashing torrent of water from his palm to knock the javelin off course.

It took her only seconds to retaliate, a shining bow bursting

– 383 –

# SKANDAR AND THE SKELETON CURSE

into her hands. Spirit arrows flew towards Skandar's chest, but he knew better than to try to block them one by one – no doubt she'd mastered illusion too. He threw up an enormous shield of sand, and Scoundrel roared a blast of cold air, freezing the shadowy arrows before they could reach his rider.

Kenna laughed and the sound had actual joy in it. 'We always dreamed of being Chaos riders together, didn't we? And now look at us – battling it out in the famous arena. But you're no match for me, little bro. Even if – for the next few minutes at least – you happen to be the Commodore.'

Kenna vaulted off Goshawk's back, her fist balled. She was holding something.

Scoundrel started to screech in warning as Kenna advanced. Skandar threw warning blasts towards her feet – fireball, ice shard, lightning strike, flint flurry. But – although she raised no shield to protect herself – none of the magic touched her.

Kenna raised her fist as she bore down on Scoundrel. She let out a terrible howl, a wild unicorn's lament. And Skandar realised what she was holding.

It was the missing top of the bone staff – the part Skandar had held as the First Rider's gift had shattered two years before on the Divide. The spirit bone.

She really was going to kill Scoundrel.

Skandar's first instinct was to fly out of there – he didn't understand Kenna's wild magic, and he didn't know if he could protect Scoundrel from it. He gathered his reins, signalling to Scoundrel that they were going to try to fly upwards, even if they couldn't get past the elemental rain, but . . .

Scoundrel wouldn't move.

Kenna was whispering something that Skandar couldn't hear, and the bone staff was brightening in her hand like a torch.

Scoundrel was mesmerised by it.

– 384 –

## IMMORTAL SECRETS

'Come on, boy,' Skandar urged, but the unicorn had completely frozen, watching as Kenna took another step and another.

'Kenna,' Skandar begged. 'Kenna, please!'

But with a swipe of her hand and a blast of spirit magic Skandar was knocked sideways out of the saddle. He hit the sand with a thump and rolled over twice with the force of it, the black-edged tendrils of Kenna's magic clinging to him like a shadow.

Kenna reached Scoundrel, running a hand down his armoured head, still whispering. Panic gripped Skandar – flashes of Isa's skeletal face and of Sunset's Blood dead on the fault line came into his mind – but as hard as he tried to crawl back to Scoundrel, he couldn't get any closer. Kenna's spirit magic weighed him down like heavy chains.

In desperation Skandar said the first thing that came into his head, for some reason remembering Sara Shekoni's words from months ago. 'Is it because you're lonely, Kenna? Is that why you've turned the unicorns wild? You don't have to be. I can help you.'

'The point of the Skeleton Curse is so we can reset the Island,' Kenna declared. 'Wild unicorns will choose their riders once more. And nobody can help me with the forged bond now Mum's . . .' She tailed off, stroking Scoundrel again. But Skandar caught the wobble at the corner of her mouth.

Skandar's breath hitched, as the pieces started to slot into place. He didn't understand it entirely, but he had enough to guess – and he could tell when his sister was afraid, even if there was so much he didn't know about her any more. 'You're scared of what the forged bond is going to do to you, aren't you? You're scared of ending up like Mum.'

There was a long silence, and then Kenna began to speak quickly, as though she'd been waiting to tell Skandar this for months.

'The Skeleton Curse works by draining the magic from a

– 385 –

# SKANDAR AND THE SKELETON CURSE

double elemental's bond. Mum's theory was that each piece of the bone staff would act as a kind of lightning rod. And she was right. In the earth zone I drained the bond between Elias and Marauding Magnet through the earth bone and into the fault line, and the magic of all the other earth bonds leaked down with it, back into the Island. That's what turned the earth unicorns wild.'

'That sounds sort of easy,' Skandar said, swallowing down the betrayal of Kenna stealing those pieces of bone from him so long ago. He had to keep her talking.

'It's not at all!' Kenna said, sounding more like herself. 'It requires an enormous amount of spirit magic to empty a bond. I don't know if anyone else could've done it. Maybe Mum when she was younger.'

'You didn't mention killing unicorns anywhere, though,' Skandar said. 'Where was the killing part?'

Kenna hesitated before answering. 'You were right, okay? The Skeleton Curse doesn't need a unicorn death to work. The thing is, when you kill a unicorn, the bond doesn't just drain – it breaks.'

'I'm aware,' Skandar murmured, glancing tensely at Scoundrel. 'I was there when you killed Arctic Swansong, remember?'

'Yes, but something else happens too.' There was no stopping Kenna's confession now. 'When a rider bonds with their destined unicorn, that unicorn gives up its immortality. That's all part of the deal – of course that didn't happen with me and Goshawk. Usually, the unicorn's immortal lifespan is compressed into the lifespan of its mortal rider. Mum told me that some spirit wielders in the old days used to study what happened at the moment they broke a bond; what happens to that compressed lifespan when the unicorn dies too soon? Before its rider.'

– 386 –

# IMMORTAL SECRETS

Skandar's heart was racing with fear. 'What happens to it?' he managed to croak.

'If the bond *hasn't* been drained, then the immortality gets mixed up in the magic flowing back into the Island and it's impossible to isolate. But once the magic is drained from a bond, the unicorn's immortality is what's left. And when the bond breaks, that life force floods into the closest bond it can find.'

'So the unicorn sacrifices – you're stealing their life force to make *yourself* immortal?!'

'I prefer *harvesting* to stealing,' Kenna said, though her voice was shaking. 'But yes, Mum thought that if I managed to harvest immortality from each of the sacrifices for the curse, then that might help me live as long as Goshawk. For ever. It might make me powerful enough to survive the forged bond.'

Skandar knew he should feel revulsion towards his sister after everything she'd told him. Feel horrified that her plan was to steal Scoundrel's immortality next. But somehow he couldn't. Somehow, he understood.

'Our mum died, Kenn. Right in front of us, and it was awful, and I miss her even though she left us when we were little. And that's really confusing, and I don't know what to do with all these feelings I have about her.'

Kenna's head snapped towards him. 'That's not why I'm doing this.'

'Isn't it?' Skandar asked gently, and he managed to crawl a tiny bit closer to Scoundrel.

'No!' Kenna said hurriedly. 'I thought you didn't care about Mum.' Kenna's fist around the spirit bone was now hanging by her thigh. 'Aren't you on Agatha's side?'

Skandar chuckled softly despite everything. 'Kenn, there *are* no sides in a family – or at least I don't think there should be. Agatha loved Erika so much. She didn't know what was going

– 387 –

# SKANDAR AND THE SKELETON CURSE

to happen when she broke her forged bond. She hates herself for it. I think sometimes she wishes she'd died instead.'

'But *she* didn't die, our mum did.' Kenna's eyes were wild with grief. 'Can't you see that this curse, her plan for my immortality – that's all she left behind, all she left for me?'

'She never should have asked this of you,' Skandar said quietly. 'You're not her, Kenn. You never have been and you never will be.'

'But I *am* like her, and if I don't do this, I'll die like her too!' Kenna cried. 'I watched her leave the world and there was nothing I could do. I felt so *powerless*, just like I have my whole life, Skar. I never had the power to make Dad better or to change my Hatchery exam result or to make you stay behind in Margate or even to change the Island's mind about me. Don't you understand that I never want to feel like that again?'

'Do you know why I never felt powerless growing up?' Skandar said very quietly. 'Because of you, Kenn. Because *you* taught me to be strong. You have no idea how powerful you were to me when we were little. From Dad's worst days, to my bullies, to the monsters under the bed – you never let me face anything alone. You made me stronger – and I think you might have forgotten how *together* we can do anything. *Together* neither of us is powerless. Don't you see?'

Kenna shook her head roughly. 'Even if that used to be true, it can't be any more. Now you're always going to see me as the villain – so that's who I've become.'

And Skandar understood then what Kenna needed to hear – that she needed to know he loved her no matter what she'd done, or what she looked like, or even whether she deserved it. There was no way out of loving her. It was a fixed point in his heart, no matter how much it hurt. So Skandar said them – the three most powerful words in any language.

– 388 –

# IMMORTAL SECRETS

'I forgive you.'

Kenna stared at him and Skandar held her gaze in one of their long looks – a look they'd perfected growing up; a look that once upon a time had allowed them to understand each other without saying a word. There was a flicker in the elemental rain as Kenna struggled to hold on to the magic that was keeping the world out.

'You can't,' she said eventually.

'I can,' Skandar said firmly. 'And I do.'

Then several things happened at once.

Falcon's Wrath – fully wild – exploded through a gap in Kenna's barrier, with Bobby shouting, 'Get away from Scoundrel right now!'

Red Night's Delight – also fully wild – followed right after her, shrieking to Scoundrel in welcome, and Mitchell was yelling at the top of his voice, 'Don't you dare hurt Skandar!'

And right behind Falcon and Red, a dapple-grey unicorn galloped through the gap in the rain and bellowed furiously at all of them.

In her shock, Kenna's spirit magic extinguished.

The elemental rain returned to sand, falling back to the arena like snow. Scoundrel was free of whatever hold she'd had over him, and he galloped over to Skandar, who was already jumping to his feet, ready to launch himself back into his Shekoni saddle.

Bobby was yelling at Kenna in rage, Falcon was shrieking at Goshawk, and Goshawk was bellowing at the dapple-grey unicorn that had halted very close to her destined rider. Meanwhile, Mitchell and Red were blocking Kenna's path towards Skandar and Scoundrel, blasting wild magic at random.

Skandar caught sight of Kenna's face as she looked from Mitchell and Bobby to the dapple-grey unicorn, and there was such pain there that he almost wanted to call out to her. Then

– 389 –

she was running over the freshly fallen sand. Goshawk escaped Falcon to gallop on Kenna's right, the dapple-grey keeping pace on her left. And in the blink of an eye Kenna was up on Goshawk's back and soaring over the stands of the arena, the dapple-grey careering out of the arena's exit to chase their flying shadows along the ground.

Bobby had already dismounted and was sprinting towards Skandar – the most enormous grin on her face, shouting, 'You won the Chaos Cup! You actually won, spirit boy!'

Mitchell was running too, saying, 'You were the last double elemental, weren't you? It was you, after all! But Kenna didn't kill Scoundrel! The Skeleton Curse, it's over! It's all going to be over!'

And then Flo was galloping Silver Blade towards the rest of her quartet, and they would all – finally – be united again.

For one glorious moment, it felt like everything was going to be okay.

Until it wasn't.

'Skandar Smith,' Flo said in a voice he had never heard her use before, 'you're under arrest.'

<sub>Kenna</sub>

# BROTHER

Kenna Everhart had been forgiven.

Back within the safety of the Eyrie, Kenna gripped the trunk in her brother's old treehouse and pressed her thumb against the different colours of elemental paint.

Fire. Water. Air. Earth. Spirit.

*I forgive you.* Skandar's voice echoed in her mind over and over again.

When she shut her eyes, she saw Mitchell and Bobby riding their wild unicorns into the arena to protect her brother. They'd had no magic, no real plan, no regard for their own safety – they'd just wanted to save Skandar.

And suddenly Kenna didn't want to be the one they were protecting him from any more. Growing up, *she* had been the protector – he'd reminded her of that. Kenna had spent so many years pretending to be fearless for Skandar that she had become truly brave. But since Goshawk and her mum, she had felt so afraid, so alone, so utterly powerless in a world that rejected her, that she'd forgotten how strong she'd once been – even without

SKANDAR AND THE SKELETON CURSE

a bond to an immortal unicorn.

*Together neither of us is powerless. Don't you see?*

Skandar was her brother. It had always been the two of them against the world, hadn't it? And in all her fear, grief and bitterness, she'd forgotten that he was the one person she could rely on. Because he saw all of her – the Kenna who'd protected him from reality in Margate so he could dream of unicorns, as well as the one who had done unforgivable things for revenge and power. Perhaps it was why she'd shut him out these past two years – afraid of how much he knew, and how he might use it to break her once and for all.

But it seemed that somewhere along the way Kenna had not only forgotten who she was but who Skandar was too. Because her little brother knew everything about her and still he loved her. Forgave her.

And it turned out she'd really needed to be forgiven.

Kenna gazed at the seascape her brother had painted on the treehouse wall. She knew that beach and that view, and there was something grounding in it. It was like time had collapsed into itself and she was back in Margate, looking out at the horizon. She felt a kind of acceptance settling over her like a sea breeze.

She'd never really been allowed to be a child. She'd never truly known her mother. She'd never properly opened the Hatchery door. She'd never recovered from her brother leaving her behind. She had done some undeniably terrible things. And the truth was, even if she stole all the immortality in the world, she'd never have the power to erase those pieces of her past. But her future could still be changed – if she gave it a chance.

If she chose living over living for ever.

Kenna left her brother's treehouse. She crossed swinging bridges and climbed down armoured trunks to the Eyrie's gate, where the leaves cast twinkling shadows on the forest floor.

– 392 –

## BROTHER

When the entrance tree opened in a beautiful tapestry of white light, she heard Albert's voice from somewhere behind her.

'Kenn, you can't go out there! They're all searching for you!'

But all she said was, 'Look after Goshawk for me.'

Kenna Smith walked out of the Eyrie into the evening sunshine, a dapple-grey unicorn matching her step for step. Because she'd finally learned the lesson Erika Everhart never had.

People aren't meant to live for ever; they're meant to live for love. That way – no matter how long they live – they leave something good behind.

And it turned out that was the most powerful thing of all.

Chapter Twenty-Five

# THE SILVER AND THE SPIRIT WIELDER

'You're under arrest,' Flo repeated. 'Please dismount from your unicorn.'

As Rex Manning and four other silvers came hurtling towards Skandar and Scoundrel, all Skandar could do was stare at Flo.

But Bobby found her voice. 'What are you *talking* about, Flo? This isn't funny!'

Rex dismounted from Silver Sorceress, and another member of the Silver Circle handed him a microphone.

Rex's voice rang out loud and clear over the speakers. 'A matter has been brought to my attention that means the result of this Chaos Cup cannot be allowed to stand.'

The crowd let out an angry roar, and Skandar realised that – even after Kenna's appearance – everyone was still in their seats.

'Skandar is the Commodore of Chaos,' Mitchell said loudly from wild Red's back. 'Who are you to—'

'*I* am the head of the Silver Circle,' Rex spoke into the microphone, 'and it is my duty to ensure that the Island is safe.

# THE SILVER AND THE SPIRIT WIELDER

*Particularly* from agents of the Mainland who are trying to threaten our way of life.'

Skandar dismounted, wanting to look Rex in the face rather than from Scoundrel's back. He tried very hard not to glance at Flo.

'I just *stopped* my sister from completing the Skeleton Curse – or were you not watching that whole thing?'

'It didn't actually look like you were doing very much at all, spirit wielder. Mostly crawling about on the sand.'

'And *you*,' Skandar shouted so the microphone picked up his voice, 'you have been *ignoring* the Skeleton Curse all year ON PURPOSE, just so you can become Commodore again and start a pointless war against—'

'SKANDAR SMITH IS THE WEAVER'S SON!' Rex's damning words echoed around the arena and whispers broke out in the crowd.

Skandar looked right at Flo then, and tears were falling freely down her cheeks.

'You told him?' Skandar said, and his words were loud and full of hurt.

'What is *wrong* with you?' Bobby hissed at Flo.

Mitchell looked completely confused.

'LET ME TELL YOU A STORY,' Rex said, speaking over the quartet and the unsettled crowd. 'Once upon a time, Erika Everhart went to the Mainland in secret, and met a man called Robert SMITH.' He jabbed a finger at Skandar. 'And she put in motion a plan that could survive me killing her. A plan that has been unfolding over the past four years before our very eyes.' Rex took a satisfied breath. 'But now I know the truth. The Weaver sent her Mainlander children to the Island to take our unicorns from us. Can any of you deny that since Skandar Smith arrived here we've seen disaster after disaster? First the Weaver killed

– 395 –

# SKANDAR AND THE SKELETON CURSE

our sentinels and stole Islanders for her wild unicorn army, then the Island's magic became unbalanced and caused mass destruction. And the next year our precious unicorn eggs were taken from the sacred Hatchery. And now? The Skeleton Curse.'

'Skandar wasn't responsible for any of those things!' Mitchell cried. 'He saved the Island every time!'

'Did he?' Rex hissed. 'Or was it all leading to this moment? To the Weaver's son becoming Commodore and her daughter taking over the Eyrie? It all seems rather convenient, doesn't it? And I for one will not stand by as the Weaver's children seize power.'

Skandar could feel the crowd's uncertainty; many were shifting in their seats, having conversations behind their hands. They were starting to believe Rex's story.

'This is madness,' Bobby said, but her eyes were fearful.

'SKANDAR SMITH,' Rex's voice boomed out, 'are you or are you not the son of Erika Everhart?'

Skandar knew that lying might save him. That there would be some who would choose to believe him over Rex Manning. But he was so sick of hiding who he was. Because he was the son of Erika Everhart, but he had also chosen *not* to join her over and over again. Agatha had once told him that being a spirit wielder meant he had to fight the pull of the darkness every day of his life. Fight the darkness and win. And he was proud that he'd done that, that he was still doing it even if he was capable of plunging the world into shadow. He could be the Weaver's son and also be a good person.

Skandar took a deep breath and leaned towards the microphone.

Rex sensed victory and there was triumph in his green eyes as Skandar spoke.

'I am the son of Erika Everhart.'

– 396 –

## THE SILVER AND THE SPIRIT WIELDER

And suddenly there were silvers rushing at him and he was being pulled away from Scoundrel as the unicorn screeched and elemental magic exploded from his horn. Bobby was yelling and Mitchell was trying to get to Skandar – his hair blazing with rage – and Falcon and Red were setting off blasts of wild unicorn magic.

But through the chaos Skandar heard Flo say, 'I'm so sorry, Skar.'

'You don't get to call me that any more,' he replied, as chains were wrapped round his wrists.

Skandar Smith sat in a dark solitary cell of the hanging prison. He had already lost any sense of how long he'd been staring at the metal bars in front of him. He had seen no one since he'd entered – no imprisoned spirit wielders, no Agatha.

The worst thing was being able to feel Scoundrel's distress through the bond. They'd been separated once before, but it hadn't been like this – Skandar had at least been able to sit outside Scoundrel's stable to reassure him. But right now neither of them knew where the other one was.

Skandar thought he might have been able to cope with everything that had happened – Kenna trying to sacrifice Scoundrel for the Skeleton Curse, Rex taking away his Chaos Cup victory, being imprisoned as the Weaver's son – if it hadn't been for Flo's betrayal. He'd been replaying the conversation they'd had in the Gilded Grove. Recalling how she'd insisted he shouldn't race because he was the last double elemental.

But nobody had made Flo arrest Skandar in the middle of the arena.

Nobody had made her give away the secret that he was the Weaver's son.

He couldn't get the words of the children's truesong out of

– 397 –

# SKANDAR AND THE SKELETON CURSE

his head: *Where love once reigned upon these shores, Now friends shall turn to foes.* He hadn't even paid attention to that line when he'd heard it. He'd been preoccupied by the war and sacrifice the song had foretold. But he'd been warned before, hadn't he? Two years ago, down in an ancient tomb:

*The one you love the most will betray you, Skandar Smith. Be wary. When it matters the most, they will turn against you.* Was this what the First Rider had meant? Had he and the truesong both been talking about *Flo*?

Skandar didn't want to believe it. He tried to search for an answer to make sense of what had happened in the arena, but darker thoughts descended – and instead, he was questioning everything.

Flo had never truly accepted that Rex had murdered Nina Kazama. Rex had promised to make Flo an Eyrie instructor, hadn't he? And it had been Flo who'd insisted that they focus on reversing the Skeleton Curse rather than fighting Rex.

Rex had somehow worked out that the Skeleton Curse was cyclical – had Flo told him that? Flo had been in the Stronghold for months, yet she'd told them nothing about Rex's plans for the Mainland. Rex had known Skandar was the double elemental, but there were only a handful of people on the Island who knew he was born in March. Had Flo told Rex that too? And what were they talking about in the Chaos Compound so secretly just before the Cup began? The betrayal felt like a gnawing hunger in his stomach, and he slipped Flo and Blade's bracelet from his arm, tossing it into a shadowed corner.

There was movement outside Skandar's cell. He squinted through the darkness – were they bringing another prisoner in? But there was no glint of a masked guard along the curved corridor. Instead, a hand curled round a bar of Skandar's cell.

'Fancy getting out of here, little bro?'

– 398 –

## THE SILVER AND THE SPIRIT WIELDER

'Kenna?'

It took a moment for Skandar to work out how he was able to see his sister's face. Then he spotted the solstice stone sitting on her right palm, glowing white – the spirit stone Agatha had thrown into the sea last year, along with four others.

'Kenn, what are you doing here? They'll arrest you!'

'They already did.' She shrugged. 'How else was I going to get you out?'

'Get me . . . out?'

'I think you should stand back,' Kenna said seriously. 'There's a lot of magic in this spirit stone. A lot of *my* magic.'

'You're going to blow the bars off?'

'That's the plan,' Kenna said, as the solstice stone glowed brighter.

'And then what?' Skandar asked desperately. He had no idea whether he could trust her, but it wasn't like he had much choice. 'What happens after that?'

Kenna fixed him with her fiercest stare.

'We fight a war.'

# EPILOGUE

Rex Manning sat in the Commodore's private quarters. It felt good to be back where he belonged.

On the floor by his yellow-striped armchair, that morning's **Hatchery Herald** announced the end of the Skeleton Curse – all bonded unicorns were now back to normal, the four riders no longer skeletons – and gave Rex the credit.

So convenient that the curse had ended at sundown on the solstice – just moments after Kenna's arrest.

Crumpled and thrown across the other side of the room, that evening's **Hatchery Herald** announced the escape of Skandar and Kenna Smith from the hanging prison.

That was less convenient.

Rex bent forward, Nina Kazama's ring glowing green on his hand. And on the coffee table in front of him was a map.

A map of the Mainland.

## EPILOGUE

*Rex dragged his finger from the edge of the Island, across the White Unicorn at Uffington and along the Mainland's coast until he reached a point that jutted out. It wasn't the best location for an invasion.*

*But as his finger pressed over the name of the town, there was something that felt so right about it.*

Yes, *Rex Manning thought.* I think we'll start with Margate.

# ACKNOWLEDGEMENTS

This book soared into the world faster than its predecessors – and as a consequence I owe so many people enormous thanks for their cheerleading and belief in both me and the *Skandar* series. First and foremost though, I want to thank my readers – for loving these books so much they have grown their own wings and taken flight in ways I never would have imagined. Thank you for reading them over and over, for creating beautiful fan art, for trading plot theories, for queuing up to meet me, for selling-out superfan events and recommending *Skandar* to your friends. I'm so grateful for you and the love you've show for Skandar and his friends as we finish their fourth adventure.

This fourth book is also longer than the third, and therefore I have the task of keeping these acknowledgements short – however much I could fill pages and pages with thanks to all those who have supported me on the journey of writing it. Wish me luck!

Thank you to my family and friends for your endless belief in me and your overflowing love – I'm so grateful. To Ruth and

Aisling, who read this fourth story first, thank you for your perfect – and sometimes CAPITALISED – reactions and for giving up your own writing time to read for me. You are selfless and wonderful.

Thank you to my agent, Sam Copeland who would fearlessly fight by my side in any Chaos Cup race – and who also didn't speak to me for hours after finishing this book (sorry!). And thank you to my film agent, Michelle Kroes, screenwriter, Jon Croker and the whole team at Sony for bringing these unicorns to the big screen. As well as David Dawson for bringing these books alive for audio – it has brought joy to so many, including me.

Winning the Chaos Cup is all about the team around you, and I have the very best in Simon & Schuster. I am so grateful to every single one of you:

To Rachel Denwood, Ian Chapman, Jonathan Karp and Justin Chanda for their fierce ambition for these bloodthirsty unicorns, and their unswerving belief in me as an author. To my UK editor, Ali Dougal for going above and beyond for this series – it is no mean feat bringing a book out six months early and I know it required superhuman effort and sacrifice. You are magic. To my US editor, Deeba Zargarpur who loved Kenna unconditionally from the start. Thank you for helping make these characters the best they can be – the heroes and the villains.

And huge thanks also to Arub Ahmed, Kathy Webb, Olive Childs and Dainese Santos for your eagle-eyed editorial expertise, as well as the copyeditors, proof readers and sensitivity readers who have made this story shine.

To Laura Hough, Dani Wilson, Rich Hawton, Leanne Nulty and the whole sales team at S&S across the world who have been relentlessly brilliant in their aim to bring bloodthirsty unicorns to every shelf. Thank you to Eve Wersocki Morris of EWM PR and to Sarah Macmillan, Jess Dean, Dan Fricker, Lizzie Irwin,

Tara Shanahan, Emily Wilson, Breanna Djamil and the rest of the S&S marketing and publicity teams both in the UK and abroad. Thank you for spreading the love for *Skandar* all over the world, and giving me the gift of meeting my readers. It is my absolute favourite thing.

To the design team at Simon & Schuster, as well as Two Dots Illustration Studio and Sorrel Packham for this emerald gem of a book. It's beautiful inside and out.

To the whole rights team and Skandar's international publishers, editors and translators – thank you for helping the Skeleton Curse cause havoc across the world. It is such an honour to see my work translated, and hear from readers enjoying it in their own languages.

I am beyond grateful to the incredible booksellers, librarians, teachers, bloggers, fellow authors and festival organisers who are passionate about getting the *Skandar* books into readers' hands. I appreciate everything you do for this series and for children's literacy in general. The real magic starts with you.

And last of all, to my husband, Joseph – for caring about these books as much as I do. For sharing my passion for bringing them to as many readers as possible, even though it means spending time apart. For listening just as carefully to my ideas for exciting plot twists, as to my queries about commas. Thank you for the infinite joy and companionship you bring to every step of this journey.